Also by Joseph Bauer

The Accidental Patriot

THE PATRIOT'S ANGELS

★ ★ ★

JOSEPH BAUER

ARCHWAY PUBLISHING

This is a work of fiction. All of the characters, names, incidents, organizations, and dialogue in this novel are either the products of the author's imagination or are used fictitiously.

Archway Publishing books may be ordered through booksellers or by contacting:

Archway Publishing
1663 Liberty Drive
Bloomington, IN 47403
www.archwaypublishing.com
844-669-3957

ISBN: 978-1-6657-0428-1 (sc)
ISBN: 978-1-6657-0426-7 (hc)
ISBN: 978-1-6657-0427-4 (e)

Library of Congress Control Number: 2021905020

Print information available on the last page.

Archway Publishing rev. date: 05/03/2021

For Gloria, who didn't give up on me, or us.

Things don't happen. Things are made to happen.
—John F. Kennedy

CONTENTS

PART 1

PART 2

PART 3

PART 4

PART 5

PART 1

1

INTERCEPTION

You could see the ritual was well practiced. Every player in the drone control center at Charleston Air Force Base knew what was expected, down to the smallest detail. Theater of war, in this place, was surely theater-like.

A large, curved screen filled the front of the room, flanked left and right by others of equal dimension. The center monitor displayed a single, highly magnified image of the next target. Side monitors displayed row upon row of separate smaller displays, each stared at intently by an assigned soldier wearing a headset. Even the lighting in the room seemed like a theater. Except for the thin red rays shedding from superfluous exit signs above the corners, the only light rose from dim floor lamps embedded in the carpeting of ascending rows in front of the screens. Many in the room talked quietly, as if patrons awaiting previews.

Only the drone pilot—Lieutenant Grey Boatwright, sitting in the center of the second row—focused exclusively on the center screen. His chair differed from all the others. It was larger and deep-seated, and the armrests on each side extended forward, dotted with color-coded switches. A joystick covered with buttons, some raised, some recessed, rose through a rubber housing atop the console in front of his chair.

A countdown clock emerged at the top of the center screen, announced by four beeps like a microwave oven signaling completion. The clock registered seven digitized minutes and began descending immediately. Every monitor brightened slightly, but nothing else seemed to change in the room. The technicians and soldiers kept talking in low tones.

Lieutenant Boatwright stood, moved away from his pilot's seat, and stretched.

"Been sitting in that thing for two hours," he said to the technician seated nearest him.

"Yeah, you flew this one a long way."

Boatwright had guided the Predator V drone and its cargo of four Hellfire III missiles from their base in Qatar to their target area seventy miles north of Mosul, Iraq. He flexed his fingers by bringing his hands together, aligning each digit with its mate, and pulsing his fingers in and out.

"My last chance to loosen up," Boatwright said. He knew he could not stand for long, and before the countdown dial reached five minutes and forty seconds he was reseated, again fingering the control stick with a typist's gentle touch.

Boatwright and the others knew that even this close to planned execution, nothing was certain. In fact, there was still no one in the room authorized to issue the strike command. The consequences of missile strikes, in terms human and political, came in just two sizes: large and extra large. Barack Obama had been the first to require explicit presidential approval for any drone strike that was not part of active combat operations or judged by military ground command as needed for the protection of engaged forces. He had issued a standing order that any drone assault on a preplanned target needed specific approval from the Oval Office. Some commanders at the time criticized him.

"What a goddamned micromanager," one protested.

But none of Obama's successors had rescinded his standing order. And more than one of them, including President Delores Winters, had privately thanked him for installing it in the first place. A career military officer herself, Del Winters appreciated, more than most, the importance of preeminent civilian authority over the armed forces. The balance between leadership and meddling could sometimes be difficult to manage, but when it came to the exercise of premeditated military power, the line was clear. It should be the president's—and only the president's—decision.

The largest image in the room displayed, ironically, the smallest land area monitored on any of them. It showed in real time six steel sheds surrounding what Special Forces had confirmed as a square underground bunker measuring one hundred feet on each side. US drones carrying specialized detection instruments revealed that the bunker was constructed of thick concrete walls further reinforced with steel cables and beams to a depth of fourteen feet. Iraqi intelligence agents had infiltrated the ISIS unit guarding the complex, posing as sympathetic insurgents delivering water supplies to the terrorists.

"It's what we thought," a CIA operative stationed in Mosul reported to military command. "It's jammed with chemical weapons supplies and warheads. Probably brought over from Syria. They're stored in the bunker, and mobile launch vehicles for deploying them are parked in the sheds around it."

Boatwright studied the center monitor and checked his flight instrumentation again, preparing to revector should the strike time be deferred. He knew it was a real possibility. Three small villages to the south of the target were a concern. The explosion of the bunker would send clouds of toxic chemicals into the air, and the prevailing wind would carry the unbreathable air to them. The president had ordered a removal plan to get the villagers out. But the evacuation of the innocents needed to happen immediately before the strike. Not hours before—minutes before. The mobile launch vehicles stored in the sheds may already be mounted and weaponized, according to the infrared aerial surveillance.

"This one might be delayed," Lieutenant Boatwright said to the technician next to him. "The president won't green light us until those people are out of the villages. I hope they get them out quick. Once the terrorists at the bunker hear about the evacuation of those villages, I'll bet they try to move or use their weapons before we can destroy them."

Boatwright had been told it would take a hundred Special Forces trained in extraction to empty the villages. He knew they had been dropped in silently two hours earlier. Transport vehicles for the civilians were already in place, secreted into the area the night before. As far as Boatwright and the soldiers in the control room knew, the forces had arrived and were clearing the villages. So far, there had been no deferral instruction, but Boatwright drew no conclusions. Some strikes had been deferred as close as fifteen seconds to launch, and he knew from the mission briefing that planners expected detection of the civilian evacuation prior to firing. Terrorist sentries would surely engage the Special Forces; it was only a question of how many and of how soon the hostiles could be dispatched and the villagers escorted out. If interference was strong, it could take longer than hoped.

Therein lay the strategic tension. It may be necessary to delay the strike to protect the civilians and troops. But any delay increased the likelihood that the terrorists at the target complex could rush their launch vehicles from the sheds to save them from the strike or—worse—unleash their chemical warheads on the evacuation force and the fleeing civilians. Boatwright could not influence these competing tensions; it was his job only to endure them.

Military meteorologists had studied the wind data around the target site for weeks, and the planned strike time was established based on their judgment that the wind from the north would be at its lowest predictable speed, four to six miles per hour, between 0415 and 0435 on this date. Drone command settled on a launch at 0420, leaving a fifteen-minute deferral window if more time was needed to clear the civilians from the villages before the wind picked up.

When the countdown clock reached three minutes, a low siren glided out from speakers around the ceiling. Boatwright raised a fist. A silence came over the control room. It was protocol. All conversation ceased instantly. From then until launch or deferral, no one was to make any sound unless it was to call out prescribed data or information to the pilot.

At two minutes twenty-eight seconds and counting, the door at the front-left side of the control room opened. All eyes went to the slender black officer who entered. They all knew him. A few liked him. All respected him. Captain Tyler Brew strode briskly to the center of the second row and greeted Boatwright flatly.

"Ready, Boat?" he asked.

"We are 'go' if you tell us we are," he replied.

"We are," Brew said. "We're not deferring. At least not yet."

It was not unusual that an officer from Special Operations Command, or SOCOM as it was called, commanded a flight center dedicated almost exclusively to planned terrorist strikes, but it *was* unusual that such a commanding officer be a Navy

SEAL. But Captain Tyler Brew's background and skills were ordinary in no sense of the word.

Now forty-two years old and by regulation aged out of special operations field assignments, he was still in top physical condition. It grated him that he was ineligible for the work on the battlefield that he had done so well for twenty years. But as a veteran of hundreds of missions, each seemingly more dangerous than the next, he knew well how every SEAL relied literally on the physical skills and capacities of every other. He did not question the judgment of those who wrote the rules; they were, he knew, designed only to protect the lives of every team member.

Most SEALs left the military at forty, or soon after, upon reaching twenty years of active service. Their training, discipline, and experience made them attractive to well-compensating employers in security-related fields, including international companies and billionaires. But some, driven by a deep desire to continue serving, transferred into civilian positions in the intelligence agencies. And a few, Tyler Brew among them, were considered by the military command as simply too valuable to leave uniform. In Brew's case, his tactical acumen in all matters terrorist, together with his natural leadership traits, made him an asset that SOCOM believed held its currency—and perhaps even increased—with age. It was not difficult to persuade him to stay on as an "out-of-theater" commander in the continuing war on terror. His only condition was that he remain a Navy SEAL while doing it. It was a bond he could not break. His request was granted immediately.

On Captain Brew's signal the young Lieutenant Boatwright, sitting at the controls, raised his right hand in the motion of an umpire laconically calling an obvious strike. The eyes of the soldiers and technicians in front and behind were locked on the young pilot, awaiting his signal. Immediately each seemed to become more serious, edging closer to their lighted panels and staring at their monitor segments.

"Wind at ground, four point eight miles, trending up," called one. She spoke through a headset to the pilot, but still loud enough to be heard in the event of failure in the wireless system.

The clock had wound down to one minute nineteen seconds. Commanding officer Brew stood behind Boatwright's right shoulder. The new wind speed data, higher than the four miles per hour reported earlier, caused Boatwright to bring the Predator down two-hundred feet from its approach altitude of eight thousand feet. Even this small increase in wind at the target site meant that he had either to raise firing velocity or decrease range; he chose the latter.

"Wind at one thousand feet, steady at five point seventy-five," another technician reported.

Boatwright executed rapid finger movements near the top of the joy stick, checking the nose temperatures of the three missiles planned for firing. All three were within optimal range, so he did not look at the fourth missile, held in reserve and not planned for use. The mission plan called for two missiles to be launched initially, merely one second apart, intended to strike the target in its northwest and southeast quadrants, destroying the sheds and their contents and compromising the cement-walled bunker between them. The pilot was then to bank the Predator sharply and release the third missile fifty seconds later, directing it in his judgment and by his own calculations to a strike point where it would be the most effective based on the impacts of the first two, presumably near the center of the storage bunker to complete the destruction.

Brew and Boatwright watched the center monitor, zoomed so closely that the target appeared to be directly beneath them.

Black-hooded men, some with automatic rifles draped over their shoulders, emerged from a stairway on the east side of the bunker and raced toward the sheds.

"Should I go early?" asked the pilot. He did not look up at Brew. His eyes were fixed on the instrumentation in front of him. His hand gripped the joystick gently. He was already computing the adjustments that would be needed.

It was tempting. The clock was down to thirty-six seconds. Two of the terrorists had entered the sheds. Brew knew it meant that the evacuation of the villages to the south had been detected; the terrorists at the target were responding. It was possible they could manage to get a vehicle out and launch a warhead. But Brew also knew that moving up the strike time, even slightly, would require instant recalibrations. If any pilot could do it correctly under such pressure, it was Grey Boatwright, in whom Brew had unreserved confidence. But the SEAL captain had personal experience with the kind of mobile missile launchers at the terrorists' disposal. In the field he had served on three missions to find and destroy them in the mountains of Afghanistan and personally had led two of them. He knew the launchers were about as maneuverable as an oversized tow truck in heavy snow. Brew judged that the risk of an error in the firing computations, able as Boatwright was, exceeded the likelihood that the awkward launchers could be moved from the sheds and oriented so quickly.

"No," Brew told the pilot. "Stay on the clock."

It is amazing how slowly thirty-six seconds seem to pass in a control room of soldiers waiting to execute a missile strike. Grey Boatwright, a strong athlete and former small-college quarterback, wondered why. When you were lining up a team at the line of scrimmage, awaiting a football snap, the seconds always seemed to rush past. There was never too much time, only not enough. Why so different here?

Captain Brew watched the instrumentation. He understood many of the dials on the console but not all of them. He knew the functions of many of the buttons on the joystick but not all. His job was both expansive and limited. In developing the mission plan, he made many decisions himself and advised on all others. But once the mission was defined, and *if* things went according to plan, his role was reduced to one of simple oversight. He conveyed the confirmation of White House authority and watched as the pilot and the technical personnel executed.

Unless events on the ground or in the air required a mission change, his decision-making role was finished. Watch the weapons deployment; report the results to central command; begin the next plan. But if execution went "off plan"—and a hundred things could cause that—the commanding officer in the control room was preeminent. Antiaircraft weapons might be detected too near the drone's flight path. Friendly forces might wander unwittingly into harm's way. Special forces elsewhere might come under fire, causing central command to redirect the Predator drone to their aid, aborting the planned mission.

No matter what the diversion, there was no time in such circumstances for discussion or debate, which is why only a single commander was ever present with the pilot and the mission team in the drone control room. No "command ambiguity," it was called. Brew and Brew alone would be responsible for any and all orders modifying the mission plan or responding to problems that might be encountered.

At ten seconds and counting, it was plain to all in the room that this mission would proceed to launch. The last audible input from the team to Boatwright came at six seconds and counting.

"Villages clear," was the report.

Everyone watched the large front screen as a bold "X" emerged in its center. Lieutenant Boatwright immediately moved it to the northwest corner of the target area where one of the sheds sat near the edge of the storage bunker. Captain Brew's decision to fire on schedule was proving wise. None of the mobile launchers had yet appeared outside of the sheds.

Four. Three. Two.

The image on the center monitor began to shake slightly from the force of the descending missile. It struck violently and precisely on-target. The shed near the bunker's northwest corner evaporated in a mushroom of flame and black earthen dust. No matter how many times you observed one of these impacts, the devastating force and sheer power was always shocking. The room erupted in a cheer, as the soldiers waited for the second impact, due in only a single second. But Captain Brew did not cheer. He did not smile. He sensed something was wrong. Had the missile been fired a fraction of a second early? He bent over, glaring at the joystick with alarmed eyes, then into pilot Boatwright's, staring back at him. The young pilot's hand trembled on the top of the stick.

"That wasn't me!" Boatwright said.

"Where's the second missile?" asked Brew. His voice was strained, each successive word elevating in volume.

"It's dead on me. It won't fire!"

Both men looked at the instrument panel. The Predator was ascending and vectoring in the reverse direction stipulated in the mission plan.

"Are you taking it there?" Brew asked.

"Hell, no!" said Boatwright. Now, everyone in the room sensed the panic. "I'm not flying the thing!"

Brew made his first off-plan decision. Perhaps five seconds had passed.

"Take it down. Now. Destruct."

Boatwright tripped three toggles on the instrument panel. Nothing happened. The self-destruction circuit had been compromised. He moved immediately to the backup switch and pounded it. Nothing. It was disabled too.

Brew sprinted for the door.

"Everybody stay put," he shouted. "Record everything you can." He stopped at the door and looked back at Grey Boatwright. "Keep trying to kill it, Boat!" he ordered. "And figure out where the goddamned thing is going."

★ ★ ★

POSTPONEMENT

The morning schedule of President Delores "Del" Winters was uncharacteristically light. The nation's first woman president was to leave in the afternoon for Atlanta to campaign for Republican Senator Will Truitt, facing a tough challenge in the upcoming midterm election from Democrat Margaret Westfall. The Georgia incumbent was not as moderate as she would prefer. But the turbulent political winds of the Trump administration, and the allied Steve Bannon populist movement that flowed from it, had effectively installed a three-party system into American democracy, at least for the present. She needed Truitt's vote dearly. It might even mean the loss of her party's control of the Senate, should he be defeated, where her Republicans held an effective edge of a single vote. Adding to the tension, two other Republican senators were wobbling in the polls in their own reelections.

The weather forecast called for the possibility of thunderstorms by late afternoon; she cleared her morning appointments in case she needed to depart early for Georgia ahead of them. She was alone at her desk in the Oval Office when the call came.

It made Atlanta weather a moot point.

Only two persons, other than her father, could reach Del Winters on a direct line bypassing the White House switchboard: Secretary of Defense Vernon Lazar and the Joint Chiefs chairman, General Silas T. Tull. The number that all others used sent the caller through the switchboard operators and then on to various staffers for vetting. Less than one out of every three hundred were deemed urgent enough to redirect at once to the president. The reasoning was simple. If the cabinet, Congressional members, other senior officials, and ordinary citizens could reach her without a rigorous filtering mechanism, the president's desk phone would be ringing all day. The only envisionable scenarios that warranted the unqualified immediate attention of the commander-in-chief were all linked to the defense of the country or its military—all the domain of the secretary of defense. And the joint chiefs' chair needed unfettered access in the event the defense secretary could not be located or was indisposed. It was common for both to be on the line when the president was needed. So it was that morning.

"I'm with Silas, Madame President. We have a large problem," Lazar said at once when she picked up the call. The president knew she needn't ask what; that would just delay what he wanted to tell her. And Lazar didn't pause to allow her time to ask because he knew better too.

"A Predator V drone piloted out of Charleston, deployed from Qatar, has left control of Tyler Brew's command and is flying either on its own or by some intervenor. It's first missile was fired at the intended target but then the drone went rogue. Now, it's carrying three Hellfire IIIs, and we can't control it."

"The mission I approved just a few minutes ago?"

"Yes," said General Tull.

"And the first missile was fired?"

"But not by Brew's pilot. At least we don't think it was."

"What about self-destruct?" she asked.

"We tried. It dysfunctioned. The backup too."

"My God. Where's it going?"

"It vectored first toward Syria, but now it's moving on a course out over the Mediterranean. Maybe toward Israel," the general said.

"I assume you've already scrambled fighters?"

"Yes, they are up now, ready for your command."

"Well, you have it," she said. "Take it down. But don't enter Israeli airspace without notice."

"I will pass on the order now, while you stay on the line with Vern. There's more I need to say."

The general left the call momentarily. It took but a few key strokes to issue the takedown order to the fighter jets, and he was back on the call almost instantly.

"I don't want to give either of you the impression it will be routine to take it down," he said.

"Really?" asked Lazar. The president had the same reaction.

"The movement capacities of that damn thing are deep," the general said. "Nobody makes a drone like we do. They are evasive as hell if someone has its controls."

She and Lazar both remembered the planning and budget meetings in which billions were committed to the sophisticated evasion systems available to the drone pilots.

"We cannot assure you we will get it down before it launches missiles. That is, if anybody *is* flying it."

"Thank God it's not an Eaglet drone," the president said.

The Eaglet series carried a small nuclear warhead, if you

could call anything nuclear *small*. She herself had commissioned the completion of its lengthy development, the fifth president to proceed with the new and frightening capability, originally authorized by George W. Bush immediately following 9/11. The Eaglets were secreted in an underground deployment facility in Kuwait designed covertly by a large, old, unassuming civilian engineer from Pittsburgh—Stanley Bigelow—only the previous year.

"Obviously, we need to understand how this happened," she said. "But that is priority two. Priority one is to blow the thing out of the air as quickly as possible."

"I think you should call the Israeli PM immediately," said Lazar.

"I will. Have you alerted his military?"

"No," said General Tull. "We felt that would be out of our province. In view of the political impact."

"I appreciate that, Silas," the president said. It was unusual for her to refer to any military officer by his first name instead of his or her rank. They both knew it reflected a personal sentiment, in this case gratitude.

"I will try to reach him immediately. But if I can't find him, I will let you know within three minutes that I haven't, so that you can tell them through your military channels. Explain that I couldn't locate the PM. I am going to tell him he should scramble with us, protecting his borders and population centers. And to take it down themselves if they can. You do the same if I don't speak with him right now."

"But if we can't get it before it reaches Israeli airspace, we *don't* continue pursuit?"

"Not without Israeli consent. I'll ask for it in my call, and you should too if I don't reach the prime minister."

"Understood."

Without even a goodbye, she hung up and reached for a small keyboard in the second drawer of her Oval Office desk. It was a telephone board listing twenty key nations—friends and foes alike. A single button touch produced a direct, secure line to the head of state. Two touches to the second in command. Three, to the third.

She was pleased that the first option worked; Ari Szell's distinctive, gravelly voice greeted her at once.

"Del," he said warmly, but nothing else. His instincts told him that an unscheduled call from the president of the United States waived unnecessary pleasantries.

"Ari, I am sorry to be making this call. An ugly thing has happened. A few minutes ago, one of our drones making a strike against terrorist armaments in Iraq was overtaken. It is flying rogue with three missiles. Toward Israeli airspace."

"What kind of missiles?"

"Hellfire IIIs."

Even on the other end of the line, Del Winters could sense the PM's silent grimace. The Hellfire III was far more destructive than the original Hellfire, still in use for smaller targets. The ordinary Hellfire had a kill zone of little more than fifty feet in any direction from its point of impact. The III's kill zone exceeded *five-hundred* feet.

"You could not destroy it at once?"

"The self-destruct controls were compromised. We have no idea who is flying it, or really if anyone is. It could be simply a technology failure."

"My God."

"We have fighters in the air now to take it down. But the drone has special evasion skills."

"We know. We wish you would tell us how you do that." He couldn't resist the comment.

"After *this*, we'll look at that again, Ari," she said. "But right now, I am suggesting you send up your own planes to protect your air space and your cities. We will try everything to destroy it before it reaches you, but if we cannot, do I have your consent to pursue it in your airspace."

The Prime Minister of Israel paused.

"Yes," he finally said. "Has your command alerted mine?"

"No. I thought you would want to know first and issue orders on your own."

"Thank you."

"And you should know, Ari, I ordered my command to stay out of your airspace without your consent."

"Thank you for that too. We are your ally. We are not your child."

"I understand that well."

"Godspeed to both of us," he said.

If only either received it.

A GENIAL YOUNG GENIUS

It was entirely coincidental, but even as the president was urgently addressing the runaway drone in the Middle East, a clean-cut young man in khakis and a polo shirt wheeled an instrument cart into a guarded state government warehouse complex on the outskirts of Augusta, Georgia. He greeted politely the uniformed officer who allowed him in with his four-digit fingerprint impression on the security pad.

"Thanks, officer," he said.

The guard nodded. He knew the young man from the National Security Agency's cybersecurity contractor, SureSecure. His name was Simon DeClerc. He had MIT credentials. He had been vetted extensively by the NSA contractor and had visited yesterday to be processed for his photo identification badge. As far as anyone knew, his record was spotless, his capability clear. He would be coming every morning for at least four days to run the diagnostics on the electronic voting machines to be used in the elections, less than a month away. He was amiable and cooperative and said he would be packing his own lunch and eating at his workstation. The guard appreciated that. He needn't be cleared back in a second time each day.

Like nearly all states, Georgia had instituted uniform electronic voting in every precinct of every one of its counties. The machines had been checked thoroughly following the US presidential election two years earlier and found to be in perfect order. But after the tumult of the Russian interference in the 2016 US election and the political turmoil it spawned—including the allegations of widespread fraud in the 2020 election—no stone could be left unturned.

By legal mandate, every voting machine in the nation was subjected to mandatory independent examination by technology experts certified for the purpose by the NSA. Even the Federal Bureau of Investigation was not deemed careful enough—or impartial enough—to certify the analytic measures, or the technologists that administered them. Perhaps unfairly, perhaps not, the FBI's standing as a purely apolitical agency had been blemished in the 2016 election mayhem and its lengthy fallout. Perhaps wisely, perhaps not, the obscure computer scientists that lined the NSA were adjudged a preferred resource to oversee the integrity of the electronic apparatus from which the results of democracy rolled out like widgets.

It was all part of a broad set of precautions produced by the histrionics of the Trump election upset in 2016 and the tumult that followed his defeat in 2020. Five Congressional investigations, a special counsel's independent one, and a polarized public taking its information as it chose from right, left, or mainstream media—but usually only one of them—culminated in the controversial Election Security Reform Act. Some said its complexities made the highly debated national health care laws look like child's play. Some on the left loved it;

some on the left despised it. Some on the right hated it; some on the right adored it. But those in the center—and the increasingly important and growing number of independents—deemed it essential for the country, notwithstanding some uncomfortable incursions on traditional notions of a democratic republic.

Signed into law by President Biden's successor, the same president who had named Del Winters to replace his original vice president upon that man's sudden death late in his first term, the framework had survived two presidential elections and three midterms without incident. Backers of the complicated new provisions and safeguards cheered its success. Even the media seemed generally to agree—for once—that the country's election integrity problems were over, at least for the time being.

Many thousands of voting precincts were spread across Georgia's 144 counties. Identical voting machines, designed to uniform federal standards, were distributed by the federal government to each state, and state elections officials decided how many were transported to each precinct site. But the new federal statute required that *all* a state's voting machines, including the internal or external wiring and devices needed to operate them, be centrally stored in approved facilities protected by round-the-clock physical security. State governments were responsible for security in the first instance, but the NSA and FBI were authorized to monitor and, if in their judgment necessary, actively manage it.

Under the law, the machines could be transported to the precinct sites no more than forty-eight hours before voting was to commence so that they were not exposed for long to tampering before Election Day. And their movement in transit, and status when positioned, were closely surveilled by federal, state, and political party personnel. It was, all observed, a "tightly closed loop," soundly designed from a security standpoint.

When the young expert arrived at the brightly lit warehouse, he found that the Georgia state employees had arranged the machines logically according to the number of registered voters in each county. Like many states, Georgia's population was very unevenly distributed between its borders. Much of southern Georgia was rural, and the same was true in its northernmost region as it stretched up toward the Great Smoky Mountains and its neighboring states. These regions were sparsely inhabited. Some counties had as few as two precincts with less than a thousand voters. In contrast, nearly two-thirds of Georgians now lived in the greater Atlanta metropolitan area, within the five counties of Fulton, Dekalb, Cobb, Clayton, and the rapidly growing Forsythe County near Lake Lanier.

The NSA supervisor, on hand to oversee and double-check young DeClerc's work, joined Simon and the guard to look over the warehouse layout. They found the machines lined up by county, and by precinct within county, with all the larger counties placed in the rear-most portion of the facility. The guard explained why, as the young cyber technician stood together with the older NSA expert assigned to oversee his work.

"Loading bays are in the rear, there." He pointed out to them. "We load the Atlanta counties first. There are so many going there, and the traffic is worse. Work our way down to the others."

"I see," said the NSA supervisor, at least twenty years senior to DeClerc. "Where will you start, Simon?"

"I'll take the bull by the horns," DeClerc said. "I'll start in the rear, on the larger counties. Get them out of the way. I'd hate to get to Friday still looking at those long rows."

And so, the courteous geek and the experienced NSA expert made their work plan. DeClerc would begin at the rear and move forward, county by county. When he had completed the analytics on all machines for a given county, he would call the overseer to check his work. It was intended as a painstaking process. The supervisor would not run his own diagnostics on just randomly selected voting machines. He would run them on *every one.*

"I'll call you when I finish a county, so you can check it," DeClerc said. "But pop down anytime you want."

Such a forthcoming young man, thought the overseer.

"Do you want me to check the surveillance cameras too?" DeClerc asked as the supervisor turned to leave. "It's not on the work order, but I could."

"Actually, that'd be good."

"Just need the ISP address."

The NSA expert thumbed through his cell phone notes.

"Got it. I'll forward it to you."

"Wonderful," DeClerc said.

To him, for good reason.

ALL GOOD, SO FAR

Young Simon DeClerc moved rapidly but carefully through the voting machines designated for Fulton County, Georgia. There were eight data input ports on each machine and one computation module. He scanned each input port with a virus detection instrument, then a separate device to check for any circuit infirmities. Then he repeated the tests to confirm that each was operating without flaw. Still another instrument was needed to verify the integrity of the computation module on the rear of each machine. The counting module was little more than a vote sorter and electronic adding machine, combined in a control device the size of a cigarette pack. For the first few machines, the warehouse guard watched and listened with curiosity.

"A voter touches this screen in the ballot box, picks the candidate she or he wants," DeClerc told the guard.

"Hell, I know that much," the guard said.

"Well, that choice enters the data input port. It gets sent by internal wires directly to the computation module. That selection is hardwired. Can't be touched before it reaches the computation module."

"Computation module?"

"Yeah, it's a little box in the back that has software in it to sort and count. Everything hardwired. Nothing wireless."

"How come, in this day and age? You can get everything wireless."

"That's the point. Anything wireless could possibly be hacked."

"Oh, I get it."

"The software directs the sorting—which candidate to count the vote for. That's got to be right."

Indeed, the accuracy of the software-directed sorting was crucial, and the protocol developed by the NSA to test the software's accuracy was scientifically sound. Before the SureSecure technician even first touched a machine, a "placebo" election had already been held; the NSA supervisor on site had simulated a dry run election by entering hundreds of thousands of votes for various candidates, offices, and voter issues. Only the federal supervisor knew what votes had been cast in the placebo contest on each precinct machine. After DeClerc verified the computation module as working properly, the same NSA expert then checked each machine's tally against the "rehearsal vote" in each precinct, and the aggregate result for the county. If there were not *exact* matches in the tallies, it was back to the drawing board for every affected precinct machine.

When he had finished the diagnostics on the last machines for Fulton County, DeClerc texted the NSA supervisor, standing by in a nearby office building.

"Fulton County anytime," the young technician texted. It was about eleven o'clock. The supervisor could do his double-check at his convenience, but DeClerc hoped he would come soon after his heads-up. He did.

"Ready with a big boy, eh?" the federal expert said to DeClerc as the guard opened the gate for him into the warehouse.

"Shoot the gorilla first," DeClerc replied. "That's my policy."

They were referring to the disproportionate size of the Fulton County voting bloc. In the 2016 presidential election, for example, 412,411 votes had been cast in Fulton, more than any other Georgia county. Hilary Clinton had received 71 percent of those votes. She also carried Dekalb and Clayton counties by large margins, and Cobb by a much lesser one. But Donald Trump's overwhelming totals in every other part of the state—solidly Republican districts—was enough to win him Georgia anyway in 2016. Not so, though, in 2020 when massive turnout in the Atlanta area carried Biden to a narrow Georgia victory.

In the NSA supervisor's placebo election used to test the Fulton County machines and DeClerc's diagnostics for the upcoming election, the simulated vote—known only to the supervisor—was much closer. The Democrat, Margaret Westfall gathered 210,819 votes in the rehearsal; the Republican incumbent, Will Truitt, 207,001. The NSA supervisor used his own equipment to see what vote count the Fulton County machines produced. As he moved down the aisles of machines, drawing a vote total from each, it was apparent that correct and exact totals were being produced by the computation modules. But he still worked meticulously at every machine, referring to his printed chart of simulated tallies before verifying each with an embossed seal on the facing of the counting module.

It was midafternoon when the verification was complete.

"All good," the supervisor said to DeClerc, as he headed out of the warehouse. "Let me know when you're ready for the next one."

"Yes, sir, Mr. Secret Agent Man."

The NSA expert didn't stop to smile.

5

★ ★ ★

STANLEY AND HELEN, AND AUGIE, OF COURSE

Pittsburgh in October delivered all the pleasures Stanley Bigelow cherished most. And especially this October.

His seventy-first birthday was behind him. But he saw the future as a fresh, mild breeze, teeming with new promise. It was not that his earlier life had abandoned him. Or he it. He held it all carefully in the hands of his memory, secure in his mind.

So much, though, was new. The last eighteen months had transformed his life. Through no initiative of his own, he had been plucked from a solitary, widower's existence, living out his years as a quiet engineer in his familiar city—an ordinary citizen. Until he was called—unsolicited and without expectation—to serve his country merely by doing what he knew how to do. He was a civil engineer with special experience in unusual metals and underground construction. His country, unknown to him, needed his skill and knowledge and sought him out for secret military work in the war against terrorism.

The public never learned of his work; as yet, neither had

the nation's enemies. The subterranean structure he designed, assembled by soldiers he secretly trained under the guidance of Navy SEAL Tyler Brew, now concealed the country's fleet of nuclearized drones in the Middle East, a valuable—and, happily, so far unused—asset against the progress of terror. Though warned, he completed the project without appreciating the personal danger to which he was exposed. Though unrewarded materially, he had met the president and earned her gratitude and, even more important to him, befriended her father, the nation's First Father, retired General Henry Winters, who admired Stanley's quiet patriotism, character, and—not incidentally—keen understanding of baseball statistics and bourbons.

And the five-month odyssey brought unexpected gifts that changed everything for the large senior citizen. More than Stanley knew, the government had been concerned for his safety during the project, and the disclosure of its purpose should he be abducted, especially after the first engineer chosen for the mission had been brutally murdered before she could commence her work, or even be told what it was about. So, the government provided Stanley the company of a trained protection dog, a German shepherd named Augie and a diligent Pittsburgh-based FBI witness protection specialist, L. T. Kitt, who had trained the dog. A strong and attractive woman in her thirties, she was moved into an adjoining apartment to ensure close tabs on his safety. Her platonic affection for the aging, childless volunteer, and his reciprocated interest in her life and well-being, developed to a strong bond. In gratitude for his service, the president herself had gifted the guard dog to him at assignment's end. Augie, who also answered to August, now lived inseparably with Stanley in his own early retirement in the comfortable Bigelow high-rise condominium overlooking the Allegheny River in downtown Pittsburgh.

But most of all, the clandestine project gifted Stanley with an even more significant, entirely unanticipated benefit. Romantic love. Who would have thought it?

To create the underground deployment base, Stanley had designed an ingenious system of interlocking panels and fittings. All were comprised of beryllium, a little-known earth metal invisible to x-ray detection and possessing unique characteristics of extreme strength, rigidity, and ultralightness. His meticulous blueprints specified exactly spaced deep cement pilings to which the components were to be bolted. After the stanchions were poured by army engineers on site, the installation was simple enough to be assembled by reserve soldiers, selected by Captain Brew and brought to a disguised training center in Charleston, South Carolina, for Stanley's instruction. But the savvy Brew foresaw the need for a qualified military engineer among the call-ups who could oversee the actual installation overseas. He chose Colonel Helen Ames, a careerist from the Army Corps of Engineers, attached to a reserves unit near St. Louis.

Helen was tall, slender, fair, and fit. Her straight auburn hair hung to her shoulders. Her default expression was an approachable smile below hazel eyes that occasionally flashed mischief. At fifty-seven and never married, she carried herself with grace and the confidence of an officer. Stanley adjudged her immediately as an engineer of the highest order. He admired her intellect and straightforward manner; she, his quiet sensitivity, gentle masculine affect, and creative mind.

Perhaps it was the fortuity of it all, the serendipity of their lives coming together in such an improbable way under delicate, secret circumstances. Perhaps the stars were simply aligned. Perhaps it was just two persons paying attention.

They opened themselves to each other by project's end in August and traveled to the White House at the president's invitation in September, where she thanked them for their work. They married in a small room of the Pittsburgh Commerce Club in February. Only Agent L. T. Kitt and Tyler Brew attended, the latter in his striking dress blues. And Augie, of course.

"Do you think you are rushing into this?" Helen asked the week of the wedding.

"I am seventy-one," said Stanley. "I am six-foot four inches tall. I weigh two hundred eighty-six pounds. *I* don't rush anywhere." He was as sure of his decision, he said, as any in his life.

Only one issue of moment had arisen in their young marriage, and it disappeared almost as rapidly as their union had formed.

"I want to stay on in the reserves, Stanley," Helen had said to her new husband. "Your home here in Pittsburgh is fine, but I want to stay with the reserves."

"In Missouri?"

"If that's what it takes."

Stanley was deeply proud of her service and rank as colonel, but he had assumed a transfer to a unit closer to Pittsburgh could be easily achieved. "But you could get a transfer," he said.

"It may not be that easy, Stanley. But, of course, I'll apply for one."

Stanley was surprised and disheartened when her formal application for reassignment to Wright Patterson Air Force Base in Dayton, a mere two-hour drive from the Steel City, was turned down. The commanding officer in St. Louis objected, stating that Colonel Ames was his brightest engineer and that her maturity and rank made her a vital mentor for younger reserves, no matter their gender.

"Don't fret over it, Stanley," she urged when Stanley pouted. "I can make the monthly trip to Missouri; it's not that bad. But you should know the Corps won't reimburse expenses because a requested transfer has been denied." But Stanley pouted.

"It's not about the money," he said.

It was probably one of the few times in the course of human events when that statement—"it's not about money"—was made truthfully. It really *wasn't* about money to him. He just didn't want to be away from her so regularly. If she served in Dayton, he could easily drive over with her. And it didn't hurt that good minor league baseball would be close by to enjoy in Columbus, Akron, and Toledo.

On one of his usual Sunday night phone calls with the president's father, Stanley mentioned Helen's situation to the retired general in a passing lament. The First Father listened without comment. Stanley asked him if he had ever met the St. Louis commander.

"No, Stanley, I'm sorry," he said. "I don't know him."

Henry Winters added nothing else. But on Thursday of the very week, certified mail arrived from the St. Louis base. Colonel Ames was reassigned to Wright Patterson, effective immediately, it declared. Henry Winters never explicitly acknowledged that he had intervened. But, elated with the news, Stanley raised the subject again with him.

"I thought you didn't know him," Stanley said.

"I don't," the First Father said. "But maybe he knows me." Nothing more was said.

Yes, all was right in the world for Stanley Bigelow—and Helen Ames too—as the October air settled in, and what it brought. Pennsylvania Octobers were always vivid with the exploding colors of the changing season. Not a complainer, Stanley didn't object openly to the humid summers in the river valley. But his extra-large frame and weight were much better suited to the crisp fall air. He could sit jacket-clad for hours on his eighth-floor balcony looking at the orange, yellow, and cranberry red hills rising high across the river. And now he could count normally on

Helen emerging from the kitchen to join him, carrying her scotch or gin martini, his bourbon. She did draw the line at fetching his cigar; but she didn't disapprove either. Stanley's cigars were of high quality; she was even beginning to enjoy their aroma, and it seemed to her a vice, albeit an expensive one, that could be overlooked. Her new husband, if overweight, was more than robust for his age, paid attention to his health and hers, and walked Augie daily on long routes, often four miles or more, occasionally in the company of their friend Agent Kitt, who had taken up residence in new townhouses just across the river.

Helen knew, nearly from first meeting, that with Stanley Bigelow came baseball. You didn't get one without the other. She was no novice to the game, having grown up with the Cardinals in the hot summers of St. Louis. But she was not a rabid follower either. Now, after living through her first season with Stanley, she found herself growing more interested. She was skeptical of some of his obtuse theories about statistical attributes—such as that what happened on a second pitch was more predictive than any other as to whether a batter would reach base—but enjoyed watching his studious recordkeeping to try to support them.

She was disinclined to abandon her Cardinals for Stanley's Pirates, and he did not expect her to. But now their allegiances were being tested by a timely coincidence in the new couple's relationship. The Cardinals had slipped into postseason play as a wild-card team and would face the division winning Pirates in the playoffs the next evening, in the ballpark just across the river.

Yes, all was right in their world, or so Stanley thought that brisk afternoon. But all was not right in the rest of the world. Helen hurried to the balcony door with Augie at her side. Stanley could hear serious tones blaring from the CNN newscast when the door cracked open.

"Stanley," she said. "Come in here and see this."

6

OBLITERATION

Israel's air force liked to "scramble thick," as one of their officers called it, often sending as many as thirty aircraft on a single sortie. Such congestion in the air was dangerous for the flyers, but their relentless training imbued confidence. Israel's pilots were among the best in the world.

This day, however, as daylight began to leave the Middle East, the Israeli commander chose differently. He knew the Americans were pursuing the runaway drone in force with their own aircraft. Twelve rocket-firing US fighter jets, positioned at four altitudes, were rushing toward Israel. His own pilots would be racing to the drone from the opposite direction. That much traffic, he reasoned, was madness. A horrific situation could too easily be made even worse. Besides, no one knew if the rogue drone was under hostile control or just running amok on its own—a technology failure. It might not intend to discharge its potent Hellfire III missiles at all. So, he decided to scramble just nine fighters, in sets of three, at three altitudes. That choice, reasonable, and prudent in the circumstances, may have made all the difference.

The runaway drone had flown northeast from the skies above Iraq, crossing Syria and Lebanon, out to the Mediterranean Sea. As it approached the thirty-second parallel, it turned sharply southeast toward Israel.

It came into sight of the American jets and the Israeli fighters streaming toward each other at nearly the same instant, just off the seacoast near Tel Aviv. Though the US airmen had been authorized to chase the drone into Israel's skies, they also had been directed to cede to Israel's forces if they were visually confirmed and comparably close to the target.

On signal from the US wing commander, the American planes peeled off in formation. The Israeli fighters filled the sky around the drone with rocket fire. All nine were firing, but the additional firepower of additional planes was sorely missed. The drone darted and leaped erratically, like a frightened butterfly in flight, startling the pilots with its evasiveness. In the first sixty seconds of fire, it remained unscathed. Inscrutably, it suddenly dove and then hovered—seemingly motionless. Now nearly under and above the drone, the nine pilots repeated their fire, relentlessly, narrowly missing each other. Pelted by rockets from both vectors, the drone imploded into a strangely silent plume as small fragments of craft debris floated and fluttered high above it. The runaway threat had been reduced to smoldering bits of drifting scrap metal and wire.

But not before it unleashed a single missile through the roof and into the bowels of the Tel Aviv Hilton Hotel.

The Hebrew American Educational Society was gathered in the hotel preparing for its annual conference, to begin formally that evening. Scholars, educators, and philanthropists from all over the world had arrived. A children's choir from Jerusalem, scheduled to sing for the plenary opening, was streaming from a bus caravan at the hotel's main entrance, just as the building collapsed in fire and fury. The force of the strike blew two of the buses to their sides like dry leaves. The grand lobby of the Hilton blazed; roofs of many floors crashed down with cacophonic slams. Guests and employees fell through the ceilings, many afire.

Heartbreaking footage, meant to memorialize the happy children trooping from their buses to their moment of recognition, instead sickened the world. It could not be described.

One of the first responders to the horror was a veteran Israeli police commander who'd been to the scenes of a dozen terrorist bombings. Hours later he was asked to compare them. He stood before the camera, trying and trying—in vain—to speak. Finally, he burst into tears, weeping uncontrollably.

In the White House, Del Winters watched the carnage on television. All regular programming was suspended; the world shook. No one could stand watching it, and no one could watch anything but it. The president did not watch for long, however.

It was imperative that the globe, and especially hostile nations, be told that world war was *not* under way. Iran had not bombed Israel, at least as far as anyone knew or could conclude. Nor had Syria. If any world player believed that one of them had, there was no predicting what misinformed calculations might follow, what military responses or misguided retaliations might be launched. She was most concerned about Russia, Iran, and Syria. Any of them might jump in if it thought an ally was at war with Israel.

She retrieved again the direct-line board from its drawer and dialed the leaders in that order. She spoke with dignity, without elevation. None of the leaders interrupted. None of the calls began with hello or ended with goodbye. The voice recognition translation technology worked without flaw. In the aggregate, the calls lasted only six minutes, Del Winters doing nearly all the talking. She was firm, unexcited, and clear. She told each that the Tel Aviv missile strike was from a commandeered or runaway United States drone. She knew not by whom.

"I make no charge of responsibility against anyone, now," she said. "That can wait. From what is known now, it could have been anyone, or no one."

"No one?" The Russian president seemed surprised.

"It could have been a technology failure sending the thing rogue."

"Oh."

"But hear me clearly. You must not react militarily. There can be no action of that kind."

"Why would we?" the Russian president said. "It would suggest culpability."

"Yes, it would. And it would lead to a chain reaction of hostilities."

"You mean Israel would retaliate."

"Not only Israel." She needn't say more. There was a brief silence on the line.

"We will do nothing," the Russian said, as did his Iranian and Syrian counterparts in the calls that followed immediately.

It may have been the most important—and successful—six minutes of emergency diplomacy ever conducted by a president.

She never discussed it publicly.

The First Father strode unannounced into the Oval Office. It was something he never did unless it was for early-morning coffee on occasions when he could not find his daughter in the upstairs residence.

"Are you okay, Delores?" He was worried about the strain on her; it had to be unbearable.

"I am going," she said.

"Going where?"

"To Tel Aviv. Right away—as soon as I talk to the country."

"You can't *do* anything there," he said.

"I can't do anything here either. And if I am not going to do anything, I am going to do it there."

She called to the Secret Service agent outside her door. She directed him to get Air Force One ready, and to reach the secretaries of defense and state to tell them they were leaving together.

"That was our goddamned missile. No matter how it did this, it was *our* goddamned missile."

It was all she said as she walked past her father.

★ ★ ★

GENIAL, YES AND ALSO EVIL

Young cyber genius DeClerc had wondered how he could be sure the warehouse guard wouldn't notice the temporary disruption of the rear-most surveillance cameras when he turned them off, but it turned out to be nothing to worry about. The guard's appetite for fast food took care of it.

"I'm going out for lunch food," the guard called in to DeClerc. "I know you've brought your lunch, but you want fries or anything?"

"Geesh, a chocolate shake would be great."

"You got it."

For an instant, DeClerc debated whether he should still shut down the cameras. If he turned them off, he could not prevent a record being made of the interruption, brief though it would be. If stoppage of the tape was noticed, suspicion might be raised. But brief service pauses were common and could be caused by any number of reasons. On the other hand, if he left the lenses running, it would be possible to observe that he had gone back to the machines *after* their verification by the NSA supervisor. *That* possibility was unacceptable. He shut them down.

He pulled a flash drive from his pocket and moved quickly down the line of the Fulton County machines, inserting it into a port on the bottom edge of the computation modules, carefully avoiding the seals that the NSA inspector had placed on each. The drive altered the sorting function of the machine's software. It would not add or delete a single vote. But it would apply an algorithm, in a constantly changing random sequence, that would pluck votes cast for the Democrat and convert them to the Republican choice before they were sent to the computation element within the module. If votes were redirected in a predictable sequence—such as every twentieth ballot—it would be more easily discoverable. But the algorithm he and his cohorts had designed would pluck erratically in no repeated sequence.

One thing was certain, though. Nineteen thousand votes cast for Margaret Westfall in Fulton County would be moved to Will Truitt's column. Over the next two days, a slightly larger number would be similarly moved in Dekalb; a slightly lesser number in Clayton and Cobb. Forsyth County, solidly Republican already, would not be touched. In all, the greater Atlanta area on Election Day would deliver sixty-six thousand more votes to the incumbent senator than he truly received and take from Democrat Westfall an equal, offsetting number.

He made the software alteration in the last machine for Fulton County just minutes before the guard returned.

"Your milkshake." The guard opened the warehouse door and handed the tall cup through.

"What do I owe you?"

"Consider it a gift of the State of Georgia," the guard said. In truth, he had paid himself for the dessert. "For your service to God and country."

★ ★ ★

THE LIEUTENANT

More than anything else, a good drone pilot is a good multitasker. There is never just one data point to react to, hardly ever merely two. Altitude, missile tip orientation, wind speed at path angle and at ground. Weapon ejection force and the audible information coming at the pilot from those in the room might influence any one or more of those variables. All had to be processed in real time.

But Lieutenant Grey Boatwright was well suited for the job. Actually, as it turned out, better suited than he would have preferred. He'd come of age during Donald Trump's presidency, earning admission to the Air Force Academy to pursue his dream of qualifying for elite fighter pilot training. He was highly disciplined, quiet in temperament, cool under stress, patriotic, and apolitical. A favorite of his training officer for all these reasons, he rated at or near the top of every skill and trait test. Except one. He failed, of all things, the eye test.

The Air Force required, at a minimum, uncorrected twenty/

twenty vision in both eyes, and highly preferred unaided eyesight exceeding that standard. In his first ophthalmology exam after the classroom portion of flight school, the young officer tested perfect in his left eye, but twenty/twenty-two in his right. Disheartened as much as the young airman, his training commander ordered a reexamination. Then a third and fourth by a different ophthalmologist. It didn't help. In fact, the second physician scored him at only twenty/twenty-*three* in the flawed eye.

Boatwright sat stunned in his commander's office when he learned the news.

"There is nothing I can do to qualify you for the air," the commander told him. "There is nothing anyone can do."

"I understand."

"But you need to fly, lieutenant. You really need to fly."

"You just said I couldn't."

"I said you can't fly *in the air.* You can't see at twenty feet what qualifiers see at twenty feet. Or further. Up there that's important. With the vibrations, your visual capabilities would be impaired more, even in daylight."

"I get it," said Boatwright.

"But to fly a *drone* you don't need to see twenty feet. You only need to see the instrument panels."

The commander lifted a thick file of test papers from his desk.

"And you have a gift that's more important down here," he said. "Your math and computational skills. Boatwright, they are crazy good." He paged through the papers, stopping to hunch over three or four pages, shaking his head. "Crazy good, lieutenant. Just insane. Unbelievable, really. And unmanned flight is the way it's going. There'll be a day when hardly anything is flown from the aircraft."

It was true that drones and manned aircraft were vastly different to fly. Sleek fighter jets and the mammoth bombers were loaded with automatic digital systems and backup redundancy devices that reduced the need for real-time computations to almost zero. But the gawky drones, even the improved Predator V series and the smaller, nuclear-capable Eaglets, relied on near constant pilot instruction and manual steps driven by computed variables by the man or woman at the control panel and joystick. Aside from runway nose attitude and liftoff speed, hardly anything was routinely preprogrammed because, unlike the "big boys," drones flew at slow airspeeds and comparatively low altitudes. To avoid detection, in-flight speed, altitude, and erratic vector changes were required, irregularly paced to be as unpredictable as possible, dodging the algorithms of surveillance technologies—and all while getting the aircraft to its target at the right time.

Now, two years later, the young lieutenant sat across a different and more solemn commander, Colonel Eugene Wilks. The air in the small office at Charleston Air Force Base seemed stuffy despite the ceiling fan spinning beneath the Spartan off-white acoustic tiles. Boatwright perspired even in his lightweight fatigues.

"We'll wait for Brew," the commander said, expressionless.

Colonel Wilks didn't cut the figure of the usual military commander. Oh, he was standard-issue tall and prone to profanity with the best of them, but he was excessively thin and looked older than his age. His hair was longer than regulation suggested and irregularly combed. The lenses of his glasses were oversized for his smallish face. You couldn't say he had rugged good looks. You couldn't say he looked even rugged. But he was keenly smart with a reputation for fairness that earned him respect from above and below.

He sat with his hands on his desk, unsmiling, looking straight at the lieutenant.

"I don't know how ...," the lieutenant began to speak.

"We'll wait for Brew," the commander interrupted, not sharply, but still unsmiling. He spoke with a smoker's throaty voice.

Two minutes passed in silence before Tyler Brew knocked once and entered. Even in a small room, the slender SEAL moved quickly. He slipped into the chair beside the lieutenant and exchanged rapid salutes with the commander.

"All right," the commander said. "I'm not much for small talk. And this is a hell of a mess. It's pouring shit around here. I don't even want to answer the phone anymore. Every third call is from the goddamned White House."

"I don't know what happened, sir," Boatwright said. "It was nuts."

"Tell that to the Israelis," the commander said. "Somehow, it *did* happen."

But the commander and Brew knew, as bad as it was, it could have been much worse. It was a sad blessing that the runaway drone had targeted an ally, and especially one so dependent on the United States for security. In deep personal love, even the worst mistakes are often accepted without reprisal. And in geopolitical terms, there is nothing that a deep ally won't forgive. The most important thing now was to understand how the lieutenant's drone acted without him—if in fact it had—and prevent it from happening again, especially against a hostile state or the homeland.

"You understand, lieutenant, the first inquiry is *you*. It's all about *you*," Commander Wilks said.

"You mean me, as *on purpose*? That I did this *on purpose*?"

"Yes."

"Do you believe that?"

"I don't *know* anything, so I don't *believe* anything. But Colonel Brew doesn't believe it."

The lieutenant looked at Tyler Brew, his supervising officer. Brew stared down, then raised his eyes to meet the lieutenant's. The two held their eye contact for seconds. The young officer wished Brew's stare was more comforting.

"I don't think you were controlling the thing, Boat," Brew said. "But something happened that you didn't notice. Or that you *did* notice and didn't tell us. Maybe because you know you should have seen it."

"I'm lost," the lieutenant said. "I don't know what you're talking about."

The commander cleared his throat and lit a cigarette. He drew on it and leaned forward over his desk.

"At five minutes thirty-eight seconds on the clock, your control panel was pinged by a satellite," he said. "Not a satellite in the command path," he said.

"What satellite?"

"I can't tell you that. As I said, Boatwright, *you're* the inquiry right now. But you're telling us you didn't observe that ping?"

"Hell no."

"It would have shown on your incoming transponder face. The stick vibrated. The seat too. The signal system recorded all of it." The commander pointed to a stack of log data on the corner of his desk.

Inadvertent satellite contacts were not uncommon. The US military had thousands of them orbiting, as did other powers, not to mention the commercial satellites that were the backbone of media communications and ordinary business transactions—millions of them every hour. Pilots and technicians called the commercial array, collectively, *The Amazon Galaxy*. The young lieutenant knew that such contacts during drone flight, even as launch approached, were just a reality and, in the normal case, no cause for concern. In the normal case. But he remembered no pings that launch morning.

"I didn't feel any vibration. There wasn't any. What satellite sent a signal?"

"I told you, we can't tell you that, Grey," Brew said. "Not now. You're going up to Langley in a couple of weeks. For a debriefing."

"You mean a grilling?"

"I won't lie to you. It won't be any fun. By the time you get there, they'll have your eighth-grade class picture and already talked to the kids in it."

"Can I study the data logs first?"

"No," the commander said, in a tone inviting no appeal. "Until then, you're on base-only leave. Do *not* try to leave base." He pushed his cigarette butt into an ashtray in his desk drawer.

"That will be all," he said. "That is, I *hope* this will be all. For all our sake."

THREAT OF A WHOLE NEW ORDER

At the Pentagon and Langley, separate teams poured over military transmissions and commercial internet intercepts trying to understand how Lieutenant Grey Boatwright's Predator V drone had been overtaken.

The possibility of such mischief in civilian transportation had been appreciated for years. Private industry and the government had collaborated to double down on the security of electronic systems in vehicles and commercial aircraft that sophisticated hackers could access through the internet. Additional measures had been taken after a demented geek managed to remotely misdirect his ex-wife and her Chevy Malibu into a California canyon a few years earlier. Vehicle and aircraft manufacturers had thereafter adopted shared proprietary guard systems; there had been no interventions since. And all the while, the deep systems of the military's communications channels, using far thicker firewalls and very few access points to the general internet, had been assumed impervious.

No longer.

The CIA and Department of Defense teams had different objectives. The former's, working with the FBI, was to understand how the craft had been intercepted and determine who did it. The latter wanted to be certain that it never happened again, *no matter who* did it.

The president gave each equal priority. She knew the perpetrator, whomever it was, posed an immediate and unique threat to national security and global stability.

"Suicide bombers, lone wolves, terrorists using trucks to mow down crowds," Del Winters said to her national security team. "They're all terrible. They're all dangerous. Every country in the world is trying to stop them. But *this*, this is a whole different category."

"Who would have thought the internet would come to this?" Vernon Lazar said.

"It's being weaponized under our noses," the president said. "It may have been used to turn an advanced weapon of the United States against our own ally. And if that can be done, it can be used against us directly. To attack our own country, our own people. The Tel Aviv death count is seven hundred and rising. This is the worst damn thing since 9/11."

The president knew that the perverse genius or geniuses who had infiltrated the military systems had to be identified and eliminated. She also knew, though, that preventing a recurrence at the hands of anyone else was vital too. It was undeniable that the nation's drone control systems were presently exposed and vulnerable. Who knew what other elements of the nation's arsenal were also? She resolved that whatever it took, no matter the cost, no matter the commitment of resources, a new and failsafe communication system for the military had to be developed as rapidly as humanly possible.

En route to Israel on Air Force One, she convened her first meeting on the subject. She shared her convictions with Vernon Lazar and the secretary of state, Harry Sells. They agreed. She asked for their ideas on resources to lead the development project.

"Wilson Bryce in my technology division would be ideal to lead the scientific team," defense secretary Lazar said. "He's a crack computer scientist. Has a rare grip on both hardware and software innovation. You'd don't see both in one guy very often."

"He could liaise with the groups within State too," Harry Sells said. "They all know him. They all like him."

"Do you remember Wilson Bryce?" Lazar asked the president.

"I remember the name."

"He worked on the Eaglets' Nest covert program last year under the Navy SEAL Tyler Brew," Lazar said.

"Yes, now I remember. But I never met him, did I?"

"He didn't attend any of the briefings in person. But he helped the civilian engineer from Pittsburgh."

"Stanley Bigelow."

"Yeah. Bryce gave him special software to encrypt his drawings."

"What's Wilson been doing since then?"

"Well, he's taken on new duties. He's now head of the whole technology division at DOD. But I could relieve him of all that to avoid distraction."

"Do it," the president said.

Lazar called Bryce at home immediately from Air Force One. Recalling the conversation later, Lazar described himself as *asking* the scientist to consider taking on a new assignment. The scientist didn't recall it exactly that way. To him, he really wasn't *asked* anything. It didn't matter. Both understood the urgency and import of the problem.

Bryce agreed to get to the Pentagon right away and draft

a work plan. When she heard that Lazar was finished with his instructions, Del Winters asked him to hand her the phone.

"Wilson," she said. "This is President Winters. Whatever it takes."

She handed the phone back to Lazar before the scientist could say a word.

10

★ ★ ★

SUSPICION

Theories abounded at the CIA and FBI as to the perpetrator of the attack on Israel. But little evidence lay beneath any of them. Of course, there were the usual suspects: the nation states of Russia, Iran, and Syria foremost among them. The CIA, in particular, believed it was probably one of them. No one believed that any of the individual jihadist groups could possibly possess the technical know-how displayed, but the action seemed so far beyond the range of rational military options—plainly risking world war—that most in the defense department, and President Del Winters too, were dubious that any nation state, however aggressive, was responsible.

The president had grown to know well the post-Putin Russian president, Dmitri Devinov. His attitudes were Putinesque, rooted in the desire, above all else, that Russia be seen and respected as a world power on equal footing with the United States. But his manner was more cerebral and contemplative. In Kremlin meetings, he was quoted as saying, "Be prepared to act at once. And then don't." She did not believe Devinov would act precipitously, and he had been anything but defensive when she had called him the day of the Tel Aviv bombing. Nor did she think the Russian would order a strike that would so surely trigger global condemnation of his proud country—and a likely war too.

Syria was a harder question, but not by much. She disliked the newest Assad and deplored his iron-fisted policies. But he was as brilliant as he was brutal. He never made that one step across the line, at least not of his own accord. His aggression always came with Russian backing, or even precipitation.

Iran? She couldn't fathom it as the actor. With the largest population in the Middle East, it had the most to lose by such a violent provocation. And consistent intelligence assessments described continued softening in the secular side of its leadership, driven principally by its younger masses anxious for educations in the West and the material prosperity they associated with it.

No, to Del Winters this whole thing just did not add up. A rogue element within a hostile country's military was more plausible, but even then, such actors would require the assistance of many minds, and probably access to American intelligence.

In the absence of rational leads, the CIA and FBI defaulted to a deeply seated core trait in each institution: suspicion. Suspicion of an inside job.

There were two likely possibilities, they reasoned. Someone on the ground at the deployment base in Qatar with access to the drone linkups and the physical crafts themselves. Or Lieutenant Grey Boatwright.

The investigators quickly ruled out sabotage on the ground in Qatar. No foreign nationals had been allowed near the aircraft. Surveillance cameras were checked and rechecked. There was no suspicious activity around the drone in question, or any of the others stationed there. It had flown perfectly nine days earlier and the digital film of every second of every day in the interim before the fateful flight was studied carefully. Nothing was done to that aircraft as it sat in its hangar.

But the case of Lieutenant Boatwright was not as clear-cut. The FBI discovered that he was disappointed when rejected for fighter pilot training. That was hardly a secret, but the investigators were surprised to learn of the depth of his unhappiness over the decision. He had told a fellow officer from the academy that the air force's ruling was unfair. He believed—erroneously—that a colonel's son with poorer vision than his had been passed. After too many drinks at the officers' club, he pressed his point with others, including a well-liked major who knew the other trainee and his father and disputed the claim. The young lieutenant lost his control, and a scuffle broke out between them. Only the intercession of the tolerant major himself saved him from a night in the brig to cool off.

Two other issues were more troubling.

The CIA unearthed a falsehood in his training application. It involved his wife. Asked whether anyone in his immediate family used narcotics or had been treated for addiction, he had written no. It could not have been a question of simply checking the wrong box. There *were* no boxes; a written and initialed response was required on the form because the military considered it such an important question for a new pilot. But the records of a VA hospital in Denver contained notes of the referral of Janice Boatwright to an opioid addiction rehabilitation facility in the area, and the government's payment for same. Twice.

Under questioning at Langley, Grey Boatwright admitted the false answer he had given three years earlier. Asked why he had done so, he was forthright; it was not because he was trying to protect his wife or himself from embarrassment, he acknowledged. No, he gave the false response because he was afraid that her problem would disqualify him. It would not be fair to hold her issue against him, he said. She had recovered fully anyway, and both were entitled to their privacy. But his principal motive, he admitted, was to avoid rejection from flight school.

The investigators believed they had, as one of them said, "an angry liar." They proceeded with an extensive polygraph examination, administered by an experienced and trusted technician, assisted by a CIA agent with intimate knowledge of drone mechanics and control. They walked the young officer through every small step of the mission that went to hell.

"Were you seated at the controls at five minutes thirty-eight seconds to intended launch?"

"Yes," he said.

"Did you observe a satellite ping on your transponder at that time?"

"No."

"Did you feel a seat vibration at that time?"

"No."

"Did you intentionally yield control of the Predator V prior to or after the first missile released?"

"No."

The examiner studied the response data assiduously. The lieutenant failed the test miserably. He was sent to a holding area below the examination room.

Within the hour, Tyler Brew received the report of the interrogation and the polygraph. He flew immediately to Langley to speak with the investigators. On his way to the hangar at Charleston Air Base, he called the CIA director, Jack Watson. He knew him well. The two had worked closely on the Eaglets Nest program a year earlier and had collaborated to protect Stanley Bigelow from near abduction at the hands of

North Korean agents suspicious of his activities. Their mutual trust was solid as rock.

"I'm coming up to Langley," he told Watson. "Are you there now?"

"Yes."

"I need you to sign something."

"I'll be waiting. I'll clear you downstairs."

Watson didn't ask if the Navy SEAL was coming concerning the interrogation of Grey Boatwright. He didn't have to.

When Brew walked into his office a hundred minutes later, the CIA chief barely glanced at the sheet the SEAL handed him before signing it. It read:

TO ALL INTERROGATION AND
SECURITY GROUP PERSONNEL:

You are directed to respond affirmatively to all requests of Captain Tyler Brew, United States Navy, SEAL, in the matter of the interrogation and custody of Lieutenant Grey Boatwright, USAF.

J.T.H. Watson
DIRECTOR
CENTRAL INTELLIGENCE AGENCY

Watson folded the order and placed it into an envelope.

"Whatever it is you're doing, Tyler," he said, "good luck." Then he moved close to Brew. "There's a lot of push to put this on somebody," he said.

"That's why I came."

"Well, if you come to the same conclusion they are, I will feel a lot better about it being correct."

"Maybe they *are* right about him," Brew said. "But I'm not convinced yet. Thanks for signing that. I owe you one, Jack."

"You will never owe me anything," Watson said, and he handed him the envelope.

11

★ ★ ★

AN ASSASSIN RETURNS

Only hours after Brew departed Charleston for Langley, another man skilled in covert actions made nearly the same trip in the opposite direction. Majir Asheed, a cool and evasive senior operative of the Syrian intelligence service, drove eight hours from Washington to Charleston. He did not know Tyler Brew, and Tyler Brew did not know him. But the past actions of each, and the future decisions of both, would change that.

Fourteen months earlier, Asheed had been sent to the American capital to find, interrogate, and kill Ruth Morgenthal, a civilian from Chicago newly selected by the Pentagon, the Syrians believed, for a secret weapons project in the Middle East or Israel. Damascus learned of the Chicago civil engineer by intercepting her daughter's communications.

It was common for foreign intelligence operatives to hack and monitor technical employees of US defense contractors, and Syrian intelligence had intercepted email traffic between a Lockheed-Martin engineer in northern Virginia—Ruth Morgenthal's former husband—and his daughter.

Ruth and the girl's father were long divorced, but they maintained cordial relations insofar as their daughter, Melinda, was concerned. About to enter college, Melinda went to Washington to help her mother get situated in the apartment provided for her by the government during the anticipated project; the daughter emailed her father to ask that he come into the city to drive her to campus at the end of her visit in the capital. She unwittingly stated that her mother had taken an assignment for the government "on some secret stuff."

Asheed and a junior agent tracked Ruth to her apartment. Her daughter was home with her, awaiting a pizza delivery. The foreign agents stormed the apartment when the delivery was made. The delivery man was slaughtered immediately. Ruth and her daughter were murdered in the apartment soon after, following Majir's interrogation of them. Neither knew any details, or even general information about the covert project that had brought the engineer to Washington—she hadn't been briefed yet. She and her daughter had nothing to give. Except their lives. Asheed's orders were to leave no witnesses. He followed them.

Perhaps, the Syrians thought, the Americans had put the project on hold when their specialist was killed. Finding nothing else to go on, Damascus eventually lost interest. Until recently.

A Russian intelligence officer bragged in a meeting with Syrian intelligence chiefs that the Russians had "put one to the North Koreans" in an odd story about assisting the Americans. According to the Russian, an old civil engineer from Pittsburgh was being hunted by the North Koreans, believing he was designing a secret military installation.

"We had a young hacker on contract in Sweden," the Russian had shared. "The kid put us onto the old American engineer.

At first it looked suspicious, but then we saw the guy was just working on a farming project, vegetable research for the US government. Someplace in South Carolina. These North Koreans hack *our* kid in Sweden and find out about the American too. Can you believe it! They send killers to Stockholm and kill our kid!"

"Really?" the Syrian in the meeting said.

"Yes! And they knew he was hacking for us. Killed him anyway."

"Did you retaliate?"

"Better!" the Russian said, smiling. "We tipped the Americans about them! Told them these idiots might come after the old American too. And they tried, too, but the Americans caught them first. And then you know what the Americans did?"

"Locked them up?"

"Better! They sent the North Koreans to *us!*"

"What did you do with them?" the Syrian asked.

The Russian grinned perniciously.

"Let us say we addressed our grievances for our lost contractor. Moscow style."

The Russians had a good laugh over it all, but in Damascus there was little amusement. The timing seemed too coincidental. And Majir Asheed had reported that the only things he learned from Ruth Morgenthal before killing her was that her expertise was *civil* engineering and that she was to work for the Pentagon.

Perhaps this old man from Pittsburgh was Morgenthal's replacement, Damascus thought. And it didn't sound like vegetables to the Syrians.

So Asheed was dispatched to Charleston to learn what he could, working from year-old news accounts of the attempted assault on an out-of-town engineer said to be working on an experimental storage facility at the United States Vegetable Laboratory on Highway 17 near the city. When he checked into his hotel an envelope was awaiting him. It contained a key wrapped in a cardboard sleeve bearing an address and a post office box number in the city. His orders were waiting in the box in a business-size envelope, together with a stack of clippings and copies of website news reports. His instructions usually came this way. Snail mail might be slow, but it was more secure nowadays than email. The orders were terse.

> What was happening last year at USDA site, Charleston?
>
> Civil engineer involved. Possible link to Morgenthal woman.
>
> News stories attached. No witnesses.

Majir received his instructions joylessly. At fifty-one, he was an experienced, careful assassin. But a weary one. There was a time when he enjoyed his work, but now it was weighing on him. Growing up in the city of Hohm, he had been attracted to the nationalistic ideas of the first Assad. Syria would shed its second-class status to the cultural histories of Egypt and Iran. It would become their equal. It would fervently pursue the elimination of Israel and the Jews. And it would never cozy up to the Americans as Saudi Arabia had.

But now, his vigor for those ideals had lessened. It was not a desire for money or interest in material comforts that diluted them. And it was certainly not sympathy for terrorism or terrorists. He detested extremist ideology and considered it a complete perversion of the Muslim faith, as did the rulers in Damascus. They had been trying to exterminate ISIS and its bedfellows for many years.

What had changed Majir was simply life—simply love.

He had fallen in love with an Indian immigrant in England after 9/11. Melaha helped manage a small, less expensive hotel in London where he often stayed on his frequent assignments there. She knew nothing of the true nature of his work until later, when Majir sought the approval of his supervisors in Syria to marry her. He was relieved when, in the end, Damascus was pleased with the arrangement. Marriage might bring a genuine UK passport, it reasoned, and it would be easier to maintain Majir's cover and explain his extensive travel through the commonwealth. Families travel. And the bride had siblings and cousins spread across Britain.

But Melaha Asheed was a deeply loving and exceptional person, and far more influential with her husband than his Syrian masters could have envisioned. The couple soon had a daughter, Desh, now sixteen and beautiful. She shared her mother's values of kindness and respect for others. This affected Majir greatly. Though he spent long periods away on orders, many of them in the United States, he worked to keep a close relationship with his daughter, who reciprocated warmly.

For her part, Melaha loved her husband dearly, as a man and as a father, despite her reservations about his work, of which she eventually knew all. As much as she worried he would lose his life, she worried he would lose his soul. He was sensitive and gentle in his heart. He was contemplative. He was never angry and only as selfish as any worthy man. And he shared his thoughts with her easily—all of them. Such a soul could not be lost, she thought. Such a loss could not be borne.

"Majir," she told him. "Pleasure is a holy gift. Pleasure is divine. It is meant to restore us. Do not foul it in killing. Take no pleasure in killing, Majir."

And he didn't. He never had derived pleasure, per se, from

the violence he practiced. But it was true that his feelings were changing about it. He used to sense nothing in the act, at most a numbness. It was necessary; it was ordered of him. He made no decisions; he was merely the instrument of a person's fate. But in recent years, he *did* begin to have feelings when he killed. He could not say they were yet feelings of revulsion. But, surely at least, feelings of reluctance. He wondered if it was enough to feel mere reluctance. Was he losing his soul anyway? Had he already lost it? His doubt spawned sorrow, beginning to approach regret, even contrition. The murder of the Morgenthals was especially worrisome. A mother and her daughter, a girl only a little older than his own. And for what? Nothing had been learned.

He was relieved when assignments did not include killing, as was beginning to be more often the case, especially his newer work as an intermediary with hate groups in the United States. Damascus had brutally extinguished its own domestic "insurgents," resorting even to repulsive chemical bombs to do so, but it sorely appreciated the damage those insurgents had leveled on governing. It thought the United States could use more insurgents of its own, and the hundreds of hate groups scattered across it were the closest equivalent. It wanted to aid them, especially with cyber technology and funding. Majir and other agents were its means of doing so.

But aiding hate was more difficult than you might think. The American groups were so different in makeup, focus, and capability. Some were just bundles of white individuals sharing an extreme dislike of blacks, but without antigovernment ideas. Others were inspired—who could know why—by century-old European notions of Nazi supremacy and its preoccupation with Jews as the source of all geopolitical evil. Still others could be classified as pure anarchists—detesting authority under any name, and especially authority in the form of government and laws of the state. And some, usually termed "militias," didn't truly hate anyone. They were just men who liked to play with guns, *sans* the rigors and commitment of regular military service. Most of their members were not racist, anti-Semitic, or even antigovernment. They viewed themselves simply as patriotic citizen soldiers, standing ready to help their country.

What the Syrians wanted were extremists who hated two things, above all else. The US government and Jews. They wanted groups as interested in playing with computers as with guns, able to ply American social media to Syria's ends and even infiltrate media outlets and cause them to advance fabricated news and propaganda. It wanted more groups like the Band of Free Brothers, from Michigan.

His work evaluating and developing domestic hate groups was why he drove, instead of flew, to Charleston. He wanted to stop in central Virginia to meet with the leaders of a group there. Damascus wanted an assessment of the group's capacities, especially the intellect and technology knowledge of its leaders. He should work it in when convenient. The new order to Charleston, Majir judged, seemed a convenient enough opportunity.

Getting a meeting with the Virginia group was not difficult. He contacted one of the leaders by phone, posing as a manufacturer's representative from Remington ammunition. *Could he meet to discuss his ability to provide ammunition supplies at terms more favorable than Cabela's, where he understood the group was presently purchasing them?* When the leader did not immediately agree to meet, Asheed noted that if a supply agreement could be arranged, he had the flexibility to include blank rounds, possibly handy for the group's training exercises, at no cost. "Why, then, let's meet," the leader replied.

Majir was not impressed, however, with what he observed

when they did. If their leaders were any indication, the Virginia group loved its national government and military as much as it deeply resented blacks and other persons of color. He doubted there was an anarchist or principled Jew-hater in the bunch. So, he proceeded to Charleston.

In his hotel room, he spread out the old news clippings and website printouts about the incident in downtown Charleston and read them carefully. The law enforcement official quoted in them was the short, old, colorful sheriff of Charleston County, Weldon Bechant. An FBI agent-in-charge, named Bobby Beach, was also mentioned. But Asheed never considered targeting them. He had not lasted twenty-three years in undercover work in the United States and England by assassinating policemen.

Instead, he researched the facility on Highway 17. Sure enough, there really was a United States Vegetable Laboratory. It was managed by a James Molineaux, who, according to the government website, had been in charge there for years. Majir concluded the manager surely would know at least whether the hubbub in Charleston last year truly related to an agricultural experiment or was cover for secret military work.

They say that a little knowledge is a dangerous thing. James Molineaux would soon learn that having a little more of it can be worse. Much worse.

★ ★ ★

THEY DIDN'T TEACH THEM THIS

Technical presentations to the president about proposed military systems normally were practiced, repracticed, and washed yet again before they were made formally to the commander-in-chief. But Wilson Bryce's new project was anything but normal. It was screaming with emergency. There was no time to stand on ceremony.

Since the call from Air Force One, he and his team had worked secretly around the clock in a cavernous space deep in the Pentagon. There were no office walls, not even cubicles. Only long laminated tables with shelves beneath, austere swivel stools, and long glossy marker boards. And drawings. Drawings and more drawings, many on architectural paper stretching for yards and held at their edges by—of all things—duct tape. Bryce himself never left the Pentagon complex for sixteen days. Many of them he worked at the tables for nearly twenty hours before sleeping on a rollaway bed set up in the building's fitness center where he could also shower and shave. He never complained. His wife may have. She was told only that he was safe, not far away, and working on something that could not be discussed.

Wilson Bryce, now forty-six, was an early member of the technology force that labored against terrorism quietly—unnoticed, uncredited. Many thousands of young Americans, inspired by the devastation of 9/11, made choices that were far from their consciences before that day. And how the nation had benefitted. Young men and women from all manner of career paths streamed into government service to lend their talents to the cause. Athletic types, some with real prospects in professional sports, signed up for military service, hoping to qualify for the Special Forces that were the point of the spear in the fight overseas. Many with language skills, and especially patriotic Muslim Americans, answered the desperate call for translators and intelligence operatives to work undercover in theater, at great personal risk. And before long, it was clear that computer technology and its possibilities were critical. For surveillance. For detection. For communication. You could not have enough of it. You could not have enough Wilson Bryces.

Most held civilian posts. No uniforms or medals, no travel to faraway places, no public acclaim. They might not be brawny or swift; they probably did not exude senses of courage or leadership. Often, they were shy, awkward, mistakenly seen as scatterbrained. But where it mattered—between the ears and in the heart—they were as strong and patriotic as any in the fight. And where it mattered in the country's leadership, including in the White House, they were as valued as any tool in the war.

Bryce had to have been utterly exhausted when he was escorted by a young marine into the wood-paneled Pentagon conference room where President Winters and the others sat awaiting him. The room was just two levels above his workspace and temporary living quarters, but it seemed a world away. The dark walnut table stretched like a highway the length of the room. One long wall was racked with video display equipment. Writing tablets lined each side of the endless table and collapsible, small white lamps beamed over each in perfect high intensity rows like the crosses at a military cemetery.

The marine knocked once and opened the door.

"Mr. Bryce," he announced. The door closed.

Bryce looked awkwardly out of place as he stood in the room. Half of those awaiting him were in uniform, sitting rock-ribbed straight, eyes trained on him. Lazar and his aides were all sharply dressed, as was the president. Tall and gangly, Bryce wore blue jeans, a loose tan T-shirt and slip-on canvas shoes, sockless. His long light hair, reaching in the back below his neckline, was tucked behind his ears and held by the bows of oddly serious black eyeglasses with thick rims. He smiled and looked nervously around the room.

Only the president rose from the table. She did not step to greet him, though. She just stood at her place, the middle seat of the far side of the table, furthest from the corner door from which he had entered.

"Wilson," she said. "We have spoken before." She was referring to the call from Air Force One not three weeks ago.

"Well, *you* did," he said.

She smiled.

"I am sorry if I appeared short," she said.

"I understood."

"Well, anyway, thank you. And for your work last year, assisting Stanley Bigelow."

Only a few in the room even knew what she was referencing; Eaglets' Nest was still classified, and most had not been aware of it even when it was under way.

"He is a fine gentleman. It was my honor. But thank you, ma'am."

"I know this new assignment has been intense. I understand you haven't left this building in weeks. And that you have something to report. So, please sit down."

She pointed to the only empty place at the table. It was directly across from her, which startled Bryce. She had asked specifically that the seating be so arranged. She wanted to see the scientist as clearly and closely as possible.

It took Bryce just a few seconds to cue up the expansive wall monitor above and behind his seat. The laptop in front of him permitted him to see the same images it displayed on the large monitor without turning away from the president. He didn't even have to adjust the bright little lamp at his place; a sensor in it dimmed it automatically. *It would have been nice to have these downstairs for the last two weeks,* he thought.

He started with an image of the entire United States, blank except for a bold outline of its border. The Hawaiian Islands, Alaska, and the US territories were included too. On the next image, the shapes were populated with hundreds of small dots, including a great number along the shorelines.

"Those are our military installations," he said. "They vary greatly in size, of course, but these markers are uniform, to keep it simple for now. Most of them along water are coast guard locations."

The president interjected almost at once.

"There are more than purely military posts up there," she said.

As a career military officer, to the rank of lieutenant general in the army prior to her sudden emergence in political life, she knew the country's military map like her father knew a baseball scorecard. The scientist's image included dots in central Missouri and western Tennessee, places she knew no military installations were located.

"Good eye," said Bryce. He meant it; he didn't think anyone would notice that fact. "We included the hidden data centers, too. Most of them are underground. Homeland Security operates them, not the military. But they're so integrated to the bases, we have them in here."

The president nodded. The public still did not appreciate the extent of the nation's hidden security and surveillance infrastructure. After 9/11, President George W. Bush had asked for repeated, secret congressional appropriations to fund dozens of specialized buildings needed to house, maintain, and analyze the enormous volume of surveillance data that began to be collected around-the-clock, around-the world. Billions had been authorized. Most of the special meetings to seek funding had been held at the Pentagon for security purposes, and to impress the congressional leaders with military gravitas. President Bush attended many of them personally. Vice President Dick Cheney attended all. Pentagon careerists joked that Cheney spent more time in the building in those months than when he ran the place under the first President Bush.

The successors to President Bush continued the funding and added to it. The Edward Snowden affair, involving the NSA contractor who leaked information about the broad personal data collection efforts of the government to WikiLeaks, raised public awareness to some extent. But not much. Most Americans believed that the collection of even private information was justified in any event, in view of the national security threats posed by advancing terrorism. Certainly, the presidents all did. The secret centers continued to be installed unnoticed, some in surprising places.

One of the largest was buried beneath a huge Walmart store

in Charlotte. The CIA had met secretly with the company's regional manager when the store was about to be built. He was a large, fit, patriotic man with a spiritual bent and a deep mellifluous voice. Now long retired to South Carolina, he was the only private citizen that even knew the underground facility existed. As the government asked, he never told a soul about it. Not his superiors in the company, not even his wife.

His discretion earned him a hand-addressed holiday card every year from the White House. His wife always puzzled over the surprising annual arrival.

"They keep sending these!" she said. "And you don't even like this one!" She was referring to a White House occupant for whom the retiree had not voted. He simply shook his head and smiled.

"It's funny the friends you make," was all he said.

Bryce then anticipated a more obvious question.

"I guess I should say up front that what we've come up with is a system where the hardware is all located within our own borders. We deal with everything else through secure satellites already in place. We will probably need more of them in the future, but we can get it up and running with what we have now."

His next image on the monitor looked like a connect-the-dots diagram from a children's coloring book. Lines, in three colors, reached maze-like to every one of the installations. He explained that each line represented physical communications cable constructed of military grade, proprietary optic fiber. Each color reflected an independent communications channel so that if any one of them was disrupted, either by force of nature or hostile intent, software systems with triple backup capability would immediately divert all traffic to an unimpaired channel.

"Will our existing aircraft need to be retrofitted to use this new system?" Lazar asked.

"Only some of them," the scientist said. "The stealth bombers will need the most, but even that is less than you'd think. Mostly, it's a matter of changing out internet modules to ones that can read these dedicated lines. We change them frequently anyway. The cost is not big."

The president extended her hands.

"*Whatever* it takes," she repeated. She did not want creative thinking inhibited by money or politics, which, she knew, often were one and the same.

Bryce showed diagrams simulating the infrastructure and interactions of the existing worldwide web. "Every electronic communication in the world enters and leaves just a few highway backbones," he said. "There are billions, even trillions of passageways, but only a few backbone channels. Think of them as on-ramps and exit ramps. The key to security is the protection of those points of access. The information and data passing through the main highway lanes is moving so fast and is so undifferentiated that its inherently damn safe. It can't be captured and made sense of. But on the ramps, it's coherent and vulnerable. Only as safe as the strength of the firewalls around them."

The only break in the scientist's presentation came in an intermission report on the security status of military and civilian communication apparatuses since the horrific incident in Israel. Susan McShane, the CIA's deputy director, delivered the update. It wasn't entirely comforting. While no other successful penetrations had been made, "edge assaults" had been attempted against communication switching systems at several air bases. Unfamiliar malware had been used to attempt break-ins to control centers. The assaults were batted away, but it was worrisome in the extreme that they had permeated outer firewalls to get that far inside. Commercial aviation systems fared better, a relief to the airlines and the national economy. Air travel had fallen precipitously in the days following the Israel bombing, but was returning to normal levels. McShane's conclusion: the sooner the military channels could be completely replaced, the better.

"You can look at this design as a whole new internet," Bryce explained when his presentation resumed. "A private, beefed-up, dedicated internet that runs through its own new backbone channel that nothing else runs through. The new backbone does have a few on-ramps to the current web backbones. Have to have them to communicate with civilian assets and as backup in case of failure in the new backbone. But we can super-firewall those ramps. There aren't many. And there are *no* ramps *from* the existing worldwide web *to* it."

The president asked if the installation could begin immediately.

"There's a problem with that, Madame President," Bryce said. "A *big* problem."

The room fell silent. He looked awkwardly around the table and closed his laptop.

"And what is that?" asked the president.

"Ma'am, we don't have *any idea* how to bury this thing. Or what to bury it *in*. Or how to house the transfer stations underground along the routes. We're not talking about simple fiber-optic in three-inch plastic conduit, a few feet below grade. We're talking about six thousand miles of much more complex fiber, through all kind of terrain. The whole system depends on the physical integrity of the pipe it runs through, and its concealability. Once it's buried, it *can't* be found, and if it is, it has to be indestructible."

"You have *no* thoughts on that?"

"Ma'am, they don't teach us that in computer school." He smiled wanly.

The president looked in turn at each person around the table. No one tried to speak. A viable solution had been presented. But it was thwarted by a sobering problem.

She thanked Bryce and adjourned the meeting. She did not smile. Wanly or otherwise.

★ ★ ★

EXCESSIVELY

It was early the next Monday morning in the East Wing residence. The president and her father sat, as they did most mornings, with coffee, toast, and newspapers. Every three minutes or so, one of them would say something. Usually, it was Henry. He was reading the *New York Times*, but next to his plate the president observed a dog-eared copy of *Baseball Week*. It triggered a thought.

"Did you talk with Stanley Bigelow last night?" she asked. She knew the two usually had a call on Sunday evenings.

He looked up over his paper and nodded.

"We talked about the playoffs," he said. Postseason play was about half done; the Pirates were still alive, having eliminated the Cardinals. "Stanley is amazing. He has a theory that late-season minor league call-ups that make the postseason roster have an 80 percent chance of outperforming their minor league numbers if they are used."

"Really," Del said flatly.

"Yeah. Did you know that Wayne Comer had a lifetime World Series batting average of *one thousand*!"

"I've never heard of Wayne Comer."

"Nobody has. The Tigers called him up in 1968. Little guy, centerfielder from West Virginia. Great glove. Batted once in the World Series against the Cardinals. And had a hit!"

"Startling," Del said dryly.

"Stanley knew that—who knows how—and it started him on this theory. Now he's pulled together all the statistics on over a hundred call-ups who appeared in postseason games in the past ten years. Hitters, pitchers, everybody. I love this guy." He pointed to the edition of *Baseball Week* on the table. "I'm listing the call-ups for this year. They've got it in there. I'll watch for them."

The president was pleased, much more than she showed, that her father and Stanley had become such friends. More and more of his old military friends had either passed away or retired to faraway places. He was losing touch with them. Without grandchildren, he needed activities and things to talk about. Del regularly invited him to join the frequent dinners she hosted at the White House, but, with a few exceptions, he didn't prefer the company of the political class. And when she hosted military chiefs, neither of them thought it appropriate for him to attend. The (Ret.) that followed his formal title was not just a trivial symbol. He needed to stay out of military affairs. Stanley presented no such conflicts and a large amount of amiability. They regarded each other equally skilled in their respective professions and equally appreciative of their favorite game.

"How's Stanley getting along?" she asked.

"Wonderfully."

"Enjoying married life?"

"Excessively." Del noticed the hint of envy in his voice.

"Healthy, then?"

"Yes. A few of the pounds may be back, he says. But he walks the dog a lot, with the FBI woman and Helen. Seems happy. Very. And Helen was reassigned to Dayton. Did you hear that?"

"No. *Should* I have heard that?" She held her paper to the side and looked at her father, a little sternly.

"No, you shouldn't have," he said. He did not look back.

She wondered if he had meddled, but there were some things you had to leave to a general's prerogative. She let it go.

"Aren't the Pirates going to be playing the Nationals here in the playoffs?" she asked. "Why don't you invite Stanley to go with you?"

"I already have. He's coming for the Sunday game."

"Where is he staying?"

"I don't know, some place he likes. You know him, he has a taste for the finer things."

"Well, have him stay here at the White House."

Her father's eyes flared as he smiled.

"Really? Why, he will love that! Helen too?"

"Of course."

They returned to their newspapers, but quickly the First Father wondered something.

"Del, you aren't thinking you need Stanley again, are you?"

She held her coffee cup near her lips.

"I am thinking the country may need him again."

"For what?" He sounded concerned.

"I can't tell you."

"Well, I hope it's not dangerous this time."

"I can't see how. It's a domestic thing, not in any hot spot. And it may not be his cup of tea anyway."

"Well, just don't expect him to start anything until after the World Series." He finished his coffee. "Please. Not until after the Series."

PART 2

14

★ ★ ★

THE ODD COUPLE OF EVIL

Lester "Buddy" Binton, rough-cut, big, and profane, didn't care much for the slender Syrian he knew only as Maji. But he did like his money and guns.

Majir Asheed, spiritual, stylish, and gentle in his own way, did not care much for Buddy Binton, founder and leader of the Band of Free Brothers. But he did appreciate his extraordinary intellect and computer science knowledge.

Buddy and the Syrian were quite different men. But as often is the case, two vastly different men will meet the other's needs if they have in common something important enough to each. And Buddy and the Syrian did.

Their bond was not born of anything you could call noble, like the stories you hear of bitter political rivals who share a love of classical music, or devotion to the same religious faith, or even the game of golf they might share together. No, the ties that bound the hate group leader from Michigan and the Middle

Eastern agent and assassin were not of love. They were ties of detestation. And, in truth, only two of them.

They detested the government of the United States. And they detested Jews.

The foundations of their hates were as polar opposite as their personalities.

Majir disliked Jews, especially those in Israel, because he saw them as illegitimate displacers, occupying the land and earth that history had devolved, in his worldview, to the Palestinian Muslims. The foundation of his hatred was political, not personal. Jews were not inferior *per se*; they were just wrongly entitled. They didn't belong there.

And Majir disliked the US government because he viewed it as the arrogant world power that had politically and militarily enabled that rearrangement of historical territorial rights, forcibly installing Israel as a nation state and then protecting it against its natural enemies.

Buddy Binton, as they say, was a horse of a different color.

His detestation of Jews was simpler to describe but harder to rationalize. He, and those who stood with him, did not claim any ancestral stake in the history of the Middle East or its political evolution. Their hatred was grounded in different earth: envy and a conviction of superiority. It was grounded in the resentment of the perceived success and wealth of Jews as a class, achieved, they convinced themselves, not through merit and education, but by wile and connivance. And this resentment-fueled envy was further stoked by the frustration inherent in observing daily the prosperity of those seen as surely inferior. How unfair; how outrageous; how deeply angering.

And the Michigander detested the US government for reasons only vaguely attached to its policy toward Israel. In truth, it wasn't about policy at all. It was about control. It was about authority and rules, and having to live under them, which he and his followers found conceptually insufferable. The federal government told *them* what to do—in all manner of things—instead of *them* telling *it* what to do. To Binton and his band, the notions of government and individual freedom were mutually exclusive. The so-called rule of law was nothing other than being told what you could do and what you couldn't. A person accepting that concept as an organizing social principle was a submissive, weak subject, trading his *absolute* right to act purely as he desired for the status of prisoner at the hands of an overbearing state, and, worse, a state manipulated by money-hungry and money-possessing Jews.

Yes, Buddy Binton and his followers were anarchists. Anarchists who hated Jews. And, oh yes, who loved guns.

"Hello, Binton," said Majir, extending his hand across the coffee shop table. His diluted accent caused him to pronounce his name Bin*teen*, which irked the big man with unkempt facial hair.

"It's Bin-TUN," he replied. "TUN, like 'ton of bricks'." He returned his hand, not vigorously, and sat down. It irritated Binton that the smooth Syrian's English diction seemed flawless except when it came to his name.

Majir looked him straight in the eye but without reaction. The Syrian had arrived first for the meeting at Joe & Rosie's in the small town of Dexter, Michigan, forty-five miles west of Detroit. He selected a table near the front of the café, several places away from the nearest other customers. He was dressed in his usual black slacks and long-sleeved black shirt. He cut a handsome figure with his trim frame, neatly groomed salt-and-pepper beard, thick black hair, and dark eyes.

Asheed's stay in Charleston to find the USDA manager had been cut short, a good thing for James Molineaux, its director. Majir went to the facility on Highway 17 posing as a professor being recruited by Clemson University. Clemson ran an extensive student program in agricultural science in partnership with the United States Vegetable Laboratory, and it was customary for faculty members to visit. But the receptionist told him that director Molineaux was midway through a touring sabbatical in Europe and Australia with a group of agronomists and botanists. She didn't have details of his itinerary, except that he was expected back in early December. Majir reported this to his supervisors in Damascus, hoping the matter would be referred to another agent. He was tired of the killing. Let a younger man deal with the lead about the old engineer, the North Koreans, and the possible vegetable laboratory ruse. But Damascus replied that he should await the manager's return and travel back to Charleston in December. Anyway, Damascus said, his ongoing work with the Michigan hate group was more pressing.

So, from balmy Charleston, the Syrian operative had traveled to the Michigan chill and the frosty Buddy Binton.

"You asked me to come," Majir said.

"We need more money," Buddy said. Whatever else you could say about the brawny Free Brother, he went straight to the point.

"So soon?"

"I said we need it. What does it matter how soon?"

Buddy's tone was provocative, but the Syrian remained calm, matter of fact.

"Because every transfer leaves a trail. A trail is a risk."

"I know about risk," Binton said. "I know about probability. I know statistical patterns. I know the technology." He turned his eyes away in an expression of self-evidence. "And you know that I do, or you wouldn't have contacted me in the first place."

That was all true. From his first meeting with Buddy Binton, Asheed believed Damascus had identified a hate group with different, rare, perhaps even unique capacities. It was not difficult to find competent, simple hackers. But hackers who truly understood the physical technologies and how they could be molded to do more than merely hack and extract—well, that was an entirely other breed. There weren't many Buddy Bintons out there. People who could *build* systems that could not only invade the internet but also *alter* its products and output. It required deep knowledge of the science of satellite communications and its capacity to interface—or not—with internet backbones and cable transmissions.

What Syrian Intelligence wanted was the disruption of news and information available to Americans and to their government. "Fake news"—*really* fake—was Syria's goal. And what Majir had been funding was to be directed to that end. Binton claimed that, with financial resources, he and his cohorts could infiltrate legitimate media satellites and physically alter their outflowing information products. To be clear, this was not the same as creating a fabricated story and publishing it on a fringe website or passing it along through social media. No, this was creating false news that carried, in every way, the credibility and gravitas of legitimate, respected, mainstream media.

Imagine a *New York Times* front-page story describing—say—a bloody riot ensuing from a panic-driven run on a California bank. A panic that never actually happened at all. That the *NYT* never truly wrote or intentionally published. And, perhaps most damaging of all, that it could not retract *for days* because the technology systems under the newspaper's control had been reconfigured.

Imagine a seemingly live *CNN* report. Isn't that Anderson Cooper standing there with the Chicago police chief? Asking him why thousands of policemen were at that very moment roaming the city's neighborhoods, rounding up every black man they could find in the city's new war on gun violence? It looked so genuine—even Anderson Cooper, as you would hope and expect, was challenging the action, declaring it un-American in the extreme and imploring the courts to intervene.

And all of it a complete fabrication; *nothing* was happening in Chicago.

Damascus knew its own citizens didn't trust or believe half of what the Syrian government permitted to be disseminated to them. It wanted the American public to be as distrustful as its own. It wanted a sustained disinformation campaign of the ages.

Buddy Binton had so far not delivered the goods. But his first prototypes looked promising, his Syrian sponsors thought. To justify its initial financial investment, Damascus had required early engineering documentation from Binton. It needed to be convinced the computer scientist had viable ideas on satellite interventions. He passed on his documentation through Asheed, and Damascus reported back that, yes, the documentation showed potential, though some of the detail had been redacted by Binton, on the ground, he claimed, of proprietary interest.

"I want the option to be the next Steve Jobs," he said. "Even though that guy didn't know shit, himself."

Modesty, like warmth, was not one of Buddy Binton's character traits.

If he had been a reclusive lone ranger working from a mountain cabin, *ala* Theodore Kaczynski, the American "Unabomber" of decades past, Damascus would not have been inclined even to pay him attention, much less money. But this man Binton had other things—among them location—that made him more credible and attractive to their designs. He founded his Band of Free Brothers in southcentral Michigan because he himself was a doctoral graduate of the School of Computer Engineering of the esteemed University of Michigan in nearby

Ann Arbor. The university was a beacon of scholarship that brought qualified scientists to study and teach from around the world. It was filled with students and professors from the Middle East, not an insignificant nicety to the comfort and easy mobility of its Syrian-born agent Majir Asheed, who looked, walked, and talked like any one of them.

And Binton had formidable human resources available to him, an important capacity Majir had verified in his vetting. It related, again, to the proximity of the university's engineering programs, as well as a large technical workforce attached to Google in that company's building in downtown Ann Arbor, formerly the corporate headquarters of the Borders Books retail chain. Binton used his channels to identify the fringe, misfit—even demented—few among them. In a large enough sample size, Binton boasted, you will always find what you are looking for. And Buddy did. He talked to students and tech employees about their personal and political philosophies. He knew a brilliant extremist when he found one. And he found more than one. He found a dozen. And then he found another dozen. They had superior brains that they believed made them superior, period. The Band was born.

Interestingly, his Band was not an all-white hate group like so many others. Far from it. Nearly a third of the group were African Americans. This intrigued Damascus and Majir and, for some reason they could not be sure of, made Binton and his group of perverted geniuses more palatable to them. Syrians had never understood the underpinning of the European and US white supremacy movements—namely, their hostile preoccupation with and against persons of color. While the Middle Eastern totalitarians welcomed any movement that infected an otherwise stable democracy, they did not see how color had much to do with national purpose or, compared to a common religious devotion, even national purity.

So, Damascus and Asheed considered it a plus, albeit a curious one, that Buddy Binton's little band was not a white supremacist group *per se* in any usually defined sense. And it didn't matter that it was also an underground armed militia; indeed, that was also desirable. Perhaps it could be put to good use in the right situation. What counted most was its vision of anarchy and resentment of governing authority—namely, the federal government of the United States. What mattered most for the present were its computer science skills and its willingness to radically misinform nearly four-hundred million American citizens. That vision and that capacity, if proven, justified continuing support.

And it didn't hurt that they disliked Jews.

"Damascus will want to know what the money is for," Majir said calmly.

"Guns and butter. Tell them it's for guns and butter."

Majir did not recognize the expression, but his own reaction did not let that on.

"A little more specificity?"

"We have new members. We need weapons for them."

"I see."

"We agreed on that, Maji. I told you the Band is a militia group."

"Geeks with guns," Majir said.

"Scientists with guns. Freedom soldiers with guns. I told you we expected help for our militia work too."

"Yes, I remember that," the Syrian said. "But we have ways of supplying weapons to you directly, you know. Instead of cash." Asheed made his point with a deceptive purpose. In truth, he did not want anything to do with furnishing guns directly, and he knew Damascus would never agree to do so. That was far too dangerous—too likely to be discovered by the FBI or the ATF. But he wanted Binton to think he was acceding to his demand. It was simply wise spy craft. Afford your contact, especially one you did not yet trust, the sense of control.

"We don't want any Middle East shit," Binton said. "We know what we want and how to get it ourselves. We want cash. Fifty thousand."

Majir turned to the side and sipped his coffee. It was, thankfully, more full-bodied than the weak brew he usually found in the United States. He raised his brow, as if surprised by the amount of the demand, and curled his lips, as if trying to think of a rejoinder. Half a minute passed before he turned back to Buddy.

"Okay," he said. "I will get back to you tomorrow. But I doubt it will be a problem."

Buddy smiled.

"I always appreciate a cooperative Syrian," he said.

Majir didn't smile. He just didn't much care for Lester "Buddy" Binton.

★ ★ ★

THE SEAL IS SKEPTICAL

They would talk at Langley for years about the night that Navy SEAL Tyler Brew walked into interrogation room 5 where young Lieutenant Grey Boatwright sat across from CIA questioners Andrew Bishop and Carlton Beal.

Six hours earlier, the two interrogators had completed their prolonged interview of the airman, repeatedly inquiring about the false answer on his flight school application, and his altercation at the officers' club. Five hours earlier, they had observed his polygraph examination, dryly administered in that very room.

Bishop and Beal were career officers with extensive experience in the field and at headquarters. Each had worked for years in the counterterrorism section of the agency. Committed. Serious. Professional. Unblemished records. And smart enough to know that when the CIA director himself had authorized the interjection of an independent person into one of their investigations, it was best not to resist. Besides, they could not help but be curious as to *this* intervenor. It was not uncommon for FBI personnel to be introduced into an inquiry, and they were often helpful. But a *navy SEAL* from SOCOM? And none other than Captain Tyler Brew, known, at least by name, throughout the agency's counterterrorism unit for his unprecedented heroism in a score of terrorist raids across a dozen countries?

When the slim black SEAL opened the door, the two CIA men stood immediately. Lieutenant Boatwright, exhausted and sluggish, rose after them.

"Everybody, please," Brew said, motioning them to sit back down. The CIA questioners did, but Lieutenant Boatwright did not. Brew looked straight into his eyes and saluted him.

"Holding up, Boat?" he asked.

"I've been better."

Brew sat down with the lieutenant and began speaking in a relaxed tone. He said he had been commanding Boatwright for nearly a year, as he had two dozen other pilots in the drone command center at Charleston. He had stood over his shoulder for sixty-seven missions. That was not an estimate, he said. He had looked it up before coming up to Langley so that he could be exact.

"Your point, Captain?" agent Bishop asked.

"I know his brain. I know his discipline. I've asked him hundreds of questions under stress. He's never given me a wrong answer or fudged anything."

Brew pulled the interrogation report from his pack. He paged through the questioner's transcribed notes.

"He lied on the application," Brew said. "Granted. He did. But he didn't lie *about* his lie, did he?" Even to Brew, it seemed at first like an unseemly argument.

"How could he lie about it? We had him dead to rights on it."

"No, you had him dead to rights on a fact he admits."

"That gets him a medal?"

"No, but it doesn't prove anything about the drone that morning either. It proves he wanted to get into flight school too much. You'd have more on him if he'd tried to cover up his reason for doing it. It was laying right out there for him. 'I was protecting my wife. I didn't want to hurt her.' Wouldn't a liar say that?"

Boatwright looked down at the table.

"But he doesn't tell you that," Brew said. "Instead, he tells you the truth. He did it to get into the program. And when he's called on it, he stands straight up and takes it."

"Okay," said Bishop. "So, he does the right thing on that. Owns up to it. What about the polygraph?"

In the field, Brew had come to know a fair amount about the new lie-detector technologies. Once a simplistic measure of galvanic skin response—determining a seemingly truthful answer from a false one, essentially on fairly primitive measurements of sweat gland changes—the newest technologies went wildly further. Probes in a headset measured tiny contractions of inner ear tissue, and powerful lenses, not unlike the ones used in eye health exams, recorded intricate physical movements in the corneas and pupils of the subject. The navy SEAL watched as they were administered to terrorist combatants to see if they were lying about their knowledge of other terrorists or their plans.

One detainee was repeatedly asked if he had met the previous day with an al Qaeda operative in a certain location. Yes, he said. Yes, yes, yes, he had, he said. But the examiners thought he might be trying to mislead them; detainees often did. Misinformation was common terrorist strategy and when successful could lead to the wasted deployment of resources—or worse, deadly ambush. It was one of the reasons torture was sometimes counterproductive, and why President Trump's Secretary of Defense James Mattis, a heralded field general himself, famously said he "could do better [obtaining information from a captive] with a few beers and a pack of cigarettes" than with torture. But the detainee that Brew saw interrogated was insistent that he had met the al Qaeda operative and described the encounter. The technology of truth, however, said otherwise.

"He's lying through his teeth," the tester in the field had concluded to Brew. He showed the SEAL the graphic displays of his answers. The lines were jumping all over the screen.

"Maybe there could be some variation," the field examiner said, "even a lot of it, on the first time or two the same question is answered. He might be telling the truth, and just be nervous. But when it scatters this much time after time, when he ought to be more relaxed because he knows he is saying the same thing, trust me, he's deceiving."

Brew had deferred the mission to take the Al Qaeda militant that otherwise he would have commissioned. After all, the test had said it was a blind alley. An hour later he received drone surveillance film made the day before. It was vivid, clear as a motel room flat screen TV image. Unmistakable. There was the detainee, standing and talking with the Al Qaeda combatant just where and when he had claimed. He had told the truth after all. The technology of truth was too advanced to serve its purpose. Brew did not forget it.

Agent Beal opened a slim binder sitting on the table.

"Have you seen the test responses?"

"I have," said Brew. "And the examiner's report and conclusions. He was thorough. A lot of control questions."

He meant questions put to Boatwright for which there were known, undebatable answers. Some would plainly call for an affirmative yes response. *Are you a lieutenant in the United States*

*Air Force? Are you stationed presently at Charleston Air Base? Do you spell your surname B-o-a-t-*w-r-*i-g-h-t?* Others would obviously be answered no. *Are you commissioned to fly manned aircraft? Are you unmarried? Were you born outside of the United States?* Since the answers to all control questions would be deemed provably and unambiguously correct, an "honesty baseline" graph was produced by them for truthful answers, to which the substantive questions and answers could be compared.

"So, what do you make of them?" Bishop asked. "Of the whole test?"

"I'll tell you after we do another exam."

Bishop and Beal were startled.

"*Another* exam?" Bishop asked. "You just said his test was done thoroughly. Why should we examine him again?"

"I didn't say another exam of the lieutenant. I said another exam."

Brew withdrew the envelope containing Jack Watson's order and placed it on the table in front of the two careerists.

"This time we'll test you, Carlton."

The two agents were stunned. They read Watson's brief direction.

"Same examiner," Brew said. "Same questions. Every one of them."

"What will that prove?"

"Nothing," said Brew. "Because we know *you* didn't do it, right?"

"So why the hell do it?"

"To see if you lie about it. According to your damn machine."

Brew pointed to the director's order, lying on the table.

"So just get the machine and the examiner in here."

★ ★ ★

HE TOOK HIS BOURBON WITH HIM

There was nothing about the White House that Stanley did not like. To the quiet, old citizen from Pittsburgh, the place stood for everything American and everything his country might be if it kept working at it.

Part of Stanley's sense of personal citizenship was ingrained in his life's work. As an engineer and designer of structures under the natural earth, he had come to understand that perfection was a never-ending pursuit. Whatever the quality, whatever the apparent genius of a design, there was always the inevitability of improvement and—with enough time—its ultimate failure.

And to Stanley, as he walked slowly through the White House rooms, stopping often to look up or bend down to examine architectural and building detail, this place embodied a people and its nation as completely as one place could. Its aspirations, its triumphs, its stuttering advances, its disconsolate retreats, its dazzling beauty, it's inevitable imperfection.

That afternoon, he learned that his Pirates weren't perfect

either. Though the best defensive team in the National League through the regular season, they committed two errors in the sixth inning and lost to the Nationals 6–1 in their playoff game. In the box seat next to him, First Father Henry Winters rejoiced. But, in truth, Stanley was not disheartened at the loss. He could not be saddened in Henry's company. To Stanley, the large general, advanced in years beyond his own, epitomized goodness in a man. He was proud but modest. Well read, balanced, and kind. Aware of his own imperfections and wisely accepting of them. Deeply loving of his daughter but realistic as to even her limitations. And he understood the game of baseball more intricately than anyone Stanley had ever known.

The president and Helen Ames Bigelow were waiting for them with cocktails in the East Wing residence when the two returned from the game. Del pulled the Secret Service agent aside as he escorted them in.

"What did they talk about on the way home?"

The agent raised his brows and rolled his eyes.

"I'm glad I didn't listen to the game," he said. "I heard it all over again."

Over the drinks, she did too. Of special interest was a controversial call in the decisive error-stained inning. A pop-up was hit by the Nationals batter toward third base that carried out barely to the left field grass near the foul line. The First Father believed the second base or home plate umpire immediately should have declared the infield fly rule, as runners were on first and second with only one out. But neither umpire did. The Pirates' manager had placed his infielders in a "shift" against the left-hand batting National at the plate, so that the shortstop was playing out of his regular position on the first base side of second, and the third baseman was stationed instead near second base, the usual position of the shortstop. The batter usually pulled the ball to the right side, and the Pirates were trying to take advantage of his habit. But this time, the lefty didn't pull the pitch, and the odd positioning made it impossible for the third baseman to reach the pop-up in time. It fell safely and opened the door to the disastrous inning for the Pirates. Had the infield fly rule been called, the pop-up would have been ruled an automatic out, whether caught or not, and the runners would have had to advance at their own peril, and probably would not have.

"That was a bad call," Henry said. "Or, really, 'noncall'."

"Even though it killed us, I don't think so, Henry." It was one of the reasons you could not dislike Stanley Bigelow. He seemed never to let his own interests lay down in front of his judgment.

There followed a discussion of the fine points of the rule. Henry maintained that any fly ball that appeared, when hit, capable of falling on the infield triggered the rule, even if its own force or the wind carried it slightly beyond. Stanley disagreed.

"That really isn't clear in the rule, Henry," he said. "It doesn't specifically say that. It's the only rule of baseball I can think of where the *full intent* of it is not obvious. Is it to be declared when the pop-up is clearly near the *infield*, or near *infielders*? You could see off the bat it was going to be trouble, just because the third baseman wasn't playing anywhere near third. Why should the fielder get the benefit of the rule, when whether it is intended to apply to the field itself or to the fielders is not clear? Maybe the batter was trying to put it there on purpose. Which isn't easy. Should the batter be penalized, and his hit called an automatic out?"

The president and Helen listened with amusement. The First Father mulled Stanley's point over his bourbon.

"Are you telling me, friend," he finally said, "that even the rules of our beloved game are imperfect?"

"I am afraid I am," said Stanley.

For the two of them, it was cause for true contemplation.

For the president, it was an opportunity to get to something on her mind.

"Stanley," she said, "have you ever worked with underground piping on a big scale?"

"What do you mean by 'big'?"

"Big big. Running very long distances."

"Well, I've certainly designed energy pipelines, if you mean something like that."

"These pipelines would house and protect communication lines. Heavy fiber-optic cables."

The president noticed that while Stanley leaned back comfortably in his wingback chair, Helen, in the chair next to him, leaned forward, listening intently, concerned.

"From where to where?" Stanley asked.

"In routes all over the country. Linking military bases and data security complexes."

"This sounds like it has to do with the sad thing in Israel."

"It does. But all the work would be here in the States."

Helen's face showed visible relief.

"We have to replace our national communication system to disconnect it as entirely as we can from the internet. From infiltration."

"I don't know anything about internet technology."

"You don't need to. We have people who know that part. Remember Wilson Bryce?"

"Sure. Brilliant man. Nice too."

"He's putting together the technical infrastructure. His team can design and build all the new fiber-optic cable and the links, all the software and hardware to make it function for the military. They already have. But they don't know how to house it underground so that it can't be detected or physically disrupted. Or at least disrupted without extraordinary effort."

"How deep does it have to go?"

"We hoped you could decide that. It sure can't be something that a dad digging posts for a swing set bumps into, or a construction crew can reach."

"Can I sit here and think for a few minutes?"

"Sure."

"And maybe a little more of this bourbon?"

"Only a little," Helen said gently.

"Why don't we leave you and Helen to think it over," the president said. "Helen would be a great help. She understands what the army engineers could do, and what they couldn't. We'll leave you to yourselves." The president looked, a little pointedly, at her father, and rose. "Maybe you will have some thoughts over dinner," she said to Stanley.

Henry lifted himself with a mild shrug and left the room with his daughter. He took his bourbon with him.

ALL PINGS ARE NOT CREATED EQUAL

It was the first good news for Lieutenant Grey Boatwright in weeks.

Brew had arranged for an additional, independent polygraph examiner to interpret the results of the proxy test administered to the CIA agent, Carlton Beal. He wanted to be sure the result of the first examiner who tested Beal, who had also tested Lieutenant Boatwright, correctly interpreted the machine's result. It turned out to be unnecessary diligence. Both examiners concluded the same thing: Beal's answers failed the exam as badly as the lieutenant's, though it was plain to all that the uninvolved CIA agent gave exclusively truthful answers to the same questions. Plainly the technology was far too sensitive to produce any result that could be considered reliable. It proved nothing—even suggested nothing—as to the culpability of Grey Boatwright in the matter of the runaway drone three weeks earlier.

Brew accompanied the young lieutenant back to Charleston Air Base, without objection by the CIA or the FBI. Agents Bishop and Beal reported up, begrudgingly, that Boatwright was still a "person of interest" but no longer a prime suspect.

But Brew was still bothered by the satellite ping that his pilot had not detected on the fatal morning. There was no doubt that a transmission had in fact been made to Boatwright's drone console about six minutes before the craft was overtaken. The data register in the central control room above the command theater recorded it clearly. Still unknown to the young lieutenant, but known to his superiors, it had been transmitted from a Ukrainian media satellite. The NSA experts were working feverishly to dissect and understand the media satellite's activity before and after the incident. So far, they were drawing blanks. But they maintained that the transmission should have triggered an immediate vibration in the console seat and, at the same time, the joystick.

Brew and Commander Wilks studied the data recording log carefully. The two senior officers wanted to believe their lieutenant; but this discrepancy required resolution. They sat together in the commander's office the morning Brew returned with Boatwright from Langley.

"What really gets me," Wilks said, "is that little bold digit in the log. The first digit for that ping." He moved the log over to Brew's side of the desk and pointed it out. "There, see it?" He withdrew a cigarette from his drawer and offered one to Brew. Brew declined.

"What's that mean?" asked the Navy SEAL.

"It means it wasn't a standard ping. It was a *hard* ping."

"And what's that mean?"

"Just what it sounds like. It was fortified. Strengthened by the sender. To be sure it got through."

Wilks explained that while he was no satellite expert, he knew that it was possible to strengthen a signal for "assurance." He said military satellite technicians did it regularly. They did it when weather was poor, or they knew something like a clutter of commercial aviation traffic might interfere with the transmission.

"A hard ping gets it there, Tyler." His cigarette smoke swirled in the small room. "The central console received it. And Boat should have felt it down there."

"Unless it reached the central console and not Boatwright's," Brew said. "I mean, just wondering."

The older commander furled his brow.

"Sonofabitch," he said. His eyes lifted behind his huge lenses. "Sonofabitch, that's possible. Kind of. Maybe you're on to something there. You've been on high-level stuff, captain. Secret stuff. Who do you know that could tell us more about satellite signals?"

Brew thought instantly of Wilson Bryce, the Department of Defense technology guru he had met in the Eaglets Nest project with Stanley Bigelow. If Bryce didn't understand what might have happened, he would know who would.

Wilks had a secure line to the Pentagon, and they had Bryce on the line within minutes.

As usual, Bryce was a quick study. And something Brew didn't know at the time, he had a head start on account of his work already designing the new internet-free communication backbones the president had commissioned because of the same incident. Wilks explained to him the data recording log and recited for him the digitized entry it showed for the transmission from the Ukrainian satellite.

"The pilot says he felt nothing in his chair or in the joystick," Wilks told Bryce. "But the log booked it."

"Give me a minute," Bryce said. "I'm going to put you on mute. I want to talk to someone here."

"Don't forget about us," Wilks said amiably.

"I don't think Captain Brew will accept being forgotten about," he said.

It was ten minutes before the Pentagon scientist came back on the line.

"Not sure if this will help you or not," he said. "I wanted to check with a satellite guy—actually a satellite woman—to be sure I was right about this."

He explained that a hard ping was actually *two* transmissions, sent in such rapid succession that, for all intents and purposes, they comprised a single signal. As Wilks had known, it was a way to strengthen a signal if conditions warranted. For commercial satellite communications, it was almost never used; many satellites didn't have even the capability. It required the sending of a "fore signal," followed at once—within milliseconds—by a second, standard transmission.

"Normally, the *content* of the fore signal and the standard one following it are identical, sending the same information," Bryce said. "Because the whole idea is to make sure a single piece of information, the intended transmission, is received clearly. But it doesn't *have* to be the same information."

"What are you getting at?" asked Brew.

"Well, it's possible to send a fore signal with content *different* than the content of the standard transmit coming after it. If you're being devious."

"Tell us more," said Wilks. He was midway through his fourth cigarette.

"You remember years ago, the thing about the Iranian utility grid. Stuxnet, they called it. Obama was president when we did it, but George W. Bush authorized the work for it before that. I think it's still all classified. We went into their power infrastructure and played around with it. Flexed a little cyber muscle. To deter them from trying anything too serious on us."

"I remember," said Brew.

"We used fore signals then. You send in a forerunning transmission to dismantle a valve, say, and the closely following standard signal is sent somewhere else where you think the recipient is expecting it, probably a central control station. It's almost like a decoy, but the decoy is sent *second*, not first. The receiving system records the standard transmission, which is actually the second signal, without always picking up the fore signal that preceded it. We disrupted the Iranian grid in places they didn't detect, because we followed with immediate decoy signals to control systems that we knew they would be recording. They picked up the second standard signal, but not the disruptor, the first signal."

"And in our case?" Wilks asked.

"A fore signal could have been altered from its standard so that it disabled the vibration alerts in the pilot's console and the transponder sensor. The standard ping follows it a nanosecond later to the central control module that registers it as hard ping. That one is logged, and the fore signal is missed altogether. It looks like the pilot's instruments must have received a hard ping. But, really, only the control console did. The pilot got hit, all right, but he couldn't know it. Not if they did it this way."

For Brew and Commander Wilks it was all coming together. They knew it was in front of them the whole time. There was no doubt that Lieutenant Boatwright's navigational and firing functions had been disabled prior to the intended launch that morning. Why had it not occurred to them that other functions, such as the vibration alert sensors, also were disabled? They stayed in Wilks's office as the older officer drafted a report to SOCOM Command in Florida, copying the CIA Director Watson, the FBI director, and, at Brew's suggestion, the White House, "For the President's Attention." Brew reviewed Wilks's draft and agreed with it. They both signed it and sent it through the secure line immediately. It read:

> CLASSIFIED—HIGHLY CONFIDENTIAL
>
> REPORT—RUNAWAY DRONE
> INCIDENT—URGENT
>
> After study of data at Charleston and consultation with DOD technology chief, Wilson Bryce, the undersigned officers have concluded that Lt. Grey Boatwright (USAF) had no intentional involvement in the commandeering of the drone originally under his control on the day of the bombing of Israel by that unmanned aircraft. Through manipulation by an unidentified external force, utilizing Ukrainian Satellite UKR19, we believe the aircraft controls in Lt. Boatwright's operating console were disabled, including the vibration warning sensors in the console seat and joystick.
>
> Lt. Boatwright, in our considered judgment, did not voluntarily relinquish control of the United States aircraft or participate in the aircraft's subsequent movements or actions.
>
> Accordingly, permission is requested to reinstate Lt. Boatwright to his duties, at once.

COLONEL EUGENE WILKS CAPTAIN TYLER BREW

COMMANDER,
CHARLESTON AIR BASE SOCOM, US NAVY, SEAL

Within minutes, Defense Secretary Lazar, the CIA's Watson, and the FBI director conferred by phone. Lazar and Watson were inclined to accept the recommendation. Each knew Brew well and trusted him. But the FBI chief was reluctant. It was unusual to clear a suspect just three weeks into an investigation, especially when there were no good leads toward another. And all three appreciated that the political optics would not be favorable, to say the least, if the US government exonerated one of its own so quickly, while Israel still mourned its unspeakable loss of life. Lazar called his personal line to the president.

"Can I bring in the others?" he asked. She had the urgent report from Charleston Air Base in front of her.

"Of course," she said.

In a moment, they were on the line together. The Defense, CIA, and FBI leaders each spoke in turn. After they had finished, the president had two questions.

"Do any of you believe Brew and Wilks are wrong about young Boatwright?"

No, each replied.

"So, it is only because of the political and public perception that we are even speaking?"

Yes, each replied.

"Well, then I thank you for calling, but then there really is no question," she said. "Let him fly. And if it's questioned, make it clear that it's on my personal order."

At Charleston, Tyler Brew was pleased, and not surprised, at the president's decision. But little did he know that three months later, he and the president would call again upon young Lieutenant Grey Boatwright. In dire need.

★ ★ ★

THE MIND OF A DOG

Who can know the mind of a dog? Who can explain the rich complexity of the canine? On the one hand, simple and predictable in its responses; on the other, capable nearly beyond measure in its instinctual and sensory gifts.

Stanley himself, even after his devotion to Augie the German shepherd was deeply cemented, didn't truly understand the full basis for the dedication he felt to the animal. Not two years earlier, he had declared himself "not a dog person," when the fit, young FBI agent, L. T. Kitt, had brought the creature to his door for the first time.

There were many things Stanley didn't understand then. And some he still did not.

For one, he never learned why Tyler Brew and the others on the secret Eaglets' Nest project were so preoccupied with his personal safety in the first place; why they worried about him even as he worked in his home and office in Pittsburgh, and later as he lived in Charleston hotels while covertly training the soldiers on the installation of his design, afterwards completed by the reservists in the Middle East under Helen Ames's supervision. Brew and the team knew, but Stanley didn't, that he was the government's *second* choice for the engineering assignment, recruited only after the first, Ruth Morgenthal, was murdered in Washington before her Pentagon vetting was even completed. They surmised—correctly—that foreign intelligence operatives had intercepted personal emails suggesting that she was about to work on a secret military program and killed her before she could begin. Stanley Bigelow, they knew, could well be their next target.

Even Agent Kitt never learned the real nature or purpose of Stanley's work. The circle of knowledge was too tight. She needed to know only her role, which was the personal protection of the overweight senior citizen, by moving into an adjoining apartment in his Pittsburgh high rise and getting him comfortable with the presence of the highly trained protection dog, August, whom she had trained and handled for six years in her witness protection assignments. She was to improve the old engineer's physical fitness, if she could, by monitoring his eating habits and taking long walks daily, with the civilian leashing the guard dog. And when Stanley was sent to Charleston for the last phase of the project, she and the dog were ordered to accompany him.

L. T. Kitt did her job with skill and professionalism. She knew dogs, and she came to know Stanley well too. Eventually, her devotion to him was almost as deep as Augie's. At project's end, in thanks for his service—and probably more out of residual concern for his ongoing safety than she let on—the president had offered the government dog to Stanley to keep as his own. By that time, he, Augie, and Agent Kitt were a strongly bonded mutual admiration society. The fourth member, Helen Ames, was welcomed in warmly when she married Stanley four months after the project's end and moved to Pittsburgh to join him and the dog.

The profound attachment between the eight-year-old shepherd and Stanley, and the speed with which it formed, may have been grounded in a commonality neither appreciated. You could say they were traits of a careful engineer and—as it happened—also of a highly trained dog. Attention to detail and particularity. Patience with complexity. Preference for simplicity. Diligence and discipline. A genuine sense that the best reward for solving a problem was having solved it and that the truest reward of work was the doing of it well.

Unmarried and living across the river in her new townhouse, Kitt welcomed the custody and company of Augie whenever Stanley and Helen traveled, usually to Dayton for Helen's monthly weekend reserve service, and this time for their visit to the White House. Her work protecting Stanley on the earlier assignment earned her praise within the bureau and, because it was known that President Winters had personal involvement in some way in it, a certain new deference. More than once she was placed on a witness protection detail that conflicted with Stanley and Helen's travel plans. As soon as she told the agent-in-charge she was expected to care for Augie, another field agent was immediately assigned, without reprobation or the hint of it.

She was waiting with the dog in their apartment when they returned on Monday evening. When the couple entered without knocking or ringing the doorbell, Augie rose instantly from his resting place in the middle of the main room and stepped quickly, but not excitedly, to Stanley's hand. He didn't bark either, which did not surprise Kitt. FBI and military-trained dogs barked rarely, unless commanded to bark, or were in attack or pursuit. Dogs trained to protect, escort, or find—including weapons or explosives sniffers—were trained to be as silent as possible and to communicate in other ways. The last thing soldiers or agents approaching in stealth needed was a barking canine to announce them.

Military and protection dogs relied principally on scent and, to some degree, voice recognition to recognize team members and friendly forces. Dogs, like people, have many individual differences, including sensory differences. Most dogs have keen olfactory skills, an order of magnitude more powerful than humans. But among dogs, smelling capacity varies widely, even within breed. Kitt had tested Augie extensively when he came into the FBI canine corps at Quantico at four months of age. His auditory range and sound differentiation were only a little above normal. But his olfactory range, and his ability to tell the difference between smells that were very similar, was extraordinary. Kitt knew Augie didn't bark that evening as Stanley and Helen approached and rattled their eighth-floor apartment door because he was unsurprised—he had smelled the couple by the time the elevator reached the fourth floor. No cause for alarm.

"So, did you approve of the White House, Stanley?" Kitt asked.

"I've been there before." Just a tinge of pride.

"Oh, pardon *me*. I forgot you were a regular."

"It was lovely," said Helen.

"Did you stay in the Lincoln Bedroom?"

"No, just a guestroom. But the president told us a funny story about it," Helen said. She repeated it for L. T.

President Bill Clinton was notorious for inviting large donors and so-called FOB—"Friends of Bill"—to stay overnight in the Lincoln Bedroom of the White House, to the point that the press began reporting the visitors' schedule like a lineup card. About that time, the Clinton's daughter, Chelsea, a teenager when the family moved into the White House, went off to college. The president was known to have a close relationship with his daughter, and a reporter asked at a press conference soon thereafter what it was like living in the White House without her.

"Terrible," the former president said, according to Del Winters. "Just terrible. I miss her so much. But it does free up another bedroom."

Kitt enjoyed Helen's rendition of the president's story, as did Stanley, even on second hearing. But Augie seemed to respond most demonstratively. Sitting at attention as she spoke, he raised his large head high and smiled broadly when she finished.

"I see he's in fine fettle," Stanley said, bending a little to rub the dog's ears.

"He was great, like always. We took long walks. Some of our old routes, Stanley."

The couple had taken a single roller bag to Washington, and Stanley was wheeling it to their bedroom when L. T. called out to say goodbye.

"I'll call you this week to walk, Stanley."

"Good, it will be like old times. I'm starting another project for the president."

"Really?"

"Don't worry. She said this one isn't dangerous."

19

★ ★ ★

THE MATHEMATICS OF THREE PARTIES

Of all its provisions, section nine of the Election Security Reform Act, entitled "Remedies," ignited the most clamor during the law's debate and passage. It was not difficult to see why. It hit the hottest buttons in the already highly emotional subject of election fraud—namely, who determined whether it truly happened or didn't? *How* was it decided, and by what standard of proof? And, if fraud *was* found to have occurred, what happened then?

Del Winters was vice president during the legislative free-for-all leading to the ESRA. She was lobbied vigorously by all sides—and there were more than two—urging their own partisan views on the act. Her high popularity since emerging into the public eye put a premium on her support, should she give it to one of them. She didn't. Wisely, thought both her father and the sitting president who had appointed her late in his first term upon the unexpected death of his first vice president, well-liked Philip Such.

"However it turns out," her predecessor president had cautioned her, "we are probably going to have something to do with it down the road. Any position either of us takes now will set us up for challenges later. Our credibility then is more important than our preferences now."

When she told her father what the president had advised, he agreed.

"That's the second-best decision he's ever made," said Henry Winters. "The first was picking you to replace Phil Such."

You could not hold a father to objectivity.

On its face, the law's framework seemed simple enough as to how election fraud could be raised and how it would be resolved. A losing candidate or political party who received at least 15 percent of the tallied vote could challenge the bona fides of the election by submitting evidence of "relevant" fraud or illegality to the national Federal Elections Commission. "Relevant" was defined by the law to mean "evidence of such a nature that, if verified, could realistically have altered the outcome of the election challenged."

Even supporters of the Election Security Reform Act worried it would be overused. It was feared that losing candidates would resort to it routinely, unless deterred from making wobbly claims. So, the law explicitly required that claims of fraud meet an extremely high standard of credibility and specificity. The formal claim had to include "not general allegations or contentions, or arguments based on historical voting trends, polls, or projections, but specific, identified instances of fraud, including the specific way it was carried out, where it was carried out, and by whom. Further, such instances must be shown to have occurred in such a number as would have realistically changed the outcome of the officially tallied vote under challenge."

That degree of evidence had proved to be a bridge too far for any would-be challengers since the law's enactment. There were always isolated instances of fraud in any large election. But they were few in actual number. The threshold for relevance that would trigger the law had not been met, in keeping with the purpose of the statute to provide a remedy, not for minor imperfections, but only for widespread, outcome-changing shenanigans.

But in addition to the standing of the parties and losing candidates, the act provided another, more controversial power to challenge an election to congressional office, this one vested exclusively in the president. Supporters of the law did not wish to leave the integrity of the election process—sacred to the core principles of democracy—solely to the discretion of party bosses, who were not answerable to the general public, and to self-interested candidates, whose motivations could not be trusted. The president, other than the vice president, was the *only* person selected by the nation as a whole. He or she, other than the vice president, was the only one who took an oath to faithfully uphold the Constitution who was accountable to *every* citizen of every state. In the event of widespread fraud or meddling, if anyone had a duty and proper standing to intervene, it was the president. So, the act provided the commander-in-chief with that power, by stating that the president, within twenty days after a national election, could directly petition the US Supreme Court on an emergency basis to set aside a House or Senate election result from any state in the nation.

The jurisdiction and powers of the high court in such an instance were carefully sculpted in the act. First, the law stated that notwithstanding the president's petition, the certified results of a state elections authority, usually the state's secretary of state, were presumed valid and were to be upheld by the court unless the president's petition was supported by "overwhelming evidence and facts of fraud or tampering clearly establishing that the outcome was illegally obtained, and the challenged office would not have been secured without it." The lawyers in Congress disliked the use of "overwhelming evidence" as a standard of proof, it being novel. But after tedious debate about the applicability of the established standards, "clear and convincing," which many feared too low a burden for such an extraordinary issue, and "beyond a reasonable doubt," which most felt should be reserved for criminal guilt, "overwhelming" won out, untested as it was.

Second, to prevent misuse of the extraordinary power by a president to favor his or her own party, the remedy to be awarded by the court depended on the political affiliation of the petitioning president and the challenged winner. If the president challenged the election of a candidate from a party other than his or her own party—an opponent—and the court agreed with the challenge on its merits, the court's remedial power was limited to ordering a new election for the seat. The outcome of the original election could not, in such case, be reversed outright by the court and the seat awarded to the candidate from the president's own party. But should the president challenge the election of a candidate from his or her *own* party, the high court could choose, in its discretion, either to order a new election *or* reverse the result and declare the defrauded candidate duly elected, without a rematch.

The act set sail onto turbulent seas in American politics. Steve Bannon's all-out assault on the traditional Republican Party apparatus, begun before the Trump administration had reached even its first-year mark, was eventually successful, if only partially. It had the effect of turning some pro-Trump "red" states into "deeply red" enclaves that stridently disfavored both Democrats *and* traditional Republicans. Eventually, the angry rightists detached from the organized Republicans and called themselves the Freedom Party, sometimes referred to as "the right right." When the Republican Party split occurred, Democrat leaders rubbed their hands cheerfully in anticipation. But the Democrats' hope that the sundering of the old GOP, the Grand Old Party, would hand to it easy majorities in Congress and a clear path to the White House went unfulfilled. It turned out that the exit of the furthest-right flank of the Republican Party made what remained of it more attractive to independent voters, and even to some moderate Democrats. This caused a handful of normally Democratic blue states to move to the traditional Republican column, enough to offset the few red ones that moved to Freedom Party deep red.

The outcome made for an uneasy coexistence of three viable parties on the national political landscape, at least insofar as the makeup of the House of Representatives and the United States Senate. None of the three parties held a mathematical majority in either chamber. "Control" had become a game of *plurality* status and the hope, and political art, of attracting defectors from one or both of the other groups to support the measure advanced by the plurality.

When it came to winning the White House, the contest remained, for all intents and purposes, between the traditional Republicans, of which Delores Winters was one, and the traditional Democratic Party. The Constitution's electoral college structure, coupled with the "winner take all" electoral vote laws in nearly every state, made it impossible as a practical matter for a Freedom Party candidate to garner a significant number of electoral votes. Since only a few states were dominated by Freedom Party voters, in presidential elections the far-rightists could not hope to capture the White House, or even affect the national selection, *unless* the Republican and Democratic candidates ran so closely that *neither* gathered the requisite 270 electoral votes required to claim the presidency outright.

That was the big catch—the big peril. If that happened, the election of the president was thrown to the House of Representatives, where each state delegation would receive one vote. The mere possibility of such an occurrence made the Freedom Party a true force indeed, since in a few state delegations it held a majority of places. It meant that it could be the swing group in the House, essentially deciding the national choice, if Republican and Democratic states were nearly evenly divided. And it further underscored the importance to any incumbent president, including Del Winters, of always having more reliable, sitting House members to bank on than the other principal presidential candidate did.

The bottom line: midterm elections had never been so important. And one was two weeks away.

The political balance for President Winters could have been better, especially in the Senate. In the House, her Republicans held a comfortable enough ten-seat plurality. But in the Senate, her plurality edge was a single vote. Republicans held forty-eight Senate seats; Democrats, forty-seven; Freedom Party rightists, five. As it was, she needed to find at least three votes from outside her natural base to assemble the fifty-one Senate votes to pass any administration initiative. She was nearly always able to do so, given her high national favorability ratings and her personal qualities and likability. But she did not relish the prospect of needing more. It was imperative that Republican Senate incumbents, including Will Truitt, hold their seats.

In all, a dozen Senate Republicans faced reelection contests in the upcoming midterm. The Georgian Truitt, running for a fourth term, appeared the most in jeopardy. His winning margin in his two prior reelections had declined *seriatim*, as the democratic stronghold of Atlanta grew. And his opponent, Margaret Westfall was formidable by all accounts. As a former Atlanta district attorney, she had strong law and order credentials, not common for modern southern Democrats. She was attractive, mature, and strong on Second Amendment gun rights, which appealed to moderate Republicans and many independents.

Political blood did not—and never had—run naturally through the veins of Del Winters. Her orientation had always been decidedly military. You didn't get *elected* to positions or responsibilities in the uniform; you *earned* them, and you progressed to them. Process, discipline, training, experience, performance. Those were the steps to military authority and station, and she believed in them. She had never held or sought public office until she was thrust into the vice presidency in a time of national tragedy. But having served in that office for five years, she grew into the rhythms of political life and came—she had to admit—to enjoy them. She appreciated the importance of relationships in the pursuit of objectives. She learned that you didn't develop relationships without engagement. Genuine engagement. It was probably the deepest mark her father, the consummate general, had made on her. She had observed him close-up as he raised her on military bases, often in the company of other officers, frequently junior to him.

"You don't have to like everybody," he said to her. "But you have to *try* to like everybody. You need to remember, they don't have to like you, either. But you want them to try. Trying is so underrated. If someone really thinks you are trying to understand them, and trying to get it right, you have their respect, whether they agree with you on something or not. In the long run, respect is a lot more important than agreement. Especially when you're the superior."

Will Truitt called her to discuss his most recent polling numbers and to urge her to come to Georgia for him. His internal polls showed the race neck and neck statewide. But his numbers in greater Atlanta were poor and getting worse.

"I didn't carry Atlanta either," she told him.

"No Republican ever does," Truitt replied. "But your approval ratings there are still good. Over 50 percent. Way higher than mine. If even a few of those would rub off on me, I can pull this thing out."

The president looked at her calendar.

"Can you have crowds ready the day after tomorrow?"

"For you, I could have them yesterday."

"I'll be there."

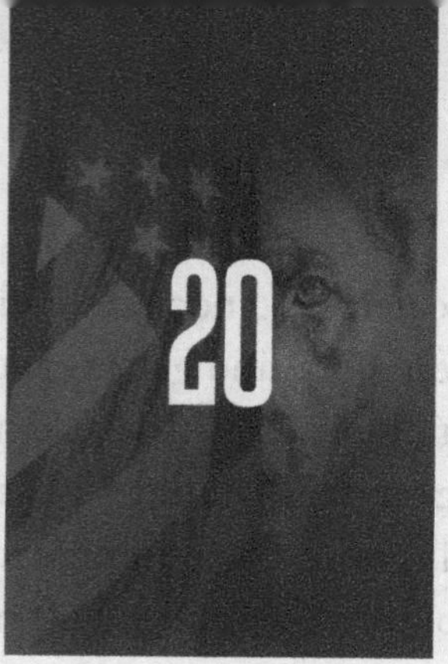

20

★ ★ ★

EXONERATION, BUT LIKE THIS?

Any remaining suspicion of Lieutenant Grey Boatwright evaporated the next morning. The world, and even the young lieutenant himself, would have preferred exoneration by other means.

He was cleared because *it happened again.*

This time, a French fighter jet flying in NATO training exercises over the Mediterranean was remotely commandeered at fifty-thousand feet. The plane careened out of formation and vectored toward Israel. Forewarned by the interception of the American drone weeks earlier, Israeli ground command and the French pilot wasted no time. As soon as he confirmed he had no control of the jet, the pilot ejected, saving his own life. The Israeli Air Force saved everyone else's, blowing the rocket-carrying fighter out of the skies ninety seconds later when it entered Israeli airspace.

The significance of the second hijacking could not be overstated. And President Winters decided immediately to acknowledge its importance, rather than minimize it.

"Are you sure about this?" Vernon Lazar asked, as she prepared to speak to the nation that afternoon from the White House. "You may scare the people."

"There is fear already," she said. "And there should be. You don't handle fear with silence."

"What do you handle it with?" Lazar asked.

"The truth. I am going to tell the people the truth," she said. "And that we are going to stop this madness. So help me God."

The globe was riveted on her words as she spoke outside the White House, without notes. She told the nation and the world that the second electronic hijacking of a military aircraft was a matter of grave concern and ongoing danger. She didn't sugarcoat it. World safety and peace depended, she said, on the correct assumption that nation states controlled their own weaponry and directed its use to legitimate and rational purposes. Every country, and every citizen, was as safe as the systems and armaments that protected them. At this moment, she said, those systems and armaments were demonstrably *not* safe.

She disclosed that the first hijacking of the US drone was carried out by remote tampering with the control systems of the aircraft, executed through subversive transmissions from a Ukrainian satellite. She stressed this did not mean that the Ukraine, or an ally of it or sister state such as Russia, was behind the interceptions. It was not even known whether the second hijacking was accomplished in the same way or from the same satellite. All that could be concluded now was that the terrorist actors possessed advanced computer science expertise.

Despite the anxiety her words otherwise surely would have produced, the president spoke in a tone of strong, calm confidence. She exuded no nervousness. She said the United States would use every ounce of its scientific knowledge to identify the perpetrators and eliminate the ongoing threat. It would seek and accept the assistance of all nations. It would use, and was already using, the best minds in government and private industry, from the United States, Britain, and elsewhere. This was not an American problem; it was not a UK problem, or a European, Asian, or African one, she said. It was a world problem.

She comforted the watching world by stating that the technical capabilities of the United States and other nations were vast beyond comprehension. Capabilities existed already that were unimaginable to most people of the world. She referred to the proven capabilities to explore and navigate outer space as one example, and of medical technology advances as another. Standing tall at the podium, looking straight ahead, and wearing a face of clear optimism, she concluded:

"We can do this. We will do this. You will be safe."

Media the world over declared her words pitch-perfect. Historians would later write that it was likely the most watched and heard speech ever made by a global leader. Confidence and hope were palpable, not only in the United States, but everywhere. Israeli Prime Minister Ari Szell summed up global reaction.

"She is the world's president today," he said.

After her speech, Del Winters walked directly from the White House lawn to the Situation Room beneath the west wing where her national security team was gathered, awaiting her. Her disclosure on the lawn that a Ukrainian satellite was used in the first hijacking was deliberate. She purposefully did not say that the second intervention came from the same satellite, though the NSA had already confirmed it. It was CIA Chief Watson's idea to divulge the limited information about the Ukrainian space vehicle. She questioned the idea, initially.

"Why tip them that we know that, Jack?" she asked.

"We lose nothing, and we might gain something," he said. He

explained that it was probable that the perpetrators had made an electronic implant of some kind in the satellite to facilitate their transmissions. Disclosure might induce them to try to remove it. His team was surveilling the Ukrainian satellite round-the-clock with what he called a "cyber blanket."

"Maybe we'll get lucky," he said. "Though anybody this smart probably won't go back there. But that isn't all bad either."

"What do you mean?" the president asked.

"If they don't go back to the same satellite, they have to set up another one. Bryce says you don't do this kind of implant overnight. At least it may buy us some time."

It was just three in the afternoon, but Delores Winters was exhausted. Buying a little time seemed a good idea.

★ ★ ★

POINT A TO POINT B

Stanley had made just three requests of President Winters when he agreed to design the subterranean system to house the new military cables. He asked for geological maps of all terrain within fifty miles on either side of the lines depicted on Wilson Bryce's national schematic; access to an expert within the Department of the Interior's US Geological Survey unit that cartographed the nation's earth surface; and a meeting with Wilson Bryce for an explanation of the devices and connection boxes to be buried with the cable. He needed to know their dimensions, and what kind of access to them would be needed and preferred.

He did not ask the president for a budget. She made it clear at the White House dinner table that expense was immaterial.

Stanley had worked before with USGS maps, as the government agency cooperated with private industry in the normal course, assisting engineers in commercial projects unrelated to national security. His design of the Eaglets' Nest deployment base a year earlier did not involve any such interaction, since that installation was constructed covertly in Kuwait. His new assignment, though, stretching across every state in the United States, would involve constant reference to the USGS mapping.

Stanley marveled at the sophistication and detail of the images provided him. They were of a different character entirely than that provided to him in his earlier commercial work. These included geothermal data and intricate bands and coded curves so that he could see the mineral makeup of the subterranean earth.

The president had stressed that the piping system had to be as impenetrable as possible and be incapable of detection from known surveillance technologies. So, Stanley's first instincts were to use once again the unusual metal he had selected for his Eaglets Nest design: beryllium. The curious fourth element of the periodic table of elements, beryllium had unique properties, including extreme strength and rigidity—seven times more rigid than steel—an extremely high melting point—in excess of four thousand degrees Fahrenheit—and, among all of the metals, unheard of lightness. It was three times lighter than even aluminum. And, Stanley knew, it was curiously invisible to x-rays and did not vibrate.

The last property was more important than it might appear. Whatever the final routing of the piping, it would certainly run frequently near expressways or even beneath them. Modern detection systems often keyed on movement and used powerful vibration sensors to isolate targets. Stanley knew that even severe movements over and near the earth surrounding the beryllium piping would not cause it to vibrate, thereby making it vulnerable to detection.

He knew from the beginning that while costs need not constrain his thinking, another practicality very much did.

Right of way. No matter how important the rapid installation of the new cable system was to national security, even it did not trump the rights of private property owners. The president worried that public easements might not be available in every location where they were needed along the cable routing. She was right. The USGS maps carefully traced all rights of way, including the many thousands of power company easements, train track rights, and state and federal highway allowances. Wilson Bryce had already developed a computer program that threaded the possible serpentine cable routes for which right of way was already in place. Stanley was surprised at how few interruptions—"terminations," Bryce's nationwide chart called them—there were. But there were still several dozen. Securing a continuous, uninterrupted route would require obtaining easements from over thirty private landowners and a dozen companies. Stanley knew this was not acceptable. It wasn't that the purpose of the cable routing couldn't be concealed. The landowners could simply be told the easements were required for possible future public transportation, water control, or internet cable needs. The problem was time. There wasn't any. The government could dispatch as many lawyers as it wanted, but there was no way to force a landowner to agree immediately, and few likely would.

Capitalism has its drawbacks.

It was Helen who had the solving insight.

"Wilson's program sure focused on the transportation easements," she observed. She leaned over Stanley's shoulder as he studied the myriad of connecting pathways.

"Yes, it does," said Stanley.

"Doesn't seem like the most efficient thing."

Stanley turned in his seat and looked up at her.

"Why not?" he said. "If you're going from Point A to Point B and all the way to Z, it seems logical."

"Yeah, logical ten and twenty miles at a time."

She had his attention.

"Sometimes even less," he said. He pointed to a section he had isolated. "Look at this one in Cleveland. Some of those sections are less than a thousand feet."

"If he rewrote his program to screen in a bias for the use of state and national parks and the national forests, you might have a lot longer runs and maybe need less private land."

Stanley smiled up at her. He knew her suggestion was brilliant. There were over four hundred national parks and forests spread across nearly every state, not to mention all the state-owned land. Most were bounded by large highways where cable line connections could be made without implicating private property routes. And the route could run, in many instances, for great distances without directional change. Helen's thought was a simple, some would say obvious, observation.

The best ideas always looked that way after someone else had them. Stanley looked up at her and pursed his lips in a kiss.

"I can see why the president wanted you involved," he said. "Don't go far."

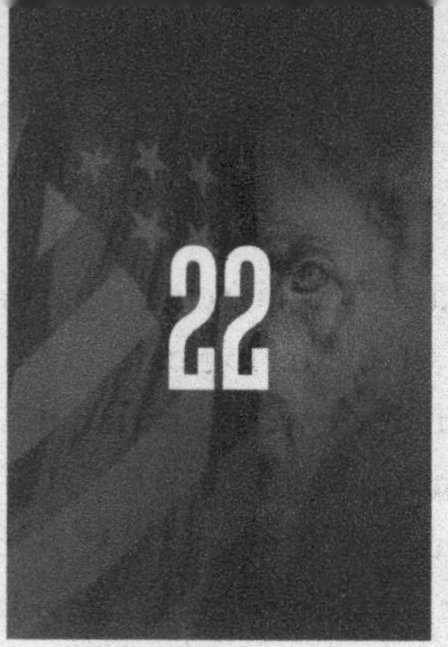

22

YOU CAN TALK A LIAR INTO ANYTHING

Senator Will Truitt beamed next to the president on the Atlanta stage. Why wouldn't he? The prodigious outdoor crowd roared as he introduced Del Winters. Its enthusiasm seemed boundless. It had been the same that morning at the first rally across town. But while his face exuded joy, in his heart the Georgia senator feared that the crowds' sentiment, like the effusive affection and large London crowds for Winston Churchill in his first campaign for prime minister after the Second World War, might not be predictive of outcome. The British citizenry had poured into the streets for Churchill, driven by deep appreciation and respect for his wartime inspiration and leadership, *not* out of desire for his continued leadership in peacetime. He lost decisively and was heartbroken. It is said his wife, Clementine, tried to console him at breakfast the morning after the defeat.

"Maybe it is a blessing in disguise," she offered.

To which the despondent leader replied, "If it be a blessing, it is indeed awfully well disguised."

Will Truitt knew that the excitement filling the Atlanta air was much more about the woman standing beside him than about himself. He was a realist. He knew the importance of the president's support. It could only help him, and the micropolling suggested he needed her critically. The race could go either way. The statistician sent from the Republican National Committee, weighing the voluminous data, pegged his chance of winning at 50 percent even, and opined that his number might be slightly optimistic. Others might interpret the data, he said, a little more favorably toward the Democrat, Westfall.

So, Truitt, the president, and the party agreed: in the Georgia Senate race there was reason for hope and none for comfort.

Truitt rode with Del back to Air Force One for her return to the Capital.

"Will you be able to come again, Madame President?" he asked. "I know that is a lot to ask. With everything happening. Israel, France. Everything."

"I will try, Will," she said. She turned to him in the Secret Service sedan and smiled warmly. "I will try very hard. You know how much we need you, Will. How much *I* need you. If you are not in the Senate, I will need to bring over Freedom people to pass anything."

"Some of them are good people," Truitt said.

"Without a doubt," Del said. "Their convictions are deep."

"And honestly held," he said.

"Agreed," she said. "Maybe that's why it is so hard to move them. You can talk a liar into anything. But convincing a believer to compromise is damn hard."

She grew pensive and didn't say more for the rest of the ride. As she stepped onto Air Force One a Secret Service agent handed her a secure cell phone.

"It's Secretary Lazar," he said.

"Yes, Vern," she said, nodding to the agent and moving toward the on-board office. "What is it?"

"My intelligence team rounded up this morning with the CIA and FBI groups," the defense secretary said. "To update each other on what they've learned about the Ukrainian satellite. The report isn't good. We're not getting very far. The satellite itself turns out to be, well, let's say, not state of the art."

"What do you mean?"

"Its transmission recording systems are outdated. No capacity to back up signals—received or sent—that are more than seventy-two hours old. We were on it quick enough to recapture its activity for about sixty-six hours before the first hijacking, but everything before that is lost."

"Does it show anything?"

"Nothing that's suspicious on its face."

"And since that day?"

"Of course, we're tracking and saving every signal in or out since that morning. But all the traffic seems unremarkable. Simple commercial stuff, mostly to and from Europe. Standard media transmissions for legitimate outlets, including the BBC. But we're running down every one of them to see if they employ any player on our terror lists or anyone associated with one. INTERPOL is throwing us good help, putting their best people on it. Plus, we have our FBI field offices over there."

"Anything else?"

"One thing. It turns out there are academics that use satellites like this for technology research. Four universities have contracts with the Ukrainian owner of this one. There are a lot of transmissions from all of them. One of them is the Max Plank Institute in Munich. We know there have been terror cells in Munich. We're putting heat on that lead." They both knew that one of the leaders of the 9/11 attack had been educated in Germany.

"What other universities?" the president asked.

"All are American," Lazar said. "MIT, RPI …"

"RPI?"

"Rensselaer Polytechnic Institute. Troy, New York. Near Schenectady."

"And the third?"

Lazar hesitated. He could not remember. He pulled the phone to his cheek and she could hear him ask for help on the other end of the line. He came back in a moment.

"The University of Michigan," he said.

PART 3

23

★ ★ ★

STANLEY'S DESIGN

Wilson Bryce looked nervous. He had met Stanley before, when the Pittsburgher had been vetted at the Pentagon for the Eaglets' Nest project a year and half earlier. Powerful people, like the ones in the Arlington conference room that day, did not intimidate Bryce. Solemn-faced military officers in uniform did not make him nervous.

A large, intently watching German shepherd did.

Augie sat erect between Stanley and the technology expert from Washington as the two stood at the broad drawing desk in Stanley's home study, looking down at the engineer's meticulous architectural compositions.

Stanley saw that Bryce was anxious about the dog and tentative when he extended his arm over the drawings, though Augie did not move a muscle, except to look up at the visitor with serious eyes.

"Oh, he *has* to sit there," Stanley said. "Don't worry about him, Wilson."

"Why?"

"Why shouldn't you worry, or why does he have to sit there?" Stanley asked.

"Why does he have to sit there? I have a good idea why I'm worried."

"Augie is a protection dog. Specially trained by the FBI. Quantico graduate," Stanley said, a note of pride evident. "And it turns out that I am his protect-*ee*. Whenever strangers are present, he always takes a position between me and them. *Always*. It's comforting."

"For you, maybe."

Stanley retreated to the kitchen for coffee, and Augie trotted with him. Bryce leaned over closely to examine the drawings on the first broadsheet, then thumbed to the center of the stack and peeled it back. He was in awe of the detail and beauty of the old man's drawings. Stanley had sequentially numbered each separately designed part, no matter how small, and then produced individual, three-dimensional drawings of each, attached in a thick appendix. So far, there were 433 individual components—elbows of every imaginable angle, specified to the tenth of a single degree, fittings, connectors, and flanges—all with detailed machining requirements. How did the president find this guy? Bryce wondered.

Stanley and Augie returned with the coffee, this time the dog leading the way until he sat precisely in his prior position next to Bryce. Stanley extended a cup to his visitor, who reached for it, hesitatingly, high above the dog's head.

"I hope you have a better feeling about my drawings than you have about my dog," he said.

"I certainly do. They're unbelievable. In six-months' time, they would be amazing. But in three weeks? Just unbelievable, Stanley."

"Thank you."

"You did a 3-D of every little part?"

"Beryllium is an unforgiving material. So hard, so unbendable. I didn't think I could leave anything to chance. The fabricator in Milwaukee is terrific. Highly skilled. But they still want my detail on everything."

"That's this Precision Beryllium outfit?"

"Yes. Every component, all of the long tubing—short tubing for that matter—will be made of pure beryllium."

"What will *that* cost?"

"I'm not asking. But, knowing it is getting this order, I'm sure not going to buy any Precision Beryllium Company stock. I suggest you don't either. They're going to have a *very* good year. I don't think even Augie could protect me from the Securities and Exchange Commission on an insider trading charge."

They spent three hours together, mainly discussing the special transfer boxes and equipment stations that Bryce's cabling design required. Stanley had dozens of questions and made careful notes of the scientist's answers. The engineer was especially interested in how moistureproof the tubing system had to be and how accessible the transfer stations for maintenance. Bryce said, yes, moisture in the cables could cause failure. Splice points were the most vulnerable, particularly if water gathered at them and was followed by freezing temperatures. Could the piping be perforated to allow it to drain? Bryce asked. Yes, Stanley said, but perforation was not effective in some soils, especially clay. Over time, it tended to seal all the perforations and trap the moisture that leached through it.

"But I can design a seal out of thermoplastic urethane and use it at every junction and connection," Stanley said. "The seals will withstand enormous temperature variation if made of that stuff. Totally nonmetallic. It won't make the tubing detectable.

Moisture will never get in to begin with. The freezing issue shouldn't be a problem in the southern climes, but I'll use it everywhere. The beryllium tubing will never bend, but a strong enough tremor might be able to break it at a joint. The seals will guard against that too."

They were nearly finished when Helen walked in. Augie gave her a brief welcome, long enough for Helen to rub his ears, then returned to separate Stanley from Bryce. She had come from the gym, wearing light blue sweatpants and a matching cotton band around her high, blushed forehead.

"So, Wilson, what do you think of his latest masterpiece?" she asked.

"Remarkable," he said. "I think it's remarkable. All this is so short a time! Has he been getting *any* sleep at all?"

"More than I favor," she said. Now it was Stanley who blushed. "But I'd say he's holding up."

Augie looked up at the three of them and smiled, his long red tongue rolling off his jaw.

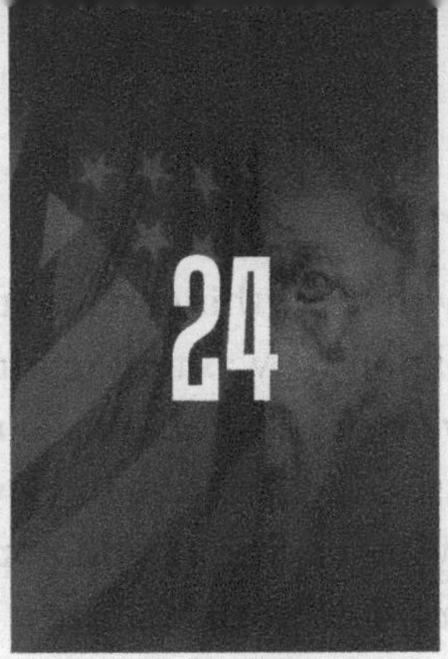

24

★ ★ ★

ELECTION NIGHT

Candidates say that when you are leading in the final days of an election race, voting day takes forever to arrive. And when you are trailing, the days seem to fly past like mile markers. Margaret Westfall, the able Democrat from Georgia, didn't know which applied to her. There was only one thing to do, she knew. Run like hell. She was.

The polling data as the race closed was utter perplexity. Statewide, Gallup and Quinnipiac had the contest too close to call. But her campaign's expensive micropolling showed her attracting more support than ever in the Atlanta metropolitan area and, oddly, slightly better than anticipated in the rural parts of the state, though Truitt's lead was still wide in them. These surprises presented a quandary. Should she step up her schedule in the urban center to hold her wide advantage there or get out into the countryside to see if even more rural support was available?

Her opponent's strategy was apparent. Will Truitt was

blanketing Atlanta with everything in his arsenal. She surmised that his own internal polling was telling him the same thing as hers. Urban voters were not sold on him, but at least there were more of them to chase. And he had a huge weapon that she did not: President Del Winters. Strong and popular, and a magnet to independent voters. The president drew large crowds in her visits to Georgia for him, and she had returned to Atlanta, as she told Truitt she would try, in the final days.

The Truitt-Westfall race in Georgia was by far the most watched contest on election night, in large part because the president had associated herself so closely with it. Some advisors felt her identification with the contest was a mistake. If Truitt did not hold his seat, it would reflect poorly on her, they said. The president should not be seen as backing a loser. And that was surely the theme of the television pundits as the returns rolled in.

She did not watch the early television coverage. She stayed in the Oval Office until seven o'clock, working with her senior staff on how to secure the special funding needed for Stanley's underground piping system. The process was as much art, judgment, and personality assessment as it was finance. The federal departments with the largest budgets all had the facility to meet some level of unbudgeted funding requests, without needing a special new appropriation. This was especially true of the defense department. But the new communication cabling system was not a $30 or $50 million expenditure that could be met by sliding money from one account to another. In fact, the ultimate cost of the new system could only, even now, be roughly estimated. "In excess of" $5 billion, Stanley and Bryce reported. That was the only estimate possible now. So, the president and her White House team were building a strategy on just how, and to whom, the appropriations requests could be made to the committees of Congress—confidentially—and then cleared for disbursement.

It was not a straightforward task. So-called "regular order"—the public introduction of a proposed bill, it's direction to committee in the House, public hearings thereafter, etc.—was out of the question. The needs of speed and secrecy ruled that out. The alternative required the navigation of arcane House and Senate procedural rules and careful management of the personalities that applied them. The president herself constructed a flow chart depicting the optional pathways to funding, and who would be needed to ensure approval in each. No matter which were selected, she knew she personally would have to manage the process. Phone calls, invitations, and bourbon would be involved, she knew. It came down to balancing and trade-offs. How could she get the money allocated rapidly—really, *instantly*—through legislators with the right authority *and* whom she could trust to hold confidentiality. The latter attribute made for some counterintuitive decisions.

"Mel Burns is chair of the Defense Technology Subcommittee," an aide said. "You're a good friend of him, aren't you?"

"Mel's wonderful," the president replied. "What a fine human being."

"Great. We can make him the point person for a chunk of the funding. Through his subcommittee."

"Forget it," the president said, bluntly. "Absolutely not."

"I thought you liked him?"

"I love the guy," she said. "But he leaks like a sieve. I'd rather work through Harry Jevins."

Jevins led the House Energy Infrastructure Subcommittee. He was a conservative Republican with libertarian leanings but mainstream enough to be part of the traditional Republican base. He was labeled a chauvinistic boor. Many thought for good enough reason. The president's staff knew she disliked him.

"Really?" the aide asked. "He's so hard to get along with."

"I dislike him. He dislikes me. But he knows I have a job to do. And mostly, I know he can keep his mouth shut. Invite him over for breakfast in the morning. Tell him it's confidential—no one should know he is coming. Just the two of us in the private dining room. I'm going up now to the residence. If he balks, call me."

Her father awaited her upstairs, watching the election coverage. Three flat-screen monitors rested on a long television stand against the wall of her study. Fox News appeared on the right, on mute. NBC stood on the left, also muted. CNN was in the center, with volume. He knew his daughter liked to move among all three, depending on content at the moment. He stood when she entered, holding his small rocks glass of bourbon. A drink for her sat on the cocktail table.

"I guessed scotch." he said.

"Good call," she said, as they sat down. "A thirty second summary? I haven't been watching."

"The polls are just beginning to close," Henry Winters said. "But there's a lot of exit polling. Bigger turnout than any midterm since 2018. Some are saying Bannon's Freedom people are showing up."

"Well, *that's* not good," she said. "They're not pulling from the liberals, that's for sure."

"Well, they're also saying my daughter is very popular." He looked at her, tilted his head slightly, and smiled. "Exit polls just about everywhere say a majority want to support your agenda. Like, 75 percent of people who say they're independents. So, let's drink to that."

They did.

As expected, the media devoted most of its attention to the Senate races where Republican incumbents were vulnerable: Maine, Nebraska, and Georgia. Especially Georgia. Commentators and analysts discussed the alternative impacts of the different possible outcomes.

"This clip from a few days ago tells you everything you need to know about tonight," the CNN election specialist said. The screen was filled with replays of the president's rallies in Atlanta. "There she is with the senator she needs tonight. Will Truitt. Seeking his fourth term. A reliable ally of the president. Well-liked across the aisle, but a traditional Republican through and through. The balance of power in the Senate hangs on him. The Republicans face challenges elsewhere, but those would be upsets. Not likely. But Truitt in Georgia, this one is a white-knuckler. And that's why you see President Winters there with him in Atlanta."

"These people sure know how to make me nervous," Del said to her father.

"Welcome to democracy," he said. "That's what they're paid to do."

As the polls closed, the networks began to fill in the counties of the state maps. Democrats and Republicans received their traditional color designations, blue and red, respectively; the Freedom Party was signified in green. Maine reported rapidly. With a state population of only about a million, and close to three fourths of it living in its southern section nearest Boston, it didn't take long to certify vote counts. By eight-thirty, all the networks called the Maine race for the Republican incumbent. The Freedom Party candidate did poorly, garnering only 4 percent of the votes.

The situation in Nebraska was not as clear, or as timely, in part because polls closed later in the central time zone. Exit polling there suggested a higher than anticipated turnout of Freedom allegiants. More than one pundit ventured that the Freedom surge would open the door to the Democrat in the race and hand the party its first senator from Nebraska since Bob Kerrey, the Vietnam war hero. It didn't happen. The vote split three ways, in surprisingly equal measures, but the Republican incumbent prevailed with a 3 percent plurality.

The president had held in two of the three battlegrounds. All eyes went to Georgia.

The returns from the small counties in the southern and northern parts of the state came in quickly. Truitt was delivering large margins there, as the pundits expected. The vote totals rolling on the television were lopsided, and misleading. At 7:50 p.m., Truitt had chalked up forty thousand votes to Westfall's eighteen hundred. In Echols County, on the southern border of the state above the Florida Panhandle, the woman from Atlanta earned just nine votes out of a thousand cast.

"I'm for Truitt and the Republicans," the president confided to her father as they watched. "But *that* is troubling."

"What is?"

"A capable woman like Margaret Westfall getting nine votes in a whole county. *Nine.*"

"Well, it's one little county down there."

"I don't care where it is. That is *not* a good thing."

"Welcome again to democracy," he said.

"Or tribalism," she replied.

The smaller counties continued to report in, and Republican Truitt's lead swelled.

"These are very large margins," one commentator proclaimed. "Truitt is getting more than he did last election in these rural counties and small towns. Not a lot more, but more.

If he can do as well as he did last time in greater Atlanta, he will win tonight. But that's a *big if*."

"To me, it's not that big of an *if*," another pundit chimed in. "Do not underestimate the impact of President Del Winters. She threw herself behind him in Atlanta. That has to help him tonight. It could well be the difference. It could carry him."

By nine thirty, the Atlanta area precincts began to report. Forsyth County was first in. Truitt carried it handily, which was not a surprise. Of the metropolitan counties, it was the most Republican. The real test would be Fulton, Dekalb, Cobb, and Clayton. Everyone knew Westfall would surely win at least Fulton and Dekalb counties, and maybe Cobb County too, but could Truitt make a stronger than predicted showing in them?

The urban precincts trickled in agonizingly. At eleven fifteen, all the networks said the Georgia Senate race was still too close to call; it would likely remain so until the final precincts reported. CNN's statistical analyst predicted that either candidate would win by fewer than thirty thousand votes, and maybe much less. Down to the wire. At the networks' headquarters, executives beamed. A bleary-eyed nation was glued to television sets across the land. Ratings, and the advertising revenues tied to them, would be through the roof.

With 90 percent of the critical Atlanta precincts reporting, and the rest of Georgia's counties already in, Truitt's statewide lead had dwindled to twenty thousand votes, and falling. It was a surmountable lead, the commentators said. Very. If candidate Westfall could match Hilary Clinton's 2016 performance in the remaining precincts, she would surpass the Republican and be the new senator from Georgia.

In Margaret Westfall's campaign hall in downtown Atlanta, there was excitement and buzzing optimism as her followers watched the huge screens. A few blocks away, the crowd at Will Truitt's election-night center was quiet, nervous, fearful.

President Del Winters sat up late with her father, just quiet and nervous. She called her chief of staff and asked him to get her a phone number for Margaret Westfall.

"You're going to call her?" asked her father.

"If she wins, yes. And it looks like she will."

"Why?"

"I tried to beat her. But she is qualified. I should congratulate her. I've only met her a few times. And I need a good relationship with her, that's for sure."

The chief of staff called back with the phone number a few minutes later, just as the banners flared across the network screens almost in unison. She told him to wait a moment.

"Republican Will Truitt has survived in Georgia!" the CNN anchor proclaimed. "The tension is over. What a night it has been. Truitt wins Georgia, retaining his seat and the Republican plurality in the United States Senate, by just *seven thousand votes*. Seven thousand and nine votes, to be exact."

Stunned silence draped the Westfall campaign hall; Truitt's ballroom was frenzied joy.

"Okay," the president said to her aide on the phone. "I don't need it now. I'm hitting the hay." After hanging up, she turned to her father.

"You too, Dad?"

"Oh, since I've watched it this far, I think I'll stay for the after-action report." You could not take the general out of a general. "Savor the victory a bit."

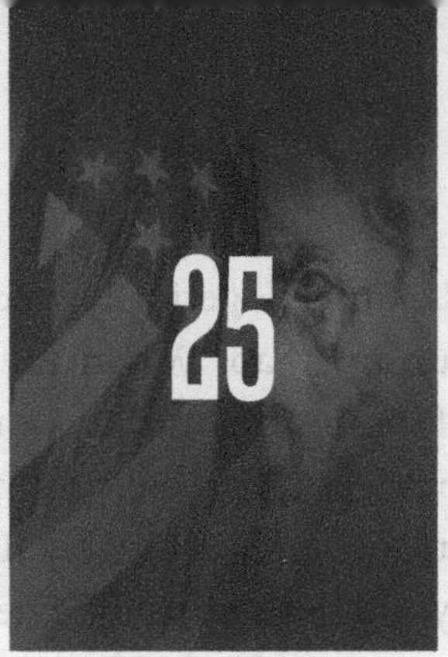

25

★ ★ ★

CACKLING AT THE CACKLING CROW TAVERN

When the Cackling Crow filled up in the evenings, patrons often shouted to be heard. No one seemed to mind. Tucked around the corner from Harvard in Cambridge, the tavern was a favorite of the academic crowd. So many intellectuals frequented the place that the bartenders joked that customers asked for C-SPAN and TED Talks on the televisions more often than sports channels.

But on election nights, no one at the tavern argued about what to show on the screens. They just argued about everything else. You'd have thought it was a presidential election, the place was so crowded. And charged.

Simon DeClerc's booth was as noisy as any of them that night. And as lubricated. More than one patron noted the way he pounded the table—bam, bam, bam—whenever the vote count in the Truitt-Westfall race was updated. Once, his histrionics jarred and wobbled a pitcher of beer on the tabletop, saved only by the quick reach of a less inebriated friend. He was drinking more than his friends, unapologetically, because he was paying for the table on a running tab. When the race was called in Truitt's favor just before midnight, the young computer genius jumped from his booth and danced around the tavern floor, pumping his fists in the air. In a relatively liberal crowd, he had the floor show pretty much to himself. The least you could say was that he drew attention to himself.

He appeared unfazed by the room's reaction to his antics. He returned to his booth where his two friends sat uncomfortably, motioning him to sit down. Reluctantly, he did.

"Simon! Simon!" one of them said. "Tighten it up, man. Cool down."

"Fuck that," blared DeClerc. "I'm *flying* tonight, man. We did it! Did you hear that margin? Seven thousand fucking votes! *Seven thousand!* We turned it! We turned it in those fucking machines!"

His friend grabbed him on the booth bench next to him and pressed his face close to Simon's.

"*Shut up,*" he said lowly. "Keep your voice down. We're getting out of here now." He looked to the bar counter. "Get up there and pay the bill."

The young cyber engineer weaved to the bar top and signed for his American Express ticket, promptly presented to him by the bartender, relieved his noisy patron was departing in less intoxicated company.

No sooner had the door closed behind Simon DeClerc and his friends than a woman in dress jeans and a black blazer stepped briskly up to the bartender. She opened her jacket and retracted her credentials. She placed them in front of him on the bar. Sophia Sikes. Federal Bureau of Investigation, Boston Field Office.

"I was sitting in the next booth to that guy," she said matter-of-factly.

"Sorry if he bothered you."

"I'm more bothered by what he said."

"Oh?"

"You know him?"

"Only that he comes in here."

"Mind showing me his credit card slip?"

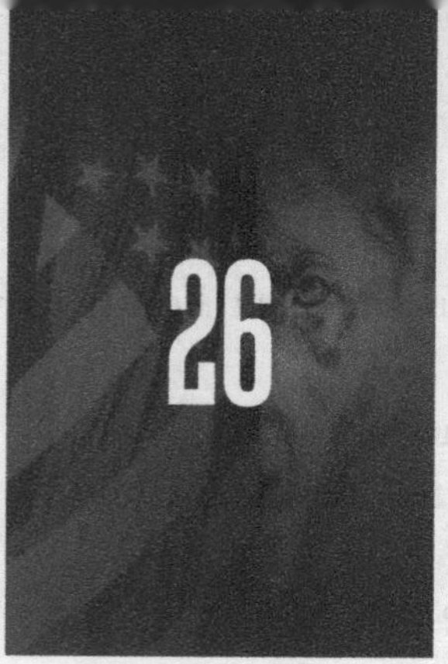

26

★ ★ ★

BLACK WEDNESDAY

Special Agent Sophia Sikes's boss in Boston agreed that what she had heard and observed at the Cambridge tavern warranted follow-up. And, in this case more importantly, *reporting* up. Since the enactment of the voting security statute, the FBI had operated a national elections integrity unit stationed in Chicago. Congress and the public thought it wise that the feds investigate voter fraud on a central, national basis. The thinking was that local politicos might influence local law enforcement. Leave it to the blue-jacketed men and women of the FBI.

The Boston agent-in-charge directed Sikes to notify the Chicago unit immediately. They would have protocols for next investigative steps and for further notifications up the chain, he told her. So, Sikes summarized her information in an email and sent it on the secure server to Chicago. Ten minutes later, she called to follow up.

Ned Thelan, the seasoned chief of the election integrity unit, took her call immediately.

"It's a busy day," he told her. "For us up here, this is like the day after Thanksgiving. All the shoppers are out. We call it Black Wednesday."

"I never thought of that," Sophia said.

"You wouldn't believe how many people say their coworker—who they just happen to hate—claims he voted twice; or their neighbor down the street had his out-of-town sister in the line with him because his wife was away. Everybody comes out of the woodwork on the day after an election. We can't possibly run down every one of these."

"How do you filter them?"

"We have a protocol. A bunch of variables. Scope of the alleged hanky-panky. Could it possibly have affected outcome? Credibility of the person making the claim. Some of these people are just serial complainers."

"How's my credibility?" asked Sophia.

"How do you usually vote?"

"Usually Republican."

"I'd say a Republican-leaning FBI agent reporting suspected activity helping a Republican is pretty damn credible."

He probed her for as much as she could recall from the evening before at the Cackling Crow. Which was just about everything. Simon DeClerc was with two companions—one male, one female. The woman said nothing that Sophie could hear. The other tried to quiet him down and get him out of the tavern. All three were Caucasian. DeClerc wore a burgundy hoodie with a Harvard logo. They left on foot and didn't get into a cab, though two were waiting at the curb outside the bar, looking for passengers.

"Did he mention Margaret Westfall's name?"

"No."

"Will Truitt's name?"

"No."

"Did the other guy?"

"No."

"How do you know DeClerc was talking about the Georgia election?"

"Because he went wacko when the TVs called it. He got out of the booth behind me and started jumping and yelling. And one of the other guys called him back, trying to settle him down. When he sat down, he said, 'Seven thousand votes … we *turned* it.'"

"Turned it *in the machines*, he said?" asked Thelan.

"Turned it 'in the *fucking* machines,'" Sikes told him.

"Just a minute," said Thelan. One of his agents in Chicago came to his desk. Sikes heard them have a brief exchange. He came back to her.

"SureSecure. Ever heard of it?" he asked Sikes.

"No."

"It's right there in Boston. A cyber consulting company."

"There are hundreds of tech outfits here."

"Well, this one is an NSA contractor. Cleared to do analytics and testing on state voting machines. We get some personnel information on the companies that get approved. One of SureSecure's employees is a Simon DeClerc. Just a minute," he said again. This time Sophia could hear him calling to an assistant, telling him to get hold of the United States attorney in Boston.

"You know Catherine O'Keane, the US attorney there in Boston?"

"Sure."

"Can you get over to her office in an hour?"

"Sure."

"We'll work with her people and put together a draft affidavit to support a warrant for the guy's employer. And for his phone and devices. You'll have to swear to it. You may be on to something."

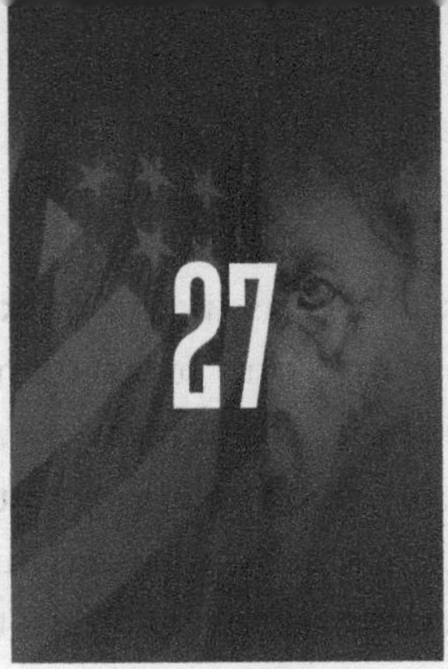

27

★ ★ ★

CALLED TO LONDON

Damascus was perplexed. It did not understand how the American drone and the French fighter jet could have been infiltrated without it knowing anything about it. Had one of its own field operatives failed to report something to central command?

The age of hacking had complicated the transfer of information between spies and their masters. In the cold war, an encrypted cable was suitable for most transmissions. Then, in the early years of email technology, before it was known to be insecure, communication was so easy that spies reminisced for the old days when meetings in dimly lit cafes were the way important information was passed. But in recent years, spymasters and their operatives had come nearly full circle. You didn't send critical information over the internet or ordinary phone lines. It was just too dangerous. No, it was back to basics. From his lips to your ears; or yours to hers.

But human communication had its own problems. Humans.

Damascus wondered if it was in the dark on the talk of the intelligence world because one of its own had erred. People forgot things. Surprisingly, sometimes even important things. And if an operative overlooked important information—and later realized his or her lapse—he or she might cover the error by going silent altogether, rather than face the embarrassment, or worse, of the miscue.

From Michigan, Majir Asheed had traveled to Oklahoma to evaluate additional hate groups. Believe it or not, there were still fringe elements in that region who revered the memory of Timothy McVeigh, the anarchist—the term *terrorist* not yet in the American public's common vernacular—who blew up the federal building in Oklahoma City in April 1995 with a truck bomb. One-hundred sixty-eight people were killed, including nineteen children. Five hundred more were injured—innocent government workers and ordinary citizens who happened to be in the building that morning to use its services. McVeigh and his accomplice, Terry Nichols, active in a subversive militia himself, shared a hatred of the US government. When arrested in a traffic stop the day of the bombing, McVeigh was wearing a T-shirt with a picture of Abraham Lincoln on the front and on the back the self-glorifying expression uttered by John Wilkes Booth after shooting him in the Ford Theatre: *Sic semper tyrannis! Thus always to tyrants!*

Damascus thought the McVeigh heritage a splendid example to be cultivated in others. It sent Majir to test the waters in the Plains states.

But now, new instructions awaited him in the Oklahoma post office outside Ponca City, near a large CITGO refinery.

Needed in London for debrief. Egerton House Hotel,
1100 hours, Thursday next.

Relief swept over him. He had been away from Melaha and Desh for over a month and missed them acutely. Now he could be with them. Once in London, Damascus normally allowed him a solid month or more before another assignment. Or more killing.

He left for London immediately.

PROBABLE CAUSE

"This isn't a TV show," Judge Eli Bidwell said. "In my room you still need probable cause."

Looking across the wide desk in his ornate chambers in Boston's federal courthouse, Judge Bidwell looked as formidable as his reputation. In some ways, he was a throwback to an earlier time.

Politics and judging were never completely independent of one another. After all, each federal judge, with only a few exceptions, such as the judges of the bankruptcy courts, was appointed by the president of the United States. There were eight hundred federal district court judges scattered across the country. Obviously, the president could not have personal experience with qualified judicial candidates in very many places. Recommendations had to be gathered, and in such a process you could not remove the influences of friendship, ideology, and—let's be honest—payback. In the end, you made the short list if you were a highly regarded lawyer and person—*and* because you knew someone powerful enough to get your name to the White House for consideration.

Yes, connections were critical. But alone, they were insufficient. The life term of the judicial appointments made by the president lent a sobriety to the selection of federal judges that was almost unique in the appointment power. Everyone in the process took it seriously, right up to the president, ordinarily. And once nominated and confirmed by the Senate, the women and men of the federal judiciary enjoyed something that hardly anyone else in government did: a presumption of integrity. Judge Eli Bidwell certainly did. He neither gave nor accepted favors. To or from anyone.

"You want warrants to seize and search the cell phone of a citizen and the records of a private company," he said. He looked down at the petition and affidavit in front of him, and then at the two women sitting in armchairs. "This company, SureSecure. Tell me about it."

"It's not just *any* company, Your Honor," said Catherine O'Keane. "It is a government contractor."

"Why is that relevant? There must be thousands of companies that do work for the government."

"Not *this* kind of work, Your Honor. It's highly sensitive. Election security. There are only three." The US attorney looked at Sophia Sikes, looking for concurrence.

"That's right, sir," Sophia said. She saw O'Keane's disapproving glance. "Your *Honor*, I mean."

Judge Bidwell didn't react; he looked down again at the affidavit. Most of the affidavits presented to support search warrants were lengthy, detailed. This one filled just two pages, and most of it was a factual recitation about the election result in the Georgia Senate race.

"What you have here are a couple sentences from a drunk

tavern patron," the judge said. "Is that probable cause to believe a crime has been committed?"

"In the context, Your Honor, I think it is," O'Keane said. "Mr. DeClerc made those statements *immediately* after the newscast declared the winning margin of the candidate. Yes, he may well have been intoxicated. Probably was. But, if anything, that lends credibility to his words. He's drunk; he's uninhibited. Had he not been drinking, who knows, maybe he would have had the composure to keep his mouth shut. As his companions apparently wanted him to. It's all in Agent Sikes's affidavit."

The judge's chair creaked as he turned to the side, thinking, looking to the wall on which was displayed the portrait of President Trump, who had appointed him. Sophia rustled in her chair, as if she was about to say something. O'Keane caught her eye and shook her head. Sophia took her cue and relaxed back in her chair. A full minute passed. Then the judge spoke.

"If this petition were supported only by a secondhand report of what this man allegedly said, if someone had called it in to you or the police, I would deny the warrant. I would make you interview him, or others, and come back with more. But this was heard by agent Sikes personally, which puts it in a different light."

"Thank you, Your Honor," the US attorney said.

"I'm not finished," he said.

O'Keane sat back, admonished.

"I'm still not convinced that a citizen loses his Fourth Amendment rights merely on the basis of a drunken comment," the judge said. "Even if it is heard by an FBI agent. But I *will* allow the warrant for the company records. That doesn't seem an invasion of anyone's privacy. As you say, the government is paying them. Why shouldn't it be able to know where this employee was working on its behalf. If you see those records and can prove this guy ... what's his name?"

"Simon DeClerc," O'Keane and Sophie chimed in simultaneously.

"Simon DeClerc," the judge resumed. "If you find that he was working on the Georgia machines, come back to me. That will be probable cause as to him and his phone." The judge reached for a pen. "Can I just cross out his name and leave the company, or do you want to prepare a new warrant for me to sign?" he asked O'Keane.

"No, that would be fine, Your Honor," she said. "We'd like to move quickly."

Judge Bidwell made a few slashes with his pen and handed the warrant over to the US attorney.

"Be sure you leave a copy with my clerk before you go," he said. "It will go in the private stack, sealed. And thanks for coming over yourself on this one, Catherine." It was rare for the US attorney herself to appear at the courthouse. She had a warehouse full of competent assistant US attorneys to send instead.

"That's kind of you, Your Honor. I didn't want to send a boy to do a woman's job." She smiled at the judge as she buckled her briefcase.

"You're not suggesting I gave you special consideration, are you?" he asked. His tone was not harsh, but not light either.

"I know better than that," she replied.

"Well, I'm glad you do. Because I didn't. And won't." He rose from his desk. "Just the same, it *was* good to see you."

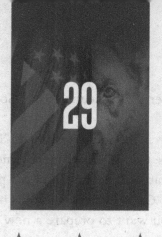

29

★ ★ ★

A MOST UNUSUAL LETTER

Inside the INTERPOL field office in Brussels, the counterterrorism unit moved quickly on the new request from American intelligence, received that morning. Could the best investigator available be dispatched to Munich to follow up on the lead at the Max Plank Institute? The institute conducted technology research utilizing the Ukrainian media satellite, the only non-American academic center to do so. Dozens of transmissions to the satellite had emanated from someone there in the days before and since the first drone hijacking.

Jacques Minter, deputy director of INTERPOL, had come from the international agency's headquarters in Lyon, France, and waited in the Brussels office for his friend Lars LaToure, the agency's head of investigations from Stockholm. LaToure had come by train to Brussels—he disdained airports—and according to the lobby security desk had just arrived. Minter was pleased. The double espresso with two sugars, sitting in a porcelain cup on the front of the desk, known to him to be the

Swedish detective's favorite morning beverage, would still be piping hot for his friend. The deputy director had brought it in even before the call came up from the lobby. Minter knew that among his virtues, Lars LaToure was never tardy.

He strode into the spacious office reserved for visiting higher-ups and reached across the desk to Minter's hand in an automatic fashion, saying nothing. He sat down in front of the desk and immediately sipped from the awaiting cup.

"You might thank me for that," Minter said.

"Yes, Jacques, very thoughtful of you."

In truth, the men were so fond of each other that ordinary courtesies were hardly necessary. What might appear to observers as a coolness between them was really an unvarnished comfort produced by decades of collaboration and mutual respect. In a way, they were the perfect team. Both highly intelligent. Each skilled and dedicated to a fault. And neither aspiring to the other's job. It had always been so, since their first assignments together thirty years ago.

Starting in the field as all INTERPOL agents did, Minter soon aspired to managerial responsibility. His friend LaToure did not. Lars relished the investigative side that he called "the hunt." He loved the pursuit, the choosing of paths, the sorting of facts. Even the writing of reports, for which his unusual one-page summaries had become a legend in the agency.

"How does Lars manage to say in a hundred words what the rest of us need five pages for?" marveled one branch supervisor to Minter.

"It has to do with sentences," Minter replied. "He doesn't use them."

"Well, I wish we could bottle it," the supervisor said.

LaToure adjusted his chair and brought his slim leather brief clutch to his lap, retrieving his signature spiral notepad.

"Where do you even *find* those things anymore, Lars?" asked the deputy director.

"It's getting troublesome," LaToure said. "Nobody has them these days. When I see them, I buy them in bulk." It was true, and even had raised an eyebrow in the finance group at Lyon. He had submitted an expense receipt for "notepads" in the amount of three hundred euros. The accountant from headquarters called to see if it might be a mistake.

"It seems like a lot of money for notepads," he said to Lars.

"They're disappearing on me," the chief investigator explained. "So, I picked up three cases. A case a year 'til I retire."

"If you won't use an electronic tablet, why not just plain legal pads?" the accountant asked. It seemed a reasonable query. "Those spiral books are getting expensive because, as you say, they are becoming rare."

"I am afraid those spiral wires are the only thing holding some of these cases together," Lars explained.

Sun streamed in through the expansive windows in the top-floor office. It was so unusually pleasant that each man paused before beginning their business to simply look out through the glass and enjoy it.

"What is Brussels coming to?" asked Lars. "So lovely today. But more to the point, what does Brussels want of *me* today?"

"The Americans need us," said Minter.

"Well that *is* cause for pause," said Lars. They both knew it happened rarely.

"It's to do with their hijacked drone."

"Oh?"

"It was misdirected through a private media satellite. Ukrainian owned."

"Yes, I was surprised the American president disclosed that," Lars said.

"Me too. But I assume she did that on purpose."

"So, what do they want from us?"

"They have evidence of transmissions to and from that satellite originating from Munich. From the Max Plank Institute, there. Apparently, there is a contract between the institute and the owner of the satellite allowing its use."

"For what?"

"Research projects. They say. Telecommunications. New technologies. Speed of light stuff." Minter seemed just a little agitated by LaToure's questions. "Anyway, how would *I* know, Lars?" he said.

"Because you are my all-knowing friend and boss."

They both laughed.

"And I expect you to keep me appearing as such," Minter said. "The Americans have sent over this dossier on the Munich connection." He handed a folder across the desk. "Very detailed. Technical. Lord knows how they do it." LaToure paged through the material as Minter continued. "They've identified the people at Max Plank known to interact with the arrangement," the deputy director said.

"They have their own FBI station in Munich," Lars said. "Another in Hamburg. Why do they desire our kind services?"

"*International cooperation* is the official justification," said Minter. "But I think the real reason is their people in Munich are weak on German. And no Russian speakers at all except in their CIA station, and of course they don't want them out in the open in Munich. How is your Russian these days, Lars? Your German *and* Russian."

"Fair to middling."

Minter smiled. He knew LaToure's German was flawless, and his Russian nearly so. Because of that he had interrogated every Russian arrested by INTERPOL in the last ten years, and most of the Germans.

"Start with the head of the contract research department there," Minter said, looking down at a note. "Dr. Neils Straak."

"Dutch or Danish?"

"Dutch, I gather."

"Well, the Ukrainian isn't making much money on that contract," LaToure said.

Minter looked across at his friend and waved his arms in feigned exasperation.

"*Lars!*" he said. "How can an investigator embrace *every* stereotype in the world and somehow still get to the truth of things every time?" His friend LaToure was revered as never having been proven wrong on a suspect he fingered. "Tell me, Lars, how do you do that?"

"It's simple, really. I never listen to myself," LaToure said. He stood to leave. "I assume you want me to get on this immediately?"

"Yes, you know the Americans. There's a high-speed train to Munich that departs in forty minutes. My assistant has a ticket for you."

"First class?"

"Need you ask?" Minter rose also. "Anything new in Stockholm?" he asked. "Besides snow and hockey?"

"Yes, actually," said Lars. "I am glad you asked. I nearly forgot." He reached into his thin leather brief clutch, barely larger than a folio. "This letter arrived in yesterday's post. Unusual to say the least."

He handed the letter to Jacque. It was a single page, handwritten on quality, heavy bond paper. The block printing was small and neat, the lines straight as a ruler's edge.

Mr. Lars LaToure,
INTERPOL Stockholm

I write seeking facilitation of asylum in Europe for myself and my family (spouse, Indian, UK residency, and daughter, age 16).

For 30 years, I have been in the service of Middle East and East Asia Intelligence. Last 25 in UK and United States. My desire to defect is not politically motivated. My motivation is based on morality. I do not want to be disloyal to my country, whose cause is just, but I do not want to continue to follow all orders.

My following of such orders in the past makes defection to the United States or Britain impossible, as I have assassinated its citizens and agents.

If I may speak with you about my desire, I will be grateful for your indication and instructions by post to Box 259, Harberton Rd. Post Office, London.

M.

"My word, Lars," said the deputy director. "You seem to have quite a fish swimming to your line. Do you have any notion as to why he is contacting *you*? Or who he is?" He paused. "I guess I should say, 'he or *she*.'"

"Not a clue."

"Spoken like a true detective."

"A clueless one, I am afraid, in this instance."

"What do you want to do about it?" asked Minter. "I *could* assign it to someone else for follow-up. But perhaps you would prefer to keep it?"

Minter's tone was clear to LaToure. The boss wanted Lars to handle it himself. He understood why. Nothing could be more sensitive or rumor-attracting than the possible defection of a foreign agent, especially one with blood on his or her hands. Right now, only two persons knew anything about it, three including the sender of the letter. The deputy director wanted to keep it that way for as long as possible.

"That seems sensible, Jacques," he said. "I'll keep you informed."

"Good. Verbal only. No texts or email."

"Of course." Lars started for the door, then stopped. "Jacques, do you know the only thing that is better in an airport than on a train?"

"What?"

"The coffee."

"I should have guessed. Take another with you."

30

WAITING, WITH DOUGHNUTS

While Lars LaToure sped to Munich at noon in Western Europe, Sophia Sikes and two fellow FBI agents pulled up at six in the morning to the downtown Boston office building that housed SureSecure Consulting. Fitting to the company's low profile, its sign was undersized and understated. It was placed in the middle of a vertical row of a dozen placards, mostly for law firms, mounted on the stone façade next to the front entrance. You had to look twice even to find it among the others.

It was typical Beantown weather for the first week of November—nipping air, bobbing at the freezing mark, and minor snow squalls. The agents knew their target occupied half of the seventh floor, facing the street. The windows were dark, and the street entrance door was locked. Knowing no one had yet arrived, they waited at the curb in their warm black Chevy Suburban, chatting amiably over takeout coffee and—yes—doughnuts.

Judge Bidwell had signed the warrant the afternoon

before—the day after the election—but Sophie had waited till now, early Thursday morning, to execute it. For one thing, she wanted physical assistance with the search and only one other agent was unoccupied when she had returned with the warrant to the office. But perhaps more importantly, she wanted time to consult with the bureau's election fraud unit in Chicago. What more could they tell her about SureSecure? Were there particular things she should be looking for in its records? Had they picked up any new information about the Georgia voting since her conversation with Ned Thelan, the unit chief, yesterday?

Her decision was wise. She learned that to date SureSecure had complied with the many reporting requirements for election security contractors. From early days under the Election Security Reform Act, the company had been approved for preelection checks of voting machines, and its work for some state election boards had even *predated* the law. One of the law's requirements mandated contractors to make semiannual notifications of personnel rolls to the FBI's fraud unit, and additional special reporting of any new hires within sixty days of a coming election. The Chicago unit told Sophia that employee turnover at SureSecure was lower than at most other contractors, and that this was considered a virtue in its security profile.

"Maybe it's Boston," one Chicago agent said to her on the phone. "They're like Red Sox fans. Loyal as hell. Even when they shouldn't be."

But there was one red flag, he told her. In the same week in early October as this election approached, three new field security specialists came on board at SureSecure: Philip Winston, Emma Kuziniak, and Simon DeClerc.

"Did you look into them in October?" she asked.

"Anything that near to voting, we always look," he said. "It was interesting because the company must have anticipated we would want more information on them. The routine notification normally sent us is just a simple form with only basic identification: address, Social Security number, driver's license detail. They sent that, but also sent resumes and the job applications for these three. Seems like they wanted to be sure they were quickly approved."

"And?"

"We worked them, and they checked out. Pretty much."

"Something didn't?" asked Sophie.

"Well, something couldn't be confirmed. Still hasn't. DeClerc's résumé and application claim a bachelor's degree in information engineering from MIT and a master's in software engineering from Tufts. His address information was verified. He lived at three addresses around Boston for the entire period. And Tufts confirmed the graduate degree. But MIT hasn't responded yet about a degree from them."

"Is that unusual?"

"Not really, but normally they get back to us by now. We just called them. They say they're still looking. The spelling of the name could be a problem. They have a DeClerk, but they haven't found a DeClerc. And the one they found in the records earned his degree fifteen years ago. That can't be your guy. He'd have been a teenager. At best."

"It smells," said Sophie.

"It does, but I wouldn't conclude anything from it yet. Résumé puffing is rampant. Even our bureau applicants do it. More than you'd think."

"You're kidding me."

"Wish I were. It's the number one reason cadets get expelled from Quantico. And if your Simon DeClerc *did* lie about his degree, that doesn't make him a saboteur. But we'll run it to ground, don't worry."

"Anything about the other two?" she asked.

"Their details were all verified. But one thing is interesting. They're both work visa holders from Europe. Winston from England. Kuziniak from Hungary. And no family for either of them in the United States."

Sophie made careful notes and thanked her Chicago colleague.

"One last thing," she asked him. "Do the rules make these contractors keep records of each assignment that a technician works on?"

"Absolutely. Every state and county, and all dates. And the NSA expert who supervised them at each site. Congress got that right. All that should be written down in their office. Let us know how it goes."

"I will."

"Are you calling first or going in cold?" the Chicago agent asked.

"Dead cold. When the doors open in the morning."

"Smart move. Take plenty of boxes."

Sophie and her fellow agents took his advice. A pile of sturdy, folded banker's boxes rose nearly to the roofline in the rear of the long Suburban, along with bubble wrap for computer equipment. As they waited in the warm, they agreed on their entry plan. They would watch for arriving persons and take turns approaching each at the entrance. SureSecure's website did not declare office hours, so there was no way to know how soon the first employee might arrive. Any number of employees from other companies in the building might appear earlier. Each arriving person would be calmly asked if he or she worked for SureSecure. FBI credentials would not be shown until someone answered yes, or, "Why do you ask?"

At six thirty, a uniformed lobby guard emerged from the

inside to unlock the revolving door. He stepped out into the cold air and kicked the corrugated mat on the sidewalk, then retreated inside. Eventually, building employees began walking up. There were eight false starts before an attractive young woman in tennis shoes and a jacket too light for the weather stepped up briskly. It was Sophie's turn. As soon as she produced her FBI credentials from her coat pocket, the other two agents jumped from the vehicle and approached.

"Yes," the woman said. "I work there. I'm the receptionist. What is this about?"

"We have a warrant to collect records and information," Sophie said matter-of-factly. "Do you have a key to the office?"

"Yes. I am supposed to get here first."

"May we go up with you?"

"I guess so."

"Good."

The woman and the three agents took the elevator to the seventh floor. As the receptionist withdrew her card key at the entrance to the company office, she turned, appearing anxious.

"Can we wait for the manager? He comes early too. Usually."

The agents were trained to accept reasonable requests, and this was an easy one.

"Of course," Sophie said.

"Would you like me to go in and make coffee? I could bring you coffee while you wait."

"No, I'm afraid we need you to stay out here with us." The young woman did not seem suspicious to her, but Sophie knew she could not take a chance. You never let someone into a search site once they knew why you were there. "If *you* want some coffee, Agent Andrews here will go out and get you some. Won't you Agent Andrews?"

Before the agent could answer, the elevator door opened,

and the manager stepped out, looking surprised. He didn't say anything and didn't step toward them. Sophie walked casually to him, as the third agent stepped quickly along the far wall, then over to a position behind the man and in front of the elevator door, now closing automatically.

"Are you the manager here, sir?" asked Sophie.

"Yes."

"And your name, sir?"

"Who are you?"

Sophie did not answer. She held up her leather credential folio and let its flap drop at his eye level.

"Your name, sir?" she repeated.

"Telsany. Edward Telsany."

"I am Special Agent Sikes. This is Agent Wells. Behind you is Agent Andrews. We have a warrant to search your offices and remove records and information." She handed him the warrant.

"Why? What for?"

"We cannot discuss that. Beyond what is stated there. In the warrant."

"Can I call a lawyer?"

"You *may*, but you are not under arrest or charged with anything." There was an anxious pause. "Assuming you are not resisting the execution of the warrant. You aren't, are you?"

"No, of course not, of course not." He withdrew his own key card and moved toward the office door. He opened the door and started in. Sophie thrust her arm in front of him, halting him.

"I'm sorry, but we will need you and your employee to remain out here in the hallway while we work," she said. "As the others arrive, they will need to wait out here too, unless you send them off for a while. If you insist on coming in, Agent Wells or Agent Andrew will need to stand with you in the reception area, and we will have to call in more officers. It will all go more easily and quickly, if the three of us do our work inside, and you all stay out here."

"That seems extreme," Telsany said.

"Really, it's just the best way, sir. For everybody."

Telsany looked at the warrant and its intimidating calligraphy.

"I hope you will do this as rapidly as you can."

Sophie nodded, and the three agents went into the office alone. A single master light switch illuminated the whole of the main floor. Telsany told the receptionist to wait for the other employees and then tell them that some special maintenance had come up. The office would not open today, she was to say.

The SureSecure manager then took the elevator to the lobby, moved to a corner for privacy, and placed a cell phone call.

To Budapest.

31

★ ★ ★
A BULLY SHE COULD TRUST

In Washington, the president's meetings with congressional leaders for the special funding of the new military communications pipeline went well, even better than expected. Her strategy was to secure the total funding, essentially in thirds, from three sets of federal committees. Vernon Lazar, the secretary of defense, was especially well-liked by two of them: the House Intelligence and Armed Services Committees, before whom he testified regularly, both publicly and in closed sessions. He attended the president's special meetings with those leaders and did most of the talking, including information about the Pittsburgh civilian, Stanley Bigelow, designing the complicated new channels.

The committees approved the entire amount requested and, moreover, as a "continuing appropriation" in the event more—even substantially more—was needed when final costs could be determined. That uncertainty was the only rough spot in the secret sessions.

"What kind of engineer can't give an accurate estimate of the real cost of such a project?" asked one of the chairmen.

"An honest one," replied the president.

The third source the president planned was the Energy Department. Most of its spending was overseen by the House Energy Infrastructure Committee chaired by Harry Jevins of Texas. Though a Republican like herself, the congressman from Dallas was independent-minded and often considered a "maverick" on key public issues. His relationship with Del Winters had been combative. The main point of contention between them involved the federal judiciary, and especially one judgeship. The president knew that Jevins had plied his network for the appointment of a certain Dallas lawyer to the federal bench when a vacancy had opened there the previous year.

"Harry Jevins is pushing this guy hard," the president's aide had said as they reviewed a short list for the seat. "We know he made a big deal out of this seat with the Texas Bar Association. They put him on their "recommended" list to satisfy him, but the guy is no legal superstar in Dallas. But, in fairness, our vetting shows he *is* capable."

"Harry can be a bully," the president said. "And I don't care for his attitude toward women. It's not that he's a harasser—he's not—but he's dismissive. He won't like it, but I am going to appoint a woman to that seat in Dallas. It's been a boys' club there for years. Twelve district judges, only two women."

At their private breakfast in the White House to discuss the special appropriation, the large Texan brought up the judicial appointment almost immediately.

"Breakfast is nice," he said. "But I would rather have had Jim Dodge on the Dallas bench. You knew I was behind his recommendation, didn't you?" He always reminded her of what she had read about LBJ in his prime, and he certainly did now, leaning across the small table and looking her straight in the eye.

"I did, Harry, yes," the president acknowledged. "I knew he was your man." She easily could have denied it, and the congressman knew that.

"Did you think he was unqualified?"

"No, he was qualified," she said, which she believed.

"Then why didn't you appoint him?"

"Because I preferred someone else who was also qualified," the president said. "And needed on that bench, in my judgment. She was confirmed ninety-nine to one by the Senate, by the way. Which I'm sure you remember, since you were the 'one.'" She could see that he was still unhappy, not letting it go, and not intending to. Momentarily, she succumbed to irritation at his presumptuousness.

"Why don't you get yourself elected president of the United States, Harry, and then *you* can make those appointments," she said, more than a trace of elevation in her voice. It was an arrogant comment, in an unnecessary tone, and she regretted it immediately. She took three sips of coffee, composing herself, as the congressman sat red-faced across from her.

"Listen, Harry," she said. "We have something important to talk about, and we need to talk about it now. This other thing, it's history. I didn't do what you wished. But you know I respect you, or I wouldn't have asked you here."

"You asked me here because you want something from me."

"That's true. Absolutely, true. But there are many others that I could get it from too. I am coming to you because I trust you."

The congressman's attention was peaked. He leaned forward in his chair.

"Trust me to do *what*, Madame President." She appreciated the salutation.

"To do the right thing, and then keep quiet about it. There are others who will do the first, but damn few you can trust to do the second." Her tone was undeniably sincere, and Harry Jevins knew it.

An hour later, Del Winters and the congressman stood at the same private side door of the White House at which he had secretly arrived earlier that morning. He asked about her father and she about his wife. She extended her hand, and he shook it firmly.

"Maybe the *next* appointment," he said as he stepped under the canopy to the waiting sedan.

"Maybe so," said the president.

In their hearts, each knew it was unlikely. But somehow it was good enough.

★ ★ ★

EGERTON HOUSE

It was the kind of quaint, cozy London hotel that if you stayed once, you stayed often. Converted red-brick row houses, the Egerton House Hotel enjoyed its tasteful, low-profile standing just off busy Brompton Road on the cusp of Chelsea and Kensington, a short walk from Herrod's Department Store. Something about its well-attired staff, interesting accommodations—just twenty-six individually appointed guest rooms—and tiny front reading room adjoining a small bar area, induced loyalty.

But, ironically, the four men and one woman who greeted each other in the little lobby afore the front desk that Thursday morning were not at the Egerton House on account of loyalty to the inn. Quite the opposite. They were there because they had never before been seen there, and never would be again.

Spies are usually big on loyalty. But they are not big at all on being noticed. And gathering in familiar places was a good way to get noticed.

Majir was the last to arrive, though he was by no means late, stepping briskly up the steps and into the lobby three minutes before eleven.

"Hello, Maji," the shortest of the men greeted him. Only first names would be used. Standard protocol.

"Yes, Amir," he answered, not as warmly.

Amir Ahmed was Majir's superior from Damascus, as he was to the other three Syrian agents whom headquarters had summoned to London. His relationship with Majir, however, was of a different order from the others by nearly every measurement. For one thing his association with the boss was of much longer standing, dating back over twenty years. At fifty-one, Majir was, save one agent presently stationed in Egypt, the oldest field operative in the Syrian secret service. Amir was three years his senior, and generally looked on as third in command of the entire Syrian intelligence apparatus. The other agents gathered that morning considered themselves privileged to work under Ahmed's supervision, and palpably endeavored to curry his satisfaction and favor. Not Majir. For no reason he consciously acknowledged, he never felt entirely at ease with the senior spymaster.

It was not that Majir distrusted Amir Ahmed. In the many years of assignments and communications, the words and actions of his Damascus handler had always been true, reliable, and clear. If they had not been all those things, Majir knew, he probably would not be alive today. It even seemed to Majir that his supervisor treated him with a sense of personal interest and affection, since Ahmed frequently asked about the well-being of Melaha and, after Desh's birth, his daughter's too.

Majir understood, though, that his lingering sense of discomfort around the Damascus chief probably was rooted in that "personal" interest, and how it began.

When Majir asked for approval to marry in England to his

Indian-born love, Damascus insisted on meeting her first. Ahmed came to London for the assessment. At that time, he had been directing Majir for only a few years. Majir and Melaha greeted him on his arrival at Heathrow and were both surprised when the spymaster suggested they go at once to Melaha's modest apartment in London's north end. It was not prepared for visitors, Melaha said, and it might be uncomfortable if tenants observed another Muslim man at her home. She had told some of them that Majir had no family. Who could this other man be? But Amir insisted, and when in the apartment he immediately went about searching it carefully, opening cupboards and every drawer.

"Must you do that?" asked Melaha.

"You know that your man is a spy, don't you?" he asked.

"Yes."

"Let's just say it would be better if you did not know that. At least, yet. But he has told you. This is why I must do this."

Majir knew that he was right. He should not have told his lover about his work. But he had done so only after he knew he wanted a life with her, and he had disclosed in his request for approval that the woman was aware of his occupation, explaining that he could not responsibly ask for marriage without her knowing it. He thought Damascus was satisfied with his reasoning; no objection or criticism had been made before Ahmed's arrival.

"I did not think that was a problem," Majir said, as Ahmed continued his look-around.

"It won't be unless I find something."

Of course, he didn't, though he asked Majir to take all the pictures off the walls so that he could see behind them before he blessed the apartment as secure.

"Well, then," the visitor finally said. "Let's go out for tea, shall we?"

It was just a twenty-minute episode, twenty years in the

past. But Majir never put it away, wherever it was you put such incidents. And Melaha certainly had not.

"I do not like him, Majir," she said seriously to him when they returned alone that evening. "Did he really think I could be a spy?"

"I am sorry, Melaha. I did not know he would do that. Perhaps I should have."

"I hope I do not have to see him ever again," she said.

She never did.

The foreign agents gathered at the Egerton House moved together to the rear of the tiny bar off the reading room, empty and quiet at that time of the morning. The small television monitor above the bar was muted on a replay of a European soccer game played the night before. Ahmed cruised lightly to the counter, located the remote, brought on the sound to a volume higher than needed even if anyone had been watching, and then joined the four field operatives at the back table.

"It is a good time to meet," he opened. "Central command is confused about the military planes—the hijackings."

"I thought maybe you called us in to say Damascus was behind them." It was the female agent, Anna Blyk, based in Prague. "No, Amir?" She sounded disappointed.

Majir had worked with Anna Blyk only twice, each time on intelligence-gathering assignments in Britain. Mature and exceptionally attractive, her specialty was seduction, to which British politicians were famously receptive. Posing as Egyptian business executives wanting to discuss legislation concerning shipping rules in the North Sea, the two had fooled their first target into dessert with Anna upstairs while Majir paid the bill in the hotel restaurant below. The Englishman learned, from Anna herself the next day, that she was in fact a Syrian operative as handy with camera technology as sexual maneuvers.

Compromised, he provided useful information to Damascus for years. She would have succeeded with the second target, months later, if the wife of that backbencher had not showed up unexpectedly during the meal, perhaps to keep an eye on her husband. Though Majir never observed them personally, others claimed that Anna's killing skills were exceptional too.

"No, no," said the supervisor. "All is dark on it. We thought it must be the Russians and were angry they said nothing to us. But Moscow denies it entirely. They even seem suspicious of *us*, and not pleased either."

Ahmed looked at the fancy coffee cups and saucers, sitting empty on the table. He pointed to his, then to the others, then to the youngest agent, motioning toward the other room. Taking his cue, the young spy rose and walked to the front desk in the lobby, asking if coffee could be delivered for them. Purposefully, he made his request in Russian, the language they had been speaking, to be sure the desk clerk could not understand it. The clerk's blank expression proved he could not, so he repeated his request in fair English, earning an eager nod from the lobby clerk. The others awaited the young spy's return before resuming.

"So," said Ahmed, "I need to know if any of you have picked up something—anything—in the field."

"I have nothing," said Anna. "But what does it matter if they are killing Jews?"

The others, except for Majir, nodded assent to her sentiment.

"Because if American and French aircraft can be taken, perhaps ours could too," Ahmed said. "Besides, if we cannot take credit for it, we surely don't want to be blamed for it!"

Majir thought the last part of his reasoning odd at best but the supervisor from Damascus took on a knowing expression, like one of a person who has uttered something profound. Such is the mental calculus, apparently, of an international spymaster.

In the end, it all came down to credit and blame. Sometimes you wanted one, sometimes you wanted the other. But usually you wanted at least one. The coffee arrived.

"You, Majir?" asked Ahmed. "What about in the States? Anything going around? Your sources in government. Have they said nothing?"

"Nothing you haven't heard in the news. The American president is said to be looking hard at it all."

"Well, you must all look for any information that might be out there," Ahmed said. "Work your assets, give it priority. Damascus thinks it's most likely a Persian operation," he said, referring to Iran's historical name, "because the drone and the fighter were both taken in the Middle East. Myself, I am keen on North Korea. I am going to our people in that region next. I will tell you what I learn, if I am permitted."

They adjourned shortly after noon, leaving separately. They could not wisely stay together for any length of time or move together for any distance, especially with closed circuit cameras mounted seemingly on every London light post. Ahmed and Majir stalled for a minute or two in the lobby and were the last to reach the street.

"And, Maji," the supervisor said, "we've learned the manager from the American laboratory has returned early."

"The agriculture man?" Majir wondered how that was known. Had another agent been dispatched to find him in Europe after all?

"Yes, he is back there," Ahmed said. "Take care of that. Take care of him. We know the North Koreans had a hand in whatever went on there. Find out. Who knows? Maybe this is all connected."

"Can it wait a few weeks? I have not been home in months."

Ahmed opened the taxi door and looked in to the driver, to

see that he was thoroughly British. Then he turned and spoke in Russian to Majir, standing on the walkway in front of the red brick hotel.

"It can wait two weeks, Maji," the man from Damascus said. "But not more than that. The Christian holidays are coming soon. Get back there, and do it before then." He climbed into the taxi and rolled the window down halfway. "And, Majir," he said, "my best, please, to Melaha and little Desh."

★ ★ ★

THE PRESIDENT IS TOLD

Del Winters first learned of the FBI's initial findings the next weekend. As soon as Sophie Sikes reported to the bureau's Chicago election fraud unit that the SureSecure records confirmed that young Simon DeClerc had in fact tested the Georgia voting machines, the group chief contacted the FBI director, suggesting notification of the attorney general. The case was still entirely circumstantial. Certainly, there was no evidence at all—yet—beyond the overheard words of the computer technician in the Boston tavern. But the enormity of the political ramifications, should the investigation turn up more support, commended a confidential alert to the top of the government sooner, not later.

The attorney general saw it the same way. She called the president immediately. Del was reading briefing papers in the White House residence, one ear on a football game that had the full attention of her father.

"Yes, Madeline," she said. "Since it's Sunday, this must be interesting."

"I am hoping it turns out to be nothing at all."

Madeline Stone had begun her career as a government prosecutor, then risen through the ranks of "skyscraper law"—the profession's somewhat cynical descriptor for the world of very large law firms—with startling speed. At age forty-five, she was managing a megafirm in Minneapolis, going toe-to-toe with usually cocky—nearly always silver-haired—male counterparts from New York, Chicago, or Washington. She endured the typical criticism of strong women in law. "She's beautiful, and that's how she wins." Only the first part was true. The president trusted her implicitly.

Del waved to her father and flapped her hand near her ear. He reached for the remote and turned the volume down.

"It's about the Georgia election," the attorney general said.

"What about it?"

"The FBI in Boston picked up a conversation about tampering with the voting machines down there. They think it's possible there may be something to it. So does the Chicago elections unit."

"*Really?* What have they got?"

"Not very much, so far," Stone said. "But a guy on election night went bonkers in a Boston bar when the final results came in on TV. Jumped around, plainly drunk, and was heard to say, "We *turned it*. We turned it *in the machines*." The attorney general added, "Actually, in the *fucking* machines."

"Who heard this?"

"Get ready for this," Stone said. "An FBI agent. Sophia Sikes, Boston field office. Happened to be sitting in the next booth with her husband. Her record is good. The director says she's a star."

"Go on."

"The guy turns out to be a computer technician employed by a cyber security company approved to check voting machines before Election Day. His company worked the Georgia machines, the whole state. And the FBI has confirmed that this is the guy who checked them."

"Only him?"

"No, every machine is double-checked by an expert from the NSA after the contractor says it's working right," Stone said. "That was done in Georgia. The expert from NSA was Homer Junes. Career guy. Straight arrow. The bureau has him and his records and are going through it with him now. But he says he thought every machine was good to go. He knows he checked their accuracy *after* this guy ran his diagnostics."

"Well, then it doesn't sound like we should hit the panic button," the president said.

"Agreed. But I thought you should know. Just in case more evidence is developed. Or this gets out."

"I appreciate it."

They both knew that Georgia's secretary of state was conducting a recount anyway in the Senate election. The margin was so close that the Democrat, Westfall, didn't even need to request it; state law made it automatic. Results of the recount were expected in a matter of days.

"Anything else you want me to do?" asked the attorney general.

"Just be sure the bureau has everything it needs to get to the bottom of it."

Henry Winters looked over from his easy chair. His face was a question mark. She nodded; he brought back the volume on his football game.

BLOODY MONDAY IN BOSTON

What the FBI's election fraud unit called "black Wednesday" was followed five days later by a bloody Monday in Boston. Very bloody, and at first even more puzzling to the Boston Police Department.

Three young Cambridge computer scientists were murdered—execution style—within ninety minutes, as best the homicide division could tell, in separate, but as would soon be evident, much related incidents.

Sophie Sikes and her team of federal agents expected to serve a search warrant on Simon DeClerc when they arrived at his tiny apartment in Somerville, adjacent to Cambridge. Judge Eli Bidwell had issued the warrant immediately upon learning that morning from the US attorney that employee DeClerc had indeed worked on the Georgia voting machines prior to the recent election.

The young computer genius never did read his own warrant. He was dead before he could be served with it, slaughtered in his second-floor loft. Five Boston police cruisers crowded against the sidewalk as Sikes, clad in an FBI windbreaker, wove through them and climbed up to the loft's entry door. A uniformed officer was guarding the doorway and stepped aside politely when she held up her credentials. He looked to a box of latex gloves and footies on the floor of the outside hall and looked at her quizzically. She nodded, and he handed her a pair of each; she put on the shoe covers, but not the gloves, and stepped inside.

Unlike urban policemen, FBI agents did not encounter scenes of violence often. Certainly, Sophia Sikes didn't. A few years earlier, she had worked a serial murderer case and had winced at the photographs and video clips viewed by the team. But seeing brutally inflicted death "live," as it were, was a wholly different experience. Standing just inside the doorway, she saw a man lying prone on the hardwood floor, ankles bound by a plastic zip cord. When she leaned, she saw that another cord wrapped his wrists behind his back. An egg-shaped pool of darkened blood extended from both sides of his head until it met the baseboard of the wall ahead.

"Why are *you* here?" asked the detective nearest the body.

"Do you have a name?" she asked, ignoring his question.

"DeClerc. Simon DeClerc," the detective said. "Twenty-eight."

"*He's* why I'm here," she said, producing the warrant from her jacket. "I came to serve him." She stepped closer to the detective and the body.

"Drugs?" the detective said, seemingly surprised. The appearance of the slender slain man and his small apartment in the gentrified neighborhood did not urge a suspicion of narcotics. "Is your warrant for drugs?"

"No."

"What then?"

"I can't say."

The detective did not react poorly, nor did he press her. He handed her his card and stepped over to confer with the officers. She overheard him mention the warrant, and soon he returned to her.

"I don't know what your warrant covers, but we haven't removed anything. And we won't until you're okay with it," he said.

"I appreciate that," she said.

"Obviously, this wasn't just a neighborhood disturbance," the detective said. "More like a mob hit, without the mob. At least not one we know about over here. This kid was killed three times over. They weren't taking any chances."

"*They?*"

"One guy can't wrap up a victim like this, at least not without a fight. One or two guys held him while another one tied him. I'd bet on it."

"Did you find his phone?" she asked.

"No."

"Any computers or tablets?"

"None. Seems odd," the detective said. "You know anything about him? That you can tell me?" His tone was professional, not cynical.

"He worked for a cyber security company downtown. SureSecure. Ever hear of it?"

"You're shitting me."

"No, he worked there," Sophie said.

The detective hurriedly retrieved his cell phone from his pocket and scrolled his text messages.

"Then we've got more going on here," he said.

"What do you mean?"

"There's another body in Cambridge," he said, "a woman about this guy's age. She was found in her own apartment, just before we found him. Same M-O." He looked at his text message. "Name is Emma Kuziniak. No phone on her either, or computers, but she had an employee badge in her purse. For SureSecure."

Even in matters of murder, when it rains it sometimes pours. The detective had barely recited the spelling of the Hungarian woman's name for the FBI agent, when his phone chimed. He backed up, as if startled, and leaned against the wall as he listened. She heard him ask the caller, oddly she thought, "as in *Churchill*?" It became clear a moment later when he pocketed his phone and walked back to Sophie.

"Philip Winston," he said to her. "Mean anything to you? He also worked for this SureSecure outfit."

"Don't tell me," said Sophie Sikes.

"He's dead too. In the North End."

★ ★ ★

A VISIT TO ARLINGTON; LOVE REMEMBERED

Ned Thelan and Sophie Sykes thought it sadly ironic that young Simon DeClerc, whose loose lips at the Cackling Crow had started the electoral odyssey now unfolding, was in the end vindicated on *one* thing, albeit posthumously. He did have that MIT degree after all. Apparently, the institution's records department was the last to get updated searching systems. Theirs was still rigidly case sensitive, and the murder victim's name had been stored as Declerc, the c uncapitalized. MIT sent his transcripts the next day. His grades were impressive indeed.

Thelan formed a fulsome team to head to Georgia and invited Sophie to join. On learning of the suspicion around Simon DeClerc, the elections fraud unit had ordered a quarantine-in-place of all the state's voting machines. At first, that order raised no undue alarm or attention from the news media, because it was known that a recount was needed and under way across the state. It made sense to keep the machines in place while the retally was completed. But when the recount was finished eight days after the election, confirming, nearly to the vote, the original result, and the machines remained under guard at the many precincts, Thelan knew it was only a matter of time before the inquiry into tampering would go viral.

Only Georgia's secretary of state was advised that an investigation had been opened into the Senate election result, and the confidential notice to him from Thelan's Chicago unit described it, somewhat disingenuously, as "a preliminary look at the mechanical functions of some machines to reconfirm preelection examinations, which showed all to be functioning properly." But the FBI team knew that once its forensic teams swarmed over the precincts, the news would be out quickly.

Of course, the triple murder in Boston of the three SureSecure cyber technicians triggered a five-alarm fire within the Justice Department, and commensurate concern at the White House. By late afternoon of "Bloody Monday" in Boston, as the national media was already calling it, Attorney General Stone had briefed the president on the severity of the concern. The nearly simultaneous execution of the three machine validators, each brought into the contractor's employ just before the election, could not sanely be viewed as an unrelated coincidence. No, what the president had perceived a week before as no cause for panic, at that time a reasonable view, now produced an undeniable sinking feeling in each of them.

"This isn't going to get better, is it, Madeline?" the president asked her attorney general.

"I don't see how."

"Do you intend to inform Truitt and Westfall?" the president asked.

"I am inclined to, yes."

"I think you should, too," said the president. "Margaret Westfall knows the recount came back against her, and Truitt thinks he's in the clear. So does the party. Westfall needs to file a challenge under the election statute by next week. She deserves to be told there may well be grounds for one."

Del Winters was well-aware that a challenge to Truitt's win in Georgia would throw her party leadership into havoc and dissension, and the holiday season, usually a respite from political furor, into a media politifest. And all while she and her national security team were engrossed—and needed to be—in running the military communications debacle to ground. Just two years into her presidency, the burdens were crushing. Her public temperament appeared unchanged, but in the privacy of the White House residence, the First Father worried about the pressure on his daughter. She was working early every morning and late every night. She was quieter than usual, preoccupied. Thanksgiving was a week away, and Congress had left town. He thought his daughter should throttle back and find relaxation some way.

It seemed counterintuitive to others, especially those fully aware of Del's personal past, but her father knew there was a certain long walk to one particular place that brought his presidential daughter serenity and refreshment like nothing else. He made a rare daytime visit to the Oval Office, after calling down to see if she was alone. It was late in the clear, crisp afternoon, two hours before sunset.

Henry slipped into a chair in front of her desk, and waited for her to greet him, before speaking. It was his habit; he thought it respectful. At any given moment, her concentration was usually devoted elsewhere, as it was now; it was better to await her than interrupt her focus. Often a full minute, even more, would pass before she redirected her attention. At last, she looked up at her father. She looked tired.

"I thought a walk to see Scotty would be good," he said. "You?"

He saw the reaction in her eyes. Not of alarm, not of pain. She didn't smile, but her face softened.

"Now?" she asked, inflecting no protest.

"Yes. Now. We can walk before sunset."

She reached for her phone to call her security detail for an escort.

"I already called them," the First Father said.

She flashed a mischievous smile, then wrinkled her face in faux disapproval.

"You know," he said in defense, "just in case you wanted to go, to give them a heads-up."

"It's fine," she said, stepping from behind her desk to join him. "It's a good idea."

Four agents were waiting with a Cadillac SUV, both front and rear passenger side doors open, when they stepped out the canopied side entrance to the West Wing. Black sedans carrying additional agents were positioned fore and aft. The First Father climbed into the open front seat, always his preference. "Makes me feel as young as you guys," he liked to say to the agents, though the truth was he felt self-conscious being chauffeured. In truth, so did his daughter, and when first elected president had requested repeatedly to sit up front too, meeting firm refusal every time until she gave up asking.

The security detail had coordinated with the Capitol and Metropolitan Police Departments—traffic arrangements were often made on a moment's notice—so that the caravan's ride from Pennsylvania Avenue to Arlington National Cemetery, only two and a half miles, took just five minutes over the cleared streets. They could have entered the cemetery from a rear service entrance, but the agents knew the president preferred to arrive through the main ceremonial gate. It was not that she hoped for attention; she simply relished the winding drive through the manicured green, rolling slopes.

On this late afternoon, three buses were parked in the area reserved for tourists, and as the presidential vehicle approached them the driver slowed and turned back to look at Del in the rear seat. She nodded no. "Maybe on the way out," she said. It was not that she couldn't be bothered with greeting the citizens. She enjoyed meeting spontaneously with the public, and especially children, which is why the driver inquired in the first place. But she knew that if she stopped now, the curious—and there were always plenty of the curious—would inevitably trail her and Henry to the northwestern boundary of the park, near the Lee Mansion and the Civil War sections, where they always began their walk. The driver cruised ahead to her usual drop-off place. They deliberately started their visit there, in the high end of the cemetery, because the view as they journeyed a mile through the sections was magnificent and, equally, because she enjoyed the time to consider her purpose and the happy recollections it produced.

Since her election, it was a walk she took nearly every month, usually with her father, to visit the grave of Captain Scott Anderson, United States Army. He rested in one of the newer sections of the national cemetery known as Section Sixty, solemnly filled since 9/11 with men and women lost in the global war on terror.

Like so many interned at Arlington, Scott Anderson was not a famous warrior. He did not come from an illustrious family. None of the tour guides mentioned him, nor would he have expected them to. Not even the long serpentine route for the tour buses, with its many stops, came near Section Sixty in the southwestern quadrant of the park where the captain lay in peace, quietly unnoticed. That would not be so if it were known that he was the only love in the life of President Del Winters.

The two officers had met in full maturity at a base holiday gathering at Fort Bragg. Both were twenty-eight, and newly minted captains. Each was committed to "career military" status, unattached, and instantly attracted. Del told her father, six months into their relationship, that the pair had enough in common to be comfortable with one another and enough so vastly different to be exciting and challenging.

Both shared a deep love of service and selflessness and eschewed material gain and affluence as life priorities. Both were serious readers with interest in history and world affairs. But their family backgrounds and upbringings were poles apart.

Del was an only child whose mother had succumbed to cancer when the future president was only ten years old. Especially since her mother had been seriously ill for years, she looked to her father—to her it seemed all her life—as her only parent. She thought of herself as a "solitary military brat," moving about with her father as he ascended in national military leadership. For his part, her father worried that his choice to remain a single career officer was damaging to his daughter and worked to introduce her to other children and families on the bases. But it was difficult. Reassignments happened on such brief intervals, especially for senior officers. It couldn't be called ideal, and neither Del nor her father did—not then, not now. But it had its own rewards, not the least of them an extraordinary closeness and trust between them.

Scott Anderson's family profile could hardly have been more different. He was the middle of seven children in a rambunctious Catholic family in St. Paul. With three brothers and three sisters, his mother called him "the tiebreaker," perhaps revealing her appreciation of Scott's gentle fairness and moderating way. As in any family, and surely any large one, there were problems, and some were not small. One of Scott's older brothers suffered from a sort of profound social awkwardness that was never fully understood, and a younger sister's early precociousness accelerated into a prolonged boy-crazy phase that exasperated everyone, culminating in a teenage pregnancy that nearly crushed her parents.

There was no deep military heritage in the Anderson family line. His father, an accountant for the 3M Company, was too young for the Korean and Vietnam wars and, though not unpatriotic, never aspired to serve. His maternal grandfather had served as a gunnery mate in the navy in World War II and seen horrifying action aboard a destroyer in the South Pacific but, like many aging veterans, had rarely spoken of it. None of his siblings expressed interest in the military academies or enlistment. But when 9/11 changed everything in America just as Scott began his junior year of high school, his impulse to serve exploded. An excellent student and a standout athlete, he wanted to enlist and "be a soldier." His mother and father, determined that he should get a college education, resisted his idea. Scott persisted. Finally, his parents suggested that if he was certain he wanted to serve, he should seek acceptance to one of the military academies.

Privately, they believed his chances slim, knowing other families who's equally gleaming children had been denied; competition for the seats was intense and the personal sponsorship of a member of the Senate or House of Representatives was a requirement for application. Even then, admission was far from assured. Only 10 percent of nominated applicants became first-year cadets. Further reducing his chances, the Anderson family, while long on togetherness and love, was unapologetically short on connections. Still, young Scott wrote and made phone calls to his congressman and both Minnesota senators. Would they nominate him for West Point consideration?

In the end, his brashness probably made the difference. He received polite letters of declination from the two senators, and no response at all from the congressman. But learning that the representative would be at his local office on a Friday near the holidays, the high school student went to the office unannounced, insisting to see him. The congressman's assistant, admiring his gumption, finally showed him in. Young Scott was clutching a dozen letters of recommendation from teachers, coaches, and his parish pastor.

"You don't have an appointment," the congressman said to him.

"No, sir. That's why I came. I want one. To West Point."

He stood tall, strong, and focused before the old congressman, who had served six years in the army, himself. He knew a future officer when he saw one. They talked for an hour and a half. The representative read all the letters.

"Do you know any of these people?" Scott asked him. He hoped that the House member might.

"No," he said. "None of them. For a change. And I like that. I'm going to call your parents. If they are okay with this, I'll nominate you."

And so began the military life of the man who would love a president.

It ended in a Somalian firefight only seventy miles from the scene of the inglorious "Blackhawk down" incident in 1993 when American marines were killed and dragged through the streets, before hardly any Americans appreciated the emerging threat of Jihadist extremism. Twenty-five years later, northern Africa had become a significant focus of the war on terror, as al Qaeda and ISIS-inspired groups took root in training camps, eager to export violence to countries near and far. A six-person Special Forces team conducting reconnaissance had come under small-arms and grenade fire from all sides. Two had been wounded, and the Americans were greatly outnumbered. Close air support was called in and two helicopters to get the men out.

The two "Super Huey" helicopters carried a total of ten Army Rangers led by Captain Scott Anderson. The choppers rained small rocket and heavy machine-gun fire around the encircled Americans, but to avoid hitting the soldiers with friendly fire, Captain Anderson ordered the gunners to keep their fire on a radial perimeter line a hundred meters from the surrounded men below, working their covering fire only *outward* from the encircled Special Forces. The barrage continued for twelve minutes, from an altitude sufficiently high to eliminate any threat to the helicopters from the small arms below. When the forces on the ground reported that incoming fire from the Jihadists had stilled, Anderson ordered his own Huey to descend to take the wounded Americans on board. He ordered the second chopper to stay aloft and continue its cover fire. Once the first Huey was loaded, the two craft would reverse roles. Anderson would send the first chopper back up, where it would provide cover for the second as it descended to pick up the rest, including the captain, who would remain on the ground, and be the last to climb on for the ride out.

Anderson had led such extractions a dozen times, in all manner of terrain. Whenever possible, he took two extraction choppers, in case enemy attackers were stronger than anticipated, or one of them was disabled in the rescue. In this case, it was clear two were needed, as the Super Huey, a mainstay in combat situations since its introduction in 2007, was not truly "super" in terms of carrying capacity. Each had lift power for only ten passengers plus its two-man crew. All of that would be needed to extract the soldiers.

The Special Forces being retrieved were well-trained on how to get to the aircraft, while protecting each other and their rescuers as best they could. A few of them would lie as low as possible on the ground and provide outgoing, nonstop cover fire as the others raced to the helicopter behind them. Even before the first craft touched ground, extraction forces would leap from it and take up covering positions on all sides. At touchdown, medics would go to the wounded, covered by the few Rangers who stayed, crouching in the open doors of the Huey once it landed.

Captain Anderson knew that even though the incoming fire had quieted, it was certain that some enemy forces remained close-in and that further assault on the helicopter was nearly as certain. Still, the first to jump from the descending helicopter would be himself, on his own order.

The next day, General Henry Winters and his daughter, then Colonel Delores Winters, sat together reading the after-action report of the mission. It described how Captain Anderson had leaped first and begun providing cover fire for the forces rushing to the Huey when, almost immediately, he was struck in the head and neck with small-arms fire. He died instantly. The general took his grieving daughter's arm.

"The best do this," he said.

"Do what?" she asked.

"Step off first. Die first."

Now, a decade later, when they reached his grave in Section Sixty at Arlington, Henry stood with her, as the Secret Service agents flared out in formation surrounding them. You might think that on these walks, and especially at the gravesite, there would generally be silence. But, instead, daughter and father spoke nearly the whole time, about Scott and their many memories of him and his expansive family; their conversation was punctuated with frequent laughter. On this day, the president asked if her father remembered the Thanksgiving in Minnesota with the entire Anderson clan. Oh, yes, he said. Who could forget it? He'd never seen such cold outside a house and such warmth inside of it, he said. There were so many nieces and nephews running around, you could fill two platoons, he said.

"And all of them wanted to talk to the general, didn't they?" she said.

He nodded. The president's eyes did not tear up; she did not become emotional. She smiled broadly in the crisp late-day air. This was why her father liked to see her come here regularly and when stressed. This place, and her memories of her captain, did not dishearten her; they relaxed and energized her.

They were approaching the SUV to begin the ride back, when one of the agents stepped toward her, extending a cell phone. It was the attorney general again. The FBI wanted to update her on the Georgia situation. Could she take a call that evening? Further, it would be necessary to go public soon with the investigation, she was told. A reporter covering the murders for the *Boston Globe* had learned that the three victims worked for the same employer. SureSecure had meant nothing to the Boston newspaper, but a *Washington Post* editor recognized the company as an election consultant. The *Post* had called the FBI for comment. None was offered, of course, but it was plain that the lid could not be kept on the story for long.

As the caravan approached the main gate, the tour buses were forming up to leave. The cemetery closed at five o'clock this time of year. She felt relief, and a sense of absolution.

She couldn't stop to greet the tourists anyway.

WHO COULD ASK FOR MORE?

All hell broke loose the day after Thanksgiving. The news media rejoiced. For once there was more to cover than Black Friday shopping mania. How many times can you show middle-of-the-night lineups outside big box stores? Who cares, really, how the day's internet shopping figures compare with last year's? No, this holiday season was beginning—thank God, they thought—with blockbuster news to report, and it had more trimmings than the grandest Thanksgiving dinner table. Intrigue. Bloody murders. Politics. Who could ask for more?

The *Washington Post* reporters discovered that SureSecure appeared on the approved list of voting machine validators and turned over stones that even Sophie Sikes couldn't reach with her search warrant. Reporters fanned out over Cambridge and found people who knew Simon DeClerc. He was a strange bird, they said. Even as a juvenile he was a computer genius and used his gift to hack into vendor and credit card accounts. He boasted to associates and students at MIT that he would earn millions and live "off the grid," while others chasing legitimate careers in technology for companies the likes of Google, Amazon, or Facebook were "little patsies." He was vocally apolitical, all agreed. His only interest in politics was an obsession with how he could exploit it for personal gain.

But the most explosive news bit the investigative reporters unearthed came from a woman DeClerc had pursued romantically. She said she was initially open to his flirtatious overtures, but soon was repulsed by his preoccupation with "stealing by keyboard," as he called it, and seeming lack of any appreciable sense of conscience. She had broken off with him. "When?" she was asked. "When he went to Georgia to work on the machines down there," she said.

Georgia? Oh, my.

The *Post* broke the news as its lead story on Black Friday.

Slain Cyber Technician Worked
on Georgia Voting Machines
FBI Investigating

read the headline. From there, it was off to the races. Conspiracy theories sprouted like daffodils on social media and the internet. Had operatives of the Republican Party stolen the election to protect its Senate plurality? Had a foreign power intervened to favor Will Truitt? Even the usually restrained Public Broadcasting Service reported that the link of the murder in Boston to the machines in Georgia raised questions as to the legitimacy of the election results there "and perhaps elsewhere."

The foggy implications of the other two murders in Boston added greatly to the intrigue. On orders of the attorney general, the FBI released a statement. The bureau was investigating all three murders, it said, and believed them to be related because of "the timing of the killings, their manner of execution, and the common employment of the victims." The statement confirmed that DeClerc had been assigned by his employer to the Georgia machines, and that the bureau had commenced an inquiry soon after the election. But it said the bureau "had not concluded, pending completion of a full investigation, that the machines were tampered with or that any of them had reported inaccurate voting results." The bureau's statement urged caution in reaching any immediate conclusions and noted that each of the Georgia machines had been independently examined by the NSA, *after* SureSecure's work and prior to the voting, and had been found to be functioning properly.

The president was pleased that the FBI's statement acknowledged that the investigation had begun weeks earlier—because it was the truth—but she knew that the disclosure would trigger uncomfortable questions. When did the government first learn that something might have happened in the Georgia voting, and how did it learn it? Why was nothing announced immediately after the murder of DeClerc and the others? Where was the president in all of this?

To the eye of the cynical mind, it looked like a cover-up.

To the eyes and minds of Ned Thelan's team in Georgia, it was utter befuddlement. Homer Junes, the NSA careerist who had personally reviewed Simon DeClerc's activities on the voting machines, was as trustworthy and diligent as they came. Even though Thelan knew the details of the inspection protocol for the voting machines, he asked Junes anyway to state them for him, step by step. His recitation was perfect. His record-keeping for the Georgia examinations was meticulous, and Thelan had it double-checked for completeness. Nothing was missing.

Of special importance to Thelan's team was the integrity of the placebo election results. No one at SureSecure, including

DeClerc, knew what ballots had been cast in the dry-run placebo voting before DeClerc had access to the machines. Only the NSA and Junes knew how many votes had been cast, precinct by precinct, machine by machine, in the simulated election. Junes had personally entered those test votes days before the young MIT genius set foot in the Augusta warehouse. And Junes himself had physically checked each machine, *after* DeClerc's testing, to see if the machines were producing the correct vote matching those he had entered earlier. That was the point of the whole exercise; an independent consultant, without knowledge of the votes cast in the simulated election, tests the machines' analytics and certifies them as functioning properly. Then a *second* independent expert, this time from the NSA, tests that conclusion by confirming that each machine produces the exact preentered vote count for each candidate, vote totals that only he or she knows.

After a full day with Homer Junes, Thelan reported to the FBI director and the attorney general that, so far, there was no physical evidence of tampering or machine malfunction. The obvious first step had been completed, the team reported, to determine whether every vote cast was in fact registered in the machines. Could it be that some number of votes cast for Margaret Westfall had somehow been deleted and removed from the count? If Truitt had won the election that way, the number of voter sign-ins across the state would have to be larger than the aggregate vote count produced by the machines—at least 7,009 larger.

So, Thelan's team tabulated the number of names appearing on every polling place sign-in sheet in the state, then compared that total to the final counts produced by the voting machines. The difference was just fourteen votes, statewide, an immaterial difference clearly attributable, the team concluded, to human error in counting lines on the sign-in sheets. No two human beings could ever count millions of names on a hundred thousand pages and come to the exact same total. It's called the human condition. No, the election had not been thrown to the Republican by the outright deletion of ballots cast for the Democrat.

"But could it have been thrown some other way?" the president asked when Thelan had finished his explanation of the work in progress.

"*Could* it?" he answered. "Sure, it could. But that would mean that somehow the ballots that were actually cast were somehow manipulated *inside* the machines. And we know they were tested and shown to be counting accurately *after* DeClerc had access to them. Plus, they've been under guard constantly since."

"Are you saying there's nothing more to look at?" she asked.

"No, there is one more thing. We could perform another placebo simulation on the machines now. We could cast a stipulated number of votes for each candidate on a set of machines. To keep it simple, we could cast an identical number for each. Say, ten thousand apiece. See if the machine records it that way."

"How long will that take?"

"Only a few hours for a randomly selected sample of a dozen or so machines."

"Good."

"But maybe weeks to do it to every machine this guy DeClerc touched. Which is every machine in Georgia. Thousands and thousands of them."

The deadline for filing a challenge petition was five days away. The president was acutely anxious. She directed Thelan to move immediately on the random sample simulation. Then she called the White House counsel to ask if it would be possible to seek an extension of the statutory deadline. She felt it was grossly unfair to Margaret Westfall that her ability to challenge the outcome might be extinguished simply because there was not enough time to explore all the tampering possibilities. As matters stood now, the evidence of election fraud, though colorful and inflammatory, was purely circumstantial, and the statute required a losing candidate to state specific facts as to *how* the results had been altered and, further, that the specifically stated acts made an outcome-changing mathematical difference. No one could make such a showing yet.

The White House counsel said the statute made no provision for extending the time. Congress would have to do it with a legislative amendment, which seemed improbable in the extreme. For one thing, the chambers were out of session until the new year.

Happily, the Justice Department and its FBI were *not* out of session. Del Winters ordered Attorney General Stone to pull resources from wherever she needed and put them under Thelan's direction in Georgia. She also sent a special directive to the NSA and to Wilson Bryce at the Defense Intelligence Agency. Their top technology people, unless personally engaged in currently mission-critical work pertaining to the nation's security, should be loaned immediately to Ned Thelan of the FBI's election fraud unit at its temporary command center in Georgia.

When Wilson Bryce received the orders, he called the White House and was sent through to the president when he told the switchboard he was responding to a directive just received from her.

"What do you mean by *immediately*?" he asked. "Is tomorrow morning okay?" It was nearly four in the afternoon.

"No, Wilson," she said. "I mean right now. A military plane is waiting at Andrews. Get them there."

Three hours and fifteen minutes later, the rear ramp of an air force C-130 transport plane closed. A cross-agency team of forty-four computer experts, including Wilson Bryce, fastened themselves in seats along its side walls. The veteran pilot later said it was the shortest flight he'd made since air school, and the lightest cargo.

He couldn't have known in the moment, but it may also have been the most important.

INTO THIN AIR

How often does a successful small company like SureSecure, with legitimate employees and services, disappear into thin air as if it never existed? *Every day,* in the world of international crime.

The Boston company never opened its doors again after the morning raid in November. For days, bewildered employees came to the floor to find the doors locked and manager Edward Telsany nowhere to be found.

Sophie Sikes smelled it the minute she had learned that all three of the newly hired technicians had been murdered on the same morning. The little Boston company was an ideal "host enterprise" for a foreign criminal syndicate looking to exploit a lucrative market that required the extraordinary skills and specialized access available in an American company.

The concept was not fundamentally different from the infiltrations used by some drug cartels to move their goods to market in the United States. In the larger trucking companies, it could be pulled off without ownership or senior management ever knowing it was happening. You identified a middle manager in Tucson, or Phoenix, or Topeka. You corrupted him. He corrupted five drivers—five soon-to-be *very rich* drivers. Within weeks, you could run a "spare room" operation, a secret unit separated from the normal trucking work of the manager's region and hidden from the larger corporation and headquarters. The illicit pickups and deliveries were all "off book." Dangerous? A little. Lucrative? Very.

But more sophisticated criminality often required a different approach. Cyber knowledge and expertise ruled the day. In banking, insurance, and credit card theft, the detection systems in the large companies were deep and too effective to permeate and stay long enough to conduct business on a running basis. Corrupting a few employees wouldn't do. No, you needed to find a specialized company or consultant with lawful access to something of great value on the criminal market—like fund transfer accounts and schedules—*acquire it outright,* get the owner out of the business, and then turn the company to your own purpose.

Of course, it was not always easy to buy such a host enterprise. Most were small firms operating out of a single location, often with family ownership. Many owners were pillars in their communities. Few were interested in leaving the company they had founded, even if they were willing to sell it. You could not approach such an owner and say, hey, we'd like to buy your company and use it to steal money, data, and personal information and then sell it through organized crime channels for a fortune. How about it?

No, you had to convince them somehow to sell the company and ride off into the sunset, to let you do what you wanted to do without telling them. You had to fool them. And international criminal syndicates knew that enough money will make many a fool.

As Sophie Sikes and the FBI would eventually learn, so it was in the case of SureSecure. A criminal syndicate in Hungary, with investors in other parts of Eastern Europe, was looking to expand its hacking product offerings into the elections business. It had made inquiries to a range of Asian and Middle East governments. If it could be shown that a US election result could be guaranteed, would you pay for the outcome you wanted? There were even more takers than the planners expected. But the foreign political regimes differed diametrically as to what they would pay for.

Iran and Saudi Arabia, for example, had opposing views on what constituted the best American outcome when hypothetical future presidential contests were proposed to them. Their responses were the seed for an even more devious thought: selling the available outcome to the highest bidder. What a business opportunity! Who knew how high the competing sovereigns would go to get their preferred candidate elected, or their despised candidate defeated? But two things were needed to capitalize on the subversive market: a cyber operative with demonstrated, verifiable access to the elections apparatus and proof that a preordained result could in fact be delivered by it.

The Hungarian syndicate sent one of its best for the project. Edward Telsany—the name he was to use in the United States, at least—was smooth, discreet, and astute in matters of finance and acquisition. For better or worse, America does not have a monopoly on investment bankers. Telsany was the top deal maker in Budapest with, it turned out, more than a little experience in transactions in the United States. Rumors—never substantiated—linked him in a previous life to Paul Manafort, the international political consultant dragged down in the outfall of the alleged Russian interference in the Trump election in 2016.

As soon as the syndicate's research team in Budapest identified SureSecure as the optimal host enterprise for the scheme, Telsany traveled to Boston to initiate discussions.

Fortune seemed to be on his side, as well as in his pockets. Many technology consulting firms were owned by young entrepreneurs. If they were profitable enterprises with plans for growth, it was difficult to entice them to sell. It took an *exceptionally* large fortune to lure them. But SureSecure's sole owner, at age fifty-two, was a dinosaur for his field. A mere *large* fortune might lure him, Telsany correctly adjudged. An innocent American investment banker who had met Telsany at a London conference years earlier made a call for the Hungarian to the owner, whom he knew from their mutual country club.

"He is legitimate, a good guy. Well thought of in Budapest," the banker told the owner.

SureSecure's annual revenues were about $10 million, about a fifth coming from its election machine work in a dozen states. The rest came from cyber security assessments for a range of financial institutions. In their meetings, Telsany never mentioned the elections work, stressing the other work and claiming that his European venture fund wanted to buy SureSecure to leverage its expertise at financial institutions abroad where the venture group had many contacts. The owner was startled at Telsany's initial offer of $50 million. He knew such a large purchase price multiple over annual sales was unheard of, but he countered anyway with $75 million.

"That is possible," Telsany said to the overwhelmed owner. "But you must understand that we see this as a clean transaction, a clean break. You personally must not stay with the company. You know these European investors. Comfortable only with their own."

For $75 million, the SureSecure owner could get comfortable

too. Easily. The deal was done rapidly, the financing adeptly. Care had to be taken in the transactional details. Under the election security statute, voting machine validators could *not* be controlled by foreign nationals. So, the purchase was made by a limited liability corporation established for the purpose under the laws of New York. But funds for the deal were transferred, moments before closing, by twelve foreign banks acting on behalf of the Hungarian syndicate.

Then came the hard part: inserting into SureSecure the clandestine capability to deliver the goods. Telsany tabbed Emma Kuziniak from the syndicate's headquarters staff, herself a deft cyber aficionado, to build the necessary software and bring on board the people to perfect and implement it. She found Simon DeClerc in a hacker's chatroom, and Philip Winston in a London bedroom. Details of the latter circumstance were never disclosed, but apparently the talented Brit made quite an impression on her. As it turned out, neither lived to describe their encounter.

The test balloon had flown successfully. All that Telsany and the syndicate had assured, a narrow win by Will Truitt, had come to pass. Rival bidders for future elections were duly impressed. The value of the infiltration offering would soar. But Telsany knew, the moment Sophia Sikes handed him the FBI search warrant, that the entire venture and all its promise had ended as suddenly, if not as savagely, as would the lives of his operatives after his call to Budapest from the lobby of the Boston office building. When he made that call to the syndicate, he did not know how the fraud had been disclosed—how the unraveling had begun with Simon DeClerc's careless blurting at the Cackling Crow. It mattered not.

All that mattered, as he fled the country under an alias *cum* passport, was the elimination of every actor in its perpetration. Every actor except himself. That is, he *hoped* except himself.

38

★ ★ ★

IN SPYCRAFT, PATIENCE PREFERRED

While Attorney General Madeline Stone was directing the feverish examination of the Georgia voting machines, the military command and intelligence agencies were nearing wit's end trying to understand the who and how of the military aircraft interceptions. So far, even the international assistance was bearing no fruit.

Lars LaToure's trip to Munich produced only a clean bill of health to the Max Plank Institute and its researchers, and no leads elsewhere. The INTERPOL director of investigations questioned Neils Straak, the Dutch physicist in charge of research, for hours. LaToure separately interviewed each of the research fellows and graduate students over the next three days. In the evenings Lars prepared and sent his emblematic one-page summary of the day's findings to his colleague Minter, by then returned to INTERPOL headquarters in Lyon, and to the NSA in Washington. The logs for the institute's transmissions to and from the Ukrainian satellite were studied methodically line-by-line and explained to the Swedish INTERPOL man and the FBI agents from the Munich station.

The research and the signals had nothing to do with control systems or intervention. Some of them used fore signals—creating so-called "hard pings"—but only to test the effect of such fore-signals on what the scientists termed "latency," essentially the speed at which a signal could be sent to and returned from the satellite. Any means of increasing that speed would have immense value, and many scientists around the world were aspiring to find it. But at least those at the Max Plank Institute weren't trying to invade military communication channels or to control systems.

Before sending his concluding report, LaToure showed it to Dr. Straak for his review and comment. As a courtesy, he wanted to be sure he had not inadvertently disclosed any information the Dutchman considered scientifically confidential.

"You know, we scientists believe all research is important, especially our own," Dr. Straak said, bemusedly, after reading the investigator's conclusion. "And if not important, at least meaningful. This is the first time I am pleased to see that my work is perfectly irrelevant."

From the bar at the Munich train station, before boarding for the long ride to Stockholm, Lars prepared a short reply to the mysterious "M.," the self-alleged Middle East intelligence officer. He had waited purposefully to reply until now. Better not to appear anxious. In spycraft, patience, when available, was nearly always the preferred option. He wrote:

> M.
>
> Your correspondence in hand. Approval to speak achieved.

Myself. Alone. No assurances of asylum, but no detention on our account.
By reply, suggest place and time to meet.

Lars LaToure
INTERPOL, Stockholm

As was his practice, he looked over the note carefully, slowly, sipping Irish whiskey in the exercise. Regrettably, the line was a complete sentence, he observed. But sometimes, grammar's confines could not be avoided and clarity still attained. Satisfied, he folded and posted it to the London post office box on Harberton Road, to the attention of M, whomever he or she truly was. He thought it possible, even likely, he would never hear another word. Even if the first message had been genuine, defectors often were mercurial, unreliable. Many changed their minds. It was, after all, a momentous and dangerous decision. Others, detected before they could complete their plan, had their minds changed for them. Figuratively speaking.

The sage INTERPOL veteran was mentally exhausted from four days of concentration. As he carried his small baggage and station espresso to his seat, he could not have known that his trip to Munich, failing of its intended purpose, would prove in the end to unravel everything, all on account of his terse note posted at journey's end.

PART 4

39

★ ★ ★

THE CHARLESTON ASSIGNMENT

Lars LaToure's reply to Majir Asheed lay in a postal box in north London, unretrieved. Its addressee was out of the country. For his part, Majir had thought it unlikely a response to his original message could come quickly. At least weeks, he had surmised. Surely, this man LaToure from INTERPOL would have to push the matter up through channels. Even the Americans might have to be consulted. Besides, he conjured, LaToure will not want to appear too anxious. He will not reply immediately, even if authorized.

No, there was ample time, the Syrian agent concluded, to go to the United States and deal with the Charleston assignment before attending to the correspondence with Mr. LaToure. He knew there was no way around the assignment in South Carolina. Any new deviation from orders would imperil his chances to defect undiscovered. He could not act in ways that would raise suspicion in Damascus. At least for the time being, he must operate as he always had—do what he was told to do. There was no choice but to deal with Mr. James Molineaux.

So Majir flew to Charlotte, North Carolina—the closest city with a large airport receiving direct flights from Europe—and drove Interstates 77 and 26 to Charleston in the bordering state, about a four-hour passage. Not two years earlier, two North Korean assassins had traveled from Miami to Charleston to hunt down Stanley Bigelow. Their abduction had been thwarted, but until it was, they had stayed at the tall Holiday Inn overlooking the downtown marina. But Majir eschewed the large hotel chains. Their internet booking and guest information systems were vast and sophisticated. You never knew what dots could be connected from the data mined in the cyberspace of the hospitality industry. Besides, nowadays the hotel chains and their franchisees seemed always to be changing hands. Hilton today, Hyatt tomorrow, who knew the next? It meant that databases, already deep, were combined with others, often even more expansive. It all made the perfect playpen for information miners, spinning algorithms to manipulate the spending tastes of consumers, and in a world of unimaginable government surveillance and hacking skills, a hazard to foreign intelligence operatives whose lives depended on invisibility.

No, Majir preferred small, independent inns and hotels with little, sleepy staffs and cranky computers. He chose the Fulton Lane Inn at the corner of King Street and Fulton Lane in historic downtown Charleston. It was comfortable, clean, and obscure, and his small standard room was priced at just $159, without breakfast. Damascus applauded thrift.

He knew he would not be long in the lovely city. Probably only three days. He needed one day to reacclimate from the long flight over, made worse by stiffer than usual headwinds from the west; another day to study the movements of the vegetable laboratory manager upon leaving the facility at day's end and plan his abduction in a suitable place; and a third to carry it out.

His earlier appearance at the USDA facility, when he first sought to take Molineaux, complicated his options this time. He had been seen by the facility's receptionist on the first visit and had used his guise as a professor under recruitment by Clemson University. He couldn't know whether the laboratory manager had reported that alias with the site's contacts at Clemson, but the Syrian considered it too possible to assume otherwise. He ruled out another direct entry into the facility. He would follow Molineaux from the laboratory complex and abduct, question, and kill him. The question was precisely where?

On his second afternoon in Charleston, he drove to the shoulder of Highway 17, the Savannah Highway as it is called, and watched as James Molineaux came out of the main entrance at five thirty. The manager, a slender man of less than average height, climbed into a red Toyota Rav 4. He was hatless and carried a soft canvas briefcase. The days were growing short in the first days of December; it was already dark.

The highway was divided at the government facility's ingress and egress points, requiring Molineaux to turn right out of the site, in a generally southerly direction; the Syrian pulled slowly from the shoulder and followed. Was this the manager's nightly route home, or was he heading south toward Savannah only because he had to begin in that direction? Majir had his answer almost immediately. A left lane was provided just five hundred feet ahead of the manager, with a median-crossing ramp for motorists desirous of the other direction, toward Charleston proper. But Molineaux ignored the opportunity, staying in the right lane and accelerating.

Any driver proceeding down Highway 17 toward Savannah, after passing the large United States Vegetable Laboratory facility on the right, will encounter the major intersection of Main Road in about three miles. Gasoline stations surround the nexus like well-lit guardhouses, keeping each other honest—one hopes—with identical fuel prices blazing from high-posted signage. On this night, the unwary Mr. Molineaux flicked the right-hand turn signal of his small vehicle and pulled adeptly into the largest, most modern of the fuel stations. The Syrian followed. He watched as the manager refueled. Molineaux's fortuitous gasoline stop on this watchful evening might appear meaningless to the mission at hand and to the agriculturist's fate. But the Syrian knew differently. By filling his tank this night, the assassin knew Molineaux would *not* need to do so the next. A significant variable—*target alters expected movement*—was removed. The little changes always caused the most trouble.

Majir saw that most southbound travelers on Highway 17 seemed to turn left and head east on Main Road, the only route to Johns Island and its companion isles, Kiawah and Seabrook. The line to turn onto Main Road was lengthy, Majir estimated at least a half mile. Molineaux had evaded that line by staying right and entering the fueling station. But upon leaving it, the Syrian wondered if his target would take the Main Road toward Kiawah Island or Seabrook like the bulk of the other motorists. He'd much rather that he didn't. Surely, the traffic would be this abundant tomorrow at this hour too. It would greatly impair any ordinary means of unwitnessed abduction. He might be forced to follow the man nearly to his home, perhaps into his own neighborhood. Even then a solitary opening might not present itself. You never killed near the target's home if you could avoid it. And besides, it was critical—the whole point, really—that he question Molineaux about his knowledge of the true happenings at his laboratory complex and the activities of the old civil engineer described in the news clippings. Depending upon how much the manager knew, it could be a lengthy interrogation. Probably, techniques of forcible persuasion would be necessary. It certainly could not be a driveway discussion.

Whatever may be said of Mr. Molineaux's luck, the Syrian's run of good fortune continued. The laboratory manager did *not* turn left onto the congested roadway. He sailed straight on through the intersection toward the village of Ravenel. Small, sparse Ravenel, five miles ahead. And along those five miles, his stalker astutely noted, any number of desolate side roads, most just dirt or gravel affairs, some bounded at the berm by murky tidewater channels, rarely visited, especially in darkness.

The next evening, one of those byways would receive two visitors.

40

★ ★ ★

IT'S PROBABLY NOTHING

It was merely a nub at the base of the dog's left ear, but Helen called it to Stanley's attention, and he, in turn, to L. T. Kitt's on his next walk with the FBI agent in Pittsburgh. Having trained Augie since he was a pup, no one knew his features like she did.

"Feel it?" Stanley asked her, as Kitt massaged the canine's ears. "Like a furry pimple, almost."

"I doubt it's serious," L. T. said. "At his age, this stuff comes up. It's not sensitive, not bothering him." She was rubbing the ear vigorously and the dog beamed, approvingly. "Have the vet look at it."

"He's due for his checkup anyway," Stanley said.

"Good," L. T. said. "It's probably nothing."

★ ★ ★

WAITING FOR MR MOLINEAUX

Majir lay in wait on the southbound shoulder of Highway 17, six miles south of the United States Vegetable Laboratory. It was five fifteen, but he had been in the vicinity for an hour and a half, scouting the roads off the highway, deciding on the place to take manager Molineaux once he secured him.

As a professional, he of course selected more than one suitable "delivery point." A backup location was needed in the event some young lovers or fisherman turned up unexpectedly and occupied the first selection when he arrived with his target. The alternative delivery point needed as much care in the choosing as the original. It had to be sufficiently far from the first, to eliminate any chance that noise could be detected, and it needed to provide egress that did not pass back in front of the original, occupied site. Anyone who happened coincidentally to place themselves out there in the darkness would be surprised enough to encounter another driver a single time. Seeing the same person twice would most surely leave an impression. Talented assassins avoid leaving impressions. Of any kind.

It was not difficult to find two suitable places. He chose one of the side roads that accessed a tidal creek. At high tide, spotted-tail bass would run in from the deep-water creeks and rivers into which it flowed. Over the years, fishermen and picnickers had trammeled out small areas along its bank every thousand yards or so. He located two places where a car could be taken off the dirt byway and snuggled out of sight beneath and behind dense overgrowth. He marked each with clumps of white paper towel, taken earlier from the restroom in the hotel lobby. He hung them low on the brush at road's edge, so that he could spot them readily when needed.

Molineaux had left the laboratory the night before at five thirty. But he had stopped for fuel, and the Syrian knew that meant he may have left early on that account. But he couldn't be sure. He needed to assume he could arrive any minute. At five twenty, he angled his rental car so that the front end hung out a foot or two into the right lane of the highway. At five twenty-two, he switched on the emergency flashers and the inside dome lights. The well-lighted car would make it less fearsome, he reasoned. Then he released the engine hood latch and got out of the car. He opened a smoke canister—the kind serious hikers, climbers, and hunters use to send danger signals when lost or in trouble and placed it under the front bumper. The white smoke billowed under and above the open hood.

He took his position at the rear of the car, arms folded, two long plastic locking ties hanging from his right rear trousers pocket. Waiting. Waiting for Mr. Molineaux in the red Rav 4.

He was checking his watch frequently. Not out of nervousness but discipline. There were parameters to every plan. Duration was one. He could not wisely wait indefinitely. Eventually, risk always outweighed probability. Majir knew it was entirely possible that Molineaux was not coming this way at all this night. Perhaps he was meeting a mistress in Charleston tonight or, more charitably, heading to a holiday concert at a child's school in the opposite direction. Who could know? There were a thousand variables, including a more likely one: that he had left work early this day and had already passed by. Majir Asheed knew, as well as any accomplished spy, that false starts in this kind of thing were more often the norm than the exception. That was what tomorrows were made for. And a false start was far superior to a law enforcement officer happening by—an increasing risk as the minutes passed.

His watch read five forty-eight when a different contingency occurred, anticipated but still unwelcomed. The wrong good Samaritan slowed and pulled over to a stop next to Majir's slanted car. He knew it was probable that others would approach if he was required to wait too long, especially as it was not that late and many of the motorists were men driving home from workplaces. The inadvertence was easy enough to dispense with, as he had planned. He made only the briefest eye contact with the benevolent soul, thanked him, said—in near perfect English—that a tow truck was en route, and waved him off. The do-gooder never left his car. But Majir was not pleased. There was now at least one witness to his presence on Highway 17.

Another minute passed without an approaching vehicle. He checked the time—five fifty—and resolved that the tipping point had been reached. He walked to the front of the car and reached for the smoke canister. As he bent, headlights of a vehicle closing range crawled around the lifted hood and into his eyes. He slid to the driver's side of the front end and raised a hand to shield his eyes and look.

His prey had arrived.

★ ★ ★

OH, OH

Wilson Bryce tucked his long hair behind the thick frames of his eyeglasses and studied the printouts Agent Ned Thelan laid before him. To all but a chosen few, the data sheets would be an indiscriminate mass of zeros, ones, and Xs. But Bryce was one of the chosen.

"This came out of which machine?" he asked Thelan. He held one of the pages before Thelan's eyes.

"Number 1621. Brantley County," Thelan said.

"And this one?"

"Number 435. Cobb County."

"Something's off, Ned," Bryce said. "The operating code in every machine should be identical, right? In the sorting and counting module of each machine, right?" he asked.

"Yes," said Thelan. "They should be the same. Identical."

"Well, these two are different," the lanky scientist said.

"How can you tell? It's just a bunch of ink." Thelan looked unconvinced.

"No, I'm sure. They're not spitting *identical* code. Very close, but not identical. I can't tell you the difference it makes in their sorting or counting. It could be minor. But these two machines are *not* sorting and computing ballots in exactly the same way."

By then, the technical team rushed by the president from Washington had run programming printouts from three dozen randomly selected machines from across Georgia. At Bryce's urging, Thelan directed priority to the computation modules instead of the touch screen panels that voters pressed to cast their ballot.

"Those screens are direct-wired to the counting and sorting modules," Bryce explained. "They're binary. Like a light switch. They're either on or they're off. Nothing else, no in-between. They can only send one signal. If a screen icon sends one vote for a candidate, it will send *every* vote from that icon for that candidate. If you tried to throw an election with the screens, you'd have a unanimous vote for somebody on each tampered machine, and we know that didn't happen. But the counting modules in the back of the thing are operated by separate software. If you're awfully good, you could manipulate the sorting and counting *after the vote leaves the screen* in a variable pattern that would not be obvious."

The conclusion that some machines were operating under different software instruction was more than significant; it was huge and frightening. Thelan immediately sent word up the chain. Not all votes were tabulated in the same way, he reported. All were counted, but some may have been slotted erroneously by altered software in selected machines. No conclusion could yet be reached as to how many machines were fouled, how many votes were misdirected, or even whether the alteration favored Truitt or Westfall. President Winters was briefed within minutes.

And Bryce's team made another important finding. The

Cobb County software was an "outlier." The thirty-six machines checked in the first sample were drawn from thirty-six different counties. Only two contained the different code. The Cobb County machine, and one taken from Dekalb County.

Thelan appreciated the significance at once. Cobb and Dekalb were among the most populated counties in Georgia, both in the Atlanta metropolitan area. He asked Bryce to do a simulated reelection on single machines from those two counties, plus machines from Clayton, Brantley, and Echols counties. Clayton was another Atlanta county, usually favoring Democrats heavily. Brantley and Echols were rural counties and overwhelmingly Republican. Echols, coincidentally, was the county whose lopsided vote, while in Truitt's favor, the president had lamented about to her father when watching the returns on election night.

"Let's use the touch screens and cast one thousand votes each for Truitt and Westfall on one machine from each of these five counties," he told Bryce. "Let's see what the machines count."

Bryce sent the directive to his team members on site in each of the five counties. Because of the small sample size, the placebo was completed quickly. In only an hour, Thelan was presented the results:

Brantley	Truitt, **R** 1,000	Westfall, **D** 1,000
Echols	Truitt, **R** 1,000	Westfall, **D** 1,000
Cobb	Truitt, **R** 1,049	Westfall, **D** 951
Dekalb	Truitt, **R** 1,052	Westfall, **D** 948
Clayton	Truitt, **R** 1,044	Westfall, **D** 956

Ten minutes later, the president picked up the call from the attorney general.

"Yes, Madeline?" she said.

"We have a problem in Georgia."

43

IT WENT POORLY

James Molineaux was not particularly athletic, but it would have made little difference if he were. It happened so rapidly, so unnaturally, and the odds were mortally stacked against the slender manager: an off guard, unarmed, unsuspecting citizen against a trained killer with an exacting plan.

Molineaux had barely stepped in front of the raised hood of the staged vehicle when, as he leaned down to get a look, his head crashed to the radiator, propelled by the palm of the Syrian agent's strong left hand. The attacker saw at once that the single blow was sufficient to its purpose. He need not lift Molineaux's collar and deliver a second slam. He could see the laboratory manager was stunned and disabled enough by the fury of the solitary blow to be wrapped without resistance. This pleased the foreign agent. He did not relish the violence or his performance of it. Quite the opposite. If it were his own prerogative, he would not continue this beating or any other. Perhaps soon he could be finished with all this, Majir thought. Hopefully, the Swedish

INTERPOL man would help him; hopefully, he could leave all of this. Perhaps he, Melaha, and Desh could all be happy. Somewhere.

In an instant, before Molineaux could raise his head from the engine—if even he tried to—Majir drew the man's arms behind his back, harshly. Already, while slamming the manager's head to the radiator with his left hand, Majir had used his other deftly to retrieve one of the plastic tying strips from his trousers and place it between his teeth. Now, bending to Molineaux's retracted wrists, he transferred the tie to his hands. Perhaps five seconds passed, in all, from the initial act of force to securement. The Syrian marched the dazed man to the trunk of the car, opened it, and—almost gently—folded him into it.

Stepping quickly, he lowered the front hood and closed off the smoke canister. He shut off the flashers and interior lights and adjusted the car safely off the highway and onto the berm. He climbed into Molineaux's little Rav 4, still running, and navigated across the grass median to the other side of Highway 17. He had chosen for the purpose an abandoned diner about three hundred yards up the road. A small parking area behind the building could not be seen from the highway. Eventually, he knew, the car would be found. But in the circumstances, this would do. He left Molineaux's ignition fob on the driver's seat of the small Toyota and left it unlocked behind the diner.

He walked briskly back to the rental car, pausing at the trunk. Molineaux, though ungagged, was making no sound. To the Syrian, his silence in confinement meant one of two things: either his captive was injured more seriously than Majir thought; or he was already growing compliant. The assassin much hoped it was the latter. For everyone's sake.

He drove to the first delivery point. As he expected, no one was there. He pulled in to the enclave's deepest corner. The dense brush provided complete cover from the tiny road. He turned off the lights and went to the trunk with a flashlight. Molineaux lay in a fetal position, just as he had left him. He directed the light to his chest, to avoid his eyes with a direct flash. It was only fifty degrees in the night air, typical for Charleston County this time of year, but the captive's forehead was beaded with sweat. The Syrian addressed him.

"Mr. Molineaux?" After all, he needed to ask.

"Yes."

The Syrian reached in and lifted out Molineaux's legs so that his belly was propped against the edge of the trunk, then pulled his shoulders out. He looked at the wrist strap. It was tight.

"Please turn around, Mr. Molineaux," he said calmly. He reached over him to close the trunk lid, extinguishing its safety light. Molineaux turned in compliance. His forehead was bruised severely, and he was cut above the left eye.

"I am sorry about that," Majir said, gesturing toward the laceration. "It was necessary." Molineaux showed no reaction.

"Can you think clearly?" the Syrian asked.

"I think so," he said. "Why did you bring me here?"

"Because this is as far as we go."

"What do you want from me?"

"Two summers ago, at the laboratory, an engineer was visiting."

Heightened fear came into the manager's eyes, but he said nothing.

"Please, Mr. Molineaux. An engineer was visiting. You know that."

The manager nodded.

"Of course, you know that. What was he doing? Who was he?"

The manager didn't answer. The Syrian took two steps back

from him. It was something he had learned about questions and frightened people. When they are not talking, you step away from them, not closer. Air. Space. A pause. It might not help an interrogation, but it never hurt. After a minute or so, he looked at the manager seriously, retaining his calm inflection.

"This can go poorly, Mr. Molineaux," he said. "Or it can go very poorly. That is up to you. I have a job to do, and I cannot leave until I have done it. I think you can see that." He tapped his open palm with the flashlight. A few seconds passed. "Who was the engineer and what was he doing with you there?"

"He wasn't working with me," the manager said. "Or with my people. We do agricultural research. Just agricultural research!"

"His work was not agricultural?"

"I never knew what it was really about."

"Truly?"

"Truly."

"Who was he working with, if it was not with your people?"

"They were soldiers."

"Soldiers?"

"Yes."

"Where from?"

"I don't know. They came every day and left every day in a laundry truck. The engineer was teaching them something, but I never knew what. I was told not to ask, and I didn't. That's all I know."

"Who was in charge?"

"A captain, a navy captain. Captain Brew."

"Was the engineer a soldier too?"

"No. He was just a citizen."

"And he worked with the captain?"

"Yes, and a woman soldier. She had a high rank, but I am not sure what exactly. She was an engineer too."

"What was her name?"

"I can't remember. It was a short name."

"Were there weapons there?"

"I don't think so."

"Were they making weapons?"

"I don't think so. The engineers were civil engineers."

"So, the citizen engineer. What was his name?"

"Stanley Bigelow."

"Age?"

"Old. Seventy, I think. At least. A very large man. He came from Pittsburgh."

Majir asked him four more times if there was more he knew, any other details he remembered. Except to say that the engineer and the soldiers came to the vegetable laboratory for about a month, he offered nothing more.

"Well, then," said the Syrian, almost sorrowfully. He stepped toward the ashen-faced manager. The blood above his eye was beginning to dry. The Syrian looked into his eyes, not unkindly. He placed his right hand on James Molineaux's shoulder.

"We are finished here," the Syrian said.

In a sense, both were.

44

DANGER FOR STANLEY

Buddy Binton was surprised to hear from Majir. No call had been scheduled by advance mail, as was the Syrian's practice. And always it was he—Binton—who initiated the requested call, Majir considering it too risky to originate cell calls himself. Binton's first impulse was fear. Perhaps Damascus was displeased. It had met each of his demands for money—a series of increasing amounts—and he had, he knew, not been honest with the Syrians. Oh, his work was successful and progressing, to be sure. Just not in the direction Damascus believed or intended.

"What is it?" Binton asked, without any greeting.

"Are you alone?" Majir asked.

"Yes."

"I'm hanging up. Go somewhere twenty miles away and call me back." Majir hung up, unceremoniously.

So, something important *was* coming from Damascus, Binton thought. Too urgent to wait for the normal, safer, communication channels. Majir wanted him to move twenty miles so that the same cell tower that pinged the Syrian's call to him, from wherever it came, would not be pinged by the Michigan extremist's return to him. It didn't feel good to Binton. It didn't feel good at all. He was at the university when he took Majir's call. He drove his pickup truck to the town of Saline, due west, then beyond another ten miles toward the area of Michigan known as the Irish Hills. It was snowing lightly and frigid. He pulled his truck into the parking area of a grain elevator, deserted for the season, and returned the Syrian's call from the warmth of his cab, the engine grumbling. Majir answered on the first ring.

"You are still alone?" the agent asked.

"Of course."

"A problem has come up, Binton."

Fear rushed into the burly militant like a knife blade.

"What kind of problem?"

Majir, trained in inflection, noted distress in the voice of his beneficiary. It was new to him. Binton had always presented himself as confident—overly so—to the border of arrogance or beyond. The Syrian paused, deliberately. He wanted to see if Binton would speak again before being spoken to. He did.

"What do you mean there is a problem? With the progress reports? Didn't you get them?"

"We received them, yes," Majir said.

Binton's tone concerned the Syrian. Was there an issue that Majir and Damascus were unaware of? But he made, as intelligence agents often must, a snap decision. He forewent inquiry for now into Binton's odd tone and moved to his immediate purpose.

"The problem is not about you, Binton," he said. "There is something new that we need you to do. This is militia duty."

It was true that Majir had considered the idea himself even before he reported to Damascus what he had learned from

James Molineaux about the secret project conducted by the citizen engineer and the soldiers at the United States Vegetable Laboratory. He knew it was certain that Damascus would want this man Stanley Bigelow located and taken immediately. And Majir knew that *he* did not want to find and take him, personally. *No more,* he thought. *No more.* Melaha had gone to the London post office box on Harberton Road. The INTERPOL man Lars LaToure had replied. A window for defection was opening. Perhaps. He could use his knowledge of the Pittsburgh engineer and the ruse at the vegetable laboratory to prove his bona fides and credibility. That is, if he could maneuver the next steps—if he could satisfy Damascus for the time being and keep Bigelow from harm.

Buddy Binton's militia in Michigan could be the means to his end. But he could not press the extremist's use to his superiors without risk of suspicion. Yes, the computer genius was an antigovernment extremist in the Timothy McVeigh mold. And, yes, he had a compound somewhere that was presumably heavily armed. Further, he was surely indebted to Damascus; funding for his technology work, yet to bear the falsified news reporting the Syrians were paying for, had swelled to nearly a million dollars.

Some of that money was used for arms and supplies for the militia activities of the Band of Free Brothers. But Binton and his people were entirely untested in traditional field work, as far as Majir knew. Did they have the skills to abduct the big engineer and get him back to Michigan? And would Damascus accept Majir's stated plan to then go to the Michigan compound to interrogate and kill Bigelow? Wouldn't Damascus surely insist instead that Majir himself conduct the abduction in Pittsburgh and *then* take him to the militia compound to be held? He considered it carefully, repeating the possible ways he could present it to his superior. He concluded Damascus would never approve abduction by the Michigan militia. So, he resolved to use the most-used, if also the most unreliable, weapon in the arsenal of a defecting intelligence operative. The lie.

He reported accurately to his supervisor Amir Ahmed all that happened in his trip to Charleston and his encounter with the vegetable laboratory manager the night before. The two had not spoken since the meeting at the Egerton House Hotel in London. Majir told his Damascus handler that, indeed, a secret military operation *had* been undertaken at the agricultural facility, directed by a US navy captain and a civil engineer, a civilian apparently drafted for the project. Soldiers were brought in surreptitiously for the work, whatever it was. The manager believed they were being trained by the engineer, but he did not know for what purpose. He was telling the truth, Majir believed.

"You must find that engineer, Majir," Ahmed said.

"I understand," Majir said.

"Where is he?"

"The manager said he was from Pittsburgh."

"Pennsylvania? That is a big city. It will be difficult to find him."

"I will find him."

"Good, Majir."

"But it will be too dangerous to hold him and interrogate him in such a place," Majir said. "Do you have any thoughts on where I should take him?"

There was silence for half a minute.

"The militia group you have developed, where are they based?" asked Ahmed. *Ah*, felt Majir, it was what he hoped for.

"In Michigan," Majir answered. His voice was restrained, his relief unbelied.

"Is that near Pennsylvania?"

"It is not very far," Majir said. "It is separated by the state of Ohio. The militia occupies a camp somewhere in the southern part of Michigan, maybe sixty kilometers from the Ohio border. Not far from the university town of Ann Arbor."

"Take the man there. Get everything out of him."

"It may take time. He is old. He must know much. I will need to be patient with him. It will not be like the manager."

"Of course," said Ahmed. "Be as patient as you must. Until the end. Then there is no patience, Majir."

"Of course. Yes, of course. I will begin right away."

And he did. From his hotel in Charleston, he scoured the internet for information on Stanley Bigelow of Pittsburgh. Almost immediately he verified that a member by that name was listed on the registry of the Pennsylvania Professional Engineers and Architects Society. The registry stated an office address for him at CSB Engineering in downtown Pittsburgh. He researched the company. Its founder was one C. Stanley Bigelow. He soon found photos from the society's annual banquet three years earlier. In two of them, Stanley was identified as he stood towering above younger colleagues. A big man, indeed, Majir thought. Bigelow was not an uncommon name in Pittsburgh. There was even a boulevard named Bigelow, a product of history unrelated to Stanley. And there was a second Stanley Bigelow in the phone directories, as well as a Stan. But there was only one C. Stanley Bigelow, listed as living in what looked to be an apartment on Fort Duquesne Boulevard. Google satellite maps showed it to be a high-rise building on the Allegheny River.

Does he live alone? the Syrian wondered. The most tedious research was through the marriage license records and death notices. Knowing that Stanley was of advanced age, he started in the public records of marriage for the earliest available decades. But the license issuances were not recorded until the 1990s. He decided to check the death notices. It was painstaking work. Three hours lapsed before he found a notice for the death of Agnes Bigelow twelve years earlier. Wife of C. Stanley Bigelow, it read. But the address—a suburban one—was different. Could he have remarried? He looked at the marriage license records month by month, year by year, finding nothing. He was about to give up when, for the sake of completeness, he searched the current year. It proved again that no detail, no diligence, should be forgone. There it was. A marriage license was issued to C. Stanley Bigelow and Helen Ames on February 12, citing a matching address for the groom at RiverBridge Place on Fort Duquesne Boulevard.

It was the composite he needed to instruct Lester Buddy Binton and his men.

"*Militia* duty?" Binton asked. Even in only two words, his inflection moved from odd tenuousness to piqued interest.

"Yes," Majir said. "Listen carefully. There is a man in Pittsburgh who has been acting for the United States government. He is a civilian. He is a civil engineer. He has been doing something for the US government that I need to learn about."

"How does that involve me and the Band?"

"We need you to take him from Pittsburgh to your camp in Michigan, so that I can come there and question him."

"We're not Uber."

"No, you're much more expensive," said Majir.

"You have my attention."

"He won't come voluntarily. You'll have to abduct him—catch him off guard and alone."

"And why bring him to our camp?"

"Pittsburgh is a big city. There are police all over. Probably, I will have to interrogate him for days before he talks. I can't do that in a big city. Your encampment is isolated, I assume?"

Majir used the word *encampment* with purpose. He thought

it would give it stature in Binton's deluded mind. From the little he understood of the place from Binton's earlier descriptions, it was more a banged-up, abandoned trailer camp than a military post, but this was not the moment for hard truth.

"Oh, it's isolated all right," Binton said.

"Well, you must have room for one more," the Syrian said. "Though I should say, he *is* a *big* man. Large and old. At least seventy. Unathletic."

Binton went quiet.

The Syrian surmised what he was awaiting from the militant in pause.

"You will be handsomely paid," Majir said, breaking the silence. "Though you've been paid very much already."

"Another hundred," Binton said.

"Thousand?"

"What else?"

"Okay. But not to any account we have used already."

"Of course not."

"Get me the numbers and the money will be transferred by tomorrow," Majir said.

"So, you want this done fast."

"Yes, as soon as possible. Right away. Time is critical."

"All right. We'll do it."

Majir gave Binton all the information he had gathered on Stanley. He recited the URL address where he told the extremist to find the target's photograph. He noted that Buddy did not seem to resent being given directions—unusual for him—and put it down to the assumption that the antigovernment computer genius had never made an abduction before. He told him to wait for Stanley outside his apartment building and never to watch from one place for more than thirty minutes. He insisted that he not attempt entry into the apartment building and that under no circumstances was Stanley's wife to be present when the taking occurred. There were two reasons, he told Binton. The Syrians wished no harm to an innocent that was not necessary. And there was nothing that would guarantee immediate pursuit like a witnessed abduction. It was important to get the engineer to Michigan before he was even noted missing, if possible. And, he stressed, the old man was not to be harmed. He had to be well and of clear mind when Majir arrived to question him.

"Do you have his car make and model?" Binton asked.

"No, sorry."

"No problem, Maji. I can hack that shit in a New York minute."

Majir found it convenient to stroke the Michigander's ego once more.

"That's what I thought," he said.

But it may have been a mistake. It seemed to revive Binton's belligerent streak.

"Where exactly is your compound there?" Majir asked.

"Not too fast," Binton said. "I never trust a Muslim until I have his money. And maybe not then. When you get to Michigan, you call me. We'll get *you* to *us*."

The Syrian did not see how he could press the point, at least in the moment. Instead, he told Binton to call him when he had Stanley Bigelow in his custody.

Then he booked a flight to Stockholm, using a credit card newly issued to Melaha in London instead of the one he normally used, one monitored by Damascus. His trip to Sweden to meet the INTERPOL man LaToure would not be detected.

Or so he hoped.

A PRESIDENT UNDER PRESSURE

You might have thought it was a Fourth of July parade without the floats, the way the flag-pin-wearing politicos were streaming in twos and threes to the White House to make their case to President Del Winters.

The deadline for a presidential petition to the Supreme Court challenging the Georgia Senate election under the election security statute was just forty-eight hours away. The president had been silent on the question of a challenge. But she had ordered the release of a statement disclosing that a special team sent to examine the voting machines had discovered that some had operated with software distorting the votes in an undetermined number of Georgia precincts. The statement said—correctly—that the suspect machines so far identified were all located in counties of the greater Atlanta metropolitan area and that the machines thus far tested had all erred in favor of the Republican incumbent, Will Truitt. But the statement also said—again correctly—that until *all* the state's machines could be examined, and test votes completed on each of them, it could not be concluded that miscounting had not also occurred in the Democrat Westfall's favor or that the miscounting as a whole was significant enough to change the outcome of the election.

Republican leaders in Congress were on edge, to put it mildly. More than a dozen asked the president to meet with them. Democratic leadership did the same. She accepted every one of the requests and cleared her schedule, except for national security matters. They all wanted to know whether she intended to challenge the result in Georgia. She said she didn't know—that there was not enough information to make that decision yet. The experts were working around the clock to test every machine in the state. She was being briefed every few hours. A pattern seemed to be emerging, but patterns could change in an instant, she said. There was no basis yet to conclude that the vote was manipulated enough to make a difference.

But what about the murders in Boston? The Democrats thought the facts of those alone warranted a challenge. She had no comment as to that view. Her Republican allies argued that if it was not proven beyond doubt that DeClerc had intentionally caused the machines to miscount, how could she justify a challenge? After all, the statute required a showing of *how* the alleged fraud was committed. She wouldn't comment on that view either. If ever a president held a poker face, it was Delores Winters in those meetings. Reporters mobbed every senator and House member leaving their sit-downs with her.

"Could you tell which way the president is leaning?" each was asked.

"Not at all," or words to the same effect, was the uniform response, usually draped in a frustrated expression.

The president herself invited only *one* person to come to the Oval Office to discuss the matter: Margaret Westfall. She had met the Georgia lawyer just three times before. The first was at a conference in San Diego addressing women in leadership in government and the military. Westfall was then the newly elected district attorney in Atlanta; Del was then the vice president. The connection was solid from the beginning. Del was struck by the Georgian's confident yet unassuming manner. Westfall was Caucasian and a lifelong southerner, but one of those—and there were more than most appreciated—deeply committed to civil rights and equal justice. They were about the same age and attractive in their own distinctive ways. Westfall was married to a mathematics professor at Emory University and had two children. In their first conversation, they discovered a common interest outside of government. They were both avid golfers with low handicaps.

"We should play sometime," the vice president said.

"I would like that," the DA said. "As long as you don't try to make me a Republican."

"Why would I?" Del said. "It's always more fun to beat a Democrat."

But the conversation in the Oval Office four years later was not as light. The president had sent a jet from the Beaufort, South Carolina, Marine Aviation Station to pick up the Senate candidate and bring her to Washington. Both agreed to keep the fact of the meeting confidential, as well as the specifics of their discussion, though the president did say that a joint statement, perhaps even a press conference, might be in order after their meeting, depending on their discussion. Westfall would not commit to that idea, which was surprising but not off-putting to the president. Apparently, the Georgian could hold a poker face too, she concluded. And Del admired the inference that the Senate candidate would not be pushed around.

It was nearly five o'clock when the black-haired candidate

arrived. A marine escorted her down the hall to the Oval Office, opened the door after a single knock, said nothing as Westfall walked past him into the room, then left. In a sense it was rude of the marine; in another a high compliment. She needed no introduction.

Ned Thelan had sent his current report just before Westfall's arrival. Immediately after greeting her visitor, the president handed a copy across her desk to her.

"We're both reading this for the first time," she said to the Georgian. "It's the latest."

The two of them sat down and read in silence. It was the principal reason Del had invited the candidate. She had directed the attorney general to keep the Senate candidate informed. But the information was coming in hour-by-hour. The picture changed with each report. The president wanted everything shared with Westfall because she felt obliged to do so out of fairness, though the statute did not speak to a candidate's rights to such information or the timing of its supply. But Del Winters had an additional reason. She knew that political history was unfolding before them, like tense acts in an unpredictable new drama. Intrigue hung in the theater air. She knew that in the final act, two players would emerge from the audience and take the stage. Ready or not, willing or not, able or not, one or both of these two actors would be choosing the ending. Del Winters and Margaret Westfall, one way or another, would be writing history.

The latest data from Thelan was painfully tentative. Twelve thousand machines across the state had been tested. The overwhelming majority of them produced accurate—flawless—counts. Will Truitt's enormously lopsided winning margins in rural county after rural county were real, verified, true. The Republican actually earned the votes credited to him in the machines in those places. But in four of the five metropolitan Atlanta counties, software in the computation module had mistranslated *some* Westfall votes, recording them as Truitt votes. The total of misdirected ballots discovered so far was 1,183, far from enough to change the outcome, since the machines on Election Day had recorded a statewide advantage of seven thousand votes for the Republican.

But many machines in the Atlanta counties remained to be tested with simulated vote counts. The report stated that it was not yet confirmed whether any counties outside of the Atlanta area were infected; the team expected to know by tomorrow. And it was known that all machines tested in *one* metropolitan Atlanta county, Forsyth, had reported *true* counts.

Especially vexing was the remaining uncertainty as to how the software had infiltrated the machines in the first place. There was no doubt that murdered Simon DeClerc and trusted civil servant Homer Junes were the two persons known to have handled the machines. But there was no evidence that anyone *else* had, and no physical evidence that either of those two had altered the machine modules, intentionally or inadvertently. Every machine in the state had remained in place since Election Day, and closed-circuit video surveillance footage, recorded from the time of their delivery before the election through the day following it had been reviewed and rechecked again. The investigators found no footage showing anyone touching them. There were very brief intermissions in the recordings made in the Augusta warehouse, which the reviewers put down to ordinary electrical current fluctuations and camera rebooting. And they noted that as closed devices unconnectable to the internet, foul play of the cyber kind, at least once the machines had reached their precincts, was impossible, even wirelessly.

"I asked you here, Margaret, to tell you in person that I

understand the position you are in," the president said. Each had finished reading the new report. "The timing of the challenge process is boxing you in."

"Boxing me *out*, actually."

"Agreed."

"Even if the discrepancy in the count grows past Truitt's margin by the deadline, how could I show that fraud was committed?" the Georgian lamented. "The whole thing might be an honest manufacturing error in the software."

"Well, if that's the case, there should be a remedy in Georgia somehow. Could you go to court down there and ask that Truitt not be seated until the state can get to the bottom of this?"

"We've thought of that," Westfall said. "If we have no other choice, we will. But they are telling me the election laws in Georgia make it hard. Kind of a 'mistakes happen' policy. If tampering didn't happen on purpose, my chances are not good under Georgia law."

"You've read the federal law carefully, I'm sure," said the president.

"Of course."

"The difference between a challenge filed by you and a petition filed by me is large," the president said.

"Tell me about it," Westfall said. Her sarcasm was gentle. Both understood that a *candidate* challenging under the federal statute must do so to the *state* elections authority, and even with winning evidence could obtain only a *revote*, a second election. So, the only remedy for Westfall if she herself filed a protest was a second chance, and she'd have to earn it from a heavily Republican state elections board. But if the *president* petitioned, the challenge was made directly to the *US Supreme Court*, and the court had the option, according to its view of the evidence, to reverse the election outcome outright and seat the cheated candidate, *so long as* that candidate, as here, was not from the president's own party.

"No one can know at this moment whether those votes were turned on purpose to defeat you, or whether enough of them were changed to make a difference," the president said. "But I want you to know that I am going to do whatever I can to protect the honesty of that election. I would do it for Truitt if it were going the other way, and I will do it for you."

"But time is running out," Westfall said.

"I know. I've asked Madeline Stone to prepare a petition to the Supreme Court so that it is ready and can be filed by the Friday deadline if the information supports it by then. It is unlikely every machine will have validated numbers by then. But it is a big team doing everything it can, as quickly as it can. It may have enough to go on by Friday. Until then, every report I receive you will receive too at the same time. You have my word on all of this."

"This is very honorable of you," Westfall said.

"It is only what should be expected of me. But I admit that I'm glad I am not having to do it for someone I dislike. Or I think is unqualified."

"I don't think your Republican members will be pleased with you."

"Tell me about it," Del said.

Touché.

46

MURDER, AND NOT BY AN AMATEUR

A deputy found the body.

The Sheriff's Department had been looking for the missing federal government employee Molineaux for three and a half days. Normally, reports of missing persons lay unattended for at least twenty-four hours before resources were deployed to search. Almost always, the person—often an upset teenager or senior citizen failing of memory and still driving the Cadillac—turned up by then. But Charleston County Sheriff Weldon Bechant chose not to defer when the call came from the wife of James Molineaux at eleven in the evening.

The sheriff was just climbing into bed when the text message dinged. He received one automatically if one of three things occurred: a report of gunfire anywhere in his county, the dispatch of more than two cruisers to a scene, or the filing of any missing person report. He'd learned long ago that part of the art of being sheriff was knowing when matters needed immediate attention and when they didn't.

Once, a county judge had reported his daughter missing when she did not appear at high school. The sheriff overheard a deputy telling a clerk to send it to the dispatcher the next afternoon, the usual practice. Weldon intervened immediately, snatching the form from the deputy's hand.

"Not *tomorrow* afternoon. Get on this *now*. Right now. And get a few others to help too," the sheriff commanded.

"How come?" the deputy asked. Then bravely, "Because this is Judge Bellamy's daughter?" Weldon didn't resent the question. He didn't avoid it either. A teaching moment.

"Your judgment needs to catch up with your instincts," the sheriff said, not overly harshly. "*Yes*, deputy, because it's the judge's girl. Everybody in this county gets justice. Some just get it a little faster. The judge is one of them. Use your head and find the child."

The girl was found two hours later. Safe, sound, and high on marijuana, with three ounces more in her school backpack. Judge Bellamy came to the jail, where Sheriff Bechant was waiting for him, deputy in tow.

"Thanks, Weldon," he said. "I came to pick up my girl."

"You mean to post her bail?" the sheriff replied. "It's a thousand dollars."

"You booked her?"

"Yes, I did, Judge. She's eighteen."

The judge stammered and paced for a moment.

"I thought you could overlook this, Weldon," he said, moving close to the sheriff. "As a favor, you know?"

"I did you a favor when we went out looking for her immediately, Judge. Now, that's my job, you could say. But the law's been broken, and it looks like you want me to look the other way about that. And that's *not* my job. No matter *who* asks."

It was a small incident, but it summed up what the citizens

of Charleston County knew intuitively about the diminutive, suspenders-wearing sheriff they returned to office time and time and time again. You could challenge his methods sometimes. You might wince at his vanity sometimes. You could question his sobriety most times. But you could never doubt his judgment, commitment, or fairness.

The deputy and the coroner waited for him to reach the secluded patch off County Road 114 before moving the body. They didn't need to touch the victim to identify him; his plastic employee badge hung exposed on a lanyard resting on the leaves next to his slashed neck. The searchers had found Molineaux's car the afternoon before behind the boarded-up diner on Highway 17. It was unlocked and appeared undisturbed, the key fob in plain view on the driver's seat.

"Whoever took him left the key there on purpose," Bechant said, when he received the news that the car had been located. "He hoped somebody'd come along and steal the damn thing. Get it far away. Have us find it somewhere else to have us search the wrong area. If Molineaux's dead, he's not far from that car."

"Then the killer's not very experienced," a deputy said.

"Or else he's very professional," Bechant said.

The sheriff was right; that was Majir Asheed's reasoning for leaving his victim's key fob. He knew that he would kill his target uncomfortably close to his abandoned car, and he hoped the body would go undiscovered for a long time. If the car turned up somewhere else because it was taken and found far away, the search for the missing man would be concentrated there, instead of the little side roads off Highway 17.

The searchers fanned out from the abandoned diner and began to walk the nearby side roads until darkness postponed the work until morning. A deputy from the department's canine unit and his German shepherd, named Nelson, discovered the manager's body just before noon.

The instant Bechant bent over the body and saw the lethal precision of the deep neck wound, recognition ran through him like electricity. He remembered the incident on King Street a year earlier and the cover story he had been provided by the Navy SEAL and Bobby Beach, the Charleston FBI agent-in-charge. He hadn't been told the details of what happened at the United States Vegetable Laboratory, but he surmised it had to do with the military. And he *was* told that the North Koreans arrested on King Street were foreign operatives trying to abduct the heavy old engineer from Pittsburgh because they believed he was doing secret work there that the government, and even the president of the United States, needed to keep secret. He himself had made the cover story stick, telling the media that the Pittsburgh engineer was simply a civilian contractor designing a vegetable storage facility.

And now this.

He looked at his cell phone anxiously. Reception this far out was often nonexistent. But there was a signal, though weak. He knew the local FBI number by heart. Fortuitously, Bobby Beach answered.

"Bobby," the sheriff said. "You'd better get a hold of that Navy SEAL captain you worked with last year."

"Tyler Brew? Why, Weldon?"

"The manager of the vegetable laboratory on Savannah Highway has been murdered. And not by any amateur."

DOG PROBLEM

It took Buddy Binton more than the New York minute he had predicted to hack into the firewalled database of the Pennsylvania Department of Motor Vehicles and find the make, model, and license number of Stanley Bigelow's automobile. It took nineteen, to be precise. But Binton would never admit that to his Syrian sponsor.

Most of his Band brothers were home at the ramshackle trailer camp on the northwestern edge of Michigan's Washtenaw County when Binton knocked at the door of the trailer occupied by Smitty Burns at ten in the morning.

"What's happening?" asked Burns, rubbing his eyes. He was clad in boxer shorts and a long-sleeved T-shirt. "It's only ten o'clock."

"Need you and your car," Binton said. "We've got militia work."

Binton would have preferred to drive his own pickup truck to Pittsburgh. It was nearly new, thanks to the diversion of funds from Damascus he'd made for its purchase. It would be more comfortable for the five-hour ride. But it lacked an essential attribute. A spacious trunk. Smitty's aged Lincoln Continental was bruised and rusted, but the engine was reliable enough, and the heater worked. It had a valid license plate, and Smitty's driver's license was current. Even if they were stopped, there would be no reason for concern. The Continental was rear-wheel drive, but the roads were clear of snow and none was forecast for the next few days. The two Free Brothers emptied the trunk of the big car, except for a tattered blanket, and drove.

Making only one brief stop at a Dunkin' Donuts on the Ohio Turnpike near the Pennsylvania border, they arrived in downtown Pittsburgh at four o'clock, taking up a position on Oliver Street, a few buildings down from the office building housing CSB Engineering. The old man was probably at work, they reasoned, and would likely emerge from the entrance in the next hour or so. They studied the photographs drawn from the internet.

They were right. At four thirty, the large engineer stepped out onto the sidewalk. But there was a problem. About 105 pounds of German shepherd. The Syrian had said nothing about a dog, especially one like this.

Stanley took Augie to the office most days, even in wintertime. The walk to and from his apartment at RiverBridge Place was less than a mile each way and he knew the dog enjoyed it. The routine pleased Helen too, who kept a gentle eye on her older husband's fitness. But on this late afternoon with crime on their minds, it did not please Buddy Binton and Smitty Burns.

"Should we go for him anyway?" Smitty asked, with a decided lack of enthusiasm.

"No fucking way," said Binton. "That dog is huge."

The two militiamen followed as Stanley and Augie made

their way home, watching as the doorman at RiverBridge Place greeted them and squatted to pet the dog as they entered. Stanley and the doorman spoke briefly, the doorman stooping down again to the dog and seeming to point out something about his ears. Stanley nodded and made a small, upward wave of his hand, as of assurance.

The surveillance was over for the night, Binton concluded, as the door closed behind the engineer and his dog.

Unknown to either the dog or his master, Augie had protected Stanley once again, deterring the abduction merely by being at his side. But as fate and sad irony would have it, it would be the loyal canine himself, and his owner's care for him, that would soon put Stanley in deadly harm's way.

ENTER BOBBY BEACH

Bobby Beach was nearing retirement. A career field agent at sixty-one, he could have retired from the FBI years ago. But when Washington enticed him to stay on by suggesting a move back to his hometown for the balance of his tenure, he readily accepted. Anyway, he was surely a young sixty-one. He was slim, strong, still quick afoot, and the picture of health. Except for his full head of neatly cropped, snow white hair—which had turned prematurely in his thirties—he could pass for a lightweight boxer in his prime. And the Charleston position was, by all accounts, a plum. But for the risk of drug importation into its spacious port, of which there had been little, the area was as genteel and quiet as you could find. Charleston was a superb final assignment indeed for the agent-in-charge.

Without doubt, the whole episode involving Stanley Bigelow the previous year was the most energizing and dangerous matter he had worked since his return to Charleston. Then he had worked daily with Captain Tyler Brew and L. T. Kitt, the dog-training agent from Pittsburgh, protecting the aging engineer while he covertly trained the reserve troops out at the USDA facility. They were successful—barely—in doing so. And through Bobby Beach's quick thinking and his engagement of his friend Sheriff Bechant, the secrecy of the work at the laboratory and Stanley's identity, important even to the president of the United States, had been preserved.

Or so they thought until now.

The news that James Molineaux had been abducted and murdered execution-style was electrifying. Bobby Beach sensed immediately, as had Sheriff Bechant, that it must be tied somehow to the Bigelow affair at the USDA site. He had heard from the Navy SEAL Tyler Brew just once since their mutual project a year earlier. The captain had emailed him to tell him that Stanley Bigelow had married Colonel Helen Ames and that they were doing well back in Pittsburgh. He also said, intriguing to the local FBI chief, that he himself had been reassigned to Charleston Air Base. The SEAL didn't describe his new duties. Maybe they could get together sometime, he said only. That would be nice, Bobby Beach had replied. He liked the no-nonsense SEAL.

Bobby Beach recalled the email as he dialed the air base. He was glad to be contacting him finally but thought it ironic and alarming that it was happening like this. When he came to the phone, the Navy SEAL began with pleasantries. Bobby Beach, a slow-talking, articulate gentleman, not prone to interruption, cut him off abruptly.

"Brew, I think Stanley Bigelow may be in danger again. In fact, I'm pretty damn sure he is."

Brew listened to the details of the killing and where it had occurred, how Sheriff Bechant had called as soon as he saw the body, not a half hour ago. Bobby Beach told him there were no clues as to the killer or killers, except that the victim's neck had been slashed deeply from ear-to-ear. Brew thought of the women executed in their Washington apartment before Stanley was first brought into the Eaglets' Nest program.

"Do you know *when* he was killed?" Brew asked.

"He was reported missing by his wife four days ago. Probably killed almost immediately. Molineaux knew who Stanley was. Knew his name."

"Oh, God," Brew said. "We need to get to Stanley. If it's not already too late. Bobby, can you get L. T. Kitt over to him in Pittsburgh? Like *now?*"

"I think so."

"Good," Brew said. "I'll call the president."

Neither even said goodbye.

49

★ ★ ★

IF, IF, IF

But it *was* too late.

The day before, Buddy Binton and Smitty Burns had resumed their surveillance from a parking lot with line of sight to RiverBridge Place. Arriving at seven in the morning, they divided their watchful responsibilities. Smitty kept his gaze fixed on the front entrance. Buddy used binoculars to study every vehicle leaving the parking ramps flanking the high-rise on either side. He knew exactly what he was hoping to see rolling down one of them. A Mercedes 8 Series sedan, bright aluminum, Pennsylvania plate number BLUPRINT.

The vanity plate was Helen's idea. She was clever in that way—part of her mischievous streak. Stanley didn't protest. Her own plate read STANBABE, also her concept. He didn't protest that one either.

At eight forty-five, Binton was rewarded for his patience. Stanley emerged slowly in his Mercedes from the left side garage. Buddy's initial elation was short-lived. Through his binoculars he saw the large German shepherd standing on his hind legs in the back seat, leaning over the console next to Stanley's head.

"He's driving out!" he said to Smitty. "But he's got the goddamned dog!"

The militiamen pulled out of the parking lot in the old Continental and followed the Mercedes down Fort Duquesne Boulevard.

"He's bound to get out of the car someplace," Binton conjectured. "Without the dog."

They followed as Stanley drove north, across the Allegheny River, and through the North Hills area. As they wound through the hills, Smitty looked out repeatedly at the mixed urban and wooded valley vistas.

"I didn't know Pittsburgh was so pretty," he said.

Binton glowered. "Would you shut the fuck up and quit sightseeing?" he snarled. "Help me watch this guy."

Stanley entered the corporate limits of Sewickley, an upscale town not far from his home for many years with Agnes. He glided down the main streets until he came to the simple, brick, free-standing enterprise near the outskirts of town. Sewickley Animal Hospital, the plain sign read.

The engineer pulled carefully into the parking lot. The militiamen followed him in, to a space not thirty feet away. Stanley sat in the car and appeared to look at his cell phone. *Maybe checking for messages,* Binton thought. In less than a minute, he dragged his heavy legs out, stood, stretched, and closed the driver's door. Binton and Smitty immediately opened the doors of their Continental and put their feet to the pavement. But before they could even bring themselves upright, Stanley had opened the driver's side rear door of the Mercedes, and Augie leaped out, unleashed. He was not aggressive, but he stepped quickly to Stanley's side, appearing attentive. Stanley raised his leash, normally Augie's cue to sit and accept latching. But the big dog did not sit. He stood, his tail looped long and low behind him, and looked to the side at the two strangers. Stanley was oblivious.

"Okay, August," he said. "Let's go see Dr. Angela." He clipped the leash and the big canine followed Stanley's steps, turning every three or four strides to look back at the two men standing motionless by their old car.

"Son of a bitch," Binton said.

"Maybe they'll stop somewhere on the way back," Smitty said. "He can't take the dog everywhere." Binton shrugged agreement.

If only Stanley or Helen or the doorman had noticed the furry nub on Augie's ear a month earlier. Even two weeks earlier. If, if, if.

Inside, Dr. Angela Lane looked at the ear in earnest as Stanley observed anxiously next to her. She probed the growth with both her thumbs, pressing aggressively at the surrounding tissue.

"Aren't you being a little rough?" Stanley said, frowning.

"Please, Stanley," she said, smiling respectfully. "I need to see how tender it is. He's a big boy." Augie glanced up at Stanley, as if in agreement.

"Okay," the veterinarian said. "It's not mobile, not loose. So, it's not just a fatty cyst. But there's no tenderness, so I doubt it's malignant."

"Just let it be, then?"

"We could. But it's getting blood supply, because his fur is growing on it. It will keep getting larger."

"So, what are you suggesting?"

"I'd like to take it off. I could do it right now. And send it to the pathology lab for tests, just to be sure."

"Would he have to stay overnight?"

"No, but I *will* need to sedate him. You could take him in a couple of hours. There will be stitches, but he'll be good as new in a couple of days."

"Well then, I'll just wait."

"There are magazines in the lobby," she said.

"Or maybe I'll just go out for a walk with a cigar. I have one in the car."

"Or that," the vet said.

Or that. If only he had simply sat and paged through the old issues of *Pennsylvania Canines* in the lobby.

If, if, if.

He never reached his cigar. He was ten steps from his Mercedes when the two abductors grabbed him in unison, from front and behind. It happened so abruptly, so quickly, that the dazed engineer stumbled on his feet, resisting only moderately, until Smitty opened the trunk of the Lincoln. Then Stanley whirled his head to see if anyone else was there who could help him. There wasn't. He kicked his legs and swung his arms as hard as he could until he felt his legs lifting into the air, then his head crashing to the bottom of the trunk. He felt his phone being ripped from his pants pocket and the deadly thud of the Lincoln truck lid slamming down over him.

50

RELIEF AND ANGUISH, BUT MORE ANGUISH

Agent L. T. Kitt was aiding a team serving arrest warrants south of Pittsburgh when the emergency call came from her superior downtown. She was responsible for canine support in the raid, conducted at a chop-shop that dismantled cars for an interstate theft ring. The dog she brought, a female named Bess, was one she had been training for three months. The dog was showing promise, Kitt adjudged. But this was only her second time in the field. Kitt had selected her for training on the raid that day only because the team's advance surveillance discerned no firearms at the shop and serious resistance was not expected.

Much less expected was what she heard on the phone as she stood on the site perimeter with Bess as the other agents went inside.

"Bobby Beach just called from Charleston," the local FBI chief said. "There's reason to think Stanley Bigelow is under immediate threat. Get over to his home right away. No one is answering the phone there. We don't know where his wife is.

Hopefully, she's not there. Stanley's not picking up his cell, and we don't have a mobile number for Helen."

"I don't either, but why do they think someone is coming after Stanley?"

"I have no details. But someone was murdered down in South Carolina, and they believe it's related to Bigelow. Could Bess help you? Take her there with you?"

"No, she's not ready."

"Then leave her with the others and get the hell over there. I've already sent two agents, and Pittsburgh PD is responding too. You have the address, right?"

"Of course."

A dozen PPD cruisers already surrounded RiverBridge Place when Kitt pulled her FBI canine unit SUV, *sans* canine, to the front curb. Officers were positioned on the eighth floor where the Bigelows lived and in the stairwells leading to and from it, above and below. Only one elevator was left operational, its door held open in the lobby, waiting for her.

"Nobody responding inside?" Kitt asked the PPD lieutenant who climbed into the elevator with her.

"Not yet. But the Bigelows know your voice. Maybe one of them is in there and afraid to answer. They may answer for you, if they can. We didn't want to take the door down until you got here. We talked to the neighbors. Nobody's heard anything or anybody, except us pounding on the door."

Kitt looked at her watch; it was approaching four o'clock.

"Obviously, you checked his office?"

"He didn't come in today. They say sometimes he doesn't."

She knew it was true that especially since Stanley and Helen had married, his daily schedule was less rigorous. He had been coming to the office for full days only about three days each week, until the new project he had taken on for the president in

October. Then he had thrown himself into that work—thousands of drawings and calculations—nearly around the clock, to the point of worry for both Helen and she herself. But since his part of the project was essentially completed by Thanksgiving, he had relaxed again.

On the eighth floor, Kitt, the PPD lieutenant, and one of the other agents sent by the FBI moved cautiously down the hall. They flanked Stanley and Helen's door. Kitt spoke loudly.

"Stanley! Helen! Are you in there? It's me, L. T. Augie! August! Are you in there, boy?"

The lieutenant was puzzled.

"Augie?" he asked.

"His dog."

"Oh."

"Not just any dog," Kitt said. "He would protect Stanley and Helen to the death. He's a trained protection shepherd."

"Really," the lieutenant said.

"And if he was in there now and if they were disabled, we wouldn't need to take this door down. He would."

"Unless the dog is dead too," said the policeman.

If ever there was a case of deep relief, and great anguish, arriving together, it happened in the next sixty seconds. The relief came when the elevator door on the eighth floor opened and out stepped Helen Ames, accompanied by a uniformed officer from below.

"What's going on, L. T.?"

"We have to get inside, Helen. I'll tell you in a minute. Give me the key and wait out here. *Don't* come in."

Kitt had barely opened the door when the phone rang on the kitchen counter. She stepped quickly to it, as the lieutenant and fellow agent scampered from room to room.

"Bigelow residence," she said.

"This is the Sewickley Animal Hospital," the voice said to L. T. Kitt's hot ear. "We're finished with Augie, and he can be picked up. He's fine. But Mr. Bigelow seems to have left. Do you know, is he coming back?"

Anguish.

51

JUST A VERY BAD NIGHT

Del Winters later would say it was the single worst night of her life as president.

There was only hard, bad, and—in one case—deeply emotional news.

Ned Thelan's latest report on the vote count in Georgia had arrived before dinner. The total of misdirected votes taken from the Democrat Westfall had swelled to over six thousand, and there were still nine hundred machines in Dekalb, Fulton, and Cobb counties to be tested. *Each* machine from those counties so far examined had misdirected an average of nearly fifty ballots. If even a fraction of that number were thrown in even some of the remaining machines, Westfall was the clear winner, and the president's plurality in the Senate was a wisp of smoke. Madeline Stone was to deliver to her later in the evening the draft petition to the Supreme Court. A critical legal, ethical, and politically charged decision remained for Del: would her presidential petition ask the court to order a new election or install Margaret Westfall *outright*?

Defense Secretary Lazar called soon after. His team had thoroughly studied the data from Munich. It agreed in full with the INTERPOL assessment. The invasion of the military communication channel did not originate in Germany, and there was nothing promising on any other lead. Even Israeli intelligence was mystified, and its sources were the most expansive in the world. US military aircraft and quite possibly civilian commercial airliners remained vulnerable. Work had begun in earnest to install the new underground cable system, but it would be months before completion.

If those reports were not disheartening enough, the last information, just received as she greeted the First Father in the residence for their customary cocktail, was devastating. Stanley Bigelow, the senior civilian, the man she had asked to come out of obscurity and serve his country—who never truly understood the threat to his safety—had been abducted in suburban Pittsburgh. His whereabouts were unknown. All that was known was that he was taken in the parking lot of a veterinarian while Augie was inside for treatment. The secrecy of the Eaglets' Nest weapons system was in plain jeopardy, as well as his current work on the new fiber optics system. But to her even more upsetting, so was Stanley's life.

She said almost nothing through dinner in the White House residence. Henry Winters was solemn too. He studied his daughter's concentration across the table.

"When I was in the field and three or four things were happening at the same time, I had a rule for myself," the general said.

"Oh?"

She thought her father would lean low and forward, the

way he often did when he thought he had something important to urge. But he didn't; he rested his fork and leaned back in his dining chair.

"I told myself to pay attention to the problem that required *my* decisions and *my* conduct. If it required that, it meant *I* could control it. The others? Leave them to people you trust. They can do it better than you anyway."

It was one of the few times that daughter did not return her father's advice with at least a semblance of a smile. But the serious, preoccupied expression she returned to him was not fueled by anger, resentment, or even irritation. Henry knew that. It was just a bad night. A very bad night.

52

★ ★ ★

A RULE OF LIFE EXPECTANCY

At least the stuffy trunk was warm enough. Stanley didn't even need the soiled blanket he could see from the pinholes of light flowing through the rusted trunk near its lock. The ride had been smooth and usually at high speed, until the last short distance over which the old Lincoln heaved and rocked slowly, almost at a crawl. His greatest discomfort, besides fear, was a bladder near bursting. He had not been out of the trunk since he was thrown into it north of Pittsburgh.

The sunlight pierced his eyes when Binton and Smitty lifted the trunk lid. Stanley thought they would blindfold him, especially when he turned his head from side to side, taking in the location. But they didn't.

"Where are we?" he asked. He tried to keep an even voice to disguise his fear.

"*You're* the engineer," said Binton. "You figure it out."

So, they knew something about him, thought Stanley. *It was not a random kidnapping.* The younger men pulled him from the trunk. Stanley did not resist. There was no point in being uncooperative. Every minute he stayed alive increased his chance of living longer, he knew. It was a basic rule of life expectancy, even in the worst of circumstances. If you wanted a short one, get yourself killed.

Stanley studied the place. He could see no roads other than the rutted dirt trail on which the Lincoln had come to rest. It ran uphill across a mounded open field of sixty acres, he guessed, heavily bordered by woods of oak, poplar, and white pines. Near the rear of the low-lying field lay a hodgepodge of rusty mobile homes and camper trailers, resting at unplanned angles, some mere feet from one another. Three drums were burning waste, or providing warmth, he couldn't tell. Some of the trailers were exhaling smoke from roof pipes. He noted the Michigan license plate on the Lincoln but knew that didn't mean he had been taken there. Stanley himself had never driven to Michigan from Pittsburgh; never farther west of Cleveland than Sandusky, about halfway across the state of Ohio, when he attended an engineering meeting there years ago. His abductors had not taken his watch, and he knew the trunk ride had lasted under five hours. *Could you even get to Michigan from Pittsburgh that quickly?* he thought. There were many other possibilities. *Pennsylvania itself is massive. You could drive five hours and never leave it. Or maybe the Catskills in New York state?*

"I have to use the bathroom," he said, when he was upright and stable.

"Take him inside, Smitty." Binton pointed to the closest camper, a dilapidated five-wheeler sitting unevenly, concrete blocks at one end, logs at the other.

"He's staying in *my* trailer?"

"Tonight, he is."

★ ★ ★

THERE ALWAYS IS

The FBI simply had nothing to go on. No one in the veterinarian's office saw anyone or remembered any vehicle in the parking lot. They recalled Stanley leaving the examination room where Dr. Lane was preparing Augie for his minor surgery and lumbering out the entrance, smiling pleasantly as he always did. Nothing more. The only surveillance cameras at the animal hospital were mounted to film the front entrance and a steel rear door. None covered the parking lot or driveway. There had been no cameras at all until a break-in the year before to steal opioids from the drug cabinets in the basement.

Within an hour, agents watched the output from the cameras. All it showed was Stanley trundling in with Augie and out twenty-eight minutes later without him.

The search was not helped by the first unwitting action of abductor Smitty Burns after the taking. Smitty was a brilliant computer science theorist who never thought inside the box in his cyber propositions, which is why Binton appreciated him. But the mentally unstable, unkempt militant was the furthest thing from practical that even a stereotyped absent-minded scientist could be. No one ever said that common sense was his forte. Most, including his leader Binton, adjudged he didn't have any at all. On that day, though, without knowing it, he had done a practical thing that set back the hunt for Stanley more than anything else. He threw the kidnapped man's cell phone out the window of the Lincoln just three blocks from the abduction site, well before the ramps of any expressway. He had no idea how tactically significant his toss was. Oh, he likely realized it meant that the phone could not be utilized as a tracking device. But because it was ejected so near the vet's office, it also provided no meaningful insight into where the takeaway vehicle was heading, even in terms of general direction.

One thing the bureau did have going for it: motivation. The White House made sure of that, calling the Pittsburgh agent-in-charge fifteen minutes after Bobby Beach's initial call from Charleston to his FBI colleague in the Steel City. The deputy chief of staff to the president asked the Pittsburgh field chief, on behalf of the president personally, to direct all available resources to the search for Stanley Bigelow and informed him that additional manpower would be arriving, including a team led by Captain Tyler Brew, a Navy SEAL.

"You're kidding," the agent-in-charge said. "*A SEAL? Military?* Why?"

"Don't ask," was the reply.

He didn't, at least not again. But he did text L. T. Kitt, who was still at the apartment with Helen.

> Stay on Bigelow case. Forget other assignments.
> Bringing in people from Scranton and Erie to assist.
> SEAL also coming to help you.

At the apartment downtown, Helen was maintaining her composure, asking what she could do to help. She wanted to fetch Augie from the vet's office. Kitt told her no; she would go herself to pick up the dog. But she did have an urgent question.

"Have you done the laundry?" L. T. asked.

"There's some to do. Why?"

"Stanley's clothes?"

"Mostly."

"Anything smelly?"

"There always is."

"Good. Don't wash them. Wrap them in a towel; make sure it's a towel that only Stanley has used. Only his things, nothing *you've* worn. I'll need them right away."

Helen stood puzzled in the kitchen. A uniformed officer stood at her door in the hallway. L. T. Kitt raced to the Sewickley Animal Hospital.

54

★ ★ ★

SNOW DID FALL

As she closed the call to the fuming chairman of the Republican National Committee, President Del Winters said the only thing to him that came to her mind.

"It's the right thing, Harry."

Her attorney general, Madeline Stone, sat across from her in the Oval Office and presented the folio to her for her signature. It contained the petition to the Supreme Court in the form Del had ordered her to write it. The petition was eighteen pages in length, reciting everything the FBI under Ned Thelan and everything Wilson Bryce and his team from the Defense Intelligence Agency had found and concluded. The election of the United States senator from Georgia had been sabotaged by the fraudulent insertion of software into the voting machines deployed to Fulton, Dekalb, and Cobb Counties, the petition stated. No one would ever know, it said, every detail and fact as to precisely how the software was placed into the ballot devices because the central actors in the fraud, including Simon DeClerc, had been murdered. The brutal destruction of evidence effectuated by their killings could not, the petition recited, be allowed to subvert the will of the citizens in a free and fair election.

The evidence was clear, the petition said, even if circumstantial. Knowing the American public would study the legal petition and strive to understand it, the attorney general, with Del's approval, explained early in the document something that the learned judges to which it was submitted—and for that matter third-year law students—knew well already: the definition and application of circumstantial evidence, and an example recited by judges in ordinary cases tens of thousands of times:

> Circumstantial evidence is of no lesser value than direct or physical evidence. For example, a person may look out his or her window before retiring for the night and see that no snow is on the ground. The same person may awake in the morning and observe that the ground is covered with snow. The person did not see any snow falling, but it is there. The fact that the snow is on the ground is circumstantial evidence that snow fell in the night while the person was not observing it fall. In such a case, it is correct to conclude that this circumstantial evidence proves beyond reasonable doubt the fact that, indeed, snow did fall.

The presidential petition stated that the sworn reports of the experts proved that, but for the placement of the manipulative software in them, the Democrat Margaret Westfall would have won the Senate election by 58,991 votes, a margin decisive enough that no recount would have been required or available to a losing candidate under Georgia election laws.

But it was the final paragraph of the president's petition that roiled her Republican friends the most. It read:

> Section Nine of the Elections Security and Reform Act vests in the president the discretion to seek either
>
> (i) an order from this Court
> for the calling of a second election to fill the challenged congressional seat *or*
>
> *(ii)* an order invalidating the outcome of the election outright and the seating of the candidate in the Congressional office to which he or she was rightfully elected based on compelling evidence, so long as the candidate to be awarded the office is not affiliated with the petitioning president's own party.
>
> The statute further states that the final decision on remedy—namely, whether to order *any* relief or the extent of same—is entirely for the Court in its discretion and final judgment. The president respects and accepts this separation of powers. But by her signature below, the president, as the duly elected representative of all of the People, states to the Court that she believes the fullest remedy—the seating of Ms. Westfall—is appropriate and just and is therefore sought by this petition.

Republican pundits excoriated her for explicitly urging the Supreme Court to reverse the election outright and hand the seat to the Democrat.

"Why in the world, in this first invocation of the election fraud law, the president would not just toss it up there and say, 'If you think it wasn't done properly the first time, do it again the right way,' is totally beyond me," railed one of them. "She's taking sides, instead of just letting the process work through the court. And taking the wrong side!"

The statements in the petition did seem a touch gratuitous, even her aides thought. But she explained it to them in a long, free-wheeling discussion late into the evening, after the attorney general had taken the signed petition to the clerk's office on Constitution Avenue. Her staff filled nearly every inch of the Oval Office as she took their questions, just as she would also the next morning from the press. Her answers were the same to both audiences. The calling of a second election was a remedy that distorted honest democracy, she believed. Who could know what influences would determine the second campaign? Perhaps—and probably—the base of one side or the other would rise in rage and dollars that were absent in the original election. What precedent would be set if an election could be fixed and the worst that could happen was a second chance to win?

But didn't it appear that she was trying to interfere with the discretion of the justices? Maybe, she conceded. They were learned men and women, and certainly did not need to be told what the law was, or their prerogatives under it. But for decades, the workings of the high court had, for better or worse, come more and more into public view. Chief Justice Roberts, now aging but still brilliant and deeply committed to the integrity of the court as an institution, assiduously toiled to keep political affiliation out of the reasoning and decisions of his brothers and sisters. He sought politicization's complete irrelevance, or as much so as the human condition would permit. Still, many rulings—not all by any means—seemed to come down along political lines and expectations.

"I wanted to let them know this is *not* about politics to me," she told her staff. "I thought I owed it to them. I haven't made an appointment to the court yet. Certainly, none of them feel *I* expect anything from them personally. But look how many of the justices were appointed by Republicans." A majority were. "If there was the slightest thought in any mind over there that I hoped for a political result on this, …, well, there isn't now."

A marine in dress blues entered the open door of the Oval Office and pushed his way to the president's desk, expressionless.

"Madame President," he said as the room fell quiet. "You are needed in the Situation Room. There is something new about the man from Pittsburgh."

★ ★ ★

THE COLORFUL SHERIFF

"We may have a break, Madame President," said Jack Watson, the usually cautious CIA director. He was in the situation room with his deputy director, Susan McShane.

"INTERPOL has information for us," he said. "I've heard only the broad outline from our station in Sweden. None of the detail. I thought you should get it unfiltered. We're connecting in Captain Brew now so he hears it too."

"What about the FBI man from Charleston? And L. T. Kitt?" she asked.

"Kitt's in the field with the dog. Refreshing him on some training. But the Charleston agent will be on the video call. And there is one thing, a little crazy, that we should go over before they get on the line."

The president took her customary chair at the center of the long table, across from Watson.

"What is it?"

"The Charleston agent you're talking about is Bobby Beach," Watson said.

"Yes, I remember him."

"He's rock solid," Watson said.

"I gather that. I know Brew was very keen on him in Eaglets' Nest."

"But do you also remember the sheriff down there?"

"The colorful fellow," the president said.

"If you ask me, 'colorful' to say the least," Watson said. "Weldon Bechant. A legend in those parts, older even than Stanley Bigelow."

"I saw him on a CNN clip after the attempt on Stanley two years ago," the president said. "He was amusing, taking the credit with his own police dog. But it worked."

"Yeah, he pulled that off, it's true," Watson acknowledged, referring to the yarn the small-statured sheriff had spun to the media that kept Stanley's identity safe and held up the cover story used all along about the research at the United States Vegetable Laboratory.

"And now?" the president asked.

"Well, he and his county deputies found Molineaux's body and saw the connection to Bigelow immediately."

"Sounds like good police work."

"It was. But the sheriff doesn't want to let go. He wants in on what happens next, with Bobby Beach and his team, and Brew."

"How do they feel about it?"

"Bobby Beach is all in. Vouches for him, totally. Thinks he is more valuable than we do."

"And Tyler Brew?"

"He likes him too."

"Well, Jack, how could he hurt?"

"He's such a publicity hog."

"Seems like he manages publicity pretty well."

"And a big drinker."

"I know a few of those around here too," Del said. She thought for a moment. "For now, let him in. We can see if there's a role for him, depending on what this lead is."

Watson nodded, and touched a button in the center of the table. Three side-by-side video monitors clicked on at one end of the room. Tyler Brew appeared on one, dressed in fatigues, from Charleston Air Base. On the second, Bobby Beach sat at a table with Sheriff Weldon Bechant in the Charleston FBI field office. On the third, a distinctly European-looking gentleman with stylish modern eyewear and a silver mustache sat studying a small spiral notebook. The president peered at the ringed pad; she had not seen one in years.

"Gentlemen, can you all see and hear each other, and us too, here in the White House?" Watson asked.

Each chimed in affirmatively—the sheriff last.

"I am honored to meet you, Lady President," he said, only then removing his large hat. Bobby Beach could be seen repressing a smile.

"And I, you, Sheriff," Del answered. "Thank you for acting so quickly to alert us about the death of Mr. Molineaux."

"Not quickly enough, I hear. But we did our best."

"We cannot ask for more."

Watson interrupted to introduce them all to the European on the video call.

"Everyone, joining us from Stockholm is Inspector Lars LaToure. Lars is sitting in our CIA station in Stockholm, so that we know the line is secure. Mr. LaToure is a senior agent with INTERPOL, in charge of its Stockholm office."

Lars nodded.

"He's the reason we're gathered," Watson said. "He has information that he and INTERPOL think we could use. Lars?"

The Swede rustled in his chair, adjusted his glasses, and turned back a few pages in his notebook.

"Madame President," he said, "fifteen days-ago I was contacted by post by a person claiming to be an intelligence officer of a Middle East government. He said he was seeking asylum in Europe for himself, his wife, and his daughter." LaToure's English was crisp and near perfect. "After getting authority, I replied to him as he asked, to a box number in the north of London. I promised nothing except that he would not be apprehended by INTERPOL, or on our account, if he still wished to meet." He paused and sipped from a cup of coffee before him. "By the way, Jack, your coffee over here is quite passable," he said.

Watson tried not to reflect impatience, but the comment may have been contagious. The president reached for her own cup.

"Anyway," LaToure continued, "you can imagine we were suspect in the extreme of this person. He said in his original inquiry that he had worked mostly in the United States and Britain for the last twenty years. He said he could not seek asylum in either place because he had killed their citizens and government agents over that time. He came to see me last evening, at a café that he selected in Stockholm, near my office. I had backup in case it was a setup. But he came alone, and we talked for two hours."

"Did he give you identification?" Watson asked.

"No, he refused," Lars said. "In his handwritten notes to me he called himself only 'M.' When we met, he said he would not identify himself unless he was assured asylum. Would not even disclose his government. He was Middle Eastern, for sure. But I couldn't tell exactly from where. Maybe Egyptian, maybe

Syrian. Possibly even Turkish. Of course, I told him asylum was impossible unless he could prove his *bona fides*, prove he was who he claimed he was." LaToure took more of his coffee.

"And then it got interesting. He said he had murdered a woman and her daughter and a third bystander in Washington early last year. He declared the woman's name as 'Morganthal.'" He turned a page of his notebook. "'Ruth Morganthal.' He said American intelligence and the Pentagon would know about the killings." There was a pause.

"That we do," said Watson.

The Swedish detective continued. "He also said he'd been sent back to America last week to kill the manager of an agricultural laboratory run by your government in South Carolina, and that he'd done it. That sounded so wild, I nearly wrote him off. Until I stepped out and asked him to wait. I called my headquarters and had them look over the last week's international homicide listings. Mr. Molineaux's murder showed up. I thought he would probably be gone when I came back to the table, but he was there. I said, 'What else?' *'Isn't that enough?'* he asked. I said if *I* could find out about Molineaux's killing, he could too. After all, I said, you claim you're a foreign agent. You can look in the same places."

"He thought about it for a few minutes and then said he knew that an American civilian from Pittsburgh, an old engineer, had been working for your government. At that very vegetable laboratory. He said that North Koreans had tried to take him last summer but had failed. The whole affair had been concealed, he said, but his own government believed this man was still valuable and wanted to find him. He said he had gone to South Carolina to find the manager, Molineaux, to learn from him who the engineer was. He said he did."

He referred again to his spiraled notes.

"He said his name is Stanley Bigelow."

"My God," the president said.

"I said if he was telling the truth, the Americans would want to protect this man from Pittsburgh. If he would help them do that, asylum would be easier. Maybe the Americans would support it, despite his past. I asked if the man was in danger now. He said yes, he had been abducted in Pittsburgh and taken away."

"By whom? To where?" asked Watson.

"He said his government did not want him to go himself to Pittsburgh; they thought it was too risky. He said in unrelated work he had been developing civilian hate groups in the United States. Private militias and such. He told one from Michigan to go get this man Bigelow in Pittsburgh. Said he paid them $100,000 to kidnap him and hold him in Michigan until he could get there to interrogate him."

"And kill him, no doubt, just like my good citizen of Charleston County," interjected Sheriff Bechant.

"Where in Michigan?" asked Bobby Beach. LaToure thumbed through his notes again.

"Is there a place called *Ann Arbor*?" the INTERPOL investigator asked. "He claimed this group has a camp near there, but he doesn't know more than that, other than he thought it was a sort of abandoned trailer park. He's never seen it and doesn't know where it is. But he told me the name of the hate group's leader. It's Lester Binton." He spelled the name, slowly. "Lester 'Buddy' Binton."

Jack Watson sat up abruptly. *"Binton?"* he said. Susan McShane, sitting next to him, reacted also.

"Yes," repeated the Stockholm investigator. "B-I-N-T-O-N."

The CIA leaders turned and look at each other.

"That name is on one of our lists," Watson said. McShane swiped images on her iPad.

"The University of Michigan list," she said. "The list of researchers using the Ukrainian satellite. Lars, did the defector say anything about Binton and the university there?"

"No," Lars answered. But he did say something else that sounded to me really—how do you say it—*nuts?*"

"Yeah," said Watson. "'*Nuts.*' It means strange, odd. Or crazy. What did he say that sounded *nuts* to you?"

"He said this man Binton and his group are not just an antigovernment armed militia. He said they are computer geniuses too."

56

FOCUS: MICHIGAN

Ann Arbor is the seat of Washtenaw County in south central Michigan, forty miles west of Detroit and home to the University of Michigan. To many it is the quintessential small town with a big college. But in truth, it is a full-fledged city, the sixth largest in Michigan, with a year-round citizenry exceeding 120,000, and swelling much larger most of the year when its massive student population is present. The formidable buildings and courtyards of the campus anchor the center of the city; lively streets dotted with restaurants, theaters and bookstores splay from them on all sides. The central business district is substantial, covering twenty square blocks, each as safe and solid as the next.

In the downtown office of the local county sheriff's department, the crew sent to save Stanley Bigelow stood the next afternoon over a large map of Washtenaw and its neighboring counties. Weldon Bechant was already proving the correctness of Bobby Beach's view of his usefulness. Within minutes of the video call with the president in the Situation Room the evening before, the South Carolinian had reached his counterpart in Michigan, sealed him to secrecy, and arranged for a local manhunt for Lester Buddy Binton and working space for the team on its way.

"It's just a sheriff's thing," Weldon explained to Brew, when the SEAL was surprised the arrangements could be made so rapidly. "We always get along. 'Course, I told him there's a goddamned Navy SEAL with us. Just in case. Adds to the atmosphere." Brew was not offended.

The local sheriff reviewed the county map with them. Essentially square-shaped, the county comprises 722 square miles of land, with many small bodies of water, most of them so-called "kettle lakes" formed by the last of ancient ice blocks melting southward in the glacial age. The city of Ann Arbor is located south and a little east of the county's center-point. The county's overall population is concentrated in and around the city limits. The areas extending south, west, and north of Ann Arbor are decidedly rural, many of them economically distressed with little or no commercial enterprises or developed housing. Eastward, toward Detroit, dense light commercial use is dominant, with modest housing clusters sprinkled in.

Brew explained to the local sheriff that Stanley was thought to be held in a camp of trailers, perhaps abandoned ones. "Are there many of those?" he asked.

"Oh, God, yes," the sheriff said.

"Dozens?"

"If you count the parts of the adjoining counties close to the Washtenaw line, there are hundreds of them. And the farther into those bordering counties you go, the more there are. I wouldn't say it's a needle in a haystack, but it's close. If you could find Binton himself, you could follow him in to his camp. But otherwise, I wouldn't know where the hell to begin."

Brew thought the place to begin was precision satellite images of the entire county, generated at night so that furnace exhaust, wood fires, moving lights, or other signs of habitation could be seen. Wherever he was, Stanley was now to begin his third night in captivity. The team surmised that before long Binton would become nervous about the late arrival of the Syrian agent whom they, but not the militiamen, knew had no intention of coming. If Binton's band concluded their foreign sponsor had abandoned them, they might move Stanley—or worse. And Brew, Beach, and Bechant knew that once the holding camp was identified, it would take another full day, at least, to assemble the right resources and script out a proper tactical plan for a rescue. The satellite images were needed yesterday. Having failed that, tonight. He called Susan McShane from the local sheriff's conference room, and she pledged to secure the images by midnight.

"Not just Washtenaw, Susan," Brew said to her. "The bordering counties too." He looked down at the maps, trying to find the names of each. Weldon Bechant was a step ahead. He had already written them in clean block letters on a slip and silently handed it up to the Navy SEAL.

"Livingston, Jackson, Monroe, Lenawee, Oakland, Ingham, and Wayne," Brew recited. Over thirty-five hundred square miles; a dauntingly large area to canvass, all agreed.

They spent the rest of the afternoon and evening doing what could be done without knowing the engineer's whereabouts. Bobby Beach dialed Washington and worked his channels for a team of eight FBI field specialists experienced in heavy arms, pursuit, and extraction. Weldon volunteered to coordinate backup resources, including perimeter security and medical treatment teams. It made sense that he should lead that part of the mission, and Beach and Brew were grateful for the sheriff's offer. Those needs would have to be filled through local government and law enforcement, and the old sheriff had the right touch for it.

Brew focused on the specific tactical needs for the assault itself. He knew that in any approach, he would need expert marksmen and physical extraction specialists. Vernon Lazar gave him carte blanche when they spoke that evening.

"Just tell me who you want, Tyler," the defense secretary said. "I'll get them to you immediately."

The captain was ready with a list, requesting by name and rank the nine SEALs he preferred, and nine alternates if any of the first nine were on deployment or too far away. Because of Stanley's age and size, he anticipated special needs in removing him, especially if he were hurt or debilitated.

"There's an Army Ranger that I fought with on a mission in Iraq," Brew said. "We had to lift a bunch of heavy equipment. I mean awfully heavy. This Ranger was unbelievable. So damn strong. Short guy, shoulders wide as a field. I'd like him too."

"You remember his name?"

"Only his nickname. 'Tug.' I know three years ago he was with the Eighty-Second Airborne."

Lazar said he would try to find him and went over the request list to be sure he had it right, including some special personal equipment that Brew described for the Army Ranger. The call went smoothly until the end. But then the civilian military chief raised, as he had to, one other issue.

"Who will lead the armed assault?" he asked.

"Me," said Brew.

"Tyler, you're forty-one."

"Forty-two," the captain corrected him.

"You're a SEAL, as you wanted to be."

"Yes."

"You know that SEALs age out at forty now. For all armed operations. Only the president can waive that."

"So, what are you talking to *me* for?" Brew said.

"Okay. I'll call her."

"You tell her, Vern. Just tell her. I have to go for Stanley."

AN IDEA IN ANN ARBOR

It didn't take L. T. Kitt and Augie anything like five hours to drive from Pittsburgh to Ann Arbor. She slapped a flasher on the roof of her unmarked Chevy Tahoe and galloped the 280 miles in three hours, ten minutes. She drove so fast that the dog in the oversized cage in the rear, sensing the rocking suspension and feeling the rat-tat-tat of the pavement joints under the tires, stood on all fours nearly the entire ride, looking happily out over the agent's shoulder and swaying in the speeding curves. She would have preferred he'd slept; it would be better if he were rested on arrival. The two of them might be able to begin his special task training right away. Sheriff Bechant had texted. He was locating a suitable place and hoped to settle on one by noon. But Augie looked so handsome and happy that she consented to his pleasure. She didn't order him down.

She arrived in Michigan to find Tyler Brew in a poor mood. The satellite imaging taken overnight was not useful. It was more or less like looking at a Wyoming sky on a clear night. Clumps of lights were everywhere in all the rural areas, and ubiquitous dim, smudgy, moving wisps, probably representing smoke and steam from occupied camps. The local sheriff's comment about haystacks and needles was truer than the three team leaders believed it would be.

"Progress on the holding place?" she asked as soon as she walked into the conference room where Bobby Beach and Brew were working.

"Zilch," the captain said. "Look at these images." He pointed to the large video monitor displaying them. "Any one of those clusters could be it. There are hundreds. This is going to take longer than I thought. But I'm glad you're here. And Augie too. The only positive is, you'll have more time to work with him."

Brew and Kitt moved to the coffee maker in the room. "We drove out to a couple of close-in trailer parks this morning," he told her. "If they have Stanley in anything like what we saw, we're really going to need to know *where* in there they've got him. There's no way we can storm twenty structures at the same time. Not and get him out alive."

Sheriff Bechant hung up on a call and slowly, stiffly rose from his chair at the table. He walked over to Kitt and Augie.

"Here are the spots that might work for you two for your practice," he said, looking down at the dog as he spoke. Standing next to Kitt, Augie looked up at the leathered lawman, as if appreciating the acknowledgment. Weldon handed her several photos. "They're campgrounds closed for the winter. This one here, it's got different bunches of campers and trailers throughout the park. Folks leave 'em there all year-round. The owner of the park says they come back and use them in season. The place would give you some variety to work him on."

"That's good, sheriff. Good work."

"I'll take you there now; you can see for yourself."

She brought food out of a backpack for the dog and a bowl for water. Augie ate and drank at once, and the three of them left for the training site within minutes in a borrowed police cruiser.

Bobby Beach and Brew stayed back, debating next steps on narrowing down the possible holding places. They knew that a large group of searchers could sweep the rural areas and cover most of the territory in a couple days' time. But that would destroy any element of surprise if they *did* find the place. Every search team would have to be large enough and skilled enough to do a spontaneous extraction facing an armed defense. It was not a reasonable option.

It was frustrating that there was no trace—none—of Lester Buddy Binton. The local sheriff confirmed that he had moved out of his last known residence six weeks earlier. Involuntarily. The Jewish landlord at the tidy apartment building, a few miles from the university near Ellsworth Road and State Street, had refused to renew his lease. About half of the tenants in the building were Jewish graduate students. Word of mouth had brought most of them there, but they didn't appreciate Binton's mouth. He repeatedly bothered them with anti-Semitic harangues and was seen bringing military-style pistols and rifles into the building. When the landlord told him he was no longer welcomed, Binton told him he would never have rented the place anyway if he'd known a Jew owned it.

If the leader of the Band of Free Brothers was driving his white pickup truck at all, it wasn't wearing his issued license plates; that seemed certain. Law enforcement in the eight-county area had made hundreds of stops in response to the all-points bulletin Weldon had put in place even before the team had arrived in Michigan. Most likely, they concluded, Binton was hunkered down in the same place Stanley was being held. The militiaman would not be leading them in.

"I'm calling the air base," Brew said.

"Charleston?" Bobby Beach seemed surprised.

"A drone could do flyovers. Low and slow. With the right pilot."

"Don't they make a lot of racket?"

"There's one that doesn't."

58

★ ★ ★

AN UNUSUAL REQUEST

Before he dialed the White House, Brew texted Vernon Lazar for approval. The captain was a supremely confident and trusted SEAL, but he wasn't born yesterday. Even generals and admirals didn't go over the head of the secretary of defense. But Lazar understood that the captain was far more knowledgeable than he was anyway on what Brew wanted to discuss with the president, and he also knew she was intensely interested in the safety of Stanley Bigelow. He readily sanctioned the direct contact.

"Captain," the president said when she lifted the handset. "I signed the waiver, already."

"I know. Thanks. I'm calling on something else."

"Oh."

He told her about the challenges in finding the camp where Stanley was captive; how the satellite imagery had revealed a virtual constellation of occupied, semioccupied, and abandoned mobile home and trailer camps within a sixty-minute drive from

Ann Arbor. Their Pittsburgh friend could be at any one of them, and they could not count on the militant Binton surfacing and leading them to him. Blunder-bussing across the whole area in a generalized sweep assault was impractical and dangerous, he said. Then he told the president something she did not know.

"You know we have two Eaglet drones at Charleston Air Base, right now?"

"No, I didn't know that," she said. It was not surprising that she was unware of such a fact. There were far too many logistical moves of military equipment, even secret armaments like the Eaglet, for the president to know of them all. "But I assume there are no Talons with them." She was referring to the small, top-secret nuclear missiles specially designed to be carried and fired by the downsized Eaglet drones. Had *they* been moved without her knowledge into the United States from their covert deployment base in Kuwait, she *would* be concerned.

"No Talons, no," Brew said. "The technical people have been fitting the Eaglets with some advanced surveillance technology. The Predator series had some of it, but those planes are so loud they have to look from at least ten thousand feet or be detected on the ground immediately."

"I know that the Eaglets are much smaller and that they're silent," the president said. "But at their speed, I thought they flew at altitudes even *higher* than the Predators."

"True usually," Brew said. "But the Eaglets have vertical lift and landing ability. They have special hydraulic systems that allow them to hover. It's not easy, and most pilots wouldn't try it, but there *is* a way to fly them low and slow by jockeying those hydraulic lift and landing controls. And still fly silent. If we flew one at night over these land areas—one from Charleston with the new detection technology and cameras—we might find who's holding Stanley without them knowing it."

"Is there a pilot who could do this?" asked the president.

"Lieutenant Grey Boatwright. He's flown the Eaglets on training exercises."

"He would fly it from the Charleston command center?"

"Yes."

"While you're there in Michigan getting your force ready?"

"Yes."

"You've talked to Boatwright?"

"Yes. He thinks he knows how to do it."

"Hold for a minute, captain."

Del muted the phone, even though she was alone in the Oval Office. It was a habit of hers, to help her concentrate when rapid decisions were necessary. She knew better, but it somehow made her feel her thoughts could not be overheard; the silence provided a semblance of privacy. This was a difficult decision. There were deep implications to Brew's request. The very existence of the Eaglet drone was a cherished secret. It was envisioned for use exclusively outside of the United States as an overpowering nuclear tool of last resort against broad-scale terrorist initiatives. Now, Tyler Brew, the antiterror Navy SEAL who had been the point man on the completion of the Eaglet program and the construction of its deployment base, Eaglets' Nest, wanted to use it for a completely different purpose—fly it in a different way in the heart of the homeland, by a young pilot who "thinks" he can fly it unconventionally. She worked the questions and risks through her mind. A minute and a half later she unmuted the phone.

"Captain, if this ends poorly, you will need to be sure you are prepared to go in and collect or destroy the aircraft—all of it. No one can learn about that craft or have any piece of it. Be certain those resources are on hand."

"Yes, Madame President."

"You call the lieutenant," she said. "I'll call Vern and tell him you are 'go' for the Eaglet."

In more ways than one, it was a decision made on the fly. She hoped she would not live to regret it.

59

★ ★ ★

DEFECTION INTERRUPTED

Lars LaToure did not wait for the European mail services. He couldn't.

He didn't know the whereabouts of the mysterious Mr. "M." He had asked him when they met at the café if he intended to stay in Stockholm. The defector wouldn't say. His government did not know he was there, he had said, and it was unsafe to stay in any unauthorized location for long. He could only stay indefinitely if asylum was assured and protection afforded.

LaToure understood. He knew the aspiring defector was at great personal risk. There were always signs, however small, of pending disloyalty; he had observed them himself in others who had "turned" over the years. The only reasonable assumption was that whoever controlled "M" occupied a position of suspicion somewhere on its long continuum. The Middle Easterner had mentioned that his wife did not get on well with his supervisor. Spies were never *fully* trusted anyway; a family man approaching fifty, as Lars assessed "M," less so.

The INTERPOL intermediary was not yet in position to guarantee asylum. Several more bridges needing crossing. But it was plain the American president was keen to find and extract the civilian from Pittsburgh, and Lars wanted to help in any way he could. Lars was the only person who knew, and was known *by*, the would-be defector. And the defector was the only person with the certain ability to contact the illusive Buddy Binton and get a clue as to where he was holding the American engineer.

Jack Watson, the CIA head, knew this too, of course. Immediately following the video call to the Situation Room, he had asked Lars to do whatever he could to contact "M" and try to convince him to affirmatively aid in the search for Binton and Stanley.

Theretofore, all contact between Lars and "M" had been by post. He knew it would take three days, at best, to get another message by normal method to the box on Harberton Road in London. Even if "M" was still in Stockholm, it was still the best way to reach him, Lars believed. The foreign agent must have had someone checking his London postal box when he wasn't in Britain. After all, he was in the United States killing Molineaux when Lars's reply to him must have been collected. Probably his wife was checking, the Swede thought. But there was no time to wait for the letter carriers. So, the INTERPOL investigator called his counterpart in London for assistance, dictated a message exhibiting his genetic brevity, and asked him to take it at once in person to the Harberton Road post center. He should use his INTERPOL credentials, Lars instructed, to persuade a clerk to deposit the note at once in Box 259:

M.

Contact in person or by phone.
As soon as possible. Imperative. Cooperation will aid asylum.

LaToure

Lars never learned whether what happened the next day resulted from his unorthodox communication. Perhaps the London box was surveilled by M's handler, grown suspicious. Or maybe the jig was up for the would-be defector well before that. It really didn't matter because just as the INTERPOL man rejoiced to see the Middle Easterner at his office door and hurried to greet him, two bulky Russians appeared in front and behind Asheed. The Russian officers knew LaToure's language skills, so they spoke in their own tongue, presenting their credentials as registered security police from the Russian embassy.

"This man is under arrest," said the older of the two. "He is going with us."

"On what charge?" asked Lars.

"Treason against the fatherland and its allies."

"You have arrest papers?"

Lars looked at the "Document for Apprehension" handed to him, bearing its embossed silver seal. The Russian embassy in Stockholm had secured it from the Swedish prosecutor. It was sad. It was tragic. It was valid.

The Syrian's face was utter blankness, a void of despair as the Russians cuffed his wrists behind his back.

"Thank you," he said dejectedly to Lars as he was led away. "I hope the old American comes to no harm." He could have been currying favor at the eleventh hour, Lars knew. Or he could be sincere. Lars thought the latter.

"What is your name?" Lars asked.

"Majir Asheed," he said. "I am Syrian."

He disappeared into the hallway, as Lars LaToure thumbed through his spiral notepad to find the phone number for Jack Watson at Langley.

★ ★ ★

TEACHING AN OLD DOG NEW TRICKS

Sheriff Weldon Bechant knew a little something about police dogs. Repeatedly, he had argued for budget funds in Charleston County to keep the ample force of canines he had maintained for decades, and he'd succeeded. When it came to the senses, including plain old common sense, he believed the dogs indispensable. Even for this case, he had prevailed on Bobby Beach to permit passage of his own department's best—six-year-old Nelson—from South Carolina to Michigan for additional police dog power.

But the elder lawman had never seen any canine team the caliber of Augie and his trainer, L. T. Kitt. The sensory connection between the two of them was so acute they seemed nearly to occupy each other's skin.

"I should only work him an hour this afternoon," Kitt said. The three of them were standing at one end of the campground that Weldon had found. Three hundred yards ahead, a dozen empty camper trailers were arranged haphazardly, divided by firepits and rusting picnic tables. "He didn't sleep on the way. The more alert he is for these exercises, the better and faster he'll learn and repeat them. And we know there'll be no rescue attempt tonight anyway. I can work with him again tomorrow."

In the trunk of the borrowed police cruiser, Kitt had sorted the unlaundered clothes Helen had given her in small piles, arranged, truth be told, by pungency. For this first day's exercise, she took an item from the most odorous stack and squatted before Augie, holding the clothing to the side. She saw that immediately the dog was energized, rising from a sitting position and moving dance-like around the outstretched item. Kitt was pleased. Augie was clearly associating the exercise with Stanley, showing excitement that he would not exhibit to an unfamiliar scent.

"Stanley!" she exclaimed, while rubbing the dog's throat and sides. "Stanley! Yes, Stanley!"

Then she placed the clothing back into the cruiser and closed the trunk. The dog leashed at her side, the two walked briskly across the field to the empty trailers while Weldon waited at the cruiser. First, the dog and his trainer walked around the perimeter of the entire area where the structures rested. After circling them all, they started approaching individual trailers, and Kitt tried to open their doors. A few were unlocked, and the agent, dog following, entered and walked through them, before returning across the field to Weldon.

"How was the tour?" the sheriff asked, bending to pet the large shepherd.

"We'll see in a minute," Kitt said. "Put Augie in the cruiser and take him out on the road, will you sheriff? Drive at least half a mile. While you're gone, I'll leave Stanley's scent over there someplace."

"In one of the open trailers?"

"No, that would be too easy. He might want to go to those first because he's been inside them. That's okay, for today, so long as he comes out and keeps looking. But it's better if I don't place the clothes anywhere we were together already."

Kitt went to the trunk of the cruiser and this time removed a moderately scented item. Augie cooperated with the sheriff and stood in the back seat as the sheriff drove off. By the time they returned, the agent had tucked the clothing high up into the wheel well of one of the locked campers near the center of the cluster. She had lowered herself to the ground to be sure the clothing could not be seen from the dog's level.

Keeping the canine leashed for the moment, Kitt squatted closely before him and looked into his eyes, fixed on hers. She said Stanley's name, again and again and again, maintaining all the while her own eye contact with the dog. Then she led him five steps or so in the direction of the trailers across the field, leaned low to his ears and said softly, "Stanley," before unleashing him. Augie bolted across the field, barely breaking speed to turn to the left and circle the perimeter, just as he had walked it with Kitt twenty minutes earlier. He did not approach any of the open trailers the two had entered before, running full speed past them until on his second lap he turned and dove toward the center of the cluster. He came to a stop, standing next to the wheel well where L. T. had planted the scent.

Now, right now, was the critical moment, Kitt knew. If the canine was treating the exercise as simply a game of play, he would free the clothing and race back to Kitt with it, seeking praise and reward. But if he understood that this was about a job, about finding and protecting Stanley, he would do what he was trained to do in protection mode. Find him. Stand guard. Sit down unless attacked. The FBI handler and the old sheriff watched from across the campground as the German shepherd thrust his snout high up into the underside of the camper without removing the clothing, then took one step toward them—and sat down.

Kitt sprinted at once toward the dog, motioning to Weldon to do the same as best he could. She hoped Augie would not disengage from the camper and begin running toward her and the sheriff. If he understood his job, he would not move from Stanley's scent. His was not to leave, attack, pursue, or be distracted. His job was to stand firm and protect. Weldon was heaving and exhausted when he reached Kitt and the dog at the trailer—and smiling from ear-to-ear. Augie sat ramrod straight, moving his eyes between Kitt and the lawman. As Kitt rubbed the dog's chest and massaged his sides, praising him, Weldon looked at his watch.

"It's been an hour, ma'am," he panted. "Are we done for today? You said he might be tired."

61

★ ★ ★

CAPTIVITY

Stanley's fourth night at the camp of the Band of Free Brothers was worse than the first three. He slept poorly—he thought less than two hours. Binton had ordered him to a different trailer each night. Smitty Burns's camper, where he was held the first night after his arrival, was the best accommodation so far. It was musty and soiled, but at least it had adequate heat and running water. Every day the cramped conditions deteriorated. Today's trailer reeked of rotting garbage, so foul that Stanley wondered how his guard could live with it. He knew complaining was not generally advised for captives, but eventually the odor became so overpowering he felt forced.

"This smell in here is terrible, don't you think?" he said.

"Gotten used to it, I guess," the guard said, sheepishly. "Is it *that* bad?"

"It really is. I couldn't even sleep."

The Brother walked from the entrance of the trailer to the

aluminum rear wall, sniffing. He turned back toward Stanley, looking embarrassed.

"Well, I can see your point," he said. He stooped to open the cabinet door beneath the sink.

"Ooooh, yeah," he said. "I sure do see your point." He rose with two plastic bags that he pinched cautiously, as if they contained a squirming rodent, and hurried out of the trailer with them.

"You can't come out!" he shouted back to Stanley. "Gotta stay in there. I'll throw these in the fire can."

Stanley followed his instruction. Mostly. He did stay inside the trailer entry, but he leaned out as far as he could balance, taking in as much of the camp as he could. So far, he had been kept inside of the trailers all the time during daylight, except for the hurried daily move in midafternoon. He was made to stay inside his designated trailer most of the time at night too. Since they had pulled him from the trunk the first day, he had sensed a strong desire to know where he was. It wasn't that knowing would improve his lot. *But a man who doesn't know where he is, is a man unanchored,* he thought. *To be in such a state is the worst kind of vulnerability and impotence. Who knows what benefit might flow from having just this morsel of knowledge?* He knew probably none. But he wanted it as much as he wanted his food and water.

Michigan is one of the states in which vehicles do not display license plates on the front end. It was maddening to Stanley that so many of the Free Brothers backed into the muddy gravel slots next to their campers so that their plates were out of view. As he looked out from the trailer, he saw nearly a dozen cars and pickup trucks; all but one was facing toward him. It was an older Land Rover utility truck parked at one of the farthest trailers. He squinted, he leaned, he squinted again. It was no use; he could not make it out. But he concluded that it was not a Michigan plate, as he had observed on Smitty's Continental. An engineer will take his data in small bits, if necessary.

His relationship with his new captor had begun on an unseemly topic, but it progressed. When he returned to his trailer, the Brother smiled at him. He returned it immediately.

"Thank you," Stanley said.

"Sorry about that."

"Sometimes you don't notice things right under your nose," Stanley said. They laughed.

"What kind of camp is this?" Stanley asked. The captor looked at him, and Stanley sensed he was going to answer but stopped himself. "I gather from Buddy that you're some sort of group," Stanley said.

"Band of Free Brothers."

"'Band' as in music? I love music."

"No, not music, man. We're a citizen militia."

"Oh. With guns?"

"Plenty." The brother stopped smiling. "But don't think about finding any. Buddy takes them out of the trailer you're going to. He says we'd have to tie you up if guns were in here."

"I've never fired one."

"Really? Old guy like you, never had a gun?"

"No."

"How about computers? Had them?"

"Sure. What's that got to do with it?"

"We're all computer guys. But we won't let you have a computer either."

"You're hackers?"

"Hacking is mostly kids' stuff. We're scientists."

"Why did you bring me here?"

"For Maji. That's all I know. He's coming."

"Maji is coming? Who's Maji?"

"That's Buddy's business. He's the boss."

"Maji's not the boss?"

"Fuck no. He's a Muslim. A Muslim with money. *Buddy's* the boss." The brother seemed agitated. "The garbage is gone, and you'll be moving in a few hours. Why don't you get some sleep?"

Stanley lay down on the lumpy bunk and drew a cover over his heavy legs. Now, he did sleep. He even dreamed. Oddly, when he awoke and recalled it, he had dreamed that Maji was an angel. An angel coming for him.

PART 5

62

Wilson Bryce was called back from Georgia to help the teams at the NSA and CIA trying to understand the new transmission data turned over by the University of Michigan. The report on the Georgia ballot sabotage was complete, and his own affidavit was among the supporting documents submitted to the Supreme Court with the president's petition challenging the election outcome. Others could do the last tidying up in Georgia.

The new lead on Lester Buddy Binton's access to the prestigious university's research systems was tantalizing, and Bryce was needed to help Jack Watson, Susan McShane, and the others. INTERPOL had chased down the transmission data from the Munich institute and cleared them as irrelevant to the interceptions of the American drone and the French fighter jet. The thought that an *American* institution might be the source—knowingly or not—of the cyber manipulation of military control channels had occurred to no one. That was, until the senior Syrian intelligence operative, trying to support his hope for asylum by providing credible information, disclosed Binton as his operative in Michigan. Buddy Binton was not a completely obscure figure to law enforcement or the university. The FBI had listed his Band of Free Brothers as a suspect antigovernment group. But that was based on only a single report from a former member who thought Binton could become dangerous if he ever found the financial resources to buy more firearms. To the bureau, there were too many hate groups and private militias who *were* dangerous, to devote attention to one that *could* become so. There was no serious follow-up. Also, the fact that the Free Brothers were not antiblack, and even had African American members, more or less immunized it from the diligent tracking of the ACLU, Southern Poverty Law Center, and other civil rights watchdogs.

As to officials and staff at the university, Binton was universally seen as a cranky, off-beat, odd, and harmless computer genius. Yes, he had extreme views and a loud mouth, but so did many others in the intellectual community, mostly on the other end of the political spectrum. And, yes, he was rumored to love and own guns—like half the population of Michigan.

He had earned a legitimate doctorate in computer sciences and engineering from the university, and that brought courtesy access to the institution's research laboratories and equipment, so long as no funding was required. As far as the university and its graduates were concerned, it was no different than a law school alumnus stopping by to use the law library. It happened all the time.

As they studied the Binton data, Bryce and the other experts benefited by the earlier work performed by Lars LaToure and the Max Plank director in Germany. The technical contrast between the character of the German students' work and Buddy Binton's was vivid and frightening. The European researchers' transmissions were, in every case, efforts merely to improve the quality and speed of the signal. But Binton's transmissions, in every case, were meant to disrupt, alter, or substitute control signals.

"This guy is throwing cyber grenades," Bryce said to the others. "One after another after another. They don't all explode. A lot are duds. But some do, and he learns from that and adjusts so that eventually he can target them with accuracy."

The team studied the work product compiled by the Michigan extremist over the past twelve months. They concluded Binton had steadily perfected the ability to send a contaminating signal to the Ukrainian satellite that then returned it to the aviation controls of a specific target. The data showed a frenzy of activity in the three weeks prior to the hijacking of the American drone in September, including transmissions that very morning. There followed a brief lull in his activity. It resumed in earnest the week before the overtaking of the French fighter jet.

Watson, McShane, and Bryce looked at each other, as if waiting to see who would make the declaration. Finally, it was Susan McShane who did.

"He's our man," she said.

A CASE OF FIRST IMPRESSION

The Supreme Court ordered expedited hearing and oral arguments on the president's petition. By law, the newly elected or reelected House and Senate members were to be sworn in on the second of January. In its order scheduling the oral argument, the court stated that it intended to rule promptly so as not to disrupt the congressional timetable.

Legal scholars agreed on one thing: if ever there was a case of true first impression, this was it. It meant that the questions before the court had never been ruled upon before. No judicial precedents applied because none existed. One of the lawyers slated to argue the case quipped that perhaps the originality of the case justified the extraordinarily brief time allowed to prepare for the hearing. "They know there's nothing to look up," he said.

To the watching public, the important question was simply who would be the next senator from Georgia. But to the court, Congress, and President Del Winters, a difficult constitutional question had to be decided first before any consideration even could be given to the issue of whether Margaret Westfall or Will Truitt would prevail electorally: Was the Elections Security and Reform Act's delegation to the president the authority to seek *federal* judicial intervention to upend an election conducted by a *state,* a violation of the Constitution's grant to the states of province over the conduct and manner of elections, including elections to congressional office?

And on this threshold issue the legal scholars were closely divided.

The State of Georgia, Senator Will Truitt, and, awkwardly, the sitting president's own party, argued it *was* such a violation and therefore unconstitutional. States controlled the polling places and the manner of casting and counting ballots, they stated. While noble in its intent—a remedy for fraud in the process—Congress had no right, and therefore neither did Del Winters, to do the state's work. The only constitutional remedy, they urged, was the one afforded under the law to candidate Westfall herself: a challenge to the *state's* election board for handling under its—and only its—discretion.

Arguing for the president and the executive branch, the solicitor general urged that Congress possessed inherent authority under the Constitution to make laws necessary for it to be effective and to protect the rights afforded under it. The right to vote, and to have one's voted counted *correctly* and free of tampering was a fundamental right that no state could claim as its exclusive province. If that were the case, the many cases striking down restrictive state rules on ballot access and voting qualification in the civil rights era, and subsequent federal statutes forbidding their reinstitution, were also invalid. Few lawyers would or could argue *that* point, the president's lawyer said.

As the single representative of the people selected by the *nation as a whole*, other than the vice president, the president was the appropriate person in whom to vest the power to seek rectification of a fraudulent federal election outcome, wheresoever it occurred. Congress, acting within its power, had chosen to so vest it.

A footnote to the president's brief noted—acidly—that among the nine-two senators voting in favor of the law when it was passed was "one Senator Will Truitt of Georgia."

Del read the brief before it was filed; she requested no changes. It was well-written and prepared, and her solicitor general was the constitutional lawyer, not her. Besides, she was preoccupied with two other issues more important to her than politics or even, for now, the constitutional balancing of federal and states' rights: the security of the nation's military arsenal from cyberspace hijacking; and the preservation of the country's nuclear secret in the war on terror—the Eaglets and their nest. And the latter depended on the safety of Stanley Bigelow, the man who modestly had called himself—in a private conversation with her eighteen months ago—an "accidental patriot" for his role in deploying the new weapons system.

Until now, no one connected the two threats. But suddenly, in the form of the perverted Lester "Buddy" Binton, they were heading toward intersection—perhaps tragically—in Michigan. She knew that as the president, she must give priority to the national security threats, notwithstanding her personal feelings for the senior citizen from Pittsburgh and his safety. Her duty was to the nation. The security of the country was more important than the well-being of any one citizen, even Stanley Bigelow. But it didn't help that her father was standing at the top of the staircase to the White House residence as she climbed the steps that evening. She was still three steps from him when he looked down to her with dour eyes sunken in a face of concern.

"Is there news on Stanley?" he asked.

Del knew there was, but that it wasn't good. The Syrian defector whose information had rushed attention to Michigan and Binton had been arrested and was in Russian custody. He could no longer help in the search for her father's friend. Stanley Bigelow's whereabouts remained unknown.

"There is, Dad," she said. "Let's go to the study."

64

★ ★ ★

THE LIEUTENANT FLIES AGAIN

Lieutenant Grey Boatwright's flight from Charleston Air Base was delayed an hour. These days, even the air force couldn't seem to fly on time.

Tyler Brew was irritated, but he should not have been. The cunctation was justified. The navigation systems at the Charleston drone command center were loaded only with international cartography, mainly of the Middle East and Africa. There were no domestic maps included in the software, and certainly none of Michigan. Base Commander Wilks had to requisition the digitized maps from Homeland Security and have a technician install them before Boatwright could fly the drone to the Midwest. It was a true achievement to complete the readiness as quickly as it was.

Captain Brew had selected the young air force lieutenant purposefully. There were other pilots with more time clocked on the small Eaglets. But no one had flown the new series under mission pressure since President Winters had ordered the drones' initial deployment two years earlier over Iran, just before Boatwright's graduation from flight school.

That maiden flight was the only one in which the secret Eaglets were armed with their nuclear payloads. They were sent up to retaliate *if* the Iranian government double-crossed the United States and bombed the thousands of vulnerable American troops then preparing to assault terrorists congregated in Afghanistan. Iran knew the attack was going to occur and had cooperated with on-the-ground advance intelligence about the terrorist positions. But the president worried it might be an ambush. American forces would be uniquely exposed before their movement against the terrorists. So, she sent up the Eaglets and their nuclear missiles to await her command. No one was more relieved than she when the Iranians kept their word, and the Eaglets were ordered back, their Talon missiles unfired.

Since then, Boatwright and others had flown the Eaglets in exercises intended to test the drones' maneuverability and surveillance capabilities. The lieutenant had excelled, showing the ability to take the craft above and below altitudes previously thought infeasible, and to cruise the drone at very low speeds and still maintain stability. Normally, high speed was a virtue in the chess game of military air war. But in the case of detailed surveillance imagery, speed was a negative. The slower the craft flew, the more concentrated and voluminous the images could be.

Boatwright's mathematical prowess and knowledge of physics made the difference. Unlike any other drone, the little Eaglet had vertical ascent and descent capability, with more precision—much more—than even the most advanced helicopters. It was designed that way so that it would never have to rest on land in open view. It could take off from and land in an underground deployment facility in Kuwait, the one secretly masterminded two years before by the civil engineer from Pittsburgh and constructed under the supervision of Colonel Helen Ames. Boatwright knew that with careful manipulation of the vertical takeoff and landing pneumatics during flight, he could reduce operating speed dramatically and, with careful steering adjustments, still maintain vibration-free control. And all in stealth.

Of course, the last thing he envisioned he'd be looking for while gliding silently over treetops were clumps of camper trailers, deserted mobile homes, and any sign of a tall, old overweight citizen. But when Brew called, he was eager, and informative too. He told the Navy SEAL that the new Eaglet surveillance package had aerial infrared sensors meant to detect concentrations of ammunition.

"I can dial up those sensors to the limit," he told Brew. "If these guys are an armed group, they'll have ammo. It will show."

"But they won't have *pallets* of ammo, Boat," Brew said. "They're not a regular army."

"Captain, these things will pick up three boxes of shotgun shells."

The lieutenant flew the drone from Charleston at high speed and military altitude until descending at ten thirty in the evening over Lake Erie near Toledo and the Michigan border. Bobby Beach had used an emergency FBI line to reach the FAA that afternoon to alert them that a federal law enforcement action required clear airspace over the eight Michigan counties between nine thirty that night until one thirty the next morning.

"*No can do* on Wayne County, or all of Oakland," the FAA official told him.

"Why not?"

"Ever heard of Detroit Metropolitan Airport? Its actual name is Detroit Metropolitan *Wayne County* Airport. It's a huge commercial hub. If you block all flights in and out of that baby, you've got a national incident on your hands."

"Can you at least divert them so that no plane flies within ten miles of the border with Washtenaw County?" Bobby Beach waited nervously for three minutes while the official conferred with the air traffic controllers in Detroit.

"That we *can* do," the official said.

"Good. That will work."

"Who do I thank for this favor?" the FAA official asked. "I'm sure about four hundred airline pilots will want to know."

"The president of the United States," Bobby Beach said.

Boatwright started at the center-point of the eight-county area and swept the drone back and forth like a lawn mower over a ballpark outfield. He managed to reduce the speed to 112 miles per hour at an average altitude of four hundred feet. Each pass canvassed a three-hundred-yard swath, the range at which the technology could deliver crystal-clear video. The cameras on the belly of the Eaglet whirled hundreds of images a minute directly to a computer at the NSA where they were sorted to cull any, all, and only images that could possibly be depicting adult persons, white pickup trucks, or structures tagged as containing ammunition by the infrared sensors. Each culled frame displayed a GPS coordinate.

A team of analysts huddled at the NSA, aided by recognition software, resorted the images as they arrived, removing thousands of irrelevant sightings. Women, children, and short men; white trucks parked in movie theatre and car lots; and thousands of infrared ammunition markers emanating from vehicles on roadways, single family residences, and gun stores.

The images that survived the cut were sent immediately to Brew, Bechant, and Bobby Beach in the Ann Arbor conference room. They divided the labor. Brew studied all the images of persons. He knew Stanley the best and as much about Buddy Binton as the other two, which was little. The defector had described him only as white, burly, and unkempt. The old sheriff poured over the images of pickup trucks. Many were partial images; the whole of the vehicle was not visible, and in some, barely viewable at all. But Bechant studied each with care. Bobby Beach took the images that revealed an ammunition marking by the infrared sensors. He wasn't an ATF agent with specialized training in weapons and ammunition types but, of the three of them, he was closest.

It was impossible to keep up with the stream of images flowing in from Boatwright's drone as the local sheriff's deputy brought in the sorted piles. A new pile was slapped on the long conference room table before a fourth of the last stack was finished.

"I feel like Lucille Ball making chocolates on an assembly line," Weldon said. The younger men were puzzled by his reference and looked at him blankly; he decided it was not the time to educate them.

But Brew, Bobby Beach, and Weldon were not deterred, working away in near silence, determined to narrow the search materially by sunrise. At three in the morning, Captain Brew suddenly stood up, holding a color image. He pulled it close to his eyes and turned it to different angles. The image had been recorded at eleven forty-four.

"Look at this, Bobby," he said, handing it to the FBI man.

The image showed a dozen men standing around two burning drums. Most were holding amber beer bottles in gloved hands. Battered trailers were partially in view around them in all directions. A propane cylinder was lying lengthwise. The roof of one of the structures could be made out, throwing smoke from a pipe in its roof. A silver-haired, heavyset man, larger than any of the others, stood hatless near one of the drums, apparently seeking warmth. His red checkered shirt collar was exposed beneath a sweater.

"Do you think that's Stanley?"

"The one without a hat?"

"Yeah."

"It *could* be," Bobby Beach said. "He's tall and big, for sure. Even slouching, he's taller than the other guys. And he looks a lot older too."

"Weldon," Brew said, "is there anything in your pile for this coordinate? Bobby, check yours too."

It took them fifteen minutes to rifle through the hundreds of images before them. It proved a valuable pause. First Bobby Beach, then Weldon, found adjoining coordinates. Taken together, the three showed a cluster of at least twenty trailers. Nineteen of the twenty, all but the one closest to the burning drums in which the men appeared, were marked with the ammunition signature. And the old sheriff's image displayed the front end of a new white pickup truck at the rear of the site, bordering a lake.

"Bingo," said Weldon. "Where the hell is this place?"

They moved down the table to the county maps.

"There," said Brew. He pointed to the extreme northwest corner of Washtenaw, near the border to Jackson County. A large area encompassing the spot was shaded. "Why is the map shaded that way?" he asked.

"The shading designates state-owned land," Weldon said. "See there, the tiny print. Waterloo State Recreation Area."

In Michigan, there are land masses designated as state parks, in which *all* the property within their confines is publicly owned and maintained. But the state has other land accumulations, some of them very expansive, in which *most*, but not all the property within its borders is state-owned. These areas are dotted with privately owned parcels, dating back to nineteenth century land grant programs encouraging western settlement. Michigan differentiates these quasi-public lands from its formal state parks by calling them state recreation areas. Waterloo is one of the largest. A dozen hiking trails and lakes run through it, and three lakeside state campgrounds are within its borders, operated seasonally by the state.

Brew called the NSA team in Washington and asked them to send immediately all imagery gathered by Boatwright within a thousand-yard radius of the promising coordinates.

"Time to get some sleep," he said. "We'll scout it at daybreak."

65

PLANNING A RESCUE

State Route 52 is the principal north-south highway through rural Michigan west of Ann Arbor. It crosses Interstate 94 at the town of Chelsea, a quiet, classic railroad town on the old line between Detroit and Chicago. Amtrak passenger service still runs through "now and again," the locals say. Unreliability forecloses more specificity. It doesn't matter, they say; the train doesn't stop in Chelsea anyway, and nobody can remember anymore when it did.

Main Street's three traffic signals were still flashing their unremitting yellow caution lights—the town dispensed with red and green between eleven at night and six in the morning—as the three leaders of the rescue team and L. T. Kitt rolled through before sunrise the next morning. Sheriff Bechant was at the wheel, in a bright mood, despite the early hour.

"Michigan is growing on me," he said. "These gentle hills are nice. All the woods. And this time of year, you can see right through them, with all the leaves and brush down. Which we've got to remember, by the way."

The southern lawman's point was sound. Care would be required in scouting the trailer grounds. Visibility from the camp up through the wooded hills surrounding it would be better than the four of them wished, owing to the sparse December leafage.

Grey Boatwright's drone surveillance placed the field of trailers—thirty-two in all—in a sixty-five-acre field bordering Cedars Lake Road at the northwestern edge of the county. To reach it, the team drove north out of Chelsea to Blue Meadow Road, then west for five, hilly, bending miles to Cedars Lake. At the intersection lay the only commerce within a five-mile radius: a sleepy beverage market catering to fishermen in the warm months and hunters in the rest. The trailer camp was less than a mile north on Cedars Lake Road.

"Our boys must frequent this place," Weldon said, as they turned left toward the camp field. "S'pose we should stop in when its opens to see if they know anything?"

If stealth were not vital to the rescue plan, the others would have agreed. But they all knew that if this encampment did in fact look to be holding Stanley, the siege to bring him out would probably occur the very next night. The odds were not high that anyone working in the market would know very much about the old engineer. They adjudged the risk greater that Binton would learn that inquiries were made about him. As is so often the case, the element of surprise was the single most important factor in getting the clumsy engineer out safely. They agreed no visit would be made to the country market.

Weldon slowly turned left onto little Belanger Road, a gravel passage that bordered the broad field on their right. Through the thicket and trees, they could see the old trailers and campers strewn low in the field near the wooded boundary on the far side. Cedars Lake, small and shallow—its surface water less than a hundred acres—bordered the field at its left rear edge, close to the structures.

"Don't stop here, Weldon," Bobby Beach said. "We might be in sight from down there if somebody looks up and across the field."

As the road climbed, a clearing in the woods appeared on the left, out of sight of the trailers. It was marked by a small wooden sign as a lake access point for small boats and fishermen. "Here we go," said Weldon. "This'll be just fine." The sheriff hopped out quickly and stepped to the back hatch. He withdrew four bright orange hunting vests and four heavy caps with matching orange bills. He handed one of each to the other three and donned his own items. Brew balked.

"Won't we be seen in these things, Weldon?" Brew said. But the Navy SEAL saw that Bobby Beach and Kitt were pulling on their bright vests and already wearing the hats.

"Best way to get noticed out here this time of year is to walk around *without* these on," Weldon said. Bobby Beach and Kitt looked at the Navy SEAL in agreement. Brew understood their point and put on his vest too. Weldon reached into the rear of the SUV and unlatched a weapons case. He extracted four shotguns and handed them out. "These too, gentlemen and lady," he said. "Don't worry, mine is the only one loaded."

"That's what worries me," said Bobby Beach. Weldon ignored him.

They walked together and took mental notes of everything they saw across the field. The structures were clustered in the northwestern quadrant of the acreage, farthest from the main road. The only driveway into the campground itself wound down a hill from that road. They saw that the entrance drive was obviously not maintained in the winter, or any other time.

It was serpentine and pockmarked with innumerable deep craters. Brew and Weldon were pleased. The only way out for the militants in vehicles would be that rough trail. They would have to drive so slowly that the assault team could pursue and overtake them on foot, if necessary.

It was still thirty minutes to sunrise. They counted sixteen structures with inside illumination; nearly all the rest were lit outside—above or next to their entry doors. Twenty-two vehicles were lodged around the site, all near the trailers, about half of them pickup trucks. The four of them divided up the trailers eight apiece and watched them intently for five minutes, looking for movement in them. Brew drew on a sketchpad. They observed moving figures or shadows in twelve structures and assumed that many of the others were also occupied by sleeping militants. No one saw Stanley, or anyone who might be him.

Bobby Beach and Weldon then walked up and around Belanger Road past the pull over area where they had parked out of view, scouting the vantage point from the lakeside to the trailers. It was marshy and easily viewable from the structures. They quickly ruled it out as either a staging area or point of assault.

Brew and Kitt walked into the field toward the trailers. The closest of the ramshackle structures sat about seven hundred yards ahead of them at a considerably lower elevation. Less than a hundred yards into the field the land dipped severely and then rose back up to form a high natural ridge across the field's entire width. Brew quickly concluded it would be the best staging place for the assault on the trailers. Even standing at full height, he could not see over the ridge to the structures beyond. It meant the militiamen would not be able to see his team either as it gathered. He climbed to the top of the ridge and studied the terrain between it and the strewn trailers. The span was not as flat as he expected from the satellite imagery. There were ample mounds and moguls to use as cover positions. Kitt especially liked one low spot that appeared deeper than the other swales, located at about the five o'clock position in front of the cluster of structures. She pointed it out to Brew.

"I can go there with Augie and wait," she said. "He and I can go down to the buildings from there once everyone else is in place." Brew nodded assent.

Fifteen minutes later they were together at the SUV in the lake access area. Weldon suggested the grassy alcove there would be a suitable holding area for the medical units. There was a looped driveway around it; the surface was gravel but smooth and surprisingly groomed. He pointed to the barren oval in the center.

"We can fit at least five medical trucks in there," he said. What happened next caused them to wish one of the units was already there. It was the only mishap of the scouting trip.

The demure sheriff loaded the shotguns and hunting apparel into the back hatch, but he struggled to reach the top of the lifted door to press its closing button. He had to get up on his tiptoes on both feet to get a finger to it, and as the heavy hatch door came down, he lost his balance and started to the ground. He reached up above the bumper for support and the descending heavy hatch gashed his left hand between the thumb and forefinger. Weldon was not given to profanity, but the circumstances produced an extended exception. Kitt retrieved a first aid kit from the glove box and Brew cleaned, gauzed, and bandaged the wound. Weldon was embarrassed, but Brew looked at him and smiled. "No problem, Weldon," he said. "Maybe this is a good omen. Maybe this will be our worst casualty."

But none of them really believed it.

With Kitt at the wheel for the drive back, they took a detour to inspect a secluded town hall building about eleven miles from the encampment. The local sheriff had suggested it to Weldon as a place where the leaders could assemble the entire team in advance of the attack. He said the force could even stay overnight there, if required. The right preassault gathering place was another thing important to preserving the element of surprise. Between the leaders and their respective subteams, the mission force would comprise over forty armed soldiers, FBI agents, and sheriff's deputies. The SEALs and special agents were en route now to Michigan. It was not a routine matter to keep such a group, most in uniform, from notice.

The Lindon Township Hall fit the bill, all agreed, when Kitt pulled into its hidden drive, just off M-52. It was a simple building, set back from the road in a wooded area. It featured an open, main meeting room on the ground floor, and a basement where arms could be stored until departure. A rear parking lot would keep the vehicles, including the local law enforcement cruisers, out of sight.

They were leaving the township hall when Brew's cell phone buzzed.

"Captain, its Vern Lazar. We found your 'Tug.' He remembers you too. He's on his way," he said. "With that harness you wanted for him."

66

★ ★ ★

BLOODSHED, AND PROBABLY MUCH OF IT

The nation reeled from the reports of election fraud in Georgia and murder in Boston. Even the mediacrats were startled at how the events held the public interest for news cycle after news cycle. The cable television torrent seemed to preoccupy everyone except President Del Winters. She was laser focused on something else: the operation to extract Stanley Bigelow from the rural, lakeside trailer park in Michigan. She thought the mission had developed with electrifying speed. Too much speed. It worried her. Tactical plans were rushed—specialized resources pulled together frantically. And all on the report of an obscure INTERPOL investigator in Stockholm relying on information from a Syrian defector.

In her two and half years in the Oval Office, Del Winters had learned to trust her instincts. To a point. When it was possible, she resisted rapid judgments based on incomplete information or made without the benefit of counsel from multiple trusted advisers. But as she looked back on her many decisions, she knew that in most of them her final call was pretty much what her instincts had instructed from the beginning. And this Michigan raid-in-the-making had unsettled her from the get-go.

Brew and Bobby Beach had been clear. Bloodshed, and probably a lot of it, was a near certainty in the raid even if it turned out that Stanley was not being held there. The paramilitary anarchists holed up in the trailer camp were armed to the teeth with automatic weapons and explosives. Negotiation was not even in the playbook, the element of surprise being deemed indispensable. A nighttime all-out assault was the only viable extraction option.

Sitting alone in the study of the White House residence, she had still withheld approval for the assault even as Brew, Bobby Beach, and Weldon Bechant gathered their team in the Lyndon Township Community Hall tucked off Michigan Route 52. She sat without any papers. Several times she rose, stretched, and paced nervously to the bookshelves, then returned to her chair.

Her father pushed the door halfway open, looking at her but saying nothing, waiting. She paused and finally nodded. He entered and took the other chair.

"I have a feeling I know what's worrying you," he said.

"And what is that?"

"It's not the political risk, Delores. Even with everything else about the election. Which, by the way, is really a dog's breakfast." It was one of those odd expressions of his that seemed truer than they should be.

"That I know," the president said.

"It's not even *all* of the human risk."

He reached to a side table and gathered a short glass and the neck of a bottle of bourbon with the same hand.

"When did we start stocking Maker's?" he asked.

"Not to your liking?"

"No, no. It's fine. Very fine."

"What do you mean about *all* the human risk?"

He poured himself two fingers of the bourbon and looked quizzically, invitingly, at his daughter. She shook her head no. He didn't press the suggestion.

"Brew, the FBI team, the old fella from Charleston, they're all in there on purpose," he said. "They know why they are there. They all signed up for it. They're good at what they do. And the militiamen are violent thugs. Homegrown terrorists."

He looked away from her, and there was a lengthy silence.

"None of *them* are your real worry," he said. "It's Stanley that worries you."

Del drew a deep breath and stirred in her chair.

"I *am* fond of him," she said.

"I am too. You know that."

"He is just a citizen doing the right thing. Because I asked him to."

"I am not saying you are wrong to be hesitant."

"Then what *are* you saying?"

The First Father got up from his chair and looked at his daughter.

"You understand, Del, I know my place."

"Yes."

"This is your decision. Yours alone."

"You know I understand that."

"But when you make it, you might consider that in a strange way, as bad as the mess is, the conditions are really so optimal. We two are not the only ones who care about Stanley. This is an unusual situation, the whole story. Kitt and that dog. They love the man like he's their father. Brew. My God, he will take any risk to himself to protect Stanley, reluctant as he may have been about him in the beginning. I have the same feeling about the FBI guy, Beach. He's become attached to old Stanley since all their time in Charleston. And the sheriff is licking his chops to see this work out and have the chance to tell about it. The bottom line is there's never been a rescue force so committed."

He paused, ostensibly for a sip of his bourbon. In truth, he wanted his daughter to have a moment to let his words sink in. "I've been around the block, Delores. In war, in peace. I doubt there's ever been a rescue force so personally motivated."

A staff aide peeked in to see if anything was needed. The president thanked him and waved him off, absent her usual smile.

"I see what you mean," Del said. "You're saying I *owe* this to Stanley. I owe him this chance. Because there may never be a better one."

Her father nodded. She picked up her secure cell phone from the cocktail table. Just two digits produced Defense Secretary Lazar's line. He answered on the first ring.

"Move on Brew's command," she said flatly.

"Yes, Madame President."

Henry Winters didn't ask this time. He reached for a second glass and poured his daughter a drink.

67

A GREEN LIGHT

Fifty-nine seconds later, Captain Brew's phone vibrated. It would have been sooner, but the communication channel had to be scrubbed three times by Pentagon software before the defense secretary could speak on the line. There was no way to reach the Navy SEAL and his team without pinging rural cell towers. And once an uncontrolled tower was pinged, the line had to be sanitized.

"You are authorized to go, Captain," Lazar said calmly. It was eight-fifteen in the evening on December 21, the winter solstice, the longest night of the year.

"When?"

"On your command."

"It may not be best tonight."

"She said, 'On *your* command.'"

"I will let you know when we intend to move," Brew said.

"Use this line. But leave yourself an extra minute to make the call. The lines will have to be cleaned up before you can talk."

It was not a trivial operational detail, and both men knew it. In a siege plan with multiple advancing components at separate intervals, not to mention the timed alignment of backup and medical resources, sixty seconds could seem like an hour, and make a fatal difference. It had already been decided by the president that real-time remote viewing would not be provided to her in the White House. And even though Brew was approved to move at any time of his choosing, his authority was, in truth he knew, to move at any time *after* a final notice to the president that the launch was about to be made. *About* to begin, not *already under way.* The final notice to her was an operational requirement in critical missions that Del Winters had insisted on from her first deployments as commander-in-chief. It was not a popular rule of engagement among some military commanders. Earlier presidents had not required such a last "check-in," as the command called it, and some of the generals didn't like it. One of them had the courage to raise it with her in a general planning review.

"Why do you need the final 'check-in' when you've already authorized the action?" he'd asked.

"Because I like the chance to change my mind, General," she'd answered.

Many in the command agreed with her, and more than a few had resolved to recommend her practice to future commanders-in-chief. World communications, and the events that they triggered, now traversed the globe at blinding speed. Who could know what might transpire in the hours, or even a quarter of a single hour, between a presidential authorization and its execution? New intelligence might erupt out of anywhere. A pertinent tyrant halfway around the world might be upended in a palace revolt. Hell, he might fall in the shower and split his head open. Yes, this president wanted the prerogative to act or not act, with the benefit of *all* available information, right down to the moment of execution. She didn't mind the fact that the general in the planning meeting had asked for her reasoning—in fact, she admired him for it. But to her answer, he was unwise.

"You know, Madame President," he had said, "a person who changes her mind at the last minute appears weak."

He never earned his next star.

At the township hall in Michigan, Brew motioned to Bobby Beach and Sheriff Bechant. He led them outside into the evening air.

"We're green lighted," Brew said. He looked up and around at the clear night sky. It was three hours past the early sunset, but the sky remained palely illuminated. "What do you think?"

"Too much light," said Bobby Beach. The quarter moon burned brightly above, the same color as the senior agent's thick crop of hair, gleaming in the lunar reflection. "At least now. We need some cloud cover to tamp this down."

"Weldon?" asked Brew.

"I'm with Bobby," the southern sheriff said. His bruised and cut hand was plainly bothering him. He rubbed its bandage gingerly against his side.

"Hurts, huh?" asked Brew.

"Worst part is it's my bourbon hand." But they all knew the old lawman's injury was irrelevant to anything but his pride. At seventy-six, he wouldn't be moving down the hill in any event. He would stay in a borrowed, unmarked car up and out of sight. He would manage communications with the medical support and off-site backup units.

The three of them and L. T. Kitt had already agreed on the tactical assault plan, insofar as it could be decided in advance. It was as detailed as possible, but the single, huge unknown variable—in *which* of the dozens of trailers was Stanley held, if any of them—made for a boggling number of contingencies. Kitt and the Charleston sheriff, experienced with canines in field work, were confident that Augie would find the right trailer if given enough time, but Brew and Bobby Beach were not so sure.

If the dog swept the camp and returned to base at the top of the hill without scenting Stanley, Bobby Beach and the sheriff would have to lead their teams on a structure by structure "knock and search" to find and arrest—or engage—Buddy Binton and his mob. If the dog *did* circle a trailer and come to rest at it, as Kitt said he would if Stanley was inside, Brew's SEAL team would have to choose *then* its precise assault approach to it. Much depended on the shape and size of the selected trailer, its placement within the camp, the number of viable points of ingress it presented, and the natural cover available for the surging rescuers.

But one physical fact applied no matter what: the *least* ambient light the better. The slight night aura rising above the tree line from the small industrial city of Jackson, just twelve miles to the west, could not be avoided. But they knew it would be foolish to move in appreciable moonlight if there was any reason to believe it might lessen in coming hours.

Brew walked to the picnic table where L. T. sat near Augie and Nelson. The dogs lay prone and unleashed, on either side of the table, their heads up and alert.

"I know I told you to be ready at dark," he said to her, looking up again into the moonlight. He pointed toward the dogs. "Will it affect them if we wait."

"How long?"

"Three, four hours. Hoping for cloud cover."

"Not if they sleep before they're sent. Nelson is in his prime; he may not need to be as rested. But Augie will have been alert six hours or more. That's on the edge, at his age."

"Then get them down," said Brew. "We'll look at it again before midnight."

L. T. nodded, rose from the picnic table, and walked under a nearby tree. Augie and Nelson followed her until she turned and knelt to speak to them. Each of the dogs then walked in a tight circle, repeating it twice, then gently collapsed to the ground and lay on his side. It seemed a welcomed order in the circumstances. A minute later they were sleeping.

68

AIR FORCE ONE

Helen Ames-Bigelow answered on the third ring.

"Helen?" the voice said.

"Yes?"

"Helen, it's the president."

Helen wondered why she didn't recognize Del Winters's voice immediately. She knew she ought to. After all, it was the president's fourth call to her since Stanley's abduction. Maybe, she thought later, it was because she hoped it was *not* her calling. Del's serious tone mirrored her timbre on the first of the calls, immediately after Stanley had been taken. On the second reach-out, merely to inform her that Bobby Beach, Tyler Brew, and Sheriff Bechant were on the ground in Ann Arbor after receiving a promising lead, her voice had been more uplifted, even casual. And on the third, to inform her that drone images may have located Stanley's holding place in rural Michigan, she had sounded energetic, optimistic. But when President Del Winters called herself "the president," as she just had, it carried gravity.

"Oh," Helen said. Then nervously, "Thank you for calling." It seemed the thing to say, though her head and heart were bursting with what she wanted truly to say, but did not: *Why* are you calling? The president mooted the question.

"We are going in for Stanley, probably tonight," the president said.

"In Michigan?"

"Yes."

"You are sure he is there?"

"No, but the odds are good."

"Who will go in for him?"

"A joint team. SEALs, the FBI, local law enforcement. Tyler Brew will lead the mission." *The "mission"*. Helen wondered if the president used that term just as a matter of course, or if she chose it because both she and Helen were military people.

"I thought Brew had aged out of field work."

"He insisted. I waived him. He handpicked the SEAL team. Nine of them. And Bobby Beach is there too, with nine other special agents. Plus L. T. Kitt and a group of Michigan county sheriff's deputies loaned to Weldon Bechant." The president paused, anticipating the question that did not come.

"And Augie is there too," the president said, finally.

"Oh."

The president could not tell whether Helen meant "Oh, good," or "Or No." It was the first time she had sensed ambiguity in the words of the usually clear and straight-speaking reserves colonel.

"They think he can help us find Stanley in there," she said. "Kitt has been working with him, using the clothes you gave her."

"So, the two males in my life are *both* in danger," Helen said, for the first time a trace of lightness in her voice.

"I am afraid so," the president reciprocated.

Neither spoke for a few moments.

"Helen, I can't tell you how badly I feel about this."

Helen didn't respond, but the president sensed she was welling up tears.

She described the location to Helen, how the many trailers were strewn over a low-lying sixty-acre rolling field abutting a small lake an hour west of Detroit near Jackson. Stanley could be in any of the ramshackle trailers, if he was there at all. At least a dozen paramilitary extremists were scattered through the camp, and there were probably more not spotted during Brew's advance surveillance. She explained that all foreseeable extraction methods had been studied and how she herself had asked whether it would be safer to wait until the militiamen tried to move Stanley, in which case his precise whereabouts would be known. But how the team leaders believed that if that option presented itself at all, the captors would be awake and alert. And worst of all, if they became convinced that the Syrian agent was not coming as promised, instead of moving Stanley they might kill him before even leaving the encampment. That outcome grew more likely the longer the rescue raid was delayed.

"I had to make the decision," the president said. "I ordered the rescue attempt on Brew's command. I could not ask you first, though I wished I could, because your husband's life is at risk."

"I understand," Helen said, now composed.

"I couldn't because it's a matter of national security on account of his earlier work. And because we believe the militia leader holding Stanley also orchestrated the drone hijacking and the attack on Israel."

"My God," Helen said.

"You mustn't share that with anyone."

"Of course."

"But I want to be there when it ends," the president said. "No matter how it ends."

Helen said nothing.

"For Stanley," the president said, "for Stanley, I want to be there. And I would like you to have the choice to be there too. If you want that."

Helen did not hesitate.

"I do," Helen said.

"Good, then. An agent from the Pittsburgh FBI office will be at your entrance in thirty minutes. Will that work for you?"

"Of course."

"She will drive you to the Pittsburgh airport to meet me at Air Force One on the tarmac. We'll fly from there to the old Willow Run air field near Ann Arbor. We won't be seen there. The Secret Service will drive us then to Washtenaw County. God willing, we'll leave together with Stanley. If he is well."

69

★ ★ ★

MOONLIGHT IN MICHIGAN

At nine thirty, Brew asked Bobby Beach to send a single FBI agent from his team to act as a sentry in the woods above the trailer camp. It was vital to monitor any comings or goings there and to confirm that all was quiet should Brew decide to mount the assault. When that time came, the extraction team would have to travel from its staging center at the township hall and assemble at the top of the hill above the trailers. Brew wanted a motionless target, if possible.

But he worried that moving the entire team together in a convoy was unwise, even though the vehicles all would be unmarked. It would be unusual for six dark SUVs and Suburbans and Tahoes to move together on the quiet country roads. Brew and Beach reasoned that the trailer camp had not been chosen by the extremists arbitrarily. It was likely that a member of the group lived nearby, and quite possibly on the route the team would have to take to reach it. And if the captors were diligent, their own sentry—or sentries—would be watching Cedars Lake

Road from both approaches to the trailers. So, they drew up two routes from Lyndon Township to the lakeside conclave. Bobby Beach and old Sheriff Bechant would lead their teams to the attack site on the most direct route, taking Blue Meadow Road west off M 52, then left on Cedars Lake. Brew would lead the SEALs on a more circuitous route, through the town of Chelsea where Interstate 94 provided access to Cedars Lake from the opposite direction.

Bobby Beach had driven both routes late the previous night, carefully timing each in the light traffic. He and Brew then charted a precise departure schedule for each vehicle. None would follow close behind another; for each route, the team's vehicles would depart at one-minute intervals and travel at stipulated speeds noted on a chart for each driver. All would extinguish their headlights, and some would slow their speed as they came near the assault site so that all six would arrive in darkness at nearly the same time.

It was important too that the team's advance sentry not be observed. So that no vehicle would be parked on the road near the site, Bobby Beach drove his agent to a spot around a bend four hundred yards east of the of the gravel drive down to the trailers and left him on the roadside next to the forest. His agent wore a Kevlar vest and thigh wraps and carried two automatic handguns with extra ammo magazines.

"If we go tonight, stay in the trees until we show up. You'll go down the hill in the second wave, with me," he told the agent. "And no cell calls to us or anyone else unless there is a disruption to report or you're in trouble. We'll text you to say that we're either on our way to launch or that we're not going tonight and are coming to pick you up."

The agent nodded and stepped out of the car, softly closing the door, and jogged into the woods.

When the FBI leader returned to the township hall, Brew was waiting for him in the drive, looking up at the night sky.

"Clouding over," Brew said. "What do you think?"

"It's better. It'll be better yet in an hour or so."

"Darker?"

"Maybe, maybe not," Bobby Beach said. "But they'll have had more to drink for sure."

Brew smiled. "So will Weldon," he said.

"Oh, not tonight, Brew. You can count on Weldon. And his men."

"He put down a third of a bottle last night."

"He knew we weren't going last night. Believe me, Brew, you can count on him."

"I'd like to pull everyone together inside and go over the plan one more time," the Navy SEAL said.

The main room of the rural township hall was what you would expect. An austere space with a gray linoleum floor, bare-bulbed fluorescent lighting, scarred metal banquet tables and a hodgepodge of folding chairs. Ventilation was poor. A tall oscillating fan hummed near the rear door, offering minor relief. Some of the team members were standing in small groups near the corners. Brew waved them to the tables and most sat down, but the SEALs and Tug stood together behind the rear tables, at attention. The captain asked Bobby Beach and the sheriff to stand with him in the front of the room. A wooden easel held a broad pad of white poster paper, placed horizontally, on which Brew drew at the top an assortment of irregularly shaped small boxes representing the trailers and sheds at the assault site.

"Not to scale, obviously," he said. "Take out your maps."

The only sounds in the room were the quiet buzz of the fan and the rustling of the thick plastic-coated single-sheet charts that each team member pulled from a pocket and unfolded. Only the three leaders and L. T. Kitt had visited the target location. The others all relied on the satellite maps that Brew had secured the day before from the Defense Intelligence Agency.

The DIA images were nothing like the foggy impressions anyone could call up on Google. They were crystal clear and, though in color, tonally adjusted to simulate how they would appear in darkness. Door and window frames were especially vivid, almost as if outlined in bold. This was important, as so many of the trailers looked similar, especially from afar. But the pictures of them on the map were highly defined, and each structure was numbered sequentially with the center-most trailer enumerated as "1," and each of the others tagged in a series of clockwise rings, like a snail. During the raid, Brew and Bobby Beach would be directing individual movements through the earpieces by reference to the numbered structures. The idea was that the calling of a low number, say 3, 4, or 5, was sending them near the inner ring of the snail. A "middigit," like 9, 10, or 11, designated a structure in the intermediate ring, and so on, to the outermost ring on which trailers 29, 30, 31, and 32 were situated.

"One more time," Brew began. "Any questions, speak up when you have them. Unless the clouds move out, we're going in an hour."

The Navy SEAL was cool, matter of fact. He drew a crescent line near the bottom of the poster.

"We gather *here*," he said. "This puts us behind a natural rise in the field about a hundred yards from the roadside. We're looking southwest. Even standing, we can't be seen from the buildings below." He drew a circle to the left of the gathering spot, nearer to the road. "Sheriff Bechant will stay here. He'll coordinate all the off-site resources, including medical support and backup if the thing goes bad and we have a battle on our hands. Once the assault is under way, Weldon will call in the medical people to have them on site and ready. There's a clearing a few yards east of his station where they will set up. Any seriously wounded are to be taken there."

"The bad guys too?" asked a SEAL from the back.

"After we stand down, yes. Only our own while there's still firing. And check with me or Bobby first. We'll be hearing from all of you about the militants' individual movements. We'll know if it's clear to get to the medics. We don't want you taking anybody up under fire."

Next Brew drew three short lines evenly spaced across the field, about a third of the distance to the first trailers below.

"On my command, SEALs will run down to each of these positions and hold there. Three to each spot. You know who you are and which place you assume." Brew had huddled earlier with the SEALs and made the assignments. "At the same time, Tug and I move to here." He drew a small circle immediately behind the three-SEAL team in the center of the forward line. "Agent Kitt and Augie come right behind us and hold in this gully," he pointed, "until we're all in position."

Brew then explained that Bobby Beach's FBI crew would position themselves in three counterpart teams *behind* the SEAL assaulters, initially behind the cover provided by the grassy natural ridge running the entire width of the field. Once the SEALs were up and running down the hill, at Brew's next command they would rush to the SEALs' original positions and, if necessary, provide cover to them from prone positions. If the SEALs made it without resistance to an inner perimeter line a mere sixty feet from the first trailers, Bobby Beach's team would then race forward and take up new positions behind the SEALs, spreading out in a crescent ninety to one-hundred feet from the trailers.

"So that's the assault team's positioning as we wait to find out where Stanley Bigelow is in there, assuming he is." Brew told them. "I'll cover what happens next in a minute. First, though, Weldon, will you talk about the outer perimeter?"

"Thank you, Captain," he said formally. "I hope you all recognize me in this outfit. Not my usual uniform, and all, and no hat. Just didn't go." Everyone laughed, even the normally serious Brew. The small old lawman did cut quite a figure in baggy camouflage pants cinched high with camouflage suspenders. No one could imagine where he had found *that* accessory.

"My team, the brave fellas from Washtenaw County, and Nelson, my Charleston dog, will hold the outer perimeter." He took the marker from Brew and drew a long horseshoe line extending from the road shoulder in both directions and then up through the woods on either side of the trailer grounds, all the way to the lake. "These militiamen might stay in their trailers and fight, or they may run like hell. If they run, my team's job is to contain and stop them."

"What about the back? The lakeside?" asked one of the deputies.

"Nothing there but real thin ice, as of the pictures we got three hours ago," the sheriff answered. "Even puddles on it. Won't hold a man. Nobody'll run in that direction."

Brew and Beach nodded agreement.

The issue of line of command remained. The sheriff addressed it and, on this point, with a serious tone. He said that Brew had overall command and that everyone should take any order he gave. If the captain went down, Bobby Beach assumed command, with the same authority. Only if both fell, would the sheriff be in charge.

Brew interjected, because he knew his men would be surprised.

"And that means, Sheriff Bechant commands everyone, including the SEALs and Tug, if it comes to that," he said.

Brew moved close to the front row in the hall, in front of L. T. Kitt.

"Agent Kitt is drawing the short straw. Once the SEALs and Bobby's teams are in position, she will go down to the trailers first, with the dog. She needs to stay close enough to the dog to read him and command him. Her eyes must stay on Augie. She'll unleash him, and he'll sniff around the trailers until he finds our package. Assuming the package *is* in any one of them. We hope he'll circle that trailer and sit down in front of it. If he does that, Tug and I will charge it for Stanley, with three SEALs backing us."

Brew explained that the highest priority was reaching Stanley and getting him out and up the hill to safety. "He's a very big man. Old, overweight, and not fit." Kitt looked up, tempted to object mildly to Brew's characterization but resisted. Augie, sitting at her side, pulled in his tongue and raised his snout seriously, appearing affronted. "He may be hurt when we find him. Or he may be very weak. We're not going to wait for him to get *himself* out of there," Brew said. "We're *pulling* him out. I'm going to strap him to Tug and Tug's going to drag him, whether he's able to keep up or not."

Tug stood up, and Brew pointed to his reinforced harness and belt, with hand grips and fasteners on each hip. It looked like a parachutist's harness with an exaggerated belt.

"If Stanley's not hurt and can move freely, he'll grab onto these rubber grips," Brew said. The thick rings hung from each side of the belt, like huge O-rings. "If he can't carry his own weight, I'll latch him to these." He pointed to a pair of padded wrist fasteners, resembling oversized handcuffs. "Tug does the rest, covered by me and the SEALs."

Tug's real name was Francis Birmingham. Brew had told Kitt he had more nicknames than any soldier he ever knew. One Rangers unit called him "Berm," another "Ham," a third "Hambone." But everyone also knew him as "Tug," coined by an early commander on account of the Ranger's short height, just five feet five inches, extra-wide girth, and tree trunk legs. "Ranger," the commander had said affectionately, "you look like a tugboat standing on end!" And to the special agent from Pittsburgh, L. T. Kitt, an attractive tugboat. Maybe it was his unusual physical build topped by a handsome, rugged face. Maybe it was the obvious confidence in him that she observed in Tyler Brew, whose own character and judgment she deeply admired. Maybe it was the connection thrust upon them now, a connection so important to her: saving Stanley Bigelow. Whatever it was, the attraction seemed mutual and rooted in at least some of the same reasons.

"Captain Brew says you're one hell of a person," the stubby Ranger said to her when they first spoke. "He's a great SEAL. Says he's glad we have you and your dog here with us."

Brew had told Kitt in advance about the plan to have the Ranger drag Stanley out during the rescue. It didn't occur to Brew that Augie might object to such a scene.

"It will look like Stanley's being hurt," she'd said to Brew. "August will not like that."

"Oh," Brew said, concerned.

"But he'll be okay if he knows the Ranger and trusts him. As soon as he gets here, I'll work him and Augie."

"Good catch, L. T.," Brew said.

Little did Tyler Brew know how true his comment would come to be.

Kitt and Francis Birmingham met at the Lyndon Township Hall when the Ranger arrived. He climbed up the front steps wearing a broad smile and embraced Captain Brew, waiting on the porch with her. Augie was standing with them. She was pleased that the new soldier seemed comfortable around the German shepherd; not all troops were, even some Special Forces.

"Beautiful guy, here," Tug said, extending an open hand, palm forward, well below Augie's face. He knows dogs, Kitt thought. It was the smart way to greet a canine for the first time.

"His name's Augie," she said. "Goes by August, too."

Tug knelt and petted the dog, first softly, then more firmly, rubbing his ears back. Augie smiled approvingly. Kitt told him that Augie was Stanley's dog and very attached to him but that before coming to Stanley he had been trained by her in the FBI's witness protection corps. At age eight, he was retired and living with the old engineer from Pittsburgh.

"And he's here to help us find the man?" Tug said.

"Yeah. And I'm glad you two get along. Otherwise, he might not take it lightly when he sees you manhandling his master. I need you to talk to him as much as you can before we go for Stanley. Use Stanley's name, over and over. In a kind tone. Like you're talking about your own brother or father. He'll connect you to him and understand you're like me and Brew. Part of the team on Stanley's side."

"And what's your name?" he asked.

"L. T. L. T. Kitt."

"What's the L. T. stand for?"

She smiled back, a little flirtatiously. "L. T. is enough for now," she said.

"Okay," Tug said. "A little mystery is all right, I guess. I sure don't want to get pushy with an FBI agent."

In the meeting room during the final briefing, Bobby Beach noticed the two were exchanging frequent glances. Brew had just explained how Tug would lead Stanley out of the camp.

"So, no shots are fired until the dog sits down, and you're charging?" a SEAL asked from the rear.

"Ideally. But if we're spotted and fired upon, we'll engage. Augie will keep doing his thing even if there's a firefight. And Kitt says he won't leave Stanley's position once he finds it. But no firing from *behind* the trailers in the direction we charge from. Those buildings are just thin aluminum and plywood. Your rounds will sail through them like fabric. We don't want anyone on our team hurt, or the dog. And remember, L. T. is vulnerable the whole time she's down there. She can't be looking around for herself, and she'll probably be the first person spotted."

Brew placed a hand on her shoulder.

"Let's take care of her," he said. "And Augie too."

They all knew what he meant, including Kitt.

Especially Kitt.

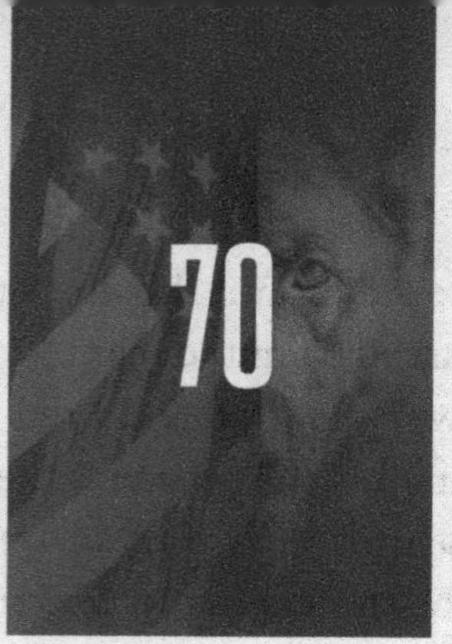

70

★ ★ ★

STANLEY IS FATIGUED

Stanley was tiring, and he knew it.

His thinking was blurring. He was not sure now how many days he had been in the trailers. He was trying to keep track of them but by the sixth day he questioned whether he may have counted one day twice, or perhaps missed one altogether. He struggled to remember. Each day was so like the next and the one before that it was hard to attach anything of significance to any of them, no hook on which to hang memory. Even the men holding him seemed so alike. They spoke little and smoked much.

A different Band Brother guarded him each day, in the Brother's own trailer. But they talked to him almost not at all. Usually, they made him sit at the back of the trailer, farthest from the door, while they stayed near the narrow entrances at the other end, working on computers most of the day, often looking at two or even three monitors at a time, all connected by cables. Stanley saw that the militiamen communicated with walkie-talkies of high quality. Probably military grade, the old man surmised. When they were moving him every afternoon, he could see guns and crates being removed from the trailer they were leading him to and loaded into the one he was departing.

Buddy was always present at moving time, watching directorially and giving instructions over the walkie-talkies. But Stanley hadn't been lodged for any night with Buddy in his trailer. Every day he watched to see where the leader retreated and saw his structure at the outer edge of the complex, on the side abutting the lake. His trailer appeared larger than the others and raised a bit higher from the ground.

Having trouble falling asleep, Stanley stayed up late in the evenings. He could not keep his mind from traveling to Helen. He worried deeply that she was harmed. She was an engineer too and had worked with him. One of the men had told him that Buddy and Smitty had been outside his apartment building watching him before he was kidnapped. *Of all the times for Helen to be without Augie*, he thought.

Only late at night did they permit him to step outside the trailers to stretch his legs. And then just briefly. He leaned to see license plates and began to believe he must be in Michigan. He saw three Michigan plates and overheard two of the men talking about a Detroit Lions game.

"Is that the home team?" he asked his guard one evening. But the Brother only glared at him silently.

At night, the men would stand around burning drums, fed with firewood and litter, drinking beer. He was invited only once, he guessed because it was a very cold night and his assigned trailer suffered from a balky furnace, spitting on and off at irregular intervals, some of them lengthy. Even his guard wanted to be out of it and with the others at the warming drum. Around midnight, the men would break up and go back to their trailers.

While they were gathered around the fires, Stanley sat in his trailer wherever he could hear the most, and he leaned as close as he could to a pried window. A few times he heard someone ask Buddy when "Maji" was coming, but Buddy's mumbled answers were unintelligible. The last time Buddy was asked, though, he thought he discerned anger in the leader's otherwise garbled reply.

This night, the weather had turned a bit colder again, he thought. He saw his guard turn up the dial on the propane furnace. He pushed aside a window curtain to see if it was still snowing lightly as it had been in the afternoon. It wasn't, and Stanley could see the night sky must be partly cloudy, as stars were bright in places and absent otherwise.

At midnight, he lowered himself into the narrow bed. Except for his wool sweater and shoes that he placed nearby, his gloves tucked inside, he had been sleeping fully clad in his unwashed clothes. He didn't want to remove them. They were his only possession, he thought, all that he had under his own control. No, he wasn't getting out of them. Besides, if his guard left in the night, maybe he could make a run for it. He pulled a blanket over himself and began to doze, resigned to face another night like the ones before it.

How wrong he was.

71

★ ★ ★

THINGS GO WRONG; THINGS GO RIGHT

Any general will tell you. Carefully drawn plans begin well. Begin.

Brew, Bobby Beach, and Sheriff Bechant arrived quietly with their teams, unnoticed on the road above and across the field. Captain Brew stepped quickly around the men and Kitt as they poured out of the vehicles and silently motioned them onto the grassy field, blotchy with light snow. He led them down to the natural ridge. One of the FBI specialists was exceedingly tall, at least six feet six, and Brew stopped him, warning him to stoop so as not to be visible above the ridgeline. The entire group, except for the sheriff and his perimeter force, descended the first part of the slope behind the Navy SEAL.

They reached the cover of the ridge undetected. Brew, Bobby Beach, Kitt, Augie, and Tug huddled immediately as the others assembled into their assigned subgroups along the ridgeline. Brew looked up and around at the sky. The quarter moon was beaming, unobstructed, but he could see a large cloud formation closely approaching it.

"Okay," he said quietly. "It'll be covered in a minute. Watch for my signal."

The next phase also proceeded without flaw. The sheriff's men and his South Carolina canine, Nelson, spread out to form their u-shaped outer perimeter encompassing the camp, all the way to water's edge on the far end. The SEALs slid rapidly down to their forward holding positions about a hundred yards from the closest trailers, just as the captain had sketched at the Township Hall. Bobby Beach's agents followed moments later, taking up their cover positions behind them. Captain Brew and Tug raced unnoticed to their planned position; Kitt and Augie to the natural foxhole Kitt had selected, slightly to the right of center, two hundred feet from the first line of trailers.

Later, Brew would acknowledge that what happened next could and should have been anticipated. He took full responsibility for it. The assault and its order of approach were his design. The contingency that materialized, while not obvious on the information known before the rescue attempt, should have been predicted and addressed in advance. Perhaps President Winters was right after all. The tactical planning was too rushed and unrehearsed. Not every possibility was accounted for. Intelligence and premission surveillance were insufficient.

It had been blind luck that Grey Boatwright's drone flight on Stanley's fifth night of captivity had recorded the old man's image. But it didn't tell the team anything about which trailer he was held in. It never occurred to any of the leaders that the captors might be moving Stanley from building to building. They wrongly assumed he had been held in the same place throughout, and that his scent in that place would attract loyal Augie to him. Had Boatwright been sent back to sweep just that area, from high altitude during daylight and low again at night, Stanley's movements, slight as they were, could have been observed, and the pandemonium that was about to take place averted, or at least anticipated.

Kitt and Augie were ready. L. T. sat in a baseball catcher's crouch in the mogul, the dog on all fours next to her. She withdrew a roll of Stanley's laundry from a zippered belly pack. She had selected articles that were only mildly odiferous. She chose the less pungent clothing because she assumed Stanley's scent would be available to the canine in only one principal place, and she wanted him to find it directly. If she primed him on the hill with something very ripe, the dog might ignore lesser similar scents—which might be Stanley's trailer—and, believing it his instruction, search only for the most pungent.

Kitt pulled the dog's face to her own and looked into his resolute eyes. She had removed his dog tags from his collar so that he could run in stealth. "Stanley, Stanley, Stanley, Stanley," she repeated into his ears—no other words—while gently wiping his snout with the ball of clothing. She felt the top of his back and his front legs tighten. She glanced at the watching Brew and unclipped the dog's short leash. Augie bounded over the mogul instantly and darted at full speed toward the trailer line. Kitt climbed out and followed, keeping her body as low to the ground as she could without falling too far behind him.

The dog ignored the first three structures he reached, racing past them, his belly slung low. But at the fourth trailer, positioned at the two o'clock position from Kitt and Brew's vantage point, he slowed, came to a brief standing halt, then circled it at moderate speed. But instead of coming to the front and sitting down, the dog looked left, then right, and ran to another trailer three places down to the left, somewhat nearer the center of the compound. Again, he circled the camper and returned to the front, standing.

But just for an instant, and not sitting. Soon, he raced to the right, turning inward in the spiral of trailers, circling still another.

"What the hell is happening?" Brew asked through his earpiece. The whole team could hear.

"He's confused. He's smelling Stanley all over the place."

"Well, he can't *be* all over the place."

"Well, he must've been before we got here."

"Will he still find him?"

"Oh, I think so. He won't give up. He's detecting differences, so he's not stopping till he's sure. But they'll find *him* first, I'm afraid."

For the next two minutes, Augie raced between and around a dozen campers. A few were partially blocked from Brew and Tug's view. Kitt scrambled, slipping in the patchy snow, keeping the dog in her sight.

It was bound to happen. As he flew across the cluster, Augie's whipping tail slapped an empty garbage drum. One of the Band Brothers peered out to see what the noise was and saw the canine disappearing around his trailer. He was on his walkie-talkie immediately to Buddy Binton. All the Band heard his squawk.

"Got a dog running through us, Buddy," he said.

"What kind of dog?"

"A big-ass dog. German shepherd, I think."

Binton froze. *Could it be the big man's dog from Pittsburgh?* "Shoot it," he said. "And everybody get your arms!" Then, "Who's got the old man?"

"Me."

"Who the fuck is *me*," Binton snarled. *Does he think I have caller ID on this thing?* the worried leader thought.

"It's Vinnie," came the voice over the walkie-talkie. It was Vincent Fearing. Even in his agitated state, Binton felt reassured.

Fearing was probably the most athletic brother in the Band, and the only one with military experience.

"Do *not* let Bigelow out of your trailer, Vinnie. No matter what. They may be coming to get him. That could be his dog."

"Well, he's a *dead* dog if he comes to *my* trailer," Fearing said.

Stanley heard it all. His heart pounded. Suddenly his feet and fingers felt cold; his blood was rushing to his gut, to his brain. He heard shots fired rapidly in succession from across the cluster of trailers. *My God, they're trying to kill Augie,* he thought. Reflexively, he tried to convince himself otherwise. *It could be any German shepherd,* he told himself. *Be rational. How could Augie even know he was in this place?*

The first shots missed Augie. Then, Smitty Burns spotted the dog racing toward the rear of his camper, positioned in the outer ring, close to the rutted driveway road, and stepped outside of it, attempting to get an angle to shoot, at about the three o'clock position in Brew and Tug's line of sight at the top of the mogul a hundred yards away. Brew trained his rifle on the militiaman's spine. He knew any shot from the outside would trigger a full state of readiness in the camp and expose the assault team's presence. If he fired, he would surely have to order a full-out charge at once. He couldn't tell whether the militant had the dog in view. But when Brew heard L. T.'s urgent call—*"Augie's running toward 30"*—signifying the trailer from which the Band Brother had stepped with rifle raised, he took Smitty Burns down with a two-bullet burst.

"Go. Go. Go." the Navy SEAL leader then instructed through the wire, oddly matter-of-factly, without exclamation. Weldon Bechant, hearing the order from his holding station far from the field—and alarmed to be receiving it so soon—told Bobby Beach later that Brew's voice was so calm and unexcited, he may as well have been ordering another at the bar of Hall's Chop House,

the sheriff's favorite drinking place in downtown Charleston, where Bobby Beach had introduced him to Captain Tyler Brew two years earlier.

Brew's rifle was tipped with a suppressor, but the shots flared through the darkness and still sent a muffled crack-crack echoing through the field and the woods behind. It was not the assault plan the captain had wanted, but it did have its advantages. The frightened militiamen holed up in their trailers panicked and began firing wildly up the black slope from camper windows and doors. In effect, each was acting as an independent sniper. And one thing a good sniper *never* does is give up his position until the last moment, *after* a kill shot. The random, rapid-fire bursts from the trailers were anything but kill shots. They allowed the charging SEALs to identify, sort, and divide their targets immediately. With the FBI specialists scampering down the slope behind them, providing cover from their flanks, the nine SEALs splayed out almost in synchronization, holding their fire until they were within ninety feet of their trailer targets. As Brew and Tug watched from their original position, they could see that at least half the time, a SEAL's initial shot felled the militant inside, and when it didn't, the continuous stream of fire racing from their rifles as they sprinted toward their targets soon did.

"Fire only at flashes!" Brew instructed as bullets sailed. "We still don't know where Bigelow is, and the dog's on the run in there with Kitt. Be careful. No extra fire!"

It was a smart directive. Even as highly trained as they were, the excitement of a full assault could lead to unnecessary firepower.

"I'm good," L. T. called in. "On the ground between 4 and 5," referencing the numbered trailers. "Augie keeps circling number 5. He must think Stanley's in there. He's hugging the edge so close the guy inside can't hit him. But he's fired at him twice.

If Augie sits down in front, he'll be wide open. The guy has an automatic rifle. I've only got my handgun and can't get a visual on him."

"Can you keep the dog circling?"

"I'm not sure, but I think so. He's following my signals so far. But, God, he's got to be tiring."

"Tug and I are coming now. Don't let the dog sit until we take out the shooter."

The captain spoke through the earpieces to the entire force, telling them he and Tug were going down to Number 5 where Kitt was pinned and believed Stanley was held. The SEAL and the Ranger descended the slope immediately. "We need cover," he called to the rest of the team. "But don't send any rounds to Number 5."

They could all see the pair advancing to the center of the snail of trailers because Tug's shiny shoulder harness glistened in the low light as he moved step for step at Brew's back. A barrage of fire protected them as they moved through the outer ring of structures toward number 5 in the center of the cluster. The two rushing soldiers pulled up under the cover of another camper, not forty feet from Number 5. They saw Augie whirl past clockwise, inches from the concrete block footings of the trailer.

Brew could see movement inside the trailer but did not want to shoot. He feared it could be Stanley he saw. "Fire on the far front edge, next to the door," he told Kitt through the wire. "Then crawl around back, try to see where Stanley is in there. But don't get anywhere near the other side of that front door. And stop the dog. Hold him with you."

Kitt didn't even take the time to verbally acknowledge the order. She fired three times at the edge of the door. A moment later, Brew and Tug could see her scissor-legging to the far rear corner of the structure, and Augie pulling to a stop next to her, at her command. The figure inside ducked expertly to the side of the door opposite Kitt's shots. Brew made his judgment in a nanosecond. The quick movement of evasion could not have been made by Stanley. For once, Stanley's great size and slowness was a virtue. With Tug Birmingham trudging behind him, the SEAL charged the trailer in full-speed strides, unleashing an unstopping stream of Z-patterned fire from his automatic rifle, beginning three feet left of the doorway—not an inch more—and extending into the door from the floor of the trailer to its ceiling. It was a deadly barrage of at least a hundred rounds.

There was no return fire. Kitt and Augie raced to the front of the trailer. Brew and the Ranger were ten feet from the door, now swinging limply in and out. Vincent Fearing lay twisted and bullet-riddled, dead against the opposite wall. Augie rushed to enter first, leaping in front of the SEAL and into the rusty camper. The dog dived left, to the rear corner where Stanley lay on his back, terrified, in a low-hanging bunk. Stanley's head was at the rear, against the wall of the trailer. Augie climbed on the bed, stepping onto the big man's abdomen and thighs, and immediately twirled his warm flanks so that he was outward facing, standing over Stanley's feet, looking at Brew, Tug, and Kitt as they came inside.

It was not a time for smiling, and only L. T. did. She went to the dog and threw her hands around his large face, praising him. Captain Brew, though, was all business.

"Are you hurt, Stanley?" he asked.

"I don't think so."

"Can you walk?"

"Yes."

"Well, we're *not* walking. We've got to get you out of here. Fast. We're not done yet. Get up."

Augie hopped off, and Kitt helped the senior Pittsburgher up from the bunk. His back was stiff from sedentary days, poor mattresses, and stooping in the trailers. Tug stepped between him and Brew.

"This is Sergeant Tug," Brew said. "He's going to pull you up the hill out there."

"Why can't I walk?"

"Because we're *not walking*," Brew snapped again. "There are nuts out there trying to kill us all." It reminded Stanley of how the Navy SEAL had treated him when they had first met at the beginning of the Eaglets' Nest project. He had learned from experience that Tyler Brew was an acquired taste. But many of the best things in life were too. And he was grateful beyond words to see him now.

"Here, hold onto these rings," Brew said, pointing to the rubber hand grabbers linked to Tug's belt. "Do what you can to keep up, but you probably won't be able to for long. When you can't keep up, just relax your legs and keep holding on to the rings. Let your legs hang limp and drag. The sarge will haul your ass up there while Kitt and I cover you."

"Who covers you two and Kitt and Augie?" Stanley asked.

"Oh, we've got people out there. They're good."

Brew thought about asking Stanley how many militiamen there were and how well they were armed, but quickly dispensed with the idea. Nothing could be changed now anyway, and there was no time to lose. The whole rescue team knew the package was in hand and would do everything they could to protect the escort to the staging area at the hilltop.

"Whatever you do, Stanley, don't let go of Tug," he said. He took off his backpack and pulled out a Kevlar jacket with a slate back plate sewed in. The engineer slid it on. It extended down below his beltline, adding forty pounds to Tug's already formidable load. "There will be gunfire, Stanley," Brew said. "If you get hit in this jacket, it will hurt, but it won't get to you. But if you get hit somewhere else and can't hold on anymore, we're going to latch your wrists up here." He showed him the cuffs hanging from the top of Tug's harness.

"My God," Stanley said.

"But one way or another, you're going home," Tyler Brew said. "I hope it's alive."

THE TAKING OF BUDDY BINTON

From his post at the top of the hill, Weldon Bechant looked down over the field like a Civil War general. He knew there were probably dead and wounded in the scattered trailers, and at least one, Smitty Burns, on the ground. He scoured the patchy field with night vision binoculars searching for anyone else lying in it. He was worried about Bobby Beach. When Brew had ordered agent L. T. Kitt to take up a position behind number 5, he saw his white-haired FBI friend from Charleston dart toward the lake and up the shoreline toward the cluster of trailers. Weldon figured he was going to her aid—without support to cover him. The sheriff had not seen Bobby Beach for eight minutes, and he did not answer his call over the earpieces.

Nervous, Weldon called to Brew, still inside number 5 with the old engineer, Kitt, the Ranger, and Augie.

"Is Bobby with you?" he asked.

"Negative," said the SEAL.

"Shit."

"What's wrong? Is he hit?" Brew asked, alarmed.

"I don't know. Last I saw him, he was down at the lake line, heading toward Kitt."

Brew thought for a moment. He knew some of the militiamen had been taken out in the frontal assault fifteen minutes ago. More remained, but their number was unknown. None had been seen fleeing toward the perimeter. All were apparently hunkered down in their trailers, and armed.

"Send four men from the perimeter to look for him, Weldon," Brew said. "We're starting up with Stanley in a minute. We need everybody else for cover as we come up."

The sheriff called to the deputies guarding the section of the perimeter line from the medical station up to the hilltop driveway. He told four of them to take his canine, Nelson, and get down to lake's edge, then move toward the trailers to see if Bobby Beach was in trouble.

The reconnaissance team was proceeding down with the dog when Bobby Beach whispered in to the old sheriff.

"I'm huddled at the shoreline near the largest trailer in the camp," the FBI man said.

"You scared the hell out of me," Weldon said.

"I couldn't talk before," the agent said. "I've got eyes on Binton in his trailer. Number 20. He's got a pile of long guns in there."

"Well, I've got a pile of long guns coming to help you right now."

"Good. I'm in the brush at the water, sixty feet from him."

"Do we need to take him alive?"

"Yes," Bobby Beach said. "That's a must. From the top."

"Because of the other thing?" Weldon surmised. The three leaders of the rescue mission had been told of the information pointing to Binton as the cyber saboteur.

"Suppose so," Bobby Beach said.

"Nelson can help with that, but you've got to keep the guy from killing him first."

The only thing better than one skilled police dog when the chips are down is two of them. The Charleston agent slid along the shoreline until he could crawl behind an unoccupied camper out of view of trailer number 20. His reinforcements arrived in minutes; they squatted in a huddle with him. Nelson, a shepherd even larger than Augie, shuffled his paws excitedly on the short leash of one of the deputies. Mindful that fire could not be sent from opposite sides of Binton's camper, Bobby Beach decided they would storm the trailer head-on, on the front long side where the only door into the camper was positioned.

"Wouldn't it be better to come from the rear side?" one of the deputies asked.

"Hell yes, but we've got to shoot the door down so the dog can go in for him. Can't fire from both sides without hitting ourselves, so we've got to take him from the front side. We can't kill him, so all your fire should be low, just above the bottom rail."

He reached to the shoulder of the deputy leashing Nelson.

"You take the door down while we're firing into the floor next to you," Bobby Beach instructed. "You'll need to get right up to it. After a few seconds of our fire, send in the dog." The FBI leader then turned to the rest of the men. "Everybody holds all fire once Nelson runs in. I'll go in first behind the dog, his handler comes in behind me. He may have to get the dog off him. If Binton is still a threat, and we *have* to fire inside, don't shoot to kill."

Buddy Binton would never admit it, but he was a far better computer scientist than he was a rifleman. Bobby Beach and the deputies flared out from behind their hiding place and commenced an onslaught of firepower into number 20, back and forth across its floor line. Nelson's handler poured a stream of bullets into the door handle, kicked the door off its hinges, and the attack canine flew inside, Bobby Beach and the handler on his tail, literally. Binton's face was flush with rage. It soon became terror. He was hit in both shins but clutching an automatic rifle, its magazine still full. He hadn't fired a single round. He never would. Nelson leaped at his right wrist with thrashing, open jaws, then swung to his left hand with equal ferocity. The gun tumbled to the plywood floor, and Binton fell backward, gashing his head on the kitchen faucet.

"Buddy Binton?" Bobby Beach said, as he cuffed him behind his back.

The leader of the Band of Free Brothers didn't answer. Bobby Beach didn't care.

"Your lucky day," the FBI man said. "Medical help's right up the hill." He pulled him to his feet. "Unless your men shoot us on the way up. Maybe you should tell them not to." He pulled Binton's walkie-talkie from its Velcro shoulder holder and held it to his face. The burly militant gave his last order. He told the Band to stand down.

"Give it again," Bobby Beach said.

Lester "Buddy" Binton repeated the order, seasoned with gratuitous expletives.

73

A HARROWING ESCORT

It could have been adrenaline. It could have been pride. Who knew? But the exhausted, seventy-two-year-old citizen from Pittsburgh was never dragged as Brew led Tug, L. T., and Augie up the hill. He didn't need to be. He threw one large, shoeless foot in front of the next with all the might he could muster behind the heels of the pulling Ranger as Augie pranced back and forth, from one side of Stanley to his other, his canine head erect and his eyes searching for any approach. For the first minute of their charge up the hill, Brew and Kitt threw automatic gunfire at any trailer showing light or the flare of a rifle from within.

Suddenly, the incoming fire stopped. Bobby Beach came through the earpieces. His tone was strong and clear, but not jubilant. "We've got Binton. He's alive. They're standing down. We're bringing him up. He's wounded."

Brew kept his escort team moving another thirty yards, testing the cease-fire, before stopping and turning to Tug and

Stanley. The three men were sweating profusely, even in the cold night air.

"Why are we stopping?" Stanley asked. Without an earpiece, he was the only one who didn't know of the militiamen's stand-down.

"We're clear now, Stanley," said Brew. A smile burst onto the SEAL's face as if released by a strong spring. He stepped behind Tug and took Stanley's hands from the rubber grips. Only then did Stanley feel the pain in his hands and fingers, cramped severely from his death grip on the handles. He flexed his thick fingers and stood up straight. Instinctively, Tug turned and hugged him. Stanley towered over the fireplug of a Ranger, so much so that his wide chin, thick with stubble from want of shaving, draped over Tug's shoulder nearly to the middle of his back. Augie sat down at the sight, resting against Stanley's leg, his long red tongue dripping to the thin snow.

L. T. Kitt lowered herself to the dog and smothered him with a praising massage of his sides and chest. She rose and embraced Stanley, saying nothing.

And then she did the same to Francis Tug Birmingham.

★ ★ ★

JUST GET US THERE

The Secret Service caravan sped through the night from the quiet egress gate at Willow Run airfield to the mission rendezvous point at the edge of Washtenaw County. The president and Helen Ames Bigelow were twenty miles from the rescue site when the firing had begun. The Secret Service was securely patched into the communications wire of Brew, Bobby Beach, and the Charleston sheriff, and followed the assault as if listening to the play-by-play of a ball game.

"The SEAL is taking them down the hill, Madame President," the agent in the front passenger seat said. "There's no gunfire yet."

It was not long before the tension in the armored sedan was unbearable.

"Agent Kitt says the dog is confused, ma'am." Minutes later: "Heavy fire in all directions."

In the rear seat, Helen clutched her hands and leaned forward. The president sat erect and reached for Helen's shoulder. "Helen, a medical team is there and ready. Trauma surgeons, the works.

If Stanley is hurt, he will not have to wait for care." Then Del leaned up toward the front seat. "Don't report anything else to us back here," she said. "Let's just get there."

"I'm sorry, ma'am," the agent said. His face showed regret. Helen said nothing.

"Just get us there," the president said, again.

When the caravan reached the crossing of Cedars Lake Road and Belanger Road beside the field, the president's driver pulled over and stopped. Two of the other Secret Service cars inched in front of and behind the presidential car, and stopped too, while the last drove up ahead to the gathering point in the woods. The president and Helen could see a sea of spinning lights spraying the sky from the police cars and rescue squads on the hill above them.

"Oh, dear," Helen said.

"I can have the agents call up to see if Brew is there," the president said. "To find out about Stanley. Do you want me to?"

"I would rather see him than hear about him."

"Okay."

In a few minutes, the vehicle sent up to scout the status turned around so that it was facing them down the hill. Its headlights flashed three times, the signal that it was safe to bring up the president. The three remaining cars from the caravan moved instantly up the road at moderate speed. When they reached the clearing to the left where Sheriff Bechant had quartered the medical vans and backup deputies, they saw Captain Brew and Bobby Beach walking quickly toward them.

"Look at them, Helen, look at them," the president said. The two leaders were smiling broadly. Breaching protocol, Del did not wait for the front passenger-side agent to get out and open her door. She opened it herself and sprang out, motioning to the agent to help Helen out instead. She saluted Brew and shook his hand.

"Is Stanley all right?" she asked quietly.

"Yes, ma'am. He's in a van being checked, but he came up under his own power. I don't think he's injured."

"And Augie?"

"Him too. He's in there with Stanley. The dog won't leave him."

"Take Helen to Stanley and the dog, Captain. Give them some time alone. And then take me."

THE CHALLENGES OF AFTERMATH

Stanley was safe. But the president and Tyler Brew knew that the national secrets about his work were not. Not by a long stretch. Once again, the threats to the public disclosure of the engineer's earlier design of the covert nuclear base in Kuwait, and now his recent underground cabling shield to protect military communications, came from home and abroad.

At home, the problem was likely discovery by the press of the extraordinary rescue in rural Michigan of an aging civil engineer by a joint team of county sheriffs' deputies, FBI extraction specialists, and—of all people—Navy SEALs. It was the stuff of media moguls' dreams. If not finessed immediately, hotels and motor inns from Detroit to Chicago would be booked solid with reporters and camera crews from the world over.

Abroad, there was the perplexing issue of the Syrian defector, Majir Asheed, now in Russian custody. Who could know what he knew about Stanley's work? How much *had* he learned from the South Carolina laboratory manager before murdering him and sending the Binton mob to take Stanley in Pittsburgh? Whatever he *did* know, the Russians soon would too.

As Air Force One escorted Stanley, Helen, and Augie back to Pittsburgh in the early-morning hours after his rescue, the president discussed the quandary by on-board phone with Brew, Bobby Beach, and Sheriff Bechant, still at the field in Michigan. It was obvious that the rescue operation just conducted could not be completely concealed. Far too many people would come to hear that something large and strange had occurred in Washtenaw County. There was already an intercepted call from a commercial airline pilot descending to Detroit, reporting to air traffic control that a disturbance was happening beneath him, complete with sustained automatic gunfire across a wide area and innumerable flashing lights from law enforcement vehicles. Detroit media were on their way to investigate.

Brew and the president felt that no matter what communications strategy was decided upon, the presence of the SEALs could not be part of it. Brew had already summoned a transport helicopter from Grayling Air Force Base, 130 miles north, and it could remove the military team within thirty minutes. The president approved.

"I think we should leave it to Weldon to talk to the press," Bobby Beach said. "He did it before, and he can do it again."

"Can you, Sheriff?" the president asked.

"Oh, with Bobby here, I'm sure I can," he said.

"What will you say?" she asked.

"I'll say an antigovernment radical murdered a fine citizen of South Carolina in my county and a lead in that investigation brought us to Michigan to this Buddy Binton outfit. Not a lie in there."

"I like it," Brew said.

"Me too," said Bobby Beach.

"How do you explain the FBI involvement?" the president asked.

"The ol' across state lines thing," Weldon said. "Best damned law there ever was." Even in the circumstance, everyone laughed, including the president.

"Sheriff, if you can button this up without exposing Stanley Bigelow, the nation will be indebted to you," she said. "Good luck. I'll be watching."

"If I'm good enough, you won't be able to," Weldon said. "Unless you can tune into local Detroit TV stations."

Captain Brew boarded the helicopter with his SEALs and the Army Ranger Tug Birmingham. The Ranger was the last to climb up. He was standing to the side with L. T. Kitt, talking quietly. Brew walked past them, leading the SEALs. "Just a minute or two, soldier," he called to the Ranger. He saw an embrace and the slipping of a piece of paper from Kitt to the fireplug.

Bobby Beach and the southern sheriff drove quickly back to the township hall. Weldon wanted to change into his regular uniform before meeting the media, and they both felt it best to keep the reporters away from the site of the assault. They cleared out the medical vans and left a team of sheriff's deputies and two FBI agents to cordon off the field. The deputies and agents were to answer no questions—none—and to direct all media representatives to the Lyndon Township Hall where the sheriff and the agent-in-charge from Charleston would be waiting for them with information.

At six thirty in the morning, the main room of the township hall was filled with reporters, cameras, and microphones from Detroit, Jackson, and Lansing. Brew and Weldon stood in the lower level.

"They're all up there, Weldon," Bobby Beach said.

"This is the closest my work gets me to feeling like a doctor," the sheriff drawled. Bobby Beach turned to him, puzzled. "I like to let 'em wait out there for twenty minutes," the sheriff said.

It was well-staged. An FBI agent finally walked to the podium at the front of the hall to check the microphone. The reporters quieted. After a brief pause, Bobby Beach and the fully attired—hat and all—sheriff climbed the platform. Bobby Beach walked straight to the wall behind Weldon's right shoulder; the sheriff walked to the podium. He raised his weathered face high and swept his eyes slowly over the whole room.

"Ladies and gentlemen, I am Weldon Bechant, sheriff of Charleston County, South Carolina. Behind me is Mr. Bobby Beach, agent-in-charge of the Charleston field office of the Federal Bureau of Investigation."

The media members were stunned to hear that South Carolina officers were briefing them. It could have been that surprise, or just the early hour, but for whatever reason, the group was more attentive than interruptive.

"I have a statement, and then Bobby and I will take a few questions." He adjusted his wide brimmed hat and began.

"The good citizens of Michigan and South Carolina are safe tonight following the successful joint operation of deputies from South Carolina, Washtenaw County, and the FBI to apprehend one Lester "Buddy" Binton and the criminal members of his Band of Free Brothers, an antigovernment hate group situated here in this county of this fine state."

With Bobby Beach standing expressionless behind him, the sheriff explained that he and his out-of-state officers were involved because a resident of Charleston County, an employee of the federal government working in, "for God's sake," an agricultural research laboratory, was murdered by an associate of the Michigan hate group leader. To establish credibility for the story, Bechant named the South Carolina victim, and spelled the

French name twice for the reporters. Weldon then said that a lead in the South Carolina investigation brought them to Michigan to find and question Binton as a "person of interest." Once the criminal activity was shown to cross state lines, the FBI was invited in for assistance.

"It turned out Mr. Binton was armed to the hilt and hunkered down in his camp of trailers in northwestern Washtenaw County near the Jackson County line. He and his men had the poor judgment to fire on us and our dog, Nelson, as we approached to question him." The old sheriff stopped and looked to his deputy at the stairway. "Get Nelson out here, deputy. He's the real hero here."

It was a touch of genius. Huge Nelson stepped out calmly with his handler and sat tall next to the short sheriff. The top of the dog's head nearly reached Weldon's shoulder as they stood on the platform. All attention quickly shifted to the canine and how he had disarmed the hate-group murder suspect inside his weapons-filled trailer. "It was Bobby Beach here that formally arrested the man in the trailer after Nelson subdued him." The reticent FBI leader smiled, almost as if embarrassed to be credited. He simply nodded. It was the closest Bobby Beach came to speaking at all.

Weldon's performance was stylish, not wildly far from at least part of the truth, and effective. He handled all questions, to Bobby Beach's relief. Was anyone killed in the operation? Yes, seven of the hate group members were dead. They would be identified in due course. Were there any casualties among law enforcement? The sheriff raised his bandaged left hand from his earlier accident, which a doctor at the medical staging area had cleaned and rewrapped for him after the assault. The new wrapping seemed enormous at the top of his thin arm. "Just this," he said. "Nothing too serious—a badge of honor." At that,

Bobby Beach could be heard to clear his throat. But he nodded again and smiled appreciatively from behind the sheriff.

Then the two of them walked immediately down the stairs, avoiding any approaches, as the officers upstairs ushered the media crews out the front door of the town hall. When all of them had driven off, Weldon and Bobby Beach came up and stepped out into the brisk air.

The sun was just beginning its rise after the longest night. Weldon's story held.

76

CHRISTMAS EVE AT THE SUPREME COURT

No one could remember when the Supreme Court last issued a decision on Christmas Eve. The nine justices assembled fully robed in their ceremonial courtroom on Constitution Avenue to publicly announce the ruling. It was not routine for the court to call itself into session solely for the purpose of reading a decision aloud from the high bench, much less on a holiday. But the national attention on *The Petition of President Delores Winters in the Matter of the Election of Willis P. Truitt to the United States Senate,* as the legal proceeding was formally titled, demanded it. At least in the view of Chief Justice John Roberts.

At the White House, Del tried to relax after the tension of the previous week. Her father was displeased that after all they had been through, his daughter had not invited his friend Stanley and his wife Helen to Washington to spend Christmas with them. But after Henry Winters called Stanley in Pittsburgh, he understood his daughter's reasoning. The old engineer was exhausted. He wanted to be alone with Helen. And the president had invited them to come early in the new year, once things had settled down and when Stanley was refreshed.

No one seemed very sure what the court would say as the justices walked in line to their places, the chief justice in the center. A clerk stood to the side of the bench with printed copies of the decision, to be distributed after the reading. Most observers expected a divided court, and even a five-to-four ruling. A dissenting justice, or more than one, might choose to read his or her differing opinion also. Deceased Justices Antonin Scalia and Ruth Bader Ginsburg, giants on the court in their day, were famous for delivering powerful dissents in person, especially in important cases.

Anyone hoping for debating opinions or a lengthy show was disappointed. The chief justice wrote and delivered the opinion. It was not verbose; it was not bombastic. Almost as a courtesy to diffuse other expectations in the packed courtroom, the chief opened by simply stating, "This decision is unanimous." Disbelieving exhalations were audible in the grand room. The graying chief justice then read unemotionally:

> The right to vote and to have that vote counted is an inherent right in our democracy. The system of government created by the United States Constitution is premised on this proposition.
>
> We address today the petition by the President of the United States to declare as invalid the election of Willis P. Truitt of Georgia to the United States Senate and further to declare that Margaret Westfall be deemed the person elected by the citizens of Georgia to fill that position.
>
> It seems to us a truism that a citizen's vote that has been misdirected to reflect a choice not made is a violation of that citizen's Constitutional

right of the most basic nature and, when such a number of other citizens' votes similarly have been misdirected so as to alter the collective will of the people *as a whole*, then the rights of the *citizenry as a whole* have been abridged.

We reject the Respondents' contention that Congress in Section IX of The Elections Security and Reform Act could not rightly give to a freely elected president, in his or her discretion in the discharge of the obligations of the Office of President, the capacity to seek relief in such an instance. While the Constitution does reserve to the states, and only the states, the actual management and conduct of elections, including to federal office, its powers in respect to assuring the fairness and correctness of elections are *not* exclusive. The Elections Clause of the Constitution states that although only the states shall conduct elections, Congress may pass laws *regulating* them. The Respondents state that the power delegated to the president to seek the outright reversal of an election cannot fairly be called a regulation, but is instead the complete abrogation of a State's right to say who has won and who has lost. We disagree, especially under the facts of this case.

Were the president in her petition seeking to reverse an election outcome so as to displace a political rival in favor of her *own* party, the Respondents' position might have more merit, and we limit our ruling today, accordingly, to the Constitutionality of the act as applied in this instance to these specific facts.

Here, the president acts *against* her own political interest, by filing her petition at all, and especially by seeking the seating of a Senator from her principal opposing party, rather than asking that a second election be held, which her own party might win if afforded a second chance. The president has concluded that her duty to uphold the Constitution and the citizens' confidence in the integrity of federal elections, wherever they may reside in the nation, requires the reversal of the election of Willis P. Truitt and the seating of Margaret Westfall in the United States Senate from the State of Georgia. On the strength of the factual evidence presented—which we find overwhelming—we unanimously defer to her judgment.

Accordingly, we order the State of Georgia to certify forthwith the election of Margaret Westfall so that she may be seated as a United States Senator from Georgia when proceedings to assemble and swear in the new Senate occur on January 2 of the coming new year.

So Ordered.

"How do you feel?" the First Father asked Del as they sat after dinner.

"Never so sorry to win," she said. "But let's toast to it anyway."

"To *it*," Henry Winters said, raising his glass. "And to Stanley. Home for Christmas. And to my daughter. For doing the right thing."

★ ★ ★

BUT WHAT OF THE SYRIAN?

There remained the thorny issue of the slender, dark Syrian. Even before Air Force One had touched down at Joint Base Andrews, bringing home the president from Michigan and Pittsburgh, she had called directly to the Russian president, Dmitri Devinov. It was Jack Watson's idea at the CIA. He did not want to contact his counterpart in Moscow cold. He wanted the president to call Devinov to introduce the purpose of his own call that would follow to the head of Russian intelligence, Marakka Yevzelsky.

"Why should I call him first?" Del had asked Watson. "Yevzelsky respects you."

"Yes, but if she's not authorized to listen seriously to me, I'll get nowhere," Watson told Del. "And there is *no one* there who can delay the interrogation of the Syrian except Devinov. Personally. It must come on *his* order, or the questioning will happen. And there is no good reason, and a lot of bad ones, to tell Yevzelsky *anything* if we believe Asheed's already talking."

Hence, the urgency. It was imperative that the defector Asheed be prevented from disclosing information about Stanley and his work to the Russians if there was any way to preempt it. Watson and the president both knew it might be too late. But Watson felt two things might work in the Americans' favor. First, Majir Asheed had been taken into custody in Stockholm. It was unlikely the Russians would question him there. They would move him, almost certainly, to a black site in Russia where professional interrogators could have at him. Christmas is a national celebration in Russia too; perhaps there would be a day or two to gain. Second, as a Syrian, Watson believed the Russians would treat the defector somewhat less severely, in deference to its ally. Probably, they would include the Syrian intelligence service in the process. Perhaps another day or two could be gained.

The whole object was to keep the Syrian's mouth and mind zipped tight, until a deal could be struck—if one could be—to get him into American hands, even if by asylum.

The American embassy in Moscow alerted the Kremlin that the US president would be calling, and the Russian president answered on the first ring. He had the ability to be friendly and icy at the same time, more so than anyone else Del Winters knew.

"Madame President, it's been too long," he said. "What is it that you want from me?"

"I *do* want something, Mr. President. And I have something to offer in return."

"I assume it is not Christmas greetings," he said, frostily. "And I hope you're not blaming us for that election fraud over there. On Lenin's grave, I know nothing about it."

Del ignored the reference. For all she knew, maybe the Russians *had* been involved.

"You have a Syrian intelligence officer in custody on suspicion of defection."

"If I did not respect you, I might consider your words 'on suspicion' an insult," Dmitri Devinov said. "The fact that you even know we have him proves you also know clearly he was trying to defect."

"I take your point," she said. "I am calling you now only to ask that you advise Marakka Yevzelsky that Jack Watson will call her shortly with particulars of what we ask and what we offer. Until you can consider our proposal, I ask merely that you keep the Syrian wherever he is. Keep the status quo, in case you want what we will offer. Because if he is harmed or interrogated—at all—there will be nothing we can offer, and Jack will not call."

"Why would I not interrogate this traitor? As soon as I can?"

"Because you have nothing to lose by pausing. And when you learn what you will gain by leaving him alone, you may think it a good exchange. It is for you to decide, of course."

There was silence on the line. Del pressed her point.

"I need your assurance, Dmitri. If I don't have it, I cannot permit Jack Watson to offer your people anything."

Another silence.

"You have my assurance," he said. "But move quickly." Without more, he hung up. Not even a Merry Christmas.

78

★ ★ ★

THE SPYMASTERS' DEAL

Marakka Yevzelsky was smart, tough, and Jack Watson knew, incorruptible. In her soul, she did not countenance *every* policy of the Russian government, especially its decidedly anti-Semitic tilt and its Neanderthal-like treatment of gays, lesbians, and transgender persons. In testament to her own talents in spycraft, she had concealed her own Jewish heritage—she was born Yevzel*man*—so that she could rise, first in the Soviet KGB and then in its successor Russian intelligence service. She reasoned that even the great societies were flawed. And to her, Russia was indeed a great one, to which she was committed to the marrow.

She had barely finished speaking with her own president when Jack Watson called.

"*Already*, Jack?"

"Your president said to act quickly."

"Well, so far you *are* trustworthy," she said.

The relationship between them was such that formalities and

pretense could be dispensed with. They spoke frankly from the beginning. There was no point, and no time, as far as Watson was concerned, to dance around a game of "who knew what."

"We want Majir Asheed. Immediately," Watson said.

"Obviously."

"We have a trade to offer."

"We are listening." *We*, Watson noted. Del's call had peaked interest.

"Asheed was useful to us in finding the source of our drone interception and the attack on Israel using it. And the French fighter too."

"If he has implicated *us*, he is lying," Marakka said.

"He hasn't."

"Good."

"Because of him, we have the group responsible. We *have* them, Marakka. We know how this was done. If you will give us Asheed, we will share with you the technical details of it. The devices, workbooks, transmission data, the manipulations, and computations. This must be of value to you. Without it, you are vulnerable to the next group, or the remnants of the first one. We cannot be sure we have *everyone* that was involved. But, in exchange for Asheed, you will have everything that we have."

"*Everything?*"

"Yes. That is the commitment of the president. So long as the Syrian is not interrogated or harmed—at all—before he is turned over."

"Give me a moment, Jack," she said. "I want to make notes before you go." A few minutes later she came back on the line.

"Is there anything I need to clarify?" the CIA chief asked. "About our offer?"

"Yes, there is. You say you will exchange everything you *have* about the hacking incidents. Will you also provide everything that you *don't* have now but learn in the future? About how it was done."

"Everything done by this group we've identified, yes. Everything we learn from them, or about them and their methods."

"That is very clear then, Jack. I cannot be sure until I speak again with my president, but I think he will be inclined. And you may take it from me. The Syrian has not been questioned yet. He has not been touched."

Watson believed her.

"One other thing," Marakka said. "If we agree to this, where do we deliver him?"

"To the place where he was arrested. INTERPOL Stockholm. To the investigator there. Lars LaToure."

79

THE PATRIOT'S ANGELS

It wasn't clear whether it was Helen or Stanley who first fully recovered from the trauma of the weeks before Christmas. But it was plain to the greeting party awaiting them at the White House in mid-January that each was in high spirits when they arrived for the Saturday afternoon reception organized by the president.

Much of the good mood was produced by the report from the trusted Swedish INTERPOL professional following his intensive debriefing of the Syrian defector. Lars LaToure concluded that Majir Asheed was truthful in every detail as he recounted his activities in Charleston—the slaying of James Molineaux and his communications with Buddy Binton. The manager of the curious vegetable laboratory on Highway 17 knew and disclosed nothing more than Stanley's name and that he was from Pittsburgh. Before killing the government manager, the Syrian had not learned what the soldiers at the research laboratory were training for or that it involved a weapons program. He did not even know Helen's last name. And—critically—Asheed had *not* disclosed Stanley's identity to his Syrian handler or to the Russian agents after his arrest in Stockholm. They knew only that the visiting engineer at the agricultural laboratory was a senior citizen from Pittsburgh.

Stanley and Helen came from Pittsburgh for the reception in an FBI Suburban with L. T. Kitt at the wheel and Augie in the rear hatch. Brew had told the president of Kitt's bravery in the rescue of Stanley, and she insisted the agent come to the gathering.

"That's a problem," Brew told the president. "Helen and Stanley leave the dog with Kitt whenever they travel," Brew told the president.

"Then the dog's invited too."

It was not a short drive, but manageable enough with Kitt's FBI "speed-limit privileges." They would be hosted by the president in the early afternoon and return immediately after.

In a way, Augie's invitation was poetic justice. It had been Nelson, the sheriff's canine from Charleston, that received the limelight after the mission, photographed next to Weldon Bechant as the demure sheriff described richly his role in the arrest of Buddy Binton. It was true, but Augie was never even mentioned; his intense training, keen adjustments, and vital behavior, so needed that night in the Michigan field, were obscured. But now, it was Augie going to the White House and, from the looks of him sitting high in the rear compartment behind the canine grate, enjoying every minute of it.

Probably not quite as much as Weldon Bechant, though. The demure old lawman, in the beginning thought by some as unnecessary, or even a hindrance, had proved a crucial planner, organizer, and, in the end, communicator for the whole team. Oh, he may have showboated his self-inflicted hand wound, and taken a touch more credit for his own dog than was merited. But Bobby Beach and Tyler Brew saw that coming. With Weldon Bechant, you got vanity; you got color. But the aging sheriff had proven once again that you also got a shrewd amiability that won over needed resources and a keen intellect to apply them efficiently. Looking back on the mission, Navy SEAL Brew could not count the number of tactical decisions and initiatives Weldon had made and managed. Now, the legend of Charleston County was getting his due—an invitation to the White House from President Del Winters. He was so bulging with pride, it was surprising his dress pants still fit as he and Bobby Beach were greeted by the president at the front entrance, the first ones to arrive.

"Sheriff, how *do* you do it?" Del greeted him.

"Now, ma'am, you wouldn't be referring to my age?" His step was quick, his smile quicker.

"I won't lie to you, Sheriff. I asked my staff to learn your age." Weldon was surprised and looked disarmed. "But they couldn't find it," Del said. "Not a trace. And with all that's been written about you down there." The president was plainly amused, and Bobby Beach too.

"Southern manners, ma'am," he said. "Which leads me to thank you for this very fine invitation and honor." He removed his hat and bowed to her. A marine came forward and took his hat. The three of them stepped inside.

The sheriff didn't know it, but his early arrival was by design. Defense Secretary Vernon Lazar had always been reluctant about the colorful southerner. He now acknowledged his clear contributions to the Michigan raid and rescue but still cautioned Del about him. He was worried that he would not keep *everything* secret, despite Bobby Beach's affirmation of his trustworthiness.

Del decided to speak to him herself, with the FBI agent-in-charge from Charleston present.

"The others will be here soon, Sheriff. We'll be gathering upstairs in the residence, and my father will be joining us. But I thought you might like to see the Oval Office and sit with me and Mr. Beach for a moment."

They ambled to the West Wing past uniformed marines at every hall intersection and into the Oval Office. She motioned Weldon and Bobby Beach to a sofa and took a seat in a wingback.

"Needless to say, Weldon, your service has been exemplary. We are all so pleased that you were willing and able to do what you did. Mr. Beach vouched for you strongly, and I can see why."

"Bobby and I work together all the time."

"I am sure you do. But not on matters of national security that must remain private," she said.

"I assume you are talking about confidentiality."

"I am. You handled the media in Michigan marvelously. And the follow-up we knew would come."

"Thank you, ma'am."

"But I need to be certain you understand the deep need that nothing more—*nothing*—be disclosed about the entire episode. To anyone."

"There's a lot I don't know in the first place. I never asked Bobby or Brew what was behind this, and they didn't offer."

"There were—*are*—reasons for that," Del said. "The identity of Stanley Bigelow has never been disclosed. It mustn't *ever* be, for his own safety and for the protection of defense secrets that I cannot go into. We live in a dangerous world. There is no end to what adversaries will do."

"I understand, *fully*," the sheriff said. "*Fully.*" He looked her directly in the eye. "You have my sworn word on it."

"And I trust you. *Fully.*" She rose and shook his hand.

A marine opened the Oval Office door. "The others have arrived, Madame President," he said.

Del had told her father that she would lead the party up to the residence, but Henry Winters couldn't resist coming down the staircase when he saw Stanley at the door. The general bounded down the stairs like a man twenty years or more younger, back straight and knees limber. He was embracing Stanley at the threshold of the entrance when Del stepped up. She gently steered the two large men to the inside and walked out to Helen, Brew, Kitt, and Augie. The dog was restless and displeased with his position, trying to edge through the group to reach Stanley's side inside the doorway. Del noticed.

"Let's allow General August through," the president said. Way was cleared.

"If he's getting a military commission," Brew said, "I think it should be in the navy."

"All right, Admiral August, then."

"Admiral? Outranking me?"

"Maybe not for long, Tyler, the way you are going. This was extraordinary work, Captain." She smiled at the Navy SEAL, who felt a bit embarrassed beneath his pride.

Upstairs, cocktails were served in the spacious foyer atop the staircase. Helen asked for a gin martini with a single olive; Stanley, Weldon, and Bobby Beach for bourbon. Kitt and Brew, light drinkers, had Bloody Mary's. Spirits were high; there was much laughter. Kitt noticed that Stanley reached often to the passing appetizer trays but took few for himself. Without bending, he lowered his hand to his side and Augie delicately took them from it. After the third time, she spoke up.

"Those are awfully rich, Stanley," Kitt said. "Remember we've got a long ride back."

"Well, this is *all* pretty rich," he said. "But I know you're right." He looked down at the dog and raised his eyebrows in a "that's it, boy" expression. Augie looked up in return in reluctant acceptance.

The residence staff said later they could not recall such a lengthy meal in the upstairs dining room. They were especially surprised to see the First Father staying so long at the table. He was usually no-nonsense about dinners and, for the most part, didn't even attend his daughter's functions. But seated next to Mr. Bigelow, he was eating slowly, talking nonstop with his friend, animated and attentive.

The staff knew that the president normally signaled that dinner was soon ending when she made a toast. She glanced at one of them and lifted a glass slightly, their cue to clear the table and bring a fresh bottle of wine.

"Stanley," she said, waiting for the voices to still. "Stanley, do you feel like the guest of honor?"

"Not really," he said. "I don't deserve honor. I am simply happy to be alive."

"Well, you surely know how much we all care about you. How grateful we are that you are safe. The weeks before Christmas were brutal for all of us, and the most brutal for you, and for Helen."

"I did not expect any of it," Stanley said. "But when it happened, I knew that at least my work was finished. I had done what I was asked. And I knew that you would not abandon me. You would look for me. Do whatever you could. I worried for Helen. I thought that she had probably been taken too, and that Augie was not able to protect her. Which he would have."

There was absolute quiet in the room. Stanley's words silenced even the gathering of the last silverware in the corner of the room. Finally, Del spoke again, from her seat.

"Two years ago," she told the table, "I told Stanley privately, after he had risked his life to use his skills for the country on another project, that he was both a citizen and a patriot. And how important citizen patriots are. He did not want credit. He did not want fame, even in secrecy. I remember him telling me, 'If I am a patriot, I am an accidental one.' Everything had happened, he thought, just because it did. We all have faith in our own way. Myself, in matters like this, my faith tells me that things never happen 'accidentally.' We can't know why events unfold exactly as they do. Often, they do not end as we would hope, or worse. But when they end well—in safety, health, and friendship—my faith tells me it is the work of angels. All of you here were Stanley's angels. And many others—Lieutenant Boatwright, Wilson Bryce, Lars LaToure, Ranger Birmingham, even the Syrian, Majir—were all Stanley's angels too."

She left her seat and walked to Stanley's shoulder. She lifted her glass.

"To the Patriot and his angels!" she said. "*All* the Patriot's angels!"

Everyone applauded, including the staff gathered near the wall. Helen beamed, but Stanley slouched at his seat, more even than usual; he lifted his head to look around the table, nodding appreciation through his self-consciousness.

Del stood outside the front entrance and said goodbye to each of them as they filed out. L. T. Kitt, leashing Augie, was near the end of the line, just before Helen and Stanley.

"Thank you for mentioning Tug Birmingham," she said to the president.

"Please tell him that I did," Del said. "And good luck to both of you."

My word, Kitt thought. *What do these people* not *know*?

The president did not say anything more to Helen or to

Stanley on the porch, and they said nothing more to her. Her eyes and heart spoke for her, and theirs for them.

Kitt raised the rear hatch of the Suburban, and Augie was about to jump in, when Stanley intervened.

"Couldn't he ride in the back seat?" he asked.

Helen was already climbing into the front of the car. Kitt knew it was out of rule for the canine to ride anywhere but behind the grate, except in emergencies. But after everything that had happened, she decided not to stand on ceremony. The dog climbed onto the rear bench seat and soon lay prone, his muzzle resting on Stanley's thigh. As he buckled his shoulder strap, Stanley saw the president walking down from the porch to his side of the car. He lowered his window.

"Thank you again, Stanley." She reached in and he put his hand in hers. "Until next time, Stanley?" She smiled at him and turned back to the White House porch.

Augie was asleep before L. T. drove through the east gate. There was no excessive speeding as they journeyed home to Pittsburgh. Kitt had enjoyed a cocktail, there was no imperative to rush, and 120 pounds of unfastened German shepherd lay on the back seat. Stanley listened to Kitt and Helen talking about the day's events, as they cruised into Pennsylvania. Not wanting to interrupt, he waited for a pause in their banter.

"What will happen to the Syrian?" he finally asked. "And his family."

"Not sure," Kitt said. "I don't think the bureau is keen on giving him asylum. I mean he killed Ruth Morgenthal and her daughter, and who knows how many others?"

"Yes, he did."

"But INTERPOL says we could hide him better in the States than anyplace in Europe. And Brew says the guy's no different than a soldier, no different than himself. He killed for his country."

Helen turned in the front seat, as if to speak, but stopped.

"What do *you* think they should do with him, Stanley?" Kitt asked.

He took a deep breath, placed his hand on Augie's chest, rising and falling evenly beside him, and looked out the window to the silver winter woods of Chester County.

"I don't like to judge angels," he said.

Twenty minutes later, he drifted to a deep sleep himself, counting his own.

AFTERWORD

The Patriot's Angels is the second book in the Stanley Bigelow series, but I wanted it to provide a satisfying reading experience independent of the first novel, *The Accidental Patriot*. I hoped that readers could enjoy this book without having read the first; that it could stand on its own as a good story. You must be the judge.

I am drawn to the ordinary man and woman presented as heroes. I am drawn to the possibilities of greatness in the average man or woman before whom fate thrusts itself. And for me at least, whether greatness is pursued or not, every average man can use a great dog.

Readers of the first book in this series will be familiar with the United States Vegetable Laboratory in Charleston, South Carolina. It *is* a real place, and the description of the roads and businesses near it on US Highway 17 are, within reason, accurate. Similarly, all the places portrayed in the scenes in Michigan are real. A few road names have been changed to avoid any awkwardness for landowners.

Whenever fiction touches political themes there is potential for unintended combustion and resentment. I hope nothing of the kind is ignited by my description of the imaginary political events or the characterization of the figures carrying the plot of this book. *The Patriot's Angels* is meant only to entertain, not to politically persuade—in any direction.

JB

ABOUT THE AUTHOR

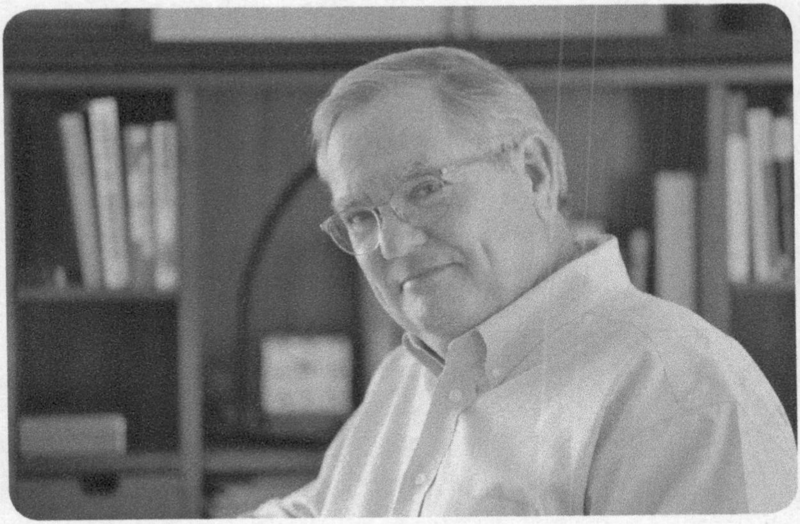

Joseph Bauer divides his time between homes in Charleston, South Carolina, and Cleveland, Ohio. He is the author of *The Accidental Patriot*, the first installment of his thriller trilogy. Bauer continues the story in the second book, *The Patriot's Angels*. For more about Joseph Bauer, his writing, and updates about the next book in the series, visit www.josephbauerauthor.com.